Natalie, 60, Looking For... What?

VAL ERASMUS

The Book Guild Ltd

First published in Great Britain in 2024 by
The Book Guild Ltd
Unit E2 Airfield Business Park,
Harrison Road, Market Harborough,
Leicestershire. LE16 7UL
Tel: 0116 2792299
www.bookguild.co.uk
Email: info@bookguild.co.uk
X: @bookguild

Copyright © 2024 Val Erasmus

The right of Val Erasmus to be identified as the author of this
work has been asserted by them in accordance with the
Copyright, Design and Patents Act 1988.

All rights reserved. No part of this publication may be
reproduced, transmitted, or stored in a retrieval system, in any form or by any means,
without permission in writing from the publisher, nor be otherwise circulated in
any form of binding or cover other than that in which it is published and without
a similar condition being imposed on the subsequent purchaser.

This work is entirely fictitious and bears no resemblance to any persons living or dead.

Typeset in 11pt Minion Pro

Printed on FSC accredited paper
Printed and bound in Great Britain by 4edge Limited

ISBN 978 1835740 521

British Library Cataloguing in Publication Data.
A catalogue record for this book is available from the British Library.

Natalie, 60, Looking For... What?

This book is dedicated to all those who can relate to it.

Chapter One

The Boeing 747 stood waiting, its huge wings spread dark and rigid against a dusty-pink sunset. It was the end of February in South Africa, mid-summer, and despite the fading light, the heat still rose from the concrete underfoot as we passengers made our way to the mobile gantry.

Step by step, with handbag and carry-all on one shoulder and boarding pass in hand, I lugged a cabin-size case up the stairs while juggling a heavy knitted poncho that would make more sense at the other end. I finally made it to the top where, waiting to welcome the weary, stood an angelic flight attendant gesturing vaguely into the interior of the plane. I followed her direction, so glad to be in this cool, dark cave with its faint smell of sanitiser (which didn't really disguise the musky odour of the previous occupants), and found my seat number. A window seat. Yay!

After the general push and shove of trying to stow cases overhead, I flopped into my seat and made myself comfortable. A couple of hours had passed since I first arrived at the airport. Josh and Mark both gave me one last hug as stoically as ever, but when Erin looked at me through tear-filled eyes I just broke down. Taking a deep breath, I closed my eyes, and thought about them. I hoped they hadn't been caught up in rush-hour traffic on the freeway. Mark would go home to Jen, who would no doubt have his supper waiting. Josh had brought Erin to the airport, so would drop her off at the garden cottage that she shared with her boyfriend, before driving a few kilometres further to his own place to eat supper alone. He'd probably be having tuna pasta. That's all he seemed to eat when he wasn't coming to me for his supper. A sudden wave of guilt and anxiety washed over me. *I can't believe I'm doing this. What am I doing? I can't leave them.*

A great weight landed in the seat next to me and I looked up to greet my seat-mate. *Or not!* I thought, as she looked down at me with total disdain.

Flight attendants walked the aisles, slamming shut the overhead lockers and checking seat belts. The sound of static came over the intercom, and then the almost bored voice of the captain announced our imminent departure. I had the sudden urge to jump up, grab my things and shout, 'Sorry, there's been a mistake – I need to get off!' But I didn't, of course, and the plane crept forwards into position for take-off. Anxiety turned to panic as in that moment I realised how much I didn't want to leave my life here; my kids, my friends, my little home – even my job.

But too late!

The plane thundered down the runway and lifted slowly, ponderously into the air. With a lump in my throat and tears in my eyes – I was on my way. Seat belts were snapping open and another smiling angel, this one pushing a drinks cart, came along, and over a large gin and tonic and a tiny packet of salted peanuts, I reconsidered my position. It was simple enough really; Mum needed me and the kids didn't. Mark certainly didn't. He would always be absolutely fine. Erin and her boyfriend, Sean, were planning to emigrate to Australia at the end of the year anyway. And Josh? He'd be over his last breakup soon. It wouldn't be long before there would be a new girl in his life to fall madly in love with. He wouldn't be able to come around for his supper two or three times a week anymore, but he could always go to Erin's.

Mum, on the other hand, needed somebody to take care of her. She had tried living in South Africa once, with my eldest sister, Cynthia. That was a while ago now. That hadn't worked out, so she'd gone back to the UK and tried living with the next eldest, Brigit – and that proved to be even more disastrous. So, she'd moved back into Greenfield Crescent, into a little bungalow three doors down from where she'd started off five years before.

But then a few years ago, her neighbour, 'Barbara-next-door' (as opposed to Barbara who she met on a coach trip one year and who has been on the Christmas card list ever since), raised the flag that Mum, at eighty-five, wasn't coping so well. Cynthia and Brigit were talking about putting her in an old age home, but Mum 'would rather die than be put in one of *those* places'.

Mum knew she'd run out of options. That's probably why, when I visited her three years ago, she had asked if I thought I would ever 'come home' to the UK. After thirty-five years in South Africa, I hadn't even considered it. She said she wanted to stay in her own bungalow, which she would leave to me when she passed on, if I felt inclined to go and live with her there in the meantime.

I hadn't given it much thought at the time, but now, with the kids all but flown the nest and retirement looming, it *was* something to think about. Mum was not an easy person to live with and I knew I was not her first choice of companion, but maybe my going over there would be a convenient fit for all. I'd spoken to big sister Cynthia about it and, with tongue in cheek, she had agreed it would solve the problem. So, here I was, on a plane, going back. Who'd have thought?

I thought about the little town house I was leaving behind. How the morning sun shone through the open-plan lounge to the kitchen, a sunny little cave of pale yellows, turquoise blues and the golden glow of the pine ceiling; how the big fern on the bookcase threw filigree shadows on the wall behind. All doors would stand open, letting in the gurgling sounds of the water feature at the front and more often than not the splashing of kids in the pool at the back. Leaving it empty and alone had been so sad, like leaving an old friend. But it would be waiting for me to come home to. If I wanted to.

We landed in Dubai at midnight with four hours to kill before the onward flight. Being to the east, Dubai was in a time warp all of its own to me, so I worked out the difference and told myself that when it was twenty past four on my watch, I had to be at Gate 11.

What a timeless, surreal place that airport is that even in the midnight hours it is as bright and hot as noon, and heaving with humanity; a crossroads for so many different cultures and tongues, all mixing in with the locals in their flowing robes and burkas – shopping, dragging luggage up escalators, taking up every seat in the cafés and bars or sleeping on rows of plastic seats. Babies cried, toddlers ran amuck, and above the din, the ascending 'ping-pong' chimes announced an arrival or departure, or requested a missing passenger to report to a desk somewhere.

I found my way to Gate 11 and went into a little coffee bar close by. The man who served me just raised his eyebrows rather than actually ask what I wanted. I asked him how much for a cappuccino, to which he just nodded and went off. When it came, I gave him twenty rands, and with a nod, he gave me change in some strange, foreign money.

I managed to get a seat by a window and looked out at the black night feeling a bit like Luke Skywalker visiting an off-planet space bar. I'd brought a book especially for this waiting time but couldn't concentrate on the words, so instead took a walk around the shops to look at the so-called duty-free merchandise. I bought Erin a little silver necklace, but heaven knows when I would be able to give it to her, I thought, my eyes tearing up again.

After another excruciating hour waiting at Gate 11, we were allowed to board, and as luck would have it I found myself sat next to the same woman again. What were the chances? And she didn't seem any more pleased to see me, either. Nor was she pleased to have to move to let me in. I smiled and apologised as she resettled herself without comment.

As soon as we were airborne the window shutters were pulled down, the lights dimmed and it was time to sleep. Seats were being reclined as people dozed, so after giving my best shot at bedtime ablutions in the tiny loo compartment (and apologising to the ogre-under-the bridge once again), I settled back into my seat. The Ogre was ready for sleep, fully reclined with neck pillow and eye mask, blanket up to her chin and sleeping socks on. Although tired, I didn't think I would be able to sleep. There was too much to think about. Tomorrow would be a new day, a new beginning... a whole new chapter, which would start the moment Alan picked me up from the airport.

Alan was the husband of my oldest friend, Maggie. I had visited them on my last visit but only very briefly, and couldn't wait to have a good old catch-up again. Maggie never changed. No matter how long it had been, it always felt as if I'd seen her just the day before.

Snuggling down under my blanket, I thought back to the day I had met her forty-odd years ago. We had both started work on the same morning in the personnel department of the local paper mill. I was eighteen and taken on as a shorthand typist. She was sixteen, and was an office junior. Pretty, fresh-faced, with auburn-blonde hair and big boobs, she was what

Mum called 'a buxom lass', with a friendly self-confidence and wicked sense of humour.

I was a size ten back then, with long brown hair trying to hide small boobs, and six-inch heals making the most of my legs. I had good legs, and (I decided years later) a pretty face, but not much in the way of self-esteem. Maggie thought I was 'dead posh and snooty' at first, but I can't think why.

We became best buddies from that first day. She had her desk in one corner of the big office, which we shared with Stinky Mavis, who didn't shave her arm pits, and who was secretary to Tom Hughes the personnel officer, and Hazel-with-the-lazy-eye, who did wages, and was engaged to one of the foremen in the mill. Both women were about ten years older, which made for a natural alliance between us two newbies. The older two seemed stuck in the fifties somehow, and this was the sixties – the age of The Beatles, Stones and Bob Dylan; the sexual revolution, miniskirts and mini-cars with flowers painted on them; hippie concerts, and demonstrations against atomic weapons and the war in Vietnam; a time when men walked on the moon, and the leader of the free world was assassinated on camera for the whole world to see. It was the age of technology; offices now had intercoms, photocopiers and telex machines. Everybody had a phone on their desk – and I even had one of the new *electric* typewriters.

On that first day I was dressed in a short, blue tunic dress, white pirate-sleeved blouse and high, black leather boots. Maggie was also in a white blouse, hers under a sleeveless, boob-hugging red tank-top, and straight skirt.

Maggie had already been shown her mail route around the offices and mill when Tom in his broad, northern accent asked me to go and get him some buttered toast 'from t'canteen' and Mavis and Hazel quickly put their orders in too. Tom asked Maggie if she could remember the way and would she mind showing me, and I wondered why she just couldn't go on her own to get it.

We had to walk right through the middle of the paper mill to get there, down a wide corridor between huge machines with thousands of rollers, over and under which ran wide rivers of paper at high speed. The heat and noise were nearly unbearable, and sweaty, half-naked men wolf-whistled their appreciation as we passed. Those were the days before political correctness and we thought it was great! We kept our eyes front and pretended not to notice, but shared a little sideways smile – and were friends from that moment on. And bonus, the toast was wonderful; an inch thick and covered with 'dripping', a dark brown sludge that looked like it could have dripped off one of the mill machines. But nothing tasted better on a cold, winter morning.

The plane bounced a little, reminding me where I was, and the captain announced that we were experiencing a little turbulence, but nothing to worry about. This proved to be the case and soon enough people were dozing off to the soft hum of the plane's engines. On my TV screen I watched a tiny yellow plane flash its way along a flight path of dots towards the Mediterranean, creeping ever closer to our destination. I think I must have fallen asleep then.

Suddenly, I woke up in a small, dark place and I couldn't breathe. Panic struck as I tried to draw in air, and couldn't. I had to get out, but the woman next to me loomed as big as a mountain. I pawed at her arm. I shook her and tried to speak, but just garbled sounds came out. Raising the eye mask, she glared at me through half-opened eyes then settled down again. So, I just scrambled over the top of her and lurched my way to the front.

'Can't... breathe!' I managed, to the two flight attendants standing chatting in the galley area.

They regarded me without concern, before one of them said, 'I'm sorry, first class is absolutely full and...' And down I went.

As the world swirled away from me, I heard a voice say, 'Uh-oh! We've got a shallow breather. You'd better tell the captain.'

When I woke, I was quite comfortably flat on my back on the galley floor with blanket and pillow, and an oxygen mask on my face. So, when the smiling angel hovered over me and told me to stay there, I was very happy to close my eyes and sleep.

The same one woke me up some time later, asking how I felt and if I'd like to return to my seat, as they would be serving breakfast soon. I guessed they didn't really need me sprawled out on the galley floor while they did so, so I let her take me back. The Ogre nearly smiled as she passed my beaker of fresh orange juice, and then my handbag, which she'd been guarding under her seat. I thanked her and was rewarded with a little smile.

Breakfast came shortly after, and then the captain announced that we were flying over the English Channel. I saw the white cliffs of Dover and the patchwork of bright greens and yellows that was the English countryside. Gradually, the cloud thickened until we were flying above a sea of bright, white cotton wool. The intercom crackled again and the captain told us that our arrival time would be 10.45am, which was ten minutes early due to a friendly tail wind. Soon after, he announced our imminent descent and that the temperature on the ground was four degrees. Four degrees? Really? Checking my watch, I realised it was 8.45 in South Africa. The kids would be at work, in the sunshine, as I, too, could have been.

The plane dropped down beneath the bright cloud into a dismal, semi-dark world. As it neared the runway, I had a glimpse of the city suburbs; bare trees, rivers of black ink and 'dark, satanic mills'. It felt more like Mordor than Manchester. With a bump we were on the ground and braking hard, then, swinging its nose towards the terminal building, the plane came to rest. Seat belts clicked open and the mad dash to be first into the overhead lockers began. I put my poncho on and waited.

***

I couldn't see Alan at first. Then this old man tapped me on the shoulder and I realised it was him.

'Hello,' he grumbled, smiling, and gave me a rough hug. 'You got here all right then?'

And without waiting for a reply, he took my trolley. Alan was a man of few words; just as well, as my teeth were chattering far too much to hold a decent conversation. I warmed up during the drive home and we spoke about the kids and how Maggie was, and my mum. He'd offered to bring her to the airport, but she had declined. It was probably too cold for her anyway. And then suddenly we were there, outside Mum's place.

'Mags says you must come for tea on Thursday night, if you want to?'

'Yes, please. That would be great,' I answered.

As Alan took my bags out of the boot, I smiled to myself, imagining the scene. Like with all old friendships, Maggie and I had shared memories that would inevitably be revisited again, and not least of which would be the time when, still in our teens, we had shared a bedsit together. Moving to a big city, i.e. Manchester, had seemed so exciting and full of promise at first, but our time there had ended in the breakup of our friendship for a while. My fault. It involved a certain DJ, lack of money, lack of fun, and a car crash. She had forgiven me but not forgotten, and we would no doubt be rehashing the whole thing yet again over a bottle of vodka. Well at least we could laugh about it these days.

Alan put the bags on the doorstep for me.

'Thanks for picking me up, Alan. Will you come in for a coffee?' I asked.

'No thanks. I'd best be getting back now.' And with a wave over his shoulder, he was gone.

Here I was, on the doorstep. Greenfield Crescent looked the same as ever, as if I'd never been away. The semi-detached, brick bungalows shrouded in white mist stood in their dismal, grey gardens, the muffled sound of the A53 coming from the gap in the hedge, and the twitch of a curtain next door.

I shivered, looking forward to a hot shower and a cup of coffee with Mum in front of the fire. I had to ring the bell twice before the door opened a crack, through which Mum blinked at me. Then she opened it wide and stood, more bent than I remembered, in a lopsided old cardigan and worn slippers; her unbrushed, white hair stuck out all over the place.

She looked at me wide-eyed. 'Natalie? Is that you? What are you doing here? Well! This is a surprise!'

Chapter Two

A few days later I was sitting on the floor in Mum's lounge, back against the sofa and legs stretched out in front of the fire as I looked out of the French windows. It was mid-morning but still semi-dark. There had been a snowfall in the night and the whiteness of the little lawn gleamed starkly against the gloom. Frost-covered spider webs festooned the low wooden fence and icicles hung from the garage roof.

Mum was still in bed and the only sounds were the tick, tick of the 'sunburst' clock above the mantlepiece, and the soft hiss of the gas fire. Otherwise, the silence defied being broken. Out in the garden, seen as a silent movie from behind the double glazing, a robin hopped down off the fence and, amid a flurry of wings, chased another one off the lawn. A speckled thrush with a snail in his beak caused a mini avalanche as he emerged from the undergrowth and looked around warily before running up the garden path; and two grey squirrels, after jerkily balancing their way along the top of the fence, climbed up into the snowy boughs of the neighbour's tree. They made their way along to the birdfeeder, where they defied gravity to get at the nuts. The tree belonged to the 'new neighbour', who had only lived there four years (as opposed to old Mr Dodd, who had been there twenty-five years before he died).

Mum's lounge was very... *Mum*. An oriental rug in front of the hearth on top of a thick, blood-red carpet; an overstuffed, sage-green suite with gold brocade, green marble coffee table, a gold lamp with tasselled shade and a porcelain bowl of porcelain fruit. All very grand for this modest lounge in Greenfield Crescent. There was a large ornate mirror on one wall but the only picture, looking down from between two gold wall lamps, was a portrait of Emma, Mum's spaniel, in her younger, slimmer days. Even then she had a mournful expression. Up to three years ago, Mum had walked her round the golf course and woods every day, but neither could manage that now. As a result, Emma had become obese, like a cocktail sausage on four toothpicks.

On the opposite wall, shallow alcoves each side of the chimney housed the TV and a display case, the latter being packed full of little china ornaments. They were everywhere else, too, on every windowsill, shelf, and any other available surface of any kind. In the kitchen that first night, I found them all along the windowsill, all over the table and even on the stove top.

In the six rooms there were twelve clocks (only one of which worked) and seven vases of silk flowers. Mum's bedroom was like Aladdin's cave with cheap beads hanging everywhere. She called it *bric-a-brac*. Not what I would have called it. She reluctantly agreed to me putting some away to make cleaning easier and I'd stowed away three boxfuls in the hall cupboard before she started to object.

I'd taken up residence in the small bedroom, which had in it a single bed. Well, that would be replaced, for a start. A dim light bulb hiding within a pink tasselled shade hung from the centre of the ceiling and the small, built-in cupboard was crammed full of all sorts of junk. The windowsill, of course, was covered in knick-knacks. It was time for a good old chucking-out session.

And there was another surprise waiting in the pantry. Every shelf, nook and cranny, was piled high with enough tins, bottles and jars to feed an army. Even the floor was three-cans deep in tomato soup, tuna, baked beans and mushrooms. She didn't even like mushrooms. There was also a big tin stuffed to the brim with little sachets of tomato sauce, mayonnaise and the like.

Some of the tins were up to ten years old, so I picked out the oldest ready for the dump. Mum was not happy. 'Tinned food doesn't go off. It'll last years!' she'd said. But then she'd agreed to let me put some in a box on the pantry floor so that we would know which ones to eat first. I filled two boxes for the pantry floor, and sneaked out more cans, one by one, and put them into empty boxes in the garage. I'd thought she wouldn't find them out there.

***

The phone rang, making me jump. It was Maggie.

'So, you're back, are you? How are you?' she asked.

'I'm fine, and you? Thanks for sending Alan to pick me up.'

'No problem. Yes, up to shit, as usual! How's your mum?'

'Not sure,' I said. 'I think she'd forgotten I was coming.'

'No – she was just hoping you wouldn't.' She chortled.

'Probably!'

'So, are you back for good now?'

'I don't know. Just going to see how things go.'

'So, are you getting on okay? Is she there with you?'

'No, she's not up yet, and yes, so far so good.'

'Mmm,' she said, unconvinced. 'And are you still fat?'

'No, I'm... er... slightly overweight.'

'No, you're not – you're still fat. Oh, good! Right then! Are you coming for tea tomorrow?'

'Yes, thanks. That'll be good.'

'Softlad'll pick you up at five, then. Okay?'

Still the same old Maggie then.

***

I heard the loo flush. Mum was up. The phone had probably woken her. A couple of minutes later she came slowly into the lounge leaning heavily on her stick, her other hand holding her back. Emma waddled along at her heels.

'Good morning,' I said. 'Is your back hurting?'

She sighed a little and I moved out of her way, offering my arm for support. Ignoring it, she dropped awkwardly onto the sofa, Emma lumbering up alongside.

'It is a bit, today,' she said, a little breathlessly.

'I'll put the kettle on. Would you like a Disprin?'

'No, you're all right. A cup of tea will do me.'

She looked up at the clock. 'What time is it? Have I overslept?'

'Not unless you were going somewhere.'

'No, I don't think so. But I like to be up by eight. Barbara-next-door always tells me if I get up late. Makes me feel a right lazy madam.'

'How does she know what time you get up? And what's it to her anyway?'

'Oh. She knows everything about everybody.'

'Well what time you get up is nothing to do with her. You don't even have to get up at all if you don't feel like it. At your age you're allowed to do whatever you like.' I smiled.

'And how old am I now?'

'You're eighty-eight.'

'I'm not, am I?' She giggled. Then noticing the gas fire, she said, 'Good Lord! What on earth have you got the fire on for? It's like an oven in here.'

'It's cold. It snowed last night. Did you see?'

'Yes, but no wonder you're cold dressed in that flimsy little thing. Go put a jersey on.'

'I'll turn it down,' I said.

'You can turn it off, for me. But suit yourself.'

I turned it off, put the kettle on, and found a jersey.

'It's not Thursday, is it?' she asked, accepting the tea.

'No, it's only Wednesday. Why?'

'I go shopping with Barbara on a Thursday. It's pensioners' day. Then we go for lunch at the Headless Horseman. They make lovely fish and chips.'

'That's nice.'

'And I play dominoes with her and Arthur on a Sunday afternoon.'

'My word! You've a better social life than me.'

'Well, you wouldn't enjoy our company, I'm afraid. Old fogies like us,' she said, suddenly very serious.

'No, I wasn't asking to be invited.' Time to change the subject. 'Now, who's Arthur? She was a widow last time I was over here.'

'Yes, she lost Bill, her husband. It was a stroke... did I tell you that already? Arthur's her fancy-man.'

'Her fancy-man?' I smiled, imagining Barbara in her eighties, having a boyfriend.

Mum leaned forwards, her voice nearly a whisper. 'She advertised for him, y' know.'

'Advertised?'

'On her computer.'

'Oh really? A dating site.' I was impressed.

She sipped her tea and squinted over the rim.

'There's something wrong when you've got to advertise for a man,' she said. 'Do you want a biscuit? They're in the pantry.'

'No, thanks. Not for me. Would you like one?'

'No. Don't get up just for me.' She frowned.

'I don't mind getting them,' I said, getting up.

'No, don't bother. I won't have one if you're not.'

'I must stop eating biscuits,' I said, sitting down again. 'It's all I've done since I arrived here.'

She looked me up and down with a critical eye. 'Yes, you'd feel much better if you lost a few pounds,' she noted.

Silence. In the past I'd have felt criticised by that remark and she would have told me I was being 'over-sensitive'.

'So, what's "Arthur" like?' I asked.

She put her cup down to answer. 'He's about eighty-seven or eighty-eight, I think. That's right, he had his eighty-eighth birthday October just gone. He's just a bit of company for her. Comes on a Friday lunchtime and goes again on Sunday night, and takes her out for a meal. They go on a coach trip now and again, too.'

'Lovely!'

'He's all right, I suppose, although I think he's been a bit of a lad in the past. Too old for all *that* now.'

'How do you mean? Bit of a lad?'

'Bit of a ladies' man, y'know. After the women.' She suddenly put down her cup and saucer and shuffled forwards to the edge of her seat quite urgently.

'Do you need a hand, Mum?' I offered.

'No, I'm fine. I'm going to get the biscuits.'

'Sit where you are. I'll get them for you.'

When I brought them to her, she looked at them and then at me.

'Aren't there any Romany Creams there?' she asked. 'Have another look.'

There were, well-hidden at the back of the pantry shelf.

'That's right!' she said, taking a couple – and then the packet, which she put down by her side. She bit off half a biscuit and gave the other half to Emma. But *I* was obviously going to be kept to my word.

'I don't think I'm the only one who would feel better for losing a few pounds,' I said, nodding towards Emma.

'Oh, don't start! The vet tells me off every time I go there with her.' She stroked Emma's grateful head. 'But you're all right, aren't you my darlin'?' Emma gazed back with mournful eyes. 'Who was on the phone?' Mum asked.

'Sorry, did it wake you up? It was Maggie. She's asked me to go to supper tomorrow night.'

'Oh, yes?' She smiled. She liked Maggie.

'I'll make your supper before I go,' I told her.

'Oh, don't worry about me. I have lunch out with Barbara on Thursdays. I shan't want tea as well.'

'Oh, of course. Right. Are you sure? I can leave some cheese and biscuits out, if you like.'

'No, you go. I can help myself if I want anything.'

'Of course you can,' I said, even though she hadn't since the day I arrived.

***

The next morning, I lay in bed wondering whether I should wake Mum up or not, or whether she would remember it was Thursday. As I lay there, willing myself to stick a toe out from under the duvet, I heard the bathroom door close and lock. Mum had beaten me to it. So, getting up anyway, I went to make coffee. There was no milk, so braving an icy blast at the front door (which sent my dressing gown flapping up around me), I brought in the two freezing pint bottles.

Mum was back in her bedroom, so I showered and dressed quickly, and went to make her some tea. But before the kettle had re-boiled, Mum came through the door with Emma at her heels. She was dressed in casual pants and top and wore decent shoes. Her hair (a little sparse these days) was neatly brushed, and there was a faint scent of 'Blue Grass' as she moved. She looked ten years younger.

'Good morning. You're looking very smart! Tea?'

'Oh! Hello,' she said. 'Yes, that would be nice.'

She seemed surprised to see me and I wondered if she

sometimes forgot I was there. She came and looked intently around the table.

'Have you lost something, Mum?'

'Yes, my tweezers. You haven't seen them, have you?'

'No. But they're probably in the lounge. I'll go look.'

I looked everywhere but couldn't find them. So, I gave her mine.

'Ah! There they are. Where were they?'

'I couldn't find yours,' I said. 'They're mine. But you can have them, if you like. I've got more.'

She looked closely. 'Are you sure they're not mine?'

'They're out of my make-up bag. But you can have them.'

'No, I'll just borrow them. You'll get them back.'

'Okay,' I said. 'What will you have for breakfast?'

'Are you making some toast?'

'Yes, I can do. Do you want something on it? How about an egg?'

'Oh, no. You know me. I only ever have a bit of toast and marmalade. I've gone off eggs.'

Not to mention the three dozen in the pantry, I thought.

'So! You're off shopping with Barbara today?'

'Yes,' she said, very capably. 'Make a list of what we need and I'll get it in.'

She became preoccupied with rummaging in her handbag, from whence came forth a pill box sectioned off into the days of the week, together with a couple of bottles of pills. She opened up each section of the box, tipped out the pills onto the kitchen table and, pushing her glasses up her nose, inspected each one.

'I think I should be taking these every day,' she said.

'What are they for?'

She didn't answer.

'When did you last have a check-up, Mum?' I asked, inspecting the bottles. 'Are you still with Dr Griffiths?'

'Yes, but you don't get to see him much now. I think he's semi-retired. You see a different face each time.'

'Maybe you should go and have a check-up. Yes?'

'Well, the district nurse, what's her name now? Er... Helen! She'll be around soon to do my blood pressure. We'll ask her.'

'This one you take twice a day,' I said, showing her the pill. 'And these once a day. If you like, I can give you them and then you don't have to worry.'

Her nose went up in the air. 'I can manage, thank you.'

But a little later, when Barbara-next-door came to pick her up and saw the pills on the table, she suggested the same thing – and Mum agreed.

Then they left on their shopping trip, leaving a very fretful Emma sitting on Mum's bed, watching the gate. I sat stroking her and tried to coax the old girl back to the warmth of the kitchen, but she was having none of it.

It seems horrible to say it, but it was really nice having the place to myself. I spent a couple of hours at my laptop at the table, sitting in the sun and watching two fat blackbirds playing hide-and-seek in the hedge outside. Then I followed the sun into the lounge and sat on the floor in the bay window, back against a chair. The warm rays made my eyes close, and listening again to the quiet tick, tick of the clock, I must have fallen asleep.

***

The doorbell woke me and I scrambled to my feet to answer it. I opened the door just in time to see Barbara-next-door retreating down the drive. I could see Mum struggling to get out of the car, so quickly went to help. Barbara was beckoning me to the open boot, out of which she was trying to lift a piece of furniture, a small bookcase in fact, which I helped lift to the ground. She stood back, straightening her matronly frame, and looked over the top of her glasses at me. She was a pleasant, round-faced woman who, despite her years, had lovely skin. And she always dressed nicely, except, perhaps, for the surgical stockings.

'Your mum just bought a bookcase,' she said, two open palms gesturing towards the piece.

'So I see!'

She gave me a meaningful nod. 'It's to put her knick-knacks on.'

She obviously knew all about them.

The bookcase was second-hand, grubby, and had chipped green paint showing through the white.

'Where on earth did she get that?' I asked.

'Down in the charity shop. She always likes to have a look in there before we come home.'

'That explains a lot.'

Barbara just smiled.

Mum had by now taken out some parcels from the back seat and was almost scurrying up the drive. I carried the bookcase to the front door and left it outside (to be taken to the garage later). Mum was in the hall, quickly jabbing silk roses – more silk roses – into an already over-full vase.

She gave a naughty little giggle. 'Oh, you're there, are you? I bought a couple more roses. They're so pretty, aren't they? I couldn't resist them.'

Barbara followed me in and asked me to fetch a couple more of Mum's things from the back seat of her car. There were three bags of shopping: eggs, tinned mushrooms, four Mills & Boon books, and a glass vase. There were also three dancing porcelain frogs, one of which wore a red spotted dress and the other two tuxedos, top-hats and canes – except one cane was broken off.

'There's some Marie biscuits in the pantry,' said Mum, nodding at me. 'Put the kettle on while you're there'.

I brought out both the Maries and the Romany Creams, although seeing Mum's slight frown when Barbara accepted a

Romany Cream, I wondered if I should have just stuck with the Maries.

'So, are you settling in okay?' asked Barbara, for the second time.

'Ja, I think so.' I smiled. 'Still feeling the cold.'

'Yes, I saw you nearly getting blown away on the doorstep this morning.' She chuckled. 'What you need is a nice warm pair of pyjamas!'

'I don't wear pyjamas,' I replied.

'So I noticed! But you'll need them *here*.'

'What?' asked Mum. 'Haven't you got pyjamas? Why didn't you say? I've got a pair for you.'

'Thanks, Mum, but I don't wear pyjamas. But thanks.'

'What do you mean, you don't wear pyjamas? What do you wear?'

'Nothing.'

'Why don't you wear pyjamas?' asked Mum, frowning.

'I don't like them. Or nighties.'

'Well, you'd better keep your curtains drawn,' said Barbara, smiling. 'There's some nosey people about.'

'Apparently!' I said, but I think the irony was lost on her.

I finished my tea and asked Mum if she was sure she didn't want me to make her a little supper for later. She said not, as they'd had a lovely fish and chips lunch.

'Your mum always has the fish and chips,' said Barbara, smiling.

And as if that prompted Mum's memory, she dug in her pockets and produced a small pile of plastic sachets of tomato sauce, salt and vinegar.

'What do you want those for, Mum?'

'Well, they're always handy for a picnic or a lunchbox, aren't they?'

Barbara gave me a knowing little smile as I wondered when Mum had last been on a picnic. And as far as I could remember, she'd never packed a lunchbox in her life. I excused myself and went to get ready to go to Maggie's.

***

Looking out of the bedroom window I saw it was getting dark already. The street lights were coming on, showing the shiny wetness of the roofs opposite. There was a telephone pole standing a few yards away at Mum's gate, its wires splayed out in all directions and criss-crossed with white vapour trails slashed across the grey sky. Liverpool, John Lennon Airport, lay just across the Mersey as the crow flies. I knew this scene intimately. In my teens I had sat looking out at the same view (except three doors down), and now it was as if all the years in between just disappeared.

Back then I couldn't wait for my life to start, and I was so scared that it never would if I stayed in Little Rutford. I'd wake up in the morning and stare at the vapour trails and imagine the people sitting in those planes, going to exciting places where the sun shone and people were happy.

That restlessness was one of the reasons Maggie and I had sought the bright lights of Manchester. Admittedly, a one-room bedsit in Chorlton-cum-Hardy, sharing a bathroom with the two guys across the landing, was a bit of a compromise – but for two young girls from Little Rutford, it was exciting stuff just the same. We'd both found jobs to go to and waited eagerly for our first payday, but the money we'd saved didn't last that long and we'd survived the last three days on baked beans, condensed milk, and desiccated coconut (handouts from Mum's larder). So, on our first pay day, we went to a Chinese restaurant and gorged ourselves silly.

When I left Manchester and returned to Little Rutford eighteen months later, I'd taken to my bed and gazed at the phone wires and vapour trails day after day. I didn't want to get up. My life was in ruins. What was there to get up for? The world was a cold, cut-throat place and I felt like a stranger in it, not even sure that I wanted to be in it. I just wanted to be left alone to sleep and forget. Manchester had chewed me up and spat me back into Little Rutford, and there I lay licking my wounds until Mum, with infinite wisdom, told me to stop feeling sorry for myself and go get a job. I did, and moved out again into a bedsit in Chester. Maggie had moved back to Little Rutford a couple of months before me and we were no longer friends. It was a long story.

A long story that had started years before in fact, when I was fourteen years old. I had been on holiday on the Isle of Man with Mum, Cynthia and Brigit (Dad had died the year before). One afternoon when Mum had gone for a nap, Cynthia was reading and Brigit had gone off somewhere, I had taken a walk down the seafront road to look at the shops. Specifically, a little boutique I had seen earlier. It looked interesting.

It was small and crammed full of stuff inside and thick with the smell of incense. And they had some nice stuff. I went to the changing rooms to try on a dress, and had quite a fright when a young man walked in on me. But it was obviously all about the dress; he helped me fit it, tugging slightly on one shoulder, and then at the waist. He seemed harmless enough. He was slight of build and wore tight-fitting jeans and a floral shirt; neat blond hair and piercing, ice-blue eyes. His nose was a little too big, but he was handsome, and very charming in a slightly effeminate kind of way. Probably queer, I thought.

It turned out that he actually owned the shop. He was also a DJ on the pirate radio ship moored off the island and quite a local celebrity. He was also a protégé of another famous DJ, who would become even more infamous in years to come. But I had no idea of any of that at the time.

Roy Trent was quite a bit older than me and I felt flattered when he asked me out that evening. So not queer! And after a chilly walk along a windswept beach, we'd ended up in the back of his van with the windows all steamed up.

After the holiday he had stayed in touch, and when he moved to Manchester a while later, I would now and again catch the train from Chester to go to see him. He had started up his own stable of DJs who he would send out to various clubs in the city, and they, 'the boys', would return from their gigs in the early hours of the morning to the dilapidated old house they rented with Roy, bringing home a percentage of the door-take and a few 'groupies' as they were known then. Just silly school girls, really. DJs were like the new royalty back then.

The boys were car mechanics by day, and Roy would pick up clapped-out old cars from the auction that they would 'do up' (usually with superglue), then resell at a profit.

I'd had a crush on Roy ever since that first night. And even though I only saw him a few times a year, I thought we had something special going on. I think he was in the back of my mind when Maggie and I decided to move to Manchester. We'd been there about three months when I told him I was now living in the suburb of Chorlton-cum-Hardy, and he immediately offered me a job as his personal assistant. I was thrilled. I even got a company car. In fact, I had a steady succession of company cars, most of which had bald tyres and very little in the way of brakes.

Such was my crush on Roy, however, that he could do nothing wrong. It was Roy's world. Whatever he said, or whatever he did, was okay. Even taking him coffee in bed in the mornings and finding him with other girls – even that had to be okay. He said they meant nothing. That he just 'serviced' them so that they would come back to the clubs and discos and bring their friends with them, and they'd take more money on the door. And that, so wrong on so many levels, had made me feel better at the time. Maggie hated him.

But every now and again he would take me out to the clubs where one of the boys would be playing the latest record releases. We would descend into dark, smoky, strobe-slashed places heaving with teenagers, but where the crowd would part before Roy like the Red Sea, and I would walk in on his arm feeling like a queen.

Wherever we went girls would immediately close in on him, smile, bat their eyelashes at him and give me the death stare. Guys would put a hand on his shoulder as if he was their best mate. They would treat me with kid gloves. I was 'Roy's girl', on whom nobody would dare make a move.

Roy didn't drink, and he would never dance. But he would watch me when I danced. I remember one particular evening when I was wearing a long, hip-hugging black dress, and I danced to 'I Heard It Through the Grapevine' – and he couldn't take his eyes off me. For once the inscrutable half-smile that was his default expression turned into something much darker. And that made me feel very good.

We bumped into George Best in a club one night. He and Roy greeted each other as old friends and stood at the bar having a chat for a minute or two. I was not introduced; the dark, brooding, Irish eyes just looked me up and down without making contact with mine. And I'd felt honoured to meet him!

Then one fateful night Maggie and I (having been home to Little Rutford for the weekend) were driving back tired, in pouring rain, in my company car. The windows were closed and it was hot and smoky inside (as we both smoked back then). Maggie, in the passenger seat, had a huge bowl of trifle on her knee (as you do!). She saw my eyes close, but there was nothing she could do in the few seconds it took for the car to mount the kerb and hit a bollard in the centre of Lymm roundabout. I'd fallen asleep at the wheel.

I will never forget the sight of Maggie just standing there, holding an empty bowl, the contents of which were all over her and being slowly sluiced off by the rain. Her expression was one of total disbelief, but for once, she was lost for words. But, thank goodness, the only injuries were a few bruises, and one very bruised and swollen ankle (Maggie's). Luckily, the authorities did not charge me because, apparently, the stretch of road leading up to the roundabout was deemed to be dangerous, as tankers slowed down and leaked oil there.

The car was a write-off, and was not insured. Roy wanted his money and I couldn't pay it all, so I made Maggie pay half – which was very unfair, of course. And she'd had enough. Roy was the reason I was never at home and we never went out or had any fun. And now this! She could just about manage to pay her half of the rent and food as it was, and having to pay for the car as well was too much. She went back to Little Rutford and moved in with her brother and family. I was not a good friend. Okay, I sucked. And karma came to bite me in the bum just weeks later when I couldn't afford to pay the rent and had to move back to Little Rutford myself.

My relationship with Roy had soured by then, and he didn't care that I was leaving. I'd come to realise exactly what I'd meant to him, and that all the silly little fantasies I'd had about being his girl were – just that. Maggie had been right and I felt so stupid, and hurt, and such a rubbish friend. So, I took to my bed and watched the vapour trails above the roofs of Greenfield Crescent.

Chapter Three

I was ready when Alan came to pick me up. As we pulled up in front of Maggie's house at the end of the terrace, I had such a strong feeling of *déjà vu*. There was the same privet hedge, the same 'clack' of the gate latch and the same little lawn with its bald spot under the tree.

The front door opened before I reached it, and there was Maggie. She had changed – not since the last time I saw her three years ago, but from the general memory I'd had of her through the years. When I visited her three years ago, I'd been shocked to see how thin she had become and the same thought struck me again now. But she looked well, and smart in her black slacks, and long cardigan jacket. Her greying hair was cropped neatly around her face, which held a familiar expression somewhere between a smile and disapproval.

'Hello! Come on in. Get a move on. It's bloody cold out here!'

She was about to turn and go back inside when I grabbed her and gave her a hug. 'Oh, it's so good to see you,' I said.

She hugged me back for a second or two, then brusquely pushed me away. 'Right! Get off me now! You know I don't do hugs.'

She led me through the narrow hall into the warmth of the lounge and took her place at one end of a black leather sofa, which with two matching single chairs pretty much filled the room.

'You've redone your lounge,' I said, taking in the mauve, silver and black theme.

'Yeah. D'you like it?'

'Mmm! Not sure. It's certainly different. Modern.'

'Well, I like it. And as it's me who sits in here the most, that's all that matters.'

Alan raised his eyebrows but said nothing.

'It looks like one of those make-overs that they do in sixty-minutes – do you watch that programme?' I asked.

'Yes, and they say that big, bold prints are in.'

I sank into a chair next to her, in a pool of light from a standard lamp that stood between us.

'Can I get anybody a drink?' Alan asked. 'Nat?'

'A cup of coffee would go down very nicely, thank you,' I said. 'Have I pinched your chair, Alan?'

'No, you're all right,' he said. 'I'm going to go and put the tea on in a minute.' He looked at Maggie with a bemused little smile. 'And what will you have, my dearest? Coffee?'

She stared at him unimpressed before turning to me. 'Do you want a vodka? I'm having vodka and coke.'

'Oh, okay. Have you got tonic? I'll have a vodka and tonic if you have, please.'

She looked at Alan in silent dismissal, and off he went.

'You've got him well-trained,' I said. '*And* he makes the supper?'

'No – he makes "the tea".'

'And why's *he* making "the tea"?'

'Because I work my arse off all day while he does stuff all, so it's the least he can do.'

'Is he not working?'

She shook her head. 'Not since the car factory closed down. Does a few odds and sods, a bit of gardening. Not much. Enough to pay for his golf, though.'

Alan came back with the drinks and we took them out of his grasp. Taking a seat, he cracked open a can of beer.

'I thought you were going to start tea,' said Maggie.

'I will. In a minute!' he answered, in a *stop nagging* kind of way.

He raised his can to me. 'Welcome home, Nat.'

'Thanks!' I said, raising my glass.

Maggie raised hers to mine. Her face was older and the thought occurred to me that I might not have recognised her if I'd met her in the street. But as we chinked glasses our eyes met, hers slate-grey and as sharp as an eagle's – and there she was.

'Cheers!' we said, in unison.

'So, how's your mum?' she asked.

'Okay,' I answered, and brought her up to date with my stay so far, the knick-knacks, the cans of food and nosy neighbour.

'Alan was round there a while back, to cut the lawn. Had to clear a space to put your cup down, didn't you?' she said to Alan, who nodded confirmation.

I nodded in agreement. 'And she doesn't want to part with them.'

'I don't think she's been looking after herself, has she?' said Alan. 'The place is always cold. I bled her radiators to make sure they were okay, but they were fine.'

'A lot of old people are like that, though,' said Maggie. 'It goes back to the war – not having much of anything.'

'I think that's it,' I said.

'Or she doesn't feel the cold,' she added. 'A lot of people can't afford the energy bills these days. They're going up all the time. But I don't think that's the case with your mum, is it?'

'Definitely not!'

'But *you'll* be feeling the cold more after South Africa,' said Alan. 'Are you missing it? Or are you glad to be here?'

'A bit of both. I'm going to miss the kids.'

'So, what did that old fart of a boss say when you gave in your notice?' asked Maggie. 'How long were you there? Eight or nine years or so, wasn't it?'

'Ten years. I didn't think I'd miss it, but I do. Well sometimes anyway. It's very strange to think of somebody else in my chair talking to the members, doing the seminars and annual dinner, or drumming up sponsorship for the golf day.'

'And you know,' said Maggie. 'In a couple of months' time it will be a case of "*Natalie who?*"'

'Yes, I know. I thought that even at my leaving do. "Old Fart" gave me the little leaving speech, which was amazingly nice considering how we used to fight.'

'Probably just glad to see the back of you!'

'Probably!' I agreed, smiling. 'How's your job going?'

'Don't ask – don't want to even think about it.'

'Mmm, like that is it?'

She rolled her eyes to the ceiling.

'I thought I might look for a little job around here. Mornings only, maybe,' I said.

Alan snorted, and an amazed Maggie asked, 'You're not serious, are you? You haven't a snowball's chance in hell!'

'It's not like it used to be,' added Alan. 'You can't just look in the paper and get a job. Those days have gone.'

'And if you're over forty – forget it,' added Maggie.

'Why d'you want to work, anyway?' asked Alan. 'Aren't you going to be your mum's carer? You can't do both. They won't let you. And you'll get more as her carer.'

'I need to work,' I said. 'Or I will go stark raving mad. I thought I'd get a little job and be a carer too.'

'No way. It's either or,' said Maggie. 'And you won't find a part-time job anyway. They're like hens' teeth.'

My future suddenly looked very bleak. 'I'll die if I don't get out now and again.'

'Don't be such a drama queen. Of course you won't! I wish I could flamin' give up work.'

She gave a quick glance in Alan's direction.

'And your car?' asked Alan, niftily changing the subject. 'You left yours in South Africa, didn't you? Will you buy a new one?'

'Yes. I left it for Erin to use. Hers was on its last legs.'

'Did your mum mention the one I told her about?'

'No. Tell me more.'

'A mate of mine who I play golf with. His mother died a couple of months back and he wants to sell her car. It's a little Matiz. Good little car.'

'Really? What colour? I'd love to be mobile again.'

'Grey,' he answered. 'Low mileage, never been in an accident. Didn't your mum mention it? She seemed quite keen on buying it when I spoke to her. You ask her about it. I'm going to get the tea now. Do you want another drink, Nat?'

Maggie and I caught up with our news. While I was in South Africa, we had kept in touch by phoning each other on our birthdays, preparing first with a 'bottle of choice' and a comfortable seat for the three- to four-hour marathon ahead. Maggie didn't want to know about video calls, or laptops, cell phones, or even how to work the TV remote. She hated Facebook and didn't want to hear about Skype, and apart from a quick visit three years ago, we hadn't had a good face-to-face chat in years.

As we tucked into our 'tea', a wonderfully sloppy lasagne, she started to tell me how things were at the hospice where she worked.

'Same old crap day in, day out,' she said. 'We used to have a lovely old girl as matron. But she retired and they put in this... this...' Her fork waved in the air as she tried to find suitable words. 'This *thing* that calls herself the matron. She's changed everything! She's made new menus, "to make them more suitable, nutritious and cost-effective", and you know, *I* always did the menus. I used to quite like going and having a little chat with the new-comers, find out what they liked to eat. And it was all good food. Nothing wrong with it. Ms Bickerstaff, she's called. She's one of these that struts round in a tight-fitted little suit, too much make-up and too much perfume, and a permanent smile on her face.'

'The smile of the tiger.'

'That's the one,' she agreed.

Alan stood, took my tray and asked if I'd like more.

'No, thank you, Alan. That was lovely,' I said, and couldn't resist adding, 'Lasagne is actually *my* signature dish, but I have to say, that was equally as good as mine.'

Alan cringed as Maggie looked at me totally aghast. Such blasphemy made her struggle for words.

'You… fuckin'… what?' she finally managed. 'You? Cook? No ways! You cook lasagne? You must be joking,' she spluttered. 'I remember your "cooking" from living in that bedsit in Manchester with you. Apart from the fact that you were never there to cook anyway, and when you were it was always tinned corned beef, baked beans and instant mash potato – and you even managed to burn that. *And* leave the pan for me to clean!'

I laughed, knowing that I had opened the floodgates, yet again, for the tirade of my failings as a flat-mate: my absence, my messiness, my lack of culinary skills, my habit of soaking my undies in a bucket of water with the then newly innovated *biological* washing powder, which if left for a few days would turn into one congealed lump in the bucket. And in particular – my choice of men.

'Lazy cow!' she finished, by which time I was laughing so hard the tears were running down my face and my ribs hurt.

Alan was laughing, too, at the stories he must have heard many times.

'You think it's funny?' she asked. 'It was a bloody nightmare living with you. Lasagne, indeed!'

Alan took the dishes, and as he went, whispered to me. 'Never challenge her cream scones, for God's sakes.'

He came back with recharged glasses and I offered to do the washing up, to which he nodded enthusiastically.

'Sit down, it's his job,' said Maggie.

'I don't mind doing it, really.'

Alan smiled and told me to sit myself down, as he disappeared back to the kitchen.

'He's very good,' I said.

'Pftt!' she said, reaching for her drink.

'So, how's life otherwise?' I asked.

She wrinkled her nose and took a slug of vodka.

'I hate it!' Nodding towards the door, she said, 'I hate him, I hate the kids, I hate the stupid cretins at work, I hate the neighbours. I hate it all!'

'No, you don't.' I laughed.

'I do, seriously,' she said. 'I think I might even hate you. The only good thing in my life is my beautiful and quite perfect little granddaughter, Julia. And she's the most beautiful, clever, wonderful little person ever.'

'It's like that, is it? And what about your grandson? Andrew's little boy – Lyle, is it?'

'*Liam*,' she corrected. 'I never see him. I told you, our Andy and Slapper-bitch moved to Milton Keynes. Didn't I?'

'Oh, yes. You did. Sorry, I forgot.'

'Yeah, well. I never see them.'

'That's sad.'

She shrugged. 'Didn't see them much even before that. That thing of a girlfriend made sure of that.'

'But why?' I asked.

She shrugged and curled her legs up under her on the sofa. 'Don't know. She's just a spiteful bitch!'

'Come on… what did you do?'

'Nothing, honestly!' she protested. 'I was always super nice with her. Even bought her expensive perfume for Christmas.'

'And you don't Skype?'

'What? I soddin' don't. You know that.'

'Have you ever been down to see them?'

'No! I've never been invited. And in any case, he knows where I am. He can come here if he wants to.'

'And Debbie? And Julia?' I asked.

'Oh, she's the sweetest little angel on this earth – Julia, I mean – not our Debbie. She's a nightmare. And I'm not biased or anything, but little Julia is brilliant. You wouldn't believe the things she comes out with. That's her.'

She nodded at a picture on the mantlepiece of a pretty little girl, cheek-to-cheek with her mother, Debbie.

'She's lovely,' I said. 'She was just a baby when I saw her last. She's like her mom, hey? How is Debs?'

'Who knows! She blows in here like a hurricane to drop Julia off or pick her up again. She's always in a rush to be off somewhere.'

'Is she still with whatssiz-name, the father?'

'No, thank the pope. She chucked that useless waste of space out a couple of years ago.'

She was thoughtful for a moment, then, 'Kids! I don't know about you but I'm not having any more, anyway.'

'Any more what?'

'Kids, stupid!'

'Me neither!' I laughed, and we clinked glasses.

Alan came and sat down again, and we chatted as he fell asleep, snoring, his specs sliding down his nose. Maggie looked at him despairingly and shook her head. Then suddenly remembered something.

'Hey! You know that Roy Trent creature went to prison, don't you? Did I tell you?'

'No!' I was amazed. 'You're joking? What for?'

'No, I'm *not* joking. About two years ago, for historical sex crimes.'

'What? He must be in his late sixties, seventy even, by now?'

'They got him! He got twenty-odd years,' she said, with satisfaction.

'He'll be lucky if he sees the outside again, then. What "historical sex crimes"?'

'Well, you should know,' she said, cynically. 'You could have given evidence yourself, if you'd been here.'

'No, I couldn't have.'

She looked over at Alan, checking that he was asleep. 'It was rape,' she whispered.

'No, it wasn't!'

'Yes, it was!'

I thought back to the holiday on the Isle of Mann and, to be honest, I wasn't sure whether it was rape or not. 'They say they can recognise a certain type, don't they? Like they can almost smell their vulnerability.'

'Well, he certainly saw you coming!'

I was just about to reply when Alan snored himself awake and looked around bewildered.

'You were snoring,' Maggie accused.

'Well, I'm tired,' he replied.

And checking the time, I apologised for staying so late.

'Don't worry, you haven't kept us up,' said Maggie. 'Don't mind him, he always falls asleep in the chair. D'you want a coffee before you go?'

'No. Thanks,' I replied. 'I've kept you up long enough.'

As I got into Alan's car, Maggie, shivering, leaned close to speak through the car window. 'D'you want to come again next Thursday?'

'Ja!' I said. 'That sounds good.'
'Well bring your own bloody vodka then.'
She waved as we drove away. Yes, same old Maggie.

Chapter Four

Within a few days I was the proud owner of a little grey Hyundai Matrix. It was wonderful to get behind the wheel again. Instant independence – instant freedom!

Putting petrol in my own car for the first time in nearly forty years was quite an experience. Getting out into the cold wind to mess around with dirty petrol caps and awkward pump nozzles was very different to how it was in South Africa, where you just sat and waited while pump attendants did everything for you. And it took me so long to work out how to use the tyre pressure gauge, that the guy behind me actually came and showed me how. Nice guy.

One sunny (if cold) morning, I thought I would drive through to Chester and visit a few old haunts. So, taking a familiar route through little hamlets and past green fields, I passed the Nag's Head, with the same white horse's head sign, the black and white beams and flower boxes. I was reminded of summer drives along these country roads with an old boyfriend. We drove in his MGB GT with the top down, my hair blowing in the wind and Booker T and the MGs playing 'Time Is Tight'.

I passed through Mickle Trafford and Hoole, and followed the sign for the city centre, soon to realise that this was now for pedestrians only. So, I drove down to the river and parked in the car park of the Boathouse. It used to be a smoky, noisy place where the in-crowd hung out on Friday and Saturday nights, three or four deep at the bar, but which was now a 'non-smoking, family-friendly, pub-restaurant'.

In the gloomy and quiet late afternoon, I walked the promenade alongside the river with a few dog walkers for company; their collars turned up against the wind, they followed their mutts through the multi-coloured autumn leaves. I remembered it as it was in summer, the river reflecting a blue sky and the Salvation Army brass band playing on the bandstand, people eating ice creams or drinking beer at the pavement cafés, or riding on the Mississippi-style river boats.

I drove back up towards the city centre, found parking behind the market, and walked the narrow, cobbled streets and alleys to Eastgate Street. I looked again at the beautiful old clock with its intricate metalwork above the Roman gateway, where it had patiently ticked away all the years I had been away. I walked along the Rows to Lower Bridge Street to see if the Falcon pub was still there. It had already weathered a few hundred years before I was even born, so I suppose it wasn't *that* surprising to find it still standing. It looked as small and crooked as ever, and I remembered the low-beamed ceilings, tiny rooms, uneven floors, and narrow wooden stairs where the plaster had been stripped back to reveal the original wattle.

Sauntering back up Bridge Street, I thought back to my secretarial college days here – the hippy era when we all wore a flower in our hair, and sat around the cenotaph and steps eating lunch in the sunshine on warm summer days. When Scott McKenzie asked *Are you going to San Francisco?*, and Bob Marley music drifted from tiny boutiques hung with bead curtains and feather boas, and which sold bongs, lava lamps and crystals. I remembered the smell of incense, the music and the psychedelic colours – even the sunshine on the cobbles.

The light was fading fast, and it was time to go home. As I drove, on impulse, I decided to swing by Brigit's place in Bromborough, just ten minutes away from Mum. I'd tried to visit her when I was over here three years ago, but her neighbour had told me she was on holiday in Greece at the time.

I parked outside her gate, and as I walked up the path a Siamese cat smiled at me from the windowsill inside the house. Its attention suddenly went to something in the room, something behind the lace curtain, and I thought there must be somebody in. Obviously not though, because I rang the bell several times and there was no answer.

When I mentioned this to Mum later, she told me that Brigit would have been in, but if she didn't have her make-up on, I would not have been allowed to see her. Nobody was.

***

So, when Mum went for an afternoon nap, I gave Brigit a call. The phone rang and rang and I was just about to hang up when a deep, husky voice came on the line.

'Hello?' she breathed, sounding posh and dramatic.

I wondered for a moment if I had dialled the right number.

'Brigit?' I asked.

'Yes, it is… who is this?' rolled the voice.

'It's Nat.'

'Oh. Hello. I heard you were coming back to the UK. I take it you're at Mum's?'

'Yes. I actually popped in to see you earlier, but you were out. I should have phoned first.'

'Yes, it's always best to, isn't it?' she purred.

Silence.

'So how are you?'

'I'm well, thanks,' she said. 'Very well.'

'So! D'you want to meet up?'

'Meet up?'

'I'd like to come visit you.'

'Oh. Okay.'

'So, when would suit you?'

'Er… er… I'm a bit bogged down at the moment. It's dress rehearsals all this week and then we open at the weekend. Maybe sometime after that?'

Mum had told me that Brigit was into amateur dramatics these days, which surprised me because I'd also heard she'd pretty much become a hermit since Peter died.

'Okay,' I said. 'That's nice. What's the production?'

'*The Importance of Being Earnest.*' She didn't elaborate.

'Okay. Well, maybe you can give me a call when it suits you for me to visit. I'm here. Not going anywhere.'

'Yes, I will do that,' she said. 'But, Natalie, can I just say one thing?'

'Of course. What is it?'

'Please don't bring Mum with you, will you? In fact, don't even tell her you're coming here. Okay?'

'Ja, don't worry. I understand.'

'Okay, I'll be in touch then. Goodbye.'

But I very much doubted that she would be.

***

Now I had my little car, I felt I should ask Barbara-next-door if she would like me to take Mum shopping, and although enthusiastic about the idea, she pointed out that it wasn't that simple.

'She likes to go to the charity shop, too,' she reminded me. 'And then to go for fish and chips.'

'Well, I'll take her for the groceries,' I said. 'And she can still come with you to do the rest, if you like?' And she did, so that was a plan.

It was a rainy Tuesday in March when Mum and I drove to the ASDA superstore and parked in its car park. I noticed each space had its own meter as Mum rooted in her purse, telling me we needed money for it.

'I can't believe you have to pay,' I said.

'Well, this is the municipal car park. I haven't got any change.'

'I haven't either. Let's just get in there. I'll get change and come back.'

'They won't give you change in there,' she warned. 'You'll have to go across the road. There's a kiosk up there.'

It was starting to rain again, so I quickly got Mum into the store and parked her on a chair just inside the door while I went in search of a pound coin. Ten minutes later, now quite wet and cold, I'd put money in the meter and was back at the lines of trollies outside the door, when I hit the next problem. The trollies were chained to each other and I couldn't work out how to free one.

A woman approached. 'Like this, luv. You put y'r pound in 'ere,' she said. And after pressing a coin into a slot, she walked off with the trolley. *I can't believe it*, I thought, envisioning another trip up to the cigarette kiosk for another pound. With hope against hope, I dug desperately in my purse for a non-existent coin. As I did, a man returned his trolley and a one-pound coin spat out. He looked at me kindly.

''Ere, take this one,' said that lovely man, giving me the coin.

At last, I walked into the warmth and brightness of the store and found Mum, who instantly commandeered the trolley to use as a walking frame. I could hardly believe the sheer size of the place. Off we went, full steam ahead past a bank of tinkling tills, the sound interspersed with occasional, crackly announcements made by a voice that could raise the dead.

When we were nearly at the end of the biscuits, crisps and snacks aisle, a little girl of about two years old whizzed around the corner and, giggling, crouched down behind a display stand. I think in her world she was playing hide-and-seek, but her mum obviously wasn't, and an angry voice boomed from the next aisle.

'Tiffany-Rose? Where the fuck are you? You bloody come 'ere, *now*!' she roared.

The little girl looked at us, a little anxiously now.

'Tiffany-Rose, I'm warnin' ya. Get back 'ere *now*!'

Tiffany-Rose wiped her nose on the padded sleeve of her bubble-gum pink jacket. I think she was just about to give herself up when her mother, a lumbering, vastly overweight woman, appeared and swooped down on her.

'Come 'ere, you!' she exploded, grabbing the child by the back of the collar and scooping her up off her feet.

'What've I told ya about fuckin' disappearin' like that,' she screeched, dropping her again. The little girl wailed loudly as the mother bent over her, mooning a plumber's crack above a pair of low-slung (but desperately hanging on) denims.

'An' shurrup!' she bellowed, pulling Tiffany-Rose to her feet.

The child wailed even more loudly as she was dragged off, her mother scowling at me as she shuffled by.

I looked to see Mum's reaction to this, but she was nowhere to be seen, and I marvelled at how quickly she had managed to disappear. It was like this store had its own Bermuda Triangle thing going on between the sweets and biscuits and the fresh fish section. I'd lost her! Panic rose as I walked along the top of the aisles, my eyes desperately searching each one but not seeing her. I was just about to go to the service desk and ask for her name to be called out when I spotted her – by the fruit, her back turned on the world as she sneakily scoffed down black grapes.

'These are nice,' she said, not even looking up at me. 'Nice and sweet. Try one.'

'Well, let's take some home,' I said, putting a pack in the trolley.

'I'm not paying that price for a few grapes!' she said, indignantly putting them back on the shelf.

I was exhausted by the time we pulled up in the driveway at home. Barbara was there in her front garden and asked me how it went. So, I told her, even about losing Mum in the store.

Barbara smiled and nodded knowingly.

'And was she by the grapes?'

'She was,' I acknowledged.

Very meaningfully she asked, 'Would you like me to take her next week?'

'Yes, please,' I replied, humbled and grateful.

***

That Thursday night, I told Maggie about Tiffany-Rose and her mother, but she didn't seem surprised. Just rolled her eyes.

'What happened to women wearing skirts and dresses and make-up and looking like women?' I asked. 'You know, from the back view, you couldn't tell if it was a woman or a man. Everybody seems to wear denims or track-suit bottoms these days.'

'What is there to get dressed up for?'

'For work. Or just for yourself. If you look nice it makes you feel good about yourself. Makes you feel more confident.'

'That one probably doesn't work. She's probably got three or four kids by different blokes and gets benefits for each child. She doesn't need to work. And she doesn't need a man.' She looked at me sadly, patiently. 'Things have changed in the last forty years, you know.'

***

On Friday night, at nine o'clock in the evening, the phone rang in the hall. Mum had already gone to bed, so I ran to answer it before it woke her, and was amazed to recognise Brigit's husky voice.

'Hello? Natalie?'

'Yes. Hello, Brigit.'

She hesitated, as if unsure whether to go on.

'What are you doing on Sunday? Do you want to come round then?'

'Yes!' I said, probably sounding a little too enthusiastic. 'What time?'

'About two-ish?'

'Yes, that will be fine,' I answered. 'I'll see you then.'

'Alone.'

'Yes, alone.'

***

Brigit had always been the black sheep of the family. Just as I had been 'nothing-but-a-damn-nuisance', she had always been 'nothing-but-trouble', justified by the fact that Nurse Cawson had apparently said so, on a visit made when Brigit was ten months old. And it had become a self-fulfilling prophecy.

I hadn't seen Brigit in fifteen years, and was nervous. It took ages for her to answer the door, then throwing it open, she quickly turned and disappeared down the hall again to the kitchen, apparently to retrieve a loaf of bread out of the oven.

'Mmm! Smells divine!' I said, closing the door.

'Yes, it does rather, doesn't it? And tastes so much nicer than bought.'

I couldn't get over the voice. She never used to speak like that: deep, dramatic and *daah-ling*!

She had always been short and slight, but seemed even more so now. Her Bette Davis eyes looked puffy and sad, but although the years had taken their toll, she was still looking pretty good for her sixty-two years.

She showed me into a neat and peaceful lounge of pastels and florals, the afternoon sun falling through the white lace curtains and across a beige carpet. It was nothing like her old bedsits where you'd be lucky to find a clean mug, or have to move stuff off a chair before you could sit. There was no hint of that in this suburban parlour. And no photos.

'Take a seat,' she said, with a tight smile.

I sat on a window seat at the table, on which sat a saucer of sweets.

'Have one. Help yourself,' she said, pushing them over to me.

'Thanks,' I said, taking one. She didn't.

'So, what can I get you to drink? Tea? Coffee? Or would you like a glass of wine? I've got wine.'

'That sounds good,' I said. 'Thanks.'

Like the last time, the cat smiled at me from the windowsill at the other end of the room, while Brigit brought the wine and poured it at the table. She was fascinating to watch – as if on stage. The long, black dress and the haughty way of her reminded me of Morticia, of Addams Family fame.

Sitting opposite me, she offered me a cigarette, which I declined.

'That's right. You gave up, didn't you?'

She smiled languidly as she lit one up and inhaled deeply, and blew smoke at the ceiling. Then her blue eyes fixed me with an intense stare.

'So, how are *you*?' she asked, as if terribly interested.

'I'm okay, thanks. How are you?'

'Oh. You know! Does Mum know you're here?'

'No. She's out with Barbara-next-door. I won't mention I've been.'

'That's probably for the best. You might think it strange, but I really can't be doing with her anymore.'

'Ja. Don't worry. I understand.'

She considered a moment. 'I don't think you do, you know. You have no idea what I've been through with her over the years while Cynthia and you have been in South Africa.'

'I can imagine. She's naughty.'

'Naughty!' She laughed, bitterly. 'Naughty?' And then the smile was replaced by an intense frown. 'She's nasty! Not naughty. Bloody evil, in fact. I'm not kidding. My nerves just can't take her anymore. It just became so toxic. So, if you've come to win me over, please, don't waste your time.'

'Nothing like that, honestly. I just wanted to see you. See how you feel about me being here.'

Brigit sipped her wine and watched me through half-closed eyes, as if still standing behind lace curtains.

'I don't mind.' She shrugged, surprised. 'Why would I?'

'Well, I don't know. Weren't you and Cynthia thinking about putting Mum in a home or something?'

'There didn't seem to be any other option. Cynthia couldn't get on with her and Mum nearly gave me a nervous breakdown living here. She didn't come and live with you, so you wouldn't know what it's like. She's a nightmare!'

'I did offer,' I protested.

'Yes, I know. But you'd just divorced Hennie and had three teenagers in the house. She wasn't going to come to you, was she!'

'She wouldn't come to me, *anyway*.' I laughed.

'Probably not.' She smiled, exhaling up to the ceiling again.

'Well, when I came over three years ago, Mum told me that if I came to live with her in her bungalow, she would leave it to me when she goes.'

'Yes, I heard something about you coming to live with her.'

'So how do you feel about that?'

'Irrelevant to me,' she said, stubbing out the cigarette. 'Has she actually made a will? I've told her she mustn't leave anything to me. I don't want a thing from her. I'd give it to the local dogs' home. And I mean it!'

'Ja, I heard that. Cynthia apparently took Mum to make a will last time she was over, but didn't go in the office and doesn't know the details.'

Brigit gave a wry smile. 'Like hell Cynthia didn't go in.'

'Ja. That's what I thought.'

'And if she did, there's no way the bungalow was left to you.'

'Well, I hadn't even given Mum an answer at that stage.'

'Cynthia's always had the lion's share of everything.' She frowned. 'Why would that change now?'

'Because Mum wants to stay in her own home and me being there allows her to, basically. Promising the bungalow to me is just the carrot.'

Brigit shrugged, bored. 'What happened between Mum and Cynthia? Did they fight? Mum never said why she came back to the UK.'

'They didn't fight, but Mum was very demanding. Cynthia would get home from work and Mum would be waiting to be taken out and entertained.'

'Oh, God! I can just imagine.'

'And you should have seen the granny flat they stuck her in. You know they converted the old garage? It was just a square little box with no view. The new garage was an extension on to the main house, with a beautiful view of the mountains. That should have been the granny flat. Mum didn't want to stay, but she couldn't come home to the UK then because old Ben was not up to the return journey.'

'Never mind the six months quarantine this end. And yes, I can just see Mum wanting to be Queen Bee and have Cynthia running around after her.'

'Exactly. And if Mum was going to stay, Cynthia needed her to pay for the old garage to be converted. Mum wasn't happy there and she tried to delay giving an answer. But Cynthia called a family meeting and said, "Right! We're not going to leave this table until we've made a decision." And apparently she thumped the table so hard it made Mum jump out of her skin!'

'Who told you this?' asked Brigit.

'Mum.'

'So Cynthia was trying to assert her authority. And Doug? Probably in the background, trying to grow a pair!'

'Well, Mum managed to fob them off. But Doug went to her room a little later and said, "Right! Mum, it's make-your-mind-up-time!"'

Brigit lit another cigarette. 'He'd probably been told to man-up and go do something.'

'Ja. Probably. And Mum just told him yes, she would stay, knowing that she didn't want to. And she paid for the conversion. But then, of course, a few months later old Ben died anyway, and she came home.'

'Then she came knocking on my door!'

'Yes. What happened? She told me she came back from walking your dog one day and found her suitcases in the hall, all packed and ready to go.'

'Ugh!' she said, shaking her head. 'This place was too small. We talked of buying a new place together, but it was hell. She didn't like what we liked, and we didn't like what she liked. But I couldn't have lived with her anyway with her nasty, manipulative little mind games. I don't even want to talk about it.' She shared out the last of the wine 'Shall I open another bottle?'

'Why not?' I said, feeling relaxed from the first one.

'Would you like something to eat? I'll just make us a little snack. You open the wine. I won't be a minute.'

I heard her rattling plates and dropping cutlery into the sink as I opened the wine, then wandered over to stroke the cat. He purred happily. I wondered what Brigit did with herself these days, and if she missed Peter. They'd never had kids. They'd tried, but it wasn't to be.

Eventually she reappeared with a feast of warm, homemade bread with things to dip it into, slices of chicken, cheese, olives and sun-dried tomatoes. My mouth was watering.

'Wow! That looks lovely.'

She smiled. 'Help yourself.'

And I did.

'How is Mum, anyway? I hear she's showing signs of dementia?'

'She forgets things. Who wouldn't at eighty-eight? She does get confused, but she's more aware than she likes to show, sometimes.'

'Mind games! I don't know how you can stand it. You know, she used to come here every Sunday with Aunty Eileen, for lunch. But she just used to work on my nerves so. I'd be downing a bottle of tranquillisers just to get through the day. And she was horrible with Eileen.'

'How d'you mean?'

'Well, you could hold a decent conversation with Eileen. She could be quite insightful at times. But if we talked about a current news item or anything vaguely intellectual, Mum would pull a face and try to shut us up; interrupt us, talk over us, turn the TV up.'

'She knows how to wind you up, doesn't she?' I laughed.

'She always did, no matter how many times I told myself I would stay calm. Do you know, on birthdays, she would always get me something she knew I wouldn't like. Or is that just me being weird?'

'Well, the last time Mum visited me in Jo'burg, we went to a flea market and she bought two skirts. Elasticated waist, layered, y'know?'

Brigit grimaced.

'Ja, I never liked them either, but she'd bought one for Cynthia and one for me, and laid them out side by side, a red one and a green one, and told me to choose. So, I chose the red one, and immediately she said that one was actually for Cynthia. The green one was for me.'

Brigit threw her hands up in the air.

'There you are,' she said. 'But it's always been like that, hasn't it?'

***

Towards the bottom of the second bottle of wine, the conversation turned to *do-you-remember-when*, and we laughed over our old escapades.

'Remember cutting up Mum's never-been-worn, fancy pink negligee to make curtains for the hamster cage?' I asked.

'Oh my God, yes! I don't know what the fuss was about. She was never going to wear the damn thing – it had been in that drawer for years.'

'Can you imagine Mum wearing something like that, anyway?'

She shook her head. 'Somebody must have bought it for her. I'm still trying to work out how she ever had three kids! It must have been by immaculate conception. But the hamsters made good use of the negligee.'

'Ja! As *bedding*. Not curtains.' I laughed.

'My God! It's a good job she doesn't know half of what we did do, isn't it? And you know what really pissed me off? The way she would say, "What've you done now?", just *assuming* that I *had* done something.'

'No,' I corrected her. 'She usually said "*What have you two little divils done now?*" when *you* had done something that I knew nothing about!'

She grinned impishly, and I caught a glimpse of the sister I once knew.

Then it was gone again and she looked thoughtfully into her wine. 'And then there was the fire,' she said.

'The fire?'

'Yes. It wasn't an electrical short. It was me!'

I sat there, dumbfounded. 'It was you? You're joking?'

'No. It was me, I'm afraid.'

'What happened?' I couldn't believe what I was hearing.

'It was a Sunday, remember? You'd gone off to Sunday school with that little friend of yours. Mum was in the kitchen, Dad down the garden, Cynthia in her room. And I was having a period and I needed to put a sanitary towel on the kitchen fire. So, while nobody was around, I opened up the glass door and popped it in. Remember those bloody great things Mum had us buy from Miss Rutter's wool shop, like a brick between your legs?'

'I do!'

'Well, I put it in the fire. Mum had just thrown new coal on and there weren't any flames but I thought, give it a minute, it will burn. But it didn't! It just sat there. Then Mum told me to call Dad for lunch, and I thought, *Oh shit! I'd better get it back out and hide it.* Couldn't let Dad see it! So, I fished it out again, wrapped it in a vest and hid it among my knickers in my underwear drawer, and went down for lunch. And the rest, as they say, is history.' She sat back, nonchalantly taking a sip of wine.

'All these years, and you didn't say a word?'

'No,' she said, flippantly. 'And that was another time when Cynthia got the best. Remember? *We* were supposed to get the new clothes with the insurance money?'

'All these years, and you said nothing?' I persisted.

'Nope!' She stubbed out her cigarette, staring at me. Challenging me.

'D'you mind if I tell Mum? I'm going to tell Mum, okay?'

'Yes, if you want to.' She looked away, as if bored with the subject.

'You know she blamed me for that, don't you?'

She pulled a fake smile. 'Sorry!' But she didn't sound very sorry.

I was shocked. I was glad that she'd told me the truth, and angry that she'd waited so long. But I'd come here to bond with my sister and I didn't want to fight with her. There was nothing to be gained in that. Not for something that happened so long ago.

We chatted a little more, and she told me all about the amateur dramatics and about her last years with Peter. But the mood for easy banter was gone. Four hours had passed and we'd said everything we had to say. It was time for me to go home.

She kissed me on the cheek, and agreeing that we must do this again soon, I went to the car. She waved from the front door, which closed before I drove away.

***

That evening, as I sat watching TV with Mum, I mentioned to her that I'd bumped into Brigit, and that we'd gone for a cup of coffee together.

'Oh, really?' she said. 'And, how is she?'

'Same as ever. But guess what? Remember when we had the fire?'

'I'll never forget it! The mess! Nearly gave me a heart attack, it did.'

'It was Brigit! Brigit caused it.'

'Brigit?' Disbelief in her eyes. 'How d'you mean?'

I told her everything that Brigit had told me.

Mum frowned. 'I see. But why didn't she say?'

'She was too embarrassed, apparently.'

'Embarrassed? After the things she used to get up to? I don't think so! Are you *sure* it was her?' she said, her eyes fixing back on the telly.

I don't think she believed a word of it.

Chapter Five

My birthday fell on a Sunday in May, and over breakfast I was touched when Mum gave me a present. I was amazed she'd even remembered. It was an old necklace of brown glass blocks along a chain of some indistinguishable, tarnished metal, which I guessed was from the charity shop. But it's the thought that counts.

'Thank you,' I said. 'It's lovely!'

'Do you like it?'

'Yes,' I said. 'It's lovely.'

'Are you sure you like it?'

'Of course.' She didn't look convinced. 'Tell you what, it's such a nice day, shall we go for a drive somewhere?'

We drove to Parkgate, where she sat on the back seat sharing an ice cream with Emma and reminiscing about her childhood visits there. She remembered her childhood, 'like it was just yesterday', but couldn't remember what she'd had for breakfast that morning. Her memory was selective, however. She would often ask what day it was, but knew when to be ready to go shopping with Barbara-next-door, or to play dominoes. Or she would ask how old she was, then giggle when I told her. But when Helen the health visitor came to visit and asked

Mum her age, Mum told her, without hesitation, that she was eighty-eight; then looked at me and added, 'Or that's what *she* says, anyway.' And when Helen asked her questions about her mobility, she was savvy enough to tell her that she did all her own housework and shopping, and even mowed the lawn herself. Helen looked at me over Mum's shoulder and, seeing my astounded expression, just winked that she understood. She whispered to me later that old people often think that they still do these things for themselves. But I think, in Mum's case, she was lying through her teeth in case anybody had any ideas about putting her in a home.

***

And so, the days passed. And then the weeks. And soon enough I was part of the furniture again. Life revolved around giving Mum her meals and her pills, shopping (alone), housework, and visiting Maggie and Alan on a Thursday night. I really did look forward to that each week. On one occasion, Maggie was throwing out an old bike and I took it eagerly, because the weather was getting warmer and the great outdoors was calling. I hadn't ridden a bike in years, but you know what they say… And after a wobbly start I got the hang of it again.

The next sunny morning, I found some sensible shoes in the hall cupboard (probably Cynthia's) and went for a ride. I headed for the woods, and was soon gliding over soft, leaf-mould paths under a canopy of newly green leaves, breathing in the wonderful, woody smells. In the deep shade, the quiet was broken only by birdsong, bike wheels splashing through puddles, and my own breathing. The sun shafted through the lichen-covered trees and glinted off the handlebars, and it felt good to be alive.

After that I was out on the bike once or twice a week, exploring the country lanes all around. I kept the bike in the garage, leaning against boxes of tinned food I'd sneaked out of the pantry. I didn't think Mum went into the garage anymore, but just in case, I thought the bike leaned up against the boxes might discourage prying eyes. Putting the bike back one day, my toe happened to kick a box, and it moved as if empty. And it *was* empty! All three of the boxes I'd filled were now miraculously… empty. No wonder the tins in the pantry never seemed to grow any fewer.

***

After three or four months in the UK I felt like I'd been there forever, and boredom was beginning to set in. South Africa was becoming just a memory, despite frequent Skype calls with Erin and the boys, which often would just make me miss them more. And Skyping is not the same as talking to someone face to face. Erin and I used to have wonderful girls' nights out together. That was before her boyfriend, Sean, moved in, that is, which was within three months of them meeting each other. Then the girls' nights out stopped. I never seemed to have time alone with her after that, as he'd always be with her when she came to visit, and he was always impatient to leave again. Even now, when we Skyped, he was usually in the background somewhere, and for some reason we couldn't have a laugh and a good old chin-wag with him there.

Within six months he'd suggested they emigrate to Australia. I thought it was all happening far too quickly, but now in her twenties, Erin wasn't going to listen to me. Within a few months, they'd be gone to start a new life halfway around the world, and which I would never be part of. And here I was in England. *Is this it? Is this the rest of my life?*

***

Then one Thursday evening when I was at Maggie's, her daughter Debbie arrived. She was a slim, self-confident young woman with straight, glossy black hair and her mum's sharp features.

'You're looking well, Nat. How are you keeping?' she asked, sinking into her dad's chair.

Alan brought her some leftovers from teatime and disappeared back to the kitchen to watch the football in peace.

Debbie sat and chatted with her mum and me, and asked about South Africa. I asked her about her life and if she had a boyfriend and she smiled, and told me there was nobody special in her life. She asked if I had anybody in my life. I laughed at the idea and told her no. So, setting her empty plate aside, she reached into her bag and brought forth a tablet.

'Oh, here we go,' said Maggie. Which didn't deter Debbie one bit.

'You don't have to roll your eyes, Mum,' she said, without looking up.

'And you don't have to bring *that* out now!' said Maggie.

'I just want to show Nat something,' she answered, and Maggie *did* roll her eyes.

'If you're going to show her that chat shop with those psycho weirdo freaks "looking for lovvvve",' she said, 'then don't bother! They're all con men or psychopaths on those things. You won't find a decent bloke. And Nat's bad enough with real men. She'd be positively dangerous on there.'

'And who says I *want* a bloke?' said Debbie, with a provocative glint in her eye. 'Why pay for the whole pig when you can just have a sausage?'

'Ugh!' said Maggie in disgust, and getting up off the sofa, she signalled for me to pass my glass. 'You can *keep* the pig… and the sausage, too!' She went off to the kitchen.

'Why haven't you got a boyfriend, Nat?' Debbie asked.

'Oh, my word! I'm too old for all that!'

'Rubbish! You're the same age as Mum, aren't you? Fifty-eight?'

'I've just turned sixty,' I told her.

'That's not old,' she said. 'Look at you. You've still *got* it. There's probably some lovely silver fox out there just waiting to meet you.'

'Are you on commission, or something?' I smiled.

'Look,' she said. 'I'll show you.'

She came to sit in her mother's seat close to mine. 'See, you just put in the age group you want…'

Maggie came back with the drinks. 'Move your bum. That's my seat,' she said to Debs.

Debbie slipped down to the floor between us, and over her shoulder I watched a succession of men's faces, an endless stream of 'mature' lonely hearts. Some of them looked quite nice. And so many.

'Put that away. She's not interested in that nonsense. Are you?' Maggie asked, turning to me.

'I'm intrigued. I can't believe there's so many!'

'Oh, my God. No! Don't you start. You're too old. Not to mention your crap choice in men. You'd probably end up with a rapist or serial killer.'

'I'll send you the link,' said Debbie with a grin.

***

That was how, a few days later, I found myself looking at a dating website, with no intention of actually signing up. But then I saw 'David'. David was fifty-nine, completely bald, and with the kindest blue eyes was smiling down at his pet Labrador. He was just made for me. My soulmate! So sure was I that I did the online questionnaire, paid the 'low introductory offer' price online, and in no time was daring myself to press the key that would, 'Send David a smile'. I pressed it as if it would electrocute me, and sat back with a guilty smile to await the response. When he read my profile, he would surely realise that we were a match made in heaven.

Well, apparently not. David never did get back to me.

But, in the meantime, a whole bunch of other guys did – with 'winks, smiles and kisses', and some very flattering messages. The sudden rush of compliments went straight to my head, of course, and like a dizzy teenager I was tapping and swiping with half a dozen guys at the same time, and getting totally confused about who I'd already messaged.

Within a couple of weeks I was going on my first date, with 'Ralph, fifty-seven years old and from Saughall'. His picture showed a blond, happy face and strong shoulders. A divorcee, he liked to go to the gym and spend time with friends, and liked to keep a positive attitude in life – which no doubt is necessary when you're only five foot tall and built like the Michelin Man. I'm only five foot two inches myself but I did need a guy to be a bit taller than me.

He wasn't short on self-confidence, however. In fact, he pitched up in a sleeveless vest designed to show off his muscles and fake tan. During the course of the date, I found out he was 'only in it for a bit of fun', which he thought was going to happen at my place. He became quite petulant when he realised it wasn't, pointing out that I was no spring chicken and that I should be grateful for his attentions.

I drove home feeling thoroughly miserable and foolish and promising myself I was going to learn how to convert centimetres to inches before looking at another man's profile on the website. Or better still, take myself off it completely. Which of course, I didn't.

Then there was 'Ricardo, 51 from Knutsford'. Going by his profile picture, he was gorgeous. He had dark hair greying slightly at the temples and dark, smouldering eyes, and he liked 'older women'. Oh, how we fool ourselves!

He fell madly in love with me within the space of three

emails, before we'd even met! And he wrote me the most wonderfully romantic messages.

We were going to meet, but he had to postpone that as he had to go back to Italy quickly, on family business. And while there he emailed me to ask a favour. He had been notified that the geyser in his flat in Knutsford had burst and it was flooding down into all the flats below. It had to be sorted out immediately and as there was nobody he could ask, and as it was difficult for him to transfer money from Italy, could I please pay the plumber to fix the problem. Of course, he would pay me back immediately on his return. Five hundred pounds should do it.

Ha! Ha! He had about as much chance of that happening as I had of a date with a good-looking Italian who liked older women.

And then there was 'Alun from North Wales', who mapped out the exact mid-way point between us, to meet.

His profile said that the first thing you notice about Alun is his warm, friendly smile. That was not true, not for me anyway. The first thing *I* noticed about Alun was the large, bright pink hearing aid over his left ear. The second thing I noticed was his warm, friendly smile. It might be very shallow of me, but that's how it was.

The Red Dragon, the pub where we met, was having an as-much-as-you-can-eat buffet and the place was packed, and so *noisy* that we battled to communicate. After we had eaten, we moved out into the beer garden, which was a little better, and I found out that he was a very nice guy. He told me that he was retired, his wife had died two years earlier of cancer and he missed her dreadfully, but realised he was still young and could move on. He loved his garden, and went on at great length about his roses, which aphids had played havoc with that year.

He shared a house with one of his daughters and her little girl, and the other daughter (and her husband and little boy) lived just three doors away. He had a caravan, and every year he and his daughters and grandchildren all went on holiday together, just up the coast about thirty miles away. However, he felt there was something missing in his life, and that a new lady might fill the gap.

To be honest, I couldn't see myself as a gap filler, living in somebody else's house with somebody else's family, and going on communal caravan holidays. So, when he mentioned a second date, I just smiled and kindly told him I didn't think so. He raised his eyebrows without comment, then checked the bill and told me how much my half came to.

Things were a little frosty as we paid the waiter (using two different cards). He walked me to my car, opened the door for me and asked if he couldn't change my mind about that second date. And then he just came out of nowhere with a big wet kiss and tried to push his tongue down my throat. That was not going to happen either.

I pushed him away with a cheery 'Bye then!' and jumped into the car, even though he was in the way of me closing the door. As I smiled up at him, he slammed it shut and left.

Again, I drove home feeling miserable and foolish and promising myself to immediately cancel my subscription on the website. And the next day I went online with that very intention, but saw I had a message. It said, *I can see you keep looking at my profile. Why won't you talk to me?*

'Richard, 59 from Leigh' sounded vaguely familiar, so I opened up his profile to see who it was and saw, too, that I had already opened it two or three times before. And it suddenly dawned on me that when I had opened somebody's profile, that person could also see that I had done so.

I hadn't contacted this one, or in fact even returned his 'smile', because he looked a grumpy old bugger. Also, he had put on his profile that he 'didn't suffer fools gladly', which I found to be a bit arrogant and condescending. But seeing as I had been busted for looking at his profile, I thought it would only be good manners to write back. So, I wrote, *I'm sorry, I must have opened your profile by mistake. But unfortunately, I was just about to take myself off the site. Thanks anyway.*

He wrote back asking, *Why?*

I wrote back, *I have come home from South Africa and need to build myself a new life, but I have come to think that people of our age, on this site, already have a life, which they would no doubt expect another person to slot into. I don't want to 'slot in' anywhere. I want to start a brand-new life with someone and realise now that there is little hope of this happening. Hope that makes sense.*

He wrote back, rather curtly, that, *If we were all happy with our lives, we wouldn't be on the site in the first place, would we?* And that he didn't expect anybody to slot into his life. He was disappointed that I wanted to give up without even giving him a chance. He sounded as angry and disillusioned as I was at that moment, which, in some strange way, gave me hope. So, I gave him my phone number and he said he would phone me that evening at eight o'clock.

At eight o'clock on the dot, my phone rang.

'Hello,' he said. 'Is that Natalie?'

'Yes. Is that Richard?' What a stupid thing to ask!

He answered politely, 'Yes. It is. How are you?'

The voice was deep, soft, and had a gentleness to it – not what I expected, going by his picture. He had quite a broad Lancashire accent, which had me saying 'pardon?' quite frequently, and he had a problem with my mumbling, which I do when I'm nervous. But we managed, and he asked if he could call back again the next night.

And I said, 'Yes.'

I may be wrong, but for me a voice says a lot about a person, and I liked his immediately. He phoned me every night after that, and it wasn't long before he asked if I would like to meet him. Trying hard to hide my excitement I told him that would be nice, and we arranged that he would come over to Little Rutford the following weekend.

Chapter Six

By the following Thursday when I visited Maggie, excitement had turned to panic. The prospect of making small talk with some strange man, even as nice as he sounded, was suddenly quite unnerving. And my expression must have given me away, because I'd hardly sat down in Maggie's lounge before she narrowed her eyes at me.

'And now?' she asked.

'What?'

'You're back on that dating thing, aren't you?'

How does she do that? 'No!' I lied. 'Why would you think that?'

'I can see it on your face,' she said. 'So, tell me?'

'Well, I never actually took myself off it. I was going to, but then I had this message from a guy… and I've been chatting with him on the phone… and he sounds really nice. He wants to come meet me.'

'Oh, for goodness' sake!' She beckoned to me to follow her to the kitchen. 'Well, don't tell him where you live.'

'Too late.'

'Oh, good God, Natalie. Will you never learn? You know, for someone who's supposed to be clever, you really are dumb.'

'You think I'm clever?' I laughed.

'Not anymore. No!'

'And anyway, I've spoken with him a few times and he sounds really nice. He's from Leigh. He's divorced, and he's got two daughters.'

'Oh, yeah? Like the last one?'

'It will be fine.'

'No, it won't! Well, if you don't pitch up next week, I'll know you're dead in a ditch, somewhere, hey?'

She made us drinks and we took them to a little garden table outside. It was still pleasantly warm out there. Alan was cutting the lawn up at the top end, but seeing me, he waved and made his way towards the kitchen.

'You know what they *should* ask on that dating thing?' she said.

'What's that?'

'What the ex-wife has to say about them. That would be interesting, wouldn't it?'

'I guess there's always two sides to every story. I suppose.'

'Well, I think you're crazy. And at your age!'

'At *my* age?' I asked, indignantly.

'You know why men go on these sites, don't you? They just want sex.'

'No, they don't. Not all of them. And what's wrong with sex, anyway? You might be too old, but I'm not sure I am yet.'

'Ugh! Really? How old are you, sixty? So, you'd probably end up with some old codger in his dotage. Are you that desperate? And for your information, no, I am not too old.'

'Oh, really?' I said with a smirk. 'Well as it happens, this guy I'm talking to is actually a year younger than me. A year and ten days, to be exact.'

'Well, he must be after your money then.'

'What money?' I laughed, and she just grimaced.

'So, you and Alan still do the deed, do you?'

'That's none of your business,' she said, her eyes flashing at me.

'No. You don't! Knew it!'

'Well, you're wrong. We do… occasionally.'

'Regularly?'

'Occasionally, I said.'

'Lights off, pyjamas on,' I teased. 'How exciting!'

'Oh, fuck off, Natalie,' she said, but she was smiling.

'Would you like to see a picture of him?' I rooted in my handbag for my phone.

'Not really. Oh, go on then!'

She reached for Alan's reading glasses on top of a newspaper on the table and, putting them on the end of her nose, took a good long look at the photo.

'He's got a face like a smacked arse!' she said, passing my phone back. 'He looks a big lad.'

'I think he looks quite handsome,' I said. 'And he comes out with things like that, too. He's got a strong Lancashire accent and says things like, "It's lookin' black over our Billy's mother's 'ouse!"'

She screwed her face up. 'What?' she barked.

'It means, it looks like it might rain later. I bet you two would get on famously together!'

'Mmm! Well just be careful, hey? Have you got Alan's number, just in case you need backup?'

'I've got it. Stop fussing, it'll be fine.'

We sat in silence for a moment, before she asked, 'Do you ever hear from Hennie these days? Is he still around?'

'No, he moved up to Tzaneen a couple of years ago. That's up in the north west of the province.'

'That's right, you told me. Do you think you'd ever get back together with him? Twenty years is a long time to write off. And didn't you tell me you were still seeing him at one stage?'

'Ja, I was seeing him, not *seeing him*. Difficult not to when you have three kids between you. There was nothing in it. We get on okay. Much better now we're divorced. And he's got a girlfriend now, too. A very young one, I believe.'

'You see! I told you, didn't I? What are they like?'

'Whatever floats your boat.' I shrugged.

'So, what actually did go wrong with you two?'

'Ah! It was lots of things.'

'Like what? You came through such a lot together, the bankruptcy and everything.'

'The bankruptcy changed everything. He was so different after that. But it started long before then.'

'So?' she asked, impatiently. 'Get on with it!'

'Well, I think it was when he got religion in his life. He needed to 'get right with the Lord', which meant confessing to me that he'd had some one-night stands, even be it many years before when he was a sales rep.'

'So why did he even tell you?'

'Well, that's just it. He didn't care how I felt as long as he and God were good pals. *I* could like it or lump it!'

'And you *did*?'

'The kids were all small, Erin just a baby still. It had happened a long time before and we were happy. We had a lovely, happy home. Why rock the boat?'

'I'd have killed the bastard! If Alan did that to me, I'd kill him. I'd chop it off,' she said, gesturing just how.

'It did take away the trust,' I said.

'And *had* he stopped screwing around?'

Just then Alan came out of the back door bearing two chicken salads, heard Maggie's words and looked at us with big eyes that begged the question, *Who are we talking about?*

'Nothing to do with you,' said Maggie, taking her plate and dismissively flicking him away.

He put the other plate down in front of me and I thanked him as he disappeared off up the garden.

'Isn't he eating?' I asked.

She shook her head. 'He's probably had his. Carry on. We'll get to the end of this story yet.'

'Can't remember what I was saying, now.'

'You didn't want to rock the boat, but let me guess – he *was* still screwing around?'

'No, I don't think so. Not while God was watching. But the thing was, he wouldn't even discuss it with me. It was like it wasn't even my business. I thought he loved me and that we had a happy marriage, but I saw then just how unimportant I was to him, because he didn't feel he had to put it right with *me*. I didn't matter as long as he and God were okay.'

I ate some salad and thought about my ex-husband. 'He was always the *main man what counts*, as he jokingly called himself; the life and soul of the party, the funny man. I was the quiet, patient little wife who would jokingly roll her eyes when he got too loud, or too near the bone with his jokes. I was just an extension of him, really. Not a person in my own right.'

'Yes?' she said, loading up a forkful of salad. 'But you allowed that, didn't you?'

'Ja, I guess. I thought that was a happy marriage. Isn't that what women do, plaster over the cracks, carry on regardless? Isn't that just life? And I did feel happy most of the time. If I didn't think about it too much, it was the happiest time of my life. But... well, then there were times when I did think about it and it just felt like we were role-playing marriage. More and more I couldn't decide if we really were in love or not. And then the financial problems started and he changed... and the *or not* seemed the most likely.'

She nodded, stirring her fork in the air for me to continue.

'And I came to realise, too, that he *could* curb his temper if he wanted to. He could turn it on and off like a tap, to control me. And if a tantrum didn't work, then he'd sulk for two days. Then I'd sulk for two days to retaliate, and it all got so predictable.'

'Sounds like us,' she said, pointing her fork up the garden at Alan.

'But if it wasn't for the bankruptcy,' I said, 'I think we would probably have stayed together. I think he had some sort of breakdown over that. It took away his whole identity somehow, or how he saw himself, at least. Not that he would ever talk to me about it. He wouldn't see anyone.

'I got a job, and he hated that, and we just didn't fit anymore. And the irony was, when I first met him, it was him who built me up and made me strong; told me to apply for jobs not as secretary to the marketing manager, but as PA to the CEO. He told me I could do it – and I did it!'

'But didn't he hit you once?'

'Ja, once. And that was the day I told him I wanted a divorce. It was a backhanded slap across my face. Mother's Day. I'd done a big Sunday roast and he was taking his time coming to the table. He'd pulled ligaments in his leg and was on crutches at the time, and he took so long to lumber around. He seemed to be taking forever that day so I said, "For goodness' sake, will you come and sit your backside down on this chair – the food's going cold". I didn't usually speak to him like that, so disrespectfully.'

'That's not disrespectful.'

'Well, he obviously thought it was, because he came through, painstakingly leaned one crutch against the table, and suddenly backhanded me through the mouth, knocking me off my chair. I didn't even see it coming.'

Her eyes narrowed. 'I'd have fuckin' killed him. What did you do?'

'I picked myself up off the floor, and with as much dignity as I could said, "I want a divorce!", and walked out.'

'And did the kids see this?'

'Yes, that was the worst part. We'd been having such a lovely day up until then. They'd been spoiling me with little cards and things and breakfast in bed. You know? Then that happened.'

'You see, right there. That would be enough for me. There's no way I could make friends with him again after that. I would have taken the kids and gone, and he would never have seen me or them ever again.'

I finished my salad and pushed the plate away. 'That was lovely, thanks.'

'Pleasure. So, what happened then?'

'Well, that was when I moved out. We didn't talk for a couple of years. But the kids came and went between us as they wanted. The boys especially. They were just in their teens then, and such a handful. Sometimes they were just too much for me and I'd phone Hennie and he would come and pick them up to go stay there with him for the night.'

'I wouldn't have let him anywhere near them,' she said.

'Looking back, I wouldn't either. I thought he was helping, but I think he was also turning them against me.'

'Of course he was. That's what they do.'

'He wasn't all bad. He could be so nice, too.'

'Just listen to yourself. Drink up,' she said.

After getting up and gathering the dirty dishes, she made her way to the kitchen. I swallowed down the last of my drink and followed.

'Did *you* ever contemplate divorce?' I asked her.

She rolled her eyes at me. 'Every day.'

'No, seriously,' I said, laughing.

'I *am* being serious.'

As she filled the sink, she pointed with a soapy finger to the vodka bottle. 'The coke's in the fridge.'

I made the drinks and listened.

'I was always the disciplinarian in our house,' she said. 'Softlad was the one to hug them better when I'd shouted at them. Wicked Witch and Mr Nice-guy, y'know?' I waited for her to go on.

She just shrugged. 'It's still like that today. They talk with him, I mean *talk*. But not with me anymore.'

Turning to me and trying to lighten the mood she said, 'But I've told you, hey? I'm not having any more.'

'Me neither!' I said, picking up the drying cloth.

She'd finished washing up, picked up her drink and leaned back against the kitchen counter while I finished drying. Through the window we could see Alan cleaning the lawn mower.

'Look at knobhead out there,' she said, shaking her head.

I picked up my vodka and joined her.

'He's not staying out of the way because I'm here, is he?'

'I don't care if he is. But no, he isn't. He's not that considerate.'

'How about you and him?' I asked. 'You okay?'

She watched him, wrinkling her nose in distaste. 'I think I might hate him,' she said, very matter-of-factly.

'No, you don't!' I laughed. But her face stayed serious.

She took in a deep breath. 'I do actually. But I'm stuck with him, so there you go.'

'Why? What happened?'

She took a swig of her drink and with two hands cradled the glass on her boobs. 'Nothin' really. He's just an arsehole,' she said as she watched him, almost kindly. 'An arsehole, all wrapped up in his own little world.'

'Shame,' I said. 'That's harsh.'

'He plays golf come hell or high water. He goes down the pub twice a week, goes to see our Debbie once or twice, potters around the garden, does a few odd jobs, and watches telly. That's it. I don't really exist, except as a kind of nagging thing that has to be picked up from work.'

'Ah, that's not fair! From where I'm sitting it looks like he dotes on you – would do anything for you!'

'Yeah, you'd think, wouldn't you? But not true.'

'I always had you two pegged for the old couple sitting hand in hand in companionable silence on the park bench, aged ninety-something.'

'We probably will be, but we won't be hand in hand, and the

only reason for us not talking will be that we've got nothing to say to each other anymore.'

'Why? What happened?' I asked again.

'It's been like that for a long time. In fact, I can't really remember how it was before, if you know what I mean.'

I just didn't know what to say. So, I didn't.

'I told you about the miscarriages, hey?'

'Yes.' I nodded.

'It was the most… awful, horrible, horrible, thing. I wanted to top myself. Really. I just couldn't get my head around it at all.'

She looked at me wanting a response, I think, but I had nothing to say.

'My little boy… I didn't want to let them take him,' she went on. 'I just wanted to hold him.' She paused. 'Alan didn't understand. He didn't get it. I know it wasn't his fault, but I just couldn't…' She broke off. 'He just said all the wrong things.'

'Maybe he didn't know how to handle it? Didn't know what to say to make it better?' I offered.

'A year later, it happened again. A little girl. I was four months. You see other mums coming out of the hospital with their newborn babies, and there's you, walking out half the person you were when you walked in. And nobody cares. You just have to get on with it.'

'But you came through it. You had Debbie. And you're still together.'

'Yeah! Then Debs came along – and we're still together.' She smiled, a quick, dead-eyed grimace.

We didn't speak for a minute.

'So, if you felt like that, why didn't you leave?' I asked.

'And go where? With what? Everything we've got is tied up in this little house.'

'But you must have loved him once. He's a good, kind man and I think he loves you very much. Have you talked with him?'

'Oh, now why didn't I think of that?' she said, sarcastically. I just shook my head at her.

She looked down into her drink. 'There was a time when I wanted to talk to him. Not anymore, 'cos I know he's not interested in listening to what I have to say.'

'Did you *ever* love him?' I asked.

'I don't know! Yeah, I suppose. I don't know!' she said, impatiently. 'What the fuck is love anyway? He asked me to marry him, and I said, "Yes."'

'So why did you marry him if you didn't know whether you loved him or not?'

Her eyes went wide and she shook her head. 'That's the million-dollar question,' she said. 'God knows! I knew I'd get him. I just knew it. So, when he asked, I just said yes.'

'Er… It's not pass the parcel, you know.'

'But it *is* really, isn't it? And what if it didn't come round to me again?'

'Of course it would. Somebody else was bound to ask you. What about that guy you were going out with from the mill? You really liked him, didn't you?'

'Colin. Liked him? I would have walked over hot coals all the way to hell for him. But he dumped me, didn't he. Then I found out he'd got that ugly, Fat Hannah thing pregnant, so he must have been cheating on me anyway.'

'Hannah? But she wasn't fat?'

'Pfft! You should've seen her a couple of years later.'

And we both grinned at that.

'And then you started as a barmaid at the Red Dragon and met Alan.'

'And then I met Alan,' she repeated. 'The landlord's son.'

She stared at him through the kitchen window while she spoke. 'I knew he fancied me right from the start. And his mum and dad liked me, and I wanted Colin to know I could also get somebody else. Alan was easy to chat with back then. We just sort of became an item. He was safe, steady, y'know? And I was sick of living with my brother Dennis, and Moira and the kids.'

I nodded that I understood, and she continued.

'And then we were a couple. And it became a habit. It was sort of expected that we'd get married. I couldn't let him down. And why would I? He was a good fella and he loved me. What else is there, anyway? Other people get married and live happily ever after, so why not us? Who's to say it was or wasn't love? Maybe it was my turn for the fairy-tale ending.'

'How many years is it now?' I asked.

'This August it will be thirty-seven years.'

'Shit, that's a helluva long time, hey?'

'Yeah! If I'd murdered him when I first felt inclined to, I'd be out of prison again by now.'

I laughed at the old joke. 'But they've been happy years… mostly?'

She thought about it. 'Yeah, we've had some happy times, with the kids and everything. And there's been shit ones, too. I don't know if we're happy anymore.' She looked directly at me. 'I don't think so,' she said sadly, and took my glass to refill it.

She came back and handed me my glass with weary eyes. 'Sometimes… sometimes… I don't know. After so many years you get to know each other so well, don't you?'

'Ja, and you don't know what you'd do without each other,' I finished for her.

'But I never felt madly in love. Not like *you* get.'

'Doesn't make it any less real, does it? Might make it more real, actually.'

She just shrugged.

'You do love him. You just don't know it,' I said.

'No. Most days I just think he's an arsehole!'

She leaned back against the counter again and we sipped our drinks in silence.

'I worked with a woman in South Africa,' I said. 'She'd been married for nearly thirty years and he'd never once said "I love you" or "I'm sorry". He'd hit her a few times in their early days. Every couple of years or so she would explode and say she'd had enough, and there were tears and drama and she swore she was going to divorce him. And then they would make up again. She explained to me once that "Donny" had had a crap childhood and he was "broken", and couldn't believe anybody could love him. So, she was going to spend her life trying to convince him that *she* did. And I thought, *why*?... Is that what love is? Maybe she's going to get more brownie points in heaven for doing that. Maybe I'm selfish thinking you only get one life and it's too precious to waste on someone who gives nothing back, and isn't going to change.'

'And you're telling me this because...?'

'I was thinking about how people stay in relationships that they would probably be happier out of.'

'And how *do* you know if you're doing the right thing or not?' asked Maggie.

'You don't,' I said.

'Bit bloody late then, isn't it!' she said. 'Did you ever meet "Donny"?'

'Ja. To me he looked like... a grumpy little man. She said he was broken but I wondered if he wasn't just enjoying that role. Maybe she goes along with it 'cos she's also broken. Maybe it's *my* brokenness that makes me cynical?'

'You say the word "broken" one more time and I'll slap you,' said Maggie.

I laughed.

'They still need each other though, don't they?' she said.

'Ja,' I agreed. 'In a broken kind of way.'

She turned to slap me but I ducked, spilling my drink.

'Now look! Mop it up!' she said, throwing a floor cloth at me.

'Did you ever regret leaving Hennie?' she asked.

I shook my head. 'No, I've never regretted it. I've often wondered if it would have been better for the kids if I'd stayed. But I don't think so.'

'I wonder if Donny thought he loved *her*? I don't know about you, but I don't believe in love. I don't think it exists. Do you?'

'I don't know, really. I think so. But I don't think it's something you *fall* into. I think it's a decision you make. I think it takes an awful lot of positive thinking to keep it going and I don't think there's many people who can keep it up for a lifetime, anyway.'

'Including you?'

'Yes, including me.'

We sat thinking about that for a moment, and then I had a brainwave.

'Maybe it's like Father Christmas,' I said. 'Maybe if you believe in him, he exists for you? Love too.'

She gave me a very jaundiced eye and said, 'But Father Christmas doesn't fuckin' exist, does he? Don't be stupid!'

'Well, you've got to believe in each other, then. And you've both got to believe you can make it work. That means keeping the respect going – and that's the hard bit, I think. You can't just get with somebody because it seems like a good idea, or because you think he would fit into your idea of what a good husband should be. When the nitty gritty of life hits the fan and you find out you don't really know him at all – well it's a bit late then, isn't it?'

'I don't know that I've ever been in love. Or been loved, either, for that matter,' she said, sipping her drink.

I thought about that one for a minute. 'I think when I married Hennie,' I said, 'I thought I was madly in love with him. And I think I was, because I was just so relieved to find somebody who wanted to stick with *me*. I felt I'd been drifting around on my own for too long. I thought being married gave you a certain status, hey? Well, your husband's anyway. And if you wanted kids you needed to get married first. But if I had my time again, I wouldn't be so desperate, so needy. I'd like myself enough not to need somebody else's approval. I think I'd be looking at *them* more closely. And I think you've got to get over yourself a bit before you can see the other person, hey!'

We stood in silence a while, then she spoke.

'But you've got to *respect* the other person for their approval to mean anything in the first place, haven't you? If you never gave a shit what they thought, then their approval won't mean anything anyway, will it?' She laughed. 'I guess that's what happens when you work out they're just another arsehole.' She looked out of the window towards Alan. 'Like him!'

'Yes, I guess so; you'd have to marry for the right reasons, or you lose respect. Familiarity breeds contempt – and then it's all over.'

'And what are the right reasons?'

'I don't know! If I knew that, I might have made a better job of it!'

'And what had you got to be insecure about anyway?' She frowned. 'You had a posh family and a posh house. What more could you have wanted?'

'Somebody to love me?' I suggested.

Her face softened some. 'Yeah, we all need some love, hey. Everybody needs somebody in life, don't they? You can't do it alone,' she said. 'Don't you ever get lonely on your own?'

'No,' I said. 'Not lonely. But sometimes I think it might be nice to have somebody else around. How about you? You lonely?'

'Fuck! I'm nothing but,' she said. 'And I'm married! But I don't think I'd have another one. Would you seriously have another fella in your life?'

'I don't know,' I said. 'Maybe. To be close to somebody. To love and be loved and all that.'

'Well, you've never been able to pick a good fella yet, so what makes you think you could now? There *are* no good ones, anyway.'

'I think I'm more mature now.'

'Mature? Ah, bless. No. You're just old!' She grinned.

'Fuck off!' I said, but laughed with her.

'One thing I can guarantee you,' she said. 'You won't find a decent man on one of those dating sites.'

'Why not?'

'I don't know. You just won't! You can't *look* for *the one*, can you? It just happens, or not.'

'Well, it's not going to happen if you don't meet people, is it?'

She shook her head. 'Well, good luck with that one! If I had my time again, I would be a real, hard bitch who made the man run around trying to please *me*. Have you noticed how some women can do that, and the men just don't seem to be able to get enough of it?'

'Er, excuse me…' I said, raising my eyebrows.

She frowned at me over the top of her glass. 'No… that is *not* me! I am not like that.'

'Are you sure?'

'You've got it all wrong. I don't exist in this house.' And after pushing herself off the cupboard she headed out through the back door.

I followed her and we sat at the little table again. It was just gone eight o'clock and the sun cast long, golden shadows down the length of the freshly mowed lawn and through the apple trees at the bottom. The smell of cut grass hung heavily on the still air, and from the fence, a blackbird sang its last song for the day. Alan was wandering around the garden inspecting his handiwork.

'He keeps out of my way as best he can,' she said. 'And he's dreading the idea of me being at home all day.'

'And I'm guessing, so are you?'

She glanced a *What do you think?* look at me.

'You know what?' she went on. 'I was so jealous when your mum told me you'd decided to stay in South Africa. I nearly packed my bags to go and join you.'

'But I asked you to. I asked you to come with me.'

'I know, but before you left you were only going for a six-week holiday. Not to stay. And then Alan proposed.'

'I remember – it was just before I went. I remember you showing me the ring. I *thought* you weren't very excited about it. Where are your rings?' I asked, noticing there were none on her fingers.

'I lost the engagement ring somewhere, years ago,' she said. 'My wedding ring's upstairs, I think. It gets in the way when I'm rolling pastry and stuff.

'I was jealous of you,' she continued, 'because you always had the guts to do the things you wanted to do, like just decide you're going to learn to drive, or emigrate halfway around the world, or divorce your husband. But that's you. Not me.'

I was truly surprised. 'You're joking,' I said. 'You were jealous of me? I've always been called foolish for being like that. "Where fools rush in!" as Mum puts it. I've always been jealous of you for being stable and sensible, having a husband-for-life, and your kids living close by.'

'Seriously?' she said, suddenly brighter.

'Of course! Here I am at sixty and at yet another crossroads. And how many more will there be?'

'Maybe crossroads are better than being stuck in a rut with nothing to look forward to anymore. I wish I had a bit more adventure in my life. If you go on any more adventures, I'm coming with you, all right?'

'For sure! Cheers to that!'

'Cheers,' she said, and we clinked glasses.

Chapter Seven

The next day I told Mum I had a date.

'Really?' she asked, wide-eyed. 'Where did you meet him?'

'Online.'

She looked confused. 'Online?'

'Yes. On… line. On the computer. On a dating site.'

'What?' she said, frowning. 'Like Barbara-next-door?'

'Yes, like that.'

'Barbara-next-door did that. That's how she found Arthur.'

'I know. Lots of people do it these days.'

'Mmm!' she said, looking at me as if she'd always known there was something wrong with me. 'Well, I hope he's nice. What's his name?'

'Richard. He's from Leigh.'

'Aaah! A Lancashire lad.' She obviously approved.

***

It was mid-July, a sunny Saturday afternoon. I'd spent most of it in a dressing gown and with my hair in rollers, desperately searching for a pair of tweezers that had just vanished into thin air (the second pair to do so). And then going through every item in my wardrobe trying to find something that would make me look wonderful – or at least a little slimmer. In the end I settled for a calf-length cream skirt and oversized, 'slouchy-chic' (hopefully), coffee-coloured cardi.

It was ten minutes to two, and my hair would only take a couple of minutes to brush through. I was just pulling out the last roller when I saw a car pull up outside Mum's gate: a shiny black Saab convertible, top down revealing the cream leather interior. *Nice!*

I quickly brushed my hair, and nervous as a teenager on her first date, peeped from behind my bedroom curtain as Richard climbed out of his car. He was tall, at least six feet or more, and built like a rugby player, big shoulders and no neck. Maggie was right, he was a big boy. Despite this, he looked very smart (if not to say dapper), in a subtly striped, maroon blazer and open-necked white shirt with grey slacks. His very short grey hair looked as if he'd just been to the barber's.

After collecting a bunch of roses off the back seat he walked almost elegantly, and far more lightly than his size would suggest, towards the front door. *Oh, yes!* I thought. *Here comes my silver fox! – or bear, as the case may be.* Nothing to do with the car or the roses, of course.

I didn't move until the doorbell rang, then taking a deep breath and a last check of hair and make-up, I went to open the door.

'Hello... Nat?'

I immediately recognised the warm, peaceful voice.

'Yes, hello,' I answered, opening the door wider. 'Come in.'

He stepped into the hall and handed over the roses, his eyes taking me in and his smile telling me that he liked what he saw.

'I got you these!'

He was a good foot taller than I, and looked down at me, shyly.

I liked what I saw, too: a big, clean-shaven, soft-skinned face and intelligent blue eyes behind nearly rimless glasses.

'Thank you. Aren't they beautiful! Come in and meet my mum while I put them in water.'

He followed me to the lounge where Mum was sitting on the sofa watching TV, and she politely turned the volume down.

'Mum, this is Richard. Richard, my mum, Margaret.'

'Hello, darlin',' he said to Mum, taking her hand in both of his. 'Pleased to meet you.'

'Hello! I'm very pleased to meet you, too,' she said, sparkly eyed and giggly.

I put the flowers in water and found my handbag, and off we went. Pushing the passenger door open from behind the wheel, he asked if it would be too windy for me with the hood down, or should he put it up.

'Don't you dare,' I said, getting in.

Smiling, he pulled smoothly off from the kerb. 'Where to?'

We went to 'The Pilot' at Eastham Ferry, which looked out over the Manchester Ship Canal and the River Mersey to Liverpool, thinly outlined on the horizon. As we walked up the steps to the patio there were other patrons sitting out enjoying the sunshine. Some turned to look at us as we arrived, and I felt proud to be with Richard. For years, I'd been telling myself that I didn't need a man to define me – but it still felt good to walk in on the arm of one.

Most of the outside tables were taken and there was a happy, lazy, people-buzz going on. He went in to order while I found a table, then he brought the drinks and sat down.

'Cheers. It's nice to meet you, Nat,' he said, downing a third of his pint in one go.

'You, too,' I said.

And there we passed the next couple of hours, chatting, getting mellow on the booze and sunshine and generally enjoying each other's company. I battled with his accent now and again, and when I'd already said '*Pardon?*' a few times, I just smiled and hoped that was the appropriate response. I think he was doing the same, too, and there were a couple of awkward little silences.

He came across as strong and calm, but there was definitely a little shyness there, too, and I wondered what kind of effort it had taken him to go on a dating site and out on dates with strange women. He must really want to find that *someone special* in his life.

But what a pleasure it was, to be with somebody who wasn't just full of themselves and who actually seemed interested in someone else, i.e. me. He wanted to know everything about me. And he was very open about himself, too, telling me about his life, his daughters and friends. He told me he was not a rich man, but had enough to live comfortably. I told him about my life, my kids and my present situation and that I still had a little place back in Jo'burg, but wasn't sure if I'd return.

I asked what he did for a living and he hesitated, as if it was a complicated situation, but then explained.

'I'm a lorry driver.'

But that was obviously the short answer.

'O… kay?' I said.

He smiled. 'I've worked in the financial services sector for most of my life, managing client investments?'

'Ja?'

'I had a partner and we had a very successful little business going. But he retired, and then they brought in all these *compliances* that had to be adhered to, which took up so much time I couldn't get out and see the clients. It just got too stressful, and I decided to go back to something basic. One of the first jobs I had was driving a truck, regular hours and stress-free. Not the most glamorous job in the world, but it suits me. I enjoy driving, and the money's good. So, what d'you think of that?' he asked.

'I think if you enjoy what you're doing, well, that's half the battle, isn't it?'

'I've got my HGV licence. You can get a job anywhere with one of those. I drive the big refrigerated jobs back and to from Leigh, to just up the road here in Bromton.'

'Oh, really? What a coincidence! I'll have to keep a look out for you on the road.'

'I get about an hour's break on the turn-around. Maybe you'd like to come up and take a look and maybe have a coffee or something, sometime?'

'Yes, that would be nice!' I said, and we both smiled at the implication of seeing each other again.

As the people started to leave, we moved to a cooler spot at a table under the trees. The time passed and he started telling me jokes and funny little anecdotes about his life. When I laughed, he laughed, and his face transformed. It was like the sun coming out.

Eventually we realised that four hours had passed and we were pretty much the last people there. It was time, in fact, for me to give Mum her tea and pills. He drove me home and walked me to the door.

'Would you like to go out again?' he asked.

'Yes.' I smiled. 'That would be nice.'

'Tomorrow?'

That totally took me by surprise. 'It's a long way for you to come again so soon. Are you sure?'

I was only thinking of the distance involved and wasn't trying to put him off. But he looked a little doubtful, perhaps thinking that I didn't really want to see him again.

'But I'd love to!' I added, quickly, and he smiled.

'Shall I come at about twelve, and maybe we could grab a bit of lunch?'

I nodded.

He smiled, and after planting the gentlest little kiss on my cheek, he left.

I floated into the house on cloud nine.

Mum looked me up and down and said, 'Oh, you're there! I wondered where you'd gone. You're all dressed up?'

'I went out with Richard, remember? He came in earlier and said hello to you?'

'Oh yes, of course! He seemed a very pleasant young man. Did you have a nice time?'

'Yes, I did, thanks.'

'Where is he now?' she asked. 'Does he want his tea?'

'No, he has to get back to Leigh. But he's coming back tomorrow. What will you have for *your* tea?'

'Oh, I don't know. Nothing much. A few fish fingers and a bit of bread and butter will do me. Don't go to any bother. And have we got any of those little mandarin oranges?'

I headed towards the kitchen to make a start.

'Natalie? Who bought me these roses?' she asked, looking at them in a vase on the coffee table.

'Richard bought them, for me.'

'Oh, of course! Aren't they pretty!'

We had tea and then sat watching television, but my mind was on Richard and our afternoon together. I went over everything that had been said, the way he looked, the subtle smell of cologne, the sound of his voice, his gentle manner. I couldn't wait for tomorrow.

Late that evening he messaged me, *Sleep tight!* x

And I wrote back, *You too!* X

***

The following morning, when Mum asked for a third time who had bought her the roses, I thought it easier just to tell her that Richard did. Satisfied, she gave a funny little smile. Later, when Richard arrived, he came in to say hello to her.

'Richard, isn't it?' said Mum. 'Did I thank you for these lovely roses?'

Richard looked at me and I just shrugged. So, taking her hand, he said, 'It's a pleasure, darlin'.'

That day was not quite as warm and sunny as the day before, but still pleasant enough to drive with the top down out into North Wales, where we found a lovely little pub with an impressive-looking menu. I noticed his hands as he read it. They were two great hams with no wrists, but the fingers were long and slender, and the nails meticulously manicured. I bet there weren't many of his work mates whose hands looked like that.

He ordered a man-size rump steak. 'So rare, a good vet could bring it back to life again!'

I chose a smaller version of the same and asked if he liked garlic sauce.

'I do!' he said, with great interest. 'Are you going to have some?'

'Yes, I think so.'

'Good. Well make that two,' he said, smiling at the waiter.

'My family tell me I overdo the garlic,' I said. 'So, I have to remind myself that not everyone likes it so much.'

He smiled broadly. 'You can never have too much garlic. And wine? Do you like red or white? How about a red wine – a nice full-bodied red?'

'I like Pinotage,' I replied, and he chose one for us.

'You're definitely more of a financial services guy than a lorry driver.'

He beamed. 'Do you think so? Well, yes, that's more who I am, really.'

By the end of the weekend I felt I had known him forever. He had such a familiar, down-to-earth way with him. I felt safe, and as if I could tell him anything and he would not be shocked or judgemental of me. He was just such a lovely, gentle soul – and I was smitten! Within a couple of days, it seemed my life had completely changed. I had purpose. I had hope. And I couldn't remember the last time I felt this happy. Could it really be, at this late stage, that I was going to get *my* happy ending after all?

The following Thursday, Barbara-next-door brought Mum back from shopping and she came in for a cup of tea with us. From the twinkle in her eye, I guessed that Mum had told her about Richard. Her gaze alighted on the roses.

'Oh, what lovely roses. Are they for you, Natalie?' said Barbara.

Mum jumped in immediately. 'No, they're mine, actually! Richard bought them for me,' she said, with a dismissive little smile in my direction.

'Well, isn't that nice!' said Barbara, with a wink.

***

It was that week, also, that Mum looked up from the TV one day, and out of the blue asked if she had a will.

'I think you do, Mum. Cynthia told me that she took you down to the solicitors to make one while she was on holiday last time. Do you remember that?'

'I don't remember. What does it say?'

'I don't know, Mum.'

'I think we must go to the solicitors and find out.'

'I can email Cynthia and ask her about it, if you like.'

'I can't remember. But don't bother Cynthia. We can just go down and find out.'

It was gone four o'clock in the afternoon. 'It's a bit late to go now,' I said. 'But we can phone them in the morning.'

'Yes. Okay then. Will you remind me?'

'I will,' I said. And in the meantime, I sent a chatty email to Cynthia giving her all the latest news and asking, by the way, had she taken Mum to the solicitors to make a will?

I don't know why I asked, because I clearly remembered her telling me she had. Sitting out on the deck in her garden, I'd told her about Mum's proposition that if I go and live with her, she would leave the bungalow to me. Cynthia had told me that she'd taken Mum to make her will, but that she didn't know anything about what was in it because she had waited outside in the car; although she did say that she didn't think Brigit's name would be in it.

Cynthia did not respond to my email, so I phoned the solicitors and made an appointment for the next day. We sat in the waiting room until a Mr Browning came to collect Mum. I hung back, but Mum told me to go in with her, and Mr Browning smiled and held the door for me. He made an over-cheerful fuss of Mum and ordered tea for us, then looked quizzically at me.

'Now, you're not Cynthia, are you?' he said. 'She's in South Africa, isn't she? So, you must be…?'

'This is my youngest daughter, Natalie. Also from South Africa, but staying here with me now.'

'Ah! That explains it.'

'That's right,' I said. 'You met Cynthia last time she was over here two years ago? When she brought Mum in to make a will?'

'Yes, that's right,' he said. 'And what can I do for you ladies today?'

'I want to look at my will,' said Mum. 'I need to make sure it's right.'

He opened a file and produced the document. 'Here it is. What is it you need to know?'

'Can you just read through it for me?' asked Mum.

He read down to the relevant part, that the bungalow was to be left jointly to Cynthia and Natalie, when Mum interrupted him.

'No, that's wrong. That needs to change. The bungalow is to be left just to Natalie.'

Mr Browning looked surprised. He looked at me, and then at Mum, and was at a loss for words. I think if I hadn't been present, he would have asked Mum why she wanted to change her will, but he didn't.

With a quick, apologetic look to me, he said, 'Mrs Sefton, are you very sure you want to do this?'

'Would you like me to wait outside?' I offered, and Mr Browning's face said that he would appreciate that. But Mum answered for him.

'No, it's fine, Natalie. Sit!'

Mr Browning sat looking at the file, obviously choosing his words carefully. 'Mrs Sefton, may I suggest that you go home and sleep on this, and if you still wish to proceed, then we will make an appointment for you to come back in.'

'I don't need to think about it,' said Mum. 'I am very sure that this is what I want to do.'

'Nevertheless,' replied Mr Browning, 'I think it would be wise for you to do so, just to make absolutely certain that this is, in fact, what you want.'

Mum muttered about having to come all the way back down again, but Mr Browning was adamant.

When we were back in the car, I said, 'He's only doing his job. It's nice to know that he has your interests at heart and is looking after you.'

'Just wants to be paid for two visits instead of one, more like.'

'Well, he probably thinks I'm trying to manipulate you into it, and I hope you don't feel like that, Mum. If you want to leave the will as it is, it's okay.'

'Nonsense! I want it changed,' she insisted.

'Well, as he says – have a think about it.'

'All right then. But you must remind me, if I forget. Okay?'

'Okay,' I agreed.

I must admit, I was surprised by Mum's tenacity. Amazed, actually. Cynthia had always been her favourite and Brigit was right in saying she had always had the lion's share. It just showed how determined Mum was not to be put in an old age home.

***

The third time Richard came to visit, he brought Mum a bag of treacle toffee, with which she was absolutely delighted.

'Oh, thank you, Richard. That is kind of you,' she said, popping one into her mouth. She offered the bag.

'No. You have them,' said Richard. 'They're for you!'

Mum giggled.

Richard and I took a drive out into the countryside again, found a pub on the canal-side overlooking three locks, and spent the afternoon sitting outside, watching long boats being raised or lowered between the various water levels.

Talking about boats and travel in general soon had us comparing the places we'd visited (a very short list for me), and those we'd still like to.

'So, have you any thoughts on what you'll do when your mum... you know... when she goes?'

'I don't think she's going anywhere just yet.' I laughed.

'Yes, but she can't go on forever, can she?'

'I think she probably will!'

Then I realised he was waiting for a serious answer.

'I don't know. I don't want to stick around Little Rutford, that's for sure. But I haven't really thought about it.'

'Do you think you will go back to South Africa?'

'I really don't know,' I repeated, with a shrug. 'Perhaps. I've always had this idea of running a little bed-and-breakfast somewhere.'

'Oh. Really? That's interesting. I'd still like to travel. Take a look around and find a nice place to settle. Somewhere with a bit of sunshine. I'm sick of this weather.'

'I'd love to travel, too,' I said. 'It's something I've always dreamed about. One day...'

'Well, maybe you and I can go somewhere.' He smiled.

'Wouldn't that be something.' I smiled back.

'Talking of which,' he said, 'and I know it isn't quite the travelling you had in mind... but I was wondering if you'd like to come over and see my place next weekend? I'd come and pick you up and take you over there.'

'I'd love to. But it's too far for you to go back and to like that. I can drive over. How long does it take?'

'About an hour. You sure? I don't mind coming over.'

'No, I'm sure,' I said, thinking to myself that I must go buy a satnav.

'You can stay over, if you like,' he said, then blushed and stammered, 'No, I don't mean... I mean, I have a spare room. You'd be perfectly happy to stay. I mean, you'd be perfectly safe to stay, and I'd be perfectly happy for you to!'

He was so cute, I had to laugh, and he relaxed.

'That would be nice. I'll have to make a plan with Mum.'

'Of course,' he said. 'Just let me know.'

That evening we went out for a meal to the Cowshed, which lived up to its reputation of having the best steaks for miles around, and again we talked of all the places it would be nice to travel to. He was amazed that I hadn't even been to Spain.

'I haven't been anywhere,' I confessed. 'I left for South Africa when I was twenty-two and there weren't any of these cheap holiday flights then.'

He'd been to quite a few places around the world, even lived in Prague for a while, and Jersey.

'When did you live in Prague?' I asked. 'Were you still married then?'

He hesitated. 'No, I was divorced by then, working for an insurance company over there.'

'Oh? You worked in insurance?'

'Jack of all trades, master of none. You'd be surprised what I've done in the past!' he said, and he laughed.

***

The following Sunday, while Mum was next door playing dominoes, on a whim I decided to chance a Skype call to Erin. *She may be close to her laptop and hear my call come in.*

To my delight, she was suddenly there, her face smiling at me through the screen.

'Hello!' I said. 'What are you up to today?'

'Hello there. This is a nice surprise! Nothing much. Just looking at stuff online. And you?'

'Where's Sean? Is he there with you?'

'Yes, he's here. He's just having a doze on the sofa. He was out on his bike this morning, so he's tired.'

She turned the laptop around to show me Sean. He waved, and I waved back.

'So, what are you up to?' she asked.

'Well,' I said, with a dramatic pause, 'my boyfriend is playing golf today, so I'm having a lazy Sunday.'

Her eyes went big. 'No!' she said, smiling. 'Which one?'

'The one that I thought looked grumpy. He wasn't so grumpy after all.'

And I told her all about him. She asked lots of questions, and I told her as much as I could think of.

'He sounds lovely, Mom. I'm so pleased for you.'

'Thank you, sweetheart.'

While chatting with her, I'd noticed that one eye looked dark. Maybe just a shadow.

'What's wrong with your eye, Erin? Is that a bruise?'

'A bruise?' she asked, frowning, her fingers finding the very spot. 'No. Where?'

'Yes, just there,' I said. 'Just as you move, it looks bruised.'

'It's probably just the light.'

Just for a split second it crossed my mind that it might be a black eye, and instantly, Sean's name popped into my head, which was so unfair, really.

'Oh, Mom! I must show you. I bought the most gorgeous

pair of shoes the other day. Wait there, I'll show you,' and off she went to fetch them.

A minute later she was back with the shoes: black, high and strappy.

'Gorgeous!' I said, and she went on to tell me about a little dress that she'd seen, about work, about her friend Amanda, and about her car getting a puncture on the highway and Sean going out to her rescue. All seemed well with her. The shadow over her eye seemed to have disappeared, so I guessed it *was* just a trick of the light.

We chatted for over an hour and it was so good to laugh with her again. I so missed her. We blew kisses while Skype closed down. And the kitchen suddenly became very quiet again.

***

That Thursday, I brought Maggie up to date on my love life and told her about my planned visit to Leigh. She looked at me with a jaundiced eye.

'You're going to drive all the way over there, on your own?'

'Ja! Why not?' Said more bravely than I felt.

'Are there any roundabouts on the way?'

'I think there's the very same one.' I laughed.

'Oh. God. They'd better move it, quick. And are you going to sleep with him?'

'Oh, let's get right to the point then, hey?'

'Well? Are you?'

'I don't know! Haven't thought about it.'

'Not much!' she scoffed.

I gave her a shrug, but she waited for an answer.

'I don't know! It's a long time since I took my clothes off in front of any man. And anyway, maybe he won't want to.'

'Yeah, right!' She gave me a cynical smirk. 'Just be careful, hey. And what about your mum?'

'I've asked Barbara-next-door if she'll keep an eye on her. Mum goes round there on Sunday afternoon anyway so Barbara's invited her over for lunch with her and Arthur.'

'Well give her Softlad's phone number too. She must phone if she needs anything, okay?'

'I think she's got it already, but I'll make sure. You know she'll probably ask him to come mow the lawn or something?'

'That's all right. That'll get him out from underfoot, hey?'

We changed the subject and she told me how her week had been. Despite the new menus, Maggie had been sneaking in the odd 'favourite dish' to some of the old ladies at the hospice. She had nearly been caught out when the matron had walked into Mrs Bryce's room just as she was taking the last bite of what was supposed to be steamed fish, but which was actually cottage pie. But Mrs Bryce had really enjoyed her 'decent meal' – which hopefully had nothing to do with the fact she died two days later.

Chapter Eight

That week couldn't go quickly enough. I bought a satnav, a pale pink blouse, and a bra and matching panties (just in case). Richard phoned me every night as usual, and we spoke very casually about me going over there. I wondered what he may or may not be anticipating.

Saturday eventually rolled around, and with my bag packed, I was on my way, allowing myself plenty of time just in case I got lost – which I have done before, even with a satnav. I smiled to myself, remembering how Erin and I had christened the satnav voice 'Jane', and how we joked about her on car trips we'd done together, saying how pissed off she sounded when informing us she was *recalculating*.

I'd filled the tank and pumped the tyres the day before, and feeling smug about being so organised, I soon found myself accelerating down the slipway onto the M6. With an amazing sense of excitement and freedom, I eased into the stream of traffic heading north east.

It was a glorious day and the motorway cut through lush green countryside. I passed Pembie Hill, its contours resembling those of a man's profile looking out over the marshes, and then Runeham Hill, and then on, into a new adventure.

The only part of the journey I didn't enjoy was Thelwell Viaduct, where a high wind buffeted the car and many streams of traffic merged into just a few lanes to cross the ancient old bridge. Cars and trucks diced around at high speed trying to get into their correct exit lanes, and huge heavy-goods vehicles closed in on me. It was no time to dither – they weren't going to slow down! And more by luck than design, I found myself in the right lane.

Leaving the motorway, I was on a narrow country lane, which eventually led into a more built-up area and ultimately to a set of traffic lights in the centre of Leigh. Within minutes, I was pulling up outside a small double-storey block of flats, which *Jane* informed me was my destination. Sure enough, a door opened and out came Richard. Smiling, he directed me to a parking bay, and I was glad to get out of the car and stretch my legs. He took my bag, gave me a little kiss, and led the way inside.

'So, this is where you live, is it?'

'It is,' he said. 'Come, I'll show you around.'

He led me into a small hallway with four doors leading off it, and opening each one, announced, 'My bedroom… the bathroom… the guest room… the lounge.' He dropped my bag in the guest room.

There was a good-sized lounge with a kitchen forming an 'L' shape off it, and a French window opening onto a small patio and communal garden. The curtains were slightly too long, and the carpet was threadbare in front of one end of the sofa; the sofa-end also looked well-used. But it was a pleasant, peaceful space and kept very neat and tidy.

'So, what do you think of it?' he asked.

'It's very nice. I like big windows.'

'This is the kitchen. And here's the kettle. Make yourself at home!'

'Thank you,' I answered, sitting down on the sofa.

'Would you like something to eat or drink? Have you had lunch?'

'No, I haven't. Have you?'

'No, not yet. I waited for you. I can offer you an egg and bacon roll, or we can go out. What do you think?'

'I think an egg and bacon roll sounds perfect,' I said. 'And a cup of coffee.'

'Okay,' he said. 'You put the kettle on while I get the other going. I'll have tea please. White with two sugars.'

'I know,' I said. 'I have made you tea before, you know.'

'Of course you have. Sorry, don't know why I said that.'

And we smiled, both knowing that it was because it was strange and different, me being there in his flat.

It felt cosy moving around the small kitchen, being domestic with him. When I gave him his tea, we were standing very close to each other and our eyes met, but I'm not sure that either of us knew what to say in that moment. Both very aware of being in a different space – just the two of us.

Then he flapped a dishcloth at me and told me to 'Move, wench! Out of my kitchen!' So, I took my coffee and perched on the end of the sofa, chatting with him from there with the smell of bacon making my mouth water.

We sat out on the little patio in the sunshine and the next couple of hours slipped away in happy conversation. Eventually we were discussing where to go that evening, which turned out to be a local pub that apparently served not-bad food.

'Then after that,' he said, 'I wondered if you'd like to come see my local and meet my friends, and maybe watch some rugby?'

'Yes, that would be nice,' I answered, pleased that he wanted me to meet them (and them, me). 'But I need to change and spruce up a bit first.'

'You're fine like that. It's not a posh place.'

'Still, I'd like to freshen up.' I was wearing denims, and wanted to look a little smarter than that to them.

'Okay, well there's a towel in the bathroom for you.'

He'd mentioned his friends to me before. I knew Jos and Estee were a lesbian couple who had been together for years. He'd known Jos since school days and liked having her on his team for pub quizzes because apparently, she was a very clever lady and 'together we make a pretty formidable team!'

Apparently, David was a quiet kind of guy who had never married and worked as a chief accountant, and Isabelle ('Belle') was a 'lovely, bubbly kind of person', and an avid rugby fan. She was married to Mike, who was the total opposite and hardly spoke. It was felt that he might have PTS disorder since coming back from Afghanistan. I looked forward to meeting them all.

I felt much more presentable in beige slacks and my new pink blouse, even though the first place we went to was nothing fancy. But when we walked into the Brewer, his local, I felt positively over-dressed. Everybody else was in denims. Except Richard, of course, who *never* wore denims. I think I was the only one wearing make-up even, except for one woman with bright red lipstick, false eyelashes and shocking pink hair, who was getting much attention at the bar. The place was what you would call a dump, and a small one at that.

As we walked in, a hand went up from a table over by a window and a voice shouted Richard's name. He waved back, asked me what I would like to drink and went to the bar. I smiled at the four friends, who smiled back at me, but decided to visit the loo before going over on my own. On my way back I met up with Richard again as he headed towards the table.

'Good evening! Good evening!' he said, putting down our drinks. We sat down to a chorus of 'Hi there. Hi, Richard!'

'This is Natalie, everyone. Natalie, this is David, Belle, Estee and...' and just at that moment the whole place broke into jubilant uproar as someone scored a try in the game on the TV. Richard stopped mid-sentence, his eyes riveted to the overhead screen.

'I'm Jos,' said the last person, who Richard hadn't managed to introduce. 'It's nice to meet you, Natalie.'

'Hi, Jos,' I said. 'You too. Please call me Nat.'

I would have known immediately that this was Jos without her even saying so, because she was, as Richard had described, 'a bit overweight'. An understatement of note.

The others were busy watching the replay and analysing the game as Estee (who on first sight I'd taken for a man), stood up and picked up her and Jos's glasses. She was as tall and lean as Jos was short and round, but had the same kind eyes, and she was friendly.

'You're from Cheshire, aren't you?' she asked. 'Did you drive over here?'

'Yes.' I smiled.

'How was it?'

'It was okay, except for Thelwell Viaduct. I got a bit nervous there. It was so windy!'

'Yeah, there was a bit of a crosswind there today. Not great.'

'Estee's a paramedic,' said Jos. 'Ambulance driver.'

'Oh, wow! That's interesting. And you? You're also working in a hospital, aren't you?'

'Well, I'm a psychiatric nurse in Her Majesty's Prison Service.' She smiled. 'And a functioning alcoholic.'

'Oh, okay,' I said, and laughed at her ironic smile. 'I bet you two have got some interesting stories to tell when you get home at night.'

'Funnily enough,' Jos said, as Estee headed towards the bar, 'we don't much talk about our jobs when we get home. It's nice to leave them behind, you know?'

'Of course, yes. I can understand that.'

'Where's Mike tonight, Belle?' asked Richard.

When I looked at Belle, I noticed that she was already looking at me, intently, through thick, bottle-bottom glasses. She quickly turned her face to Richard.

'No, he didn't want to turn out t'neet,' she said. 'He thinks he's comin' down with summat.'

Richard downed half his pint without answering her, his attention back on the game. Belle turned to me.

'So, Natalie, are you a rugby fan?'

They say your mind decides in the first few seconds whether you like somebody or not. That was certainly the case with Belle. I disliked her on sight, and I'm pretty sure the feeling was mutual. She was short and fat, and had far too much to say in her unrepentantly raucous voice. She laughed loudly and often, at virtually anything, and reminded me of Miss Piggy with piggy little eyes and nose.

'Not at all, I'm afraid,' I said, shaking my head.

She didn't answer but looked at Richard wide-eyed, as if expecting an explanation, the thick lenses magnifying her eyes. Then she wrinkled her nose and pushed her glasses up, further completing the piggy look.

'We'll have to *convert* her, won't we!' he said with a wide grin. The pun was lost on Belle, but not on Jos, who pretended to smack him across the ear.

He grinned wider, pleased with his little joke.

David, sitting next to Belle, lifted his glass in my direction and nodded at me almost apologetically. I nodded back. He was a mild man with thinning hair and a sad smile.

'So, what chance d'you think Saints have got on Sat'dy then, Richard?' asked Belle, and as he gave his considered opinion on the matter the conversation turned to rugby, and the spotlight, thankfully, turned away from me.

It was going dark outside, and street lights started to flicker on in the gloom. They lit a scene that was typical of any working-class, northern town – a mishmash of terraced shops, soot-blackened brick walls splashed with graffiti and flashing neon signs advertising fish 'n' chips, curry and kebabs.

The curtains in the pub looked like they'd hung there since the Second World War. I couldn't even tell you what colour they were supposed to be. And the polished table where we sat, which stood on bare wooden floorboards, was thick with dust in the carved places around the base. It was an old place that smelled of stale beer, rotting wood and damp, and a particularly bad smell that came from the gents' toilet, which Richard told me was due to blocked drains that the brewery was not interested in fixing.

I imagined that it once had been a place where sooty-faced, cloth-capped, Lancashire coal miners came for a drink at the end of their shift, and that it hadn't changed much since. All it was missing was a spittoon. Its nod to the twenty-first century was a karaoke stage up at one end with an empty space in front (a dance floor?), five TV screens (all showing rugby), and a couple of slot machines flashing lights in one corner.

But everybody seemed to know each other and there was a happy vibe as they watched the match. Apparently, it was an important game – World Cup or something.

Everybody in our group was drinking beer, except me, and so quickly that I couldn't keep up. Richard must have downed about four or five pints while we sat there, and had already had two with his meal earlier. Maybe it was just the excitement of the game. Eventually, the game ended, and from the jubilation I gathered that England had won.

Soon after, people started to leave and Jos and Estee made ready to go, followed by Belle. David stood up, too, and offered to walk her to the corner. Which left just Richard and me. We also decided to go. We finished our drinks and I stood at the end of the bar waiting for him while he went to the loo. And as I idly watched the TV screen above me, two guys who were standing at the bar turned to speak to me.

'Hello, luv,' said one, smiling. 'So, what's a nice girl like you doing with an arsehole like Richard?'

Obviously friends of his, having a joke, I thought. Giving them a raised eyebrow, I told them I had no idea. They exchanged a look that made me wonder if they *were* joking. Richard joined us.

'We're just asking your lovely lady here what she's doing with an arsehole like you, Richard,' said the other guy.

Both of them were well-spoken despite their choice of words, and again, the cold smiles made me wonder if they really were joking.

Richard just looked smug and put his arm around me. 'Well, *you* can get your eyes off her for a start!' he said, and walked me out.

'Who was *that*?' I asked.

'Nobody,' he said. 'So, what did you think of my friends?'

When we got back to his place, he poured us both a glass of wine and asked if I was hungry.

'I'm going to have a slice of bread and butter. D'you want one?'

I said I did, and what came was an inch-thick wedge of crusty bread with real butter blobbed on it, as it was too cold to spread. It was divine, and washed down surprisingly well with the red wine.

We talked about rugby, which I already knew he loved, but I didn't know that he had once played it himself, 'to quite a high standard'. And apparently that meant being good enough to travel on a team bus to away games, on which everybody would get drunk and rowdy on the return trip. He told me of their various escapades.

Eventually I was stifling yawns.

'Yeah, I'm tired, too. Time for bed, I think.'

'Oh. I'm sorry,' I said, stifling another one. 'Tiredness has just hit me.'

'It's been a long day.' He smiled, understandingly. 'Off you go,' he said. 'I'll just wash these glasses.'

I came out of the bathroom with a big, fluffy guest towel wrapped around me and headed for the spare room opposite, when suddenly he was right there, apparently waiting to turn the hall light off.

'Have you got everything you need?' he asked, his eyes twinkling in the gloom.

'Yes, I'm sure I have, thanks.'

'Well, good night then,' he said, giving me a little kiss on my cheek. That turned into a more passionate one, and when we separated, he didn't move away. We just stood in the semi-dark, our faces close together. I could smell his cologne.

I felt it was my turn to say something. I *could* just have said, 'Good night, then,' and gone into the spare room. But I didn't, of course.

'You're not really going to make me sleep on my own in there, are you?'

His whole body relaxed. 'Oh, thank God!' he said, and kissed me again.

***

Who says old fogies can't make love? Or that it's, as Josh would say, 'just wrong'. Because what came next was very right. Passionate, loving, and breath-taking. He had the softest skin and smelled of soap, and I revelled in the feel of his big shoulders, the strength and warmth of him, and the gentleness of him. I lay there in his big-bear embrace, my body tingling with a feeling I hardly remembered. He kissed me, and snuggled down beside me.

'Phew! That was something, hey?' he said.

'It certainly was! I thought I'd forgotten how.'

'Oooh, noooo!' He chuckled. 'I don't think you have.'

'If my kids could see me now.'

'What would they say?'

'I think they'd probably be shocked.'

'You should shock 'em a bit more, then, and tell them you've got yourself a toy-boy.'

'Toy-boy!' I repeated. 'You're not that much younger than me.'

'A year and ten days,' he said, as if it were ten times that.

'I don't think that qualifies you for "toy-boy",' I said, tweaking the grizzle of grey hair on his chest.

'Ouch!' he cried. 'How about "boyfriend", then?'

'No, you're too old for "boyfriend".'

'What? Well, it will do,' he said, smiling. 'For now.'

'Let's just take it as it comes. No promises. No expectations. Because you never know, we might just as easily end up calling each other "ex".'

'Agreed!' he said. 'We'll just see where this road takes us.' He kissed my forehead. 'But I'm thinking neither of us went on that dating site just to find a new friend, did we?' He smiled.

I felt safe, and warm, and loved, and it was marvellous. *Could this be it? Could we two, at our age, have found the real thing?* And feeling like the luckiest person alive, I fell asleep in his arms.

***

When I woke up the next morning, the bed beside me was empty. Grey light filled the room as rain trickled down the window, casting rippling shadows on the ceiling. Then I heard sounds coming from the kitchen and a minute later he appeared with nothing but a towel tied around his waist, and two steaming mugs – and balanced on top of each was a thick slice of toast with butter melting into it. He deposited one on my side table. It smelled wonderful.

'Good morning! And how are you this morning?' he said cheerily. After taking his mug around to his side, he lost the towel and jumped back into bed.

'Ooh! Thank you,' I said. 'I'm wonderful. And you?'

'Cold!' And he grinned as he cuddled up and wrapped his cold body around me.

'Get off! You're freezing!' I complained, pushing him away – but I didn't fight very hard. 'Where's your pyjamas?'

'Don't have any. Can't stand the things.'

'Really? Me too! Whatever would Barbara-next-door think?'

'And what's Barbara-next-door got to do with it?' he asked.

I told him the story, and he told me about his neighbours: two old dears who lived either side of him, who fed him lamb hotpot and tended his patch of garden for him.

We had a lovely, long lie-in, neither of us wanting to leave the snug warmth of the bed, or each other. So, we didn't. It was about eleven o'clock when we finally crawled out and went for a pub brunch at a place called the Moorings, where we sat and watched a dozen or so little boats bobbing about on the canal.

I had told Barbara that I would be home by three o'clock though, so all too soon it was time for me to say goodbye. He said he'd phone me later to say goodnight, and he stood for a long time with his arms around me before I actually climbed into the car. Then he waved and smiled as I drove away.

I travelled the same route home that I'd come by, but it was a whole new world now; everything was different, almost surreal. *I* was different. I'd never thought of myself as a lonely person. I enjoyed my own company. But now life promised to be even better with someone else to share it with. I must have driven that whole journey on autopilot because my mind certainly wasn't on the road. *I could love this man*, I thought, and my heart felt so full of joy, I thought it would burst.

Chapter Nine

We'd arranged that Richard would come and stay over at Mum's the following weekend, which couldn't come soon enough for me. On the Friday morning I was up early, happily anticipating Richard coming over that evening even though I still hadn't asked Mum if she would mind if he stayed. I didn't think it would be a problem.

It was September, and the early morning sun shone through the open back door, just outside of which I could see the yellow blossoms of the climbing rose that surrounded it. Drawing closer, I watched the biggest bumble bee I think I'd ever seen navigate its way from the secret, golden heart of one sunlit bloom to the next. I stood for a moment enjoying the sun's warmth on my face. I was just about to make tea and toast for Mum, when she came shuffling into the kitchen in her dressing gown.

'Good morning,' I said. 'You're up early. I was just making you a cup of tea.'

She sat down at the table with a sigh, her face red and angry.

'Are you okay? Mum? Is everything all right?'

Out of her dressing gown pocket she pulled a folded piece of A4 paper and opened it up.

'What do you think of this?' she said, handing it over.

It was the print-out of an email addressed to Barbara-next-door, and it was from Cynthia.

'Where's this come from?' I asked, looking at Mum.

'Barbara gave it to me yesterday, when I went round there. I forgot to show you last night. Read it!'

The first few lines were a personal message from Cynthia to Barbara, asking her to give the letter attached to Mum, 'preferably when Natalie isn't around to interfere'. The letter itself (which I'm guessing was the only bit Mum was supposed to have seen) read...

Dear Mum,
    Natalie has asked about your will, and I wonder why, and what's going on? I do hope she's not interfering in things that don't concern her? Or worse! You were happy with the will as it was, and it was very fair. So please don't let anybody brainwash you into thinking otherwise.

    If you are now thinking of changing it, or, for instance, leaving the bungalow to Natalie, please talk to me first before you do anything. To do such a thing would be extremely unfair. Daddy would turn in his grave at the thought. He would never have condoned such a thing. And if this is what you intend to do and if this is what you think of me, then I can't think of any good reason why I would come over to see you ever again. I really can't believe you would do this.

    Love, Cynthia.

I was truly shocked at the nasty tone of it. I would never speak to Mum like that (not these days anyway), and was amazed that Cynthia would use such blatant, moral blackmail. I looked at Mum in amazement.

'Who does she think she is, speaking to me like that?' she said.

Her mouth made a tight, straight line and her eyes sparkled with anger.

'Wow! I can't believe how nasty this is,' I said, reading it again. 'I can't believe this.'

'How does she know about it? And what business is it of hers? It's nothing to do with her. How dare she speak to me like that?'

'I sent her an email a couple of weeks ago when you first asked about your will. I wanted to ask her if you'd made one. But she never replied.'

'You shouldn't discuss such things with her! It's none of her business. And it's not like she's not had enough out of me already.'

I know, I thought.

'But she and I spoke before I left South Africa and she told me she had taken you to make a will. I told her about you offering to leave the bungalow to me if I came over – and she seemed fine with it.'

'None of her business! They rented out that granny flat, you know?' She nodded at me, confirming her own words. 'I paid for that! And they've been getting rent on it all these years I've been back here. Not that they even need it. They don't want for anything! And he'll be on a good pension as well, now.'

'I know. He brags about that every time I visit them.'

'It's just greed!' she said, getting redder and redder in the face.

'Ah, Mum. Don't let it upset you. Just ignore her.'

'And you had no right to discuss these things with her. We need to go down to the solicitors – today! I'm going to do what needs to be done. Will you take me down?'

'We'll have to make an appointment first.'

'Well phone them now and ask them. What time is it? Are they open?'

'It's twenty past nine,' I said. 'They should be.'

'Well, the number's there in my book. Phone them.'

'Mum, are you really sure you want to do this?'

'Yes, of course! Go on. But don't be telling Cynthia everything I do. It's nothing to do with her.'

I brought the phone through to the kitchen and tapped in the number. The receptionist answered and I asked for an appointment for Mrs Sefton. The receptionist wanted to know what it was in connection with and had Mrs Sefton been there before and who was her solicitor, etc. Mum gestured impatiently for me to give her the phone.

'Hello?' she said. 'This is Mrs Sefton speaking. I'd like to speak to the young man I saw last time about my will.'

'Mr Browning,' I whispered.

'Mr Browning,' she repeated, with authority, nose in the air. Then she listened for a few seconds and said, 'Thank you!' She was apparently put straight through, and a moment later she was talking to him.

'Yes, I understand that,' she said, 'and I have thought about it, long and hard, and it is definitely what I want to do… Right. Okay. Can't I come down today? Tuesday?'

She looked at me for confirmation and I nodded.

'Yes,' she continued, 'Tuesday will be fine. Okay, yes. Eleven o'clock. We'll see you then. Thank you. Goodbye.'

She passed the phone back to me. 'Tuesday morning. Is that all right?'

'Fine with me.'

'Right!' she said, smiling. 'We'll get this settled once and for all. And I'll have that cup of tea now.'

I felt strangely close to Mum just then. Perhaps that smile had been for me?

Richard came over that evening. He arrived with his overnight bag in one hand and a bag of liquorice all-sorts, for Mum, in the other.

'So, where's *my* liquorice all-sorts then?' I teased.

'I've got something else for you.' He grinned, pulling me to him for a kiss. 'I missed you,' he whispered. 'Is your mum okay with me staying over?'

'No problem at all. She said I could share her bed, and give *you* mine.'

'Oh, okay,' he said, obviously not sure if I meant it.

'Don't worry, that's not going to happen.'

He smiled. 'I think your mum likes me, doesn't she?'

'Oh, for sure! Not to mention the liquorice all-sorts, of course.'

Mum was delighted with the sweets and ate half the bag before her tea, for which, and although she mostly lived on the sofa these days, she joined us at the kitchen table. Despite her protests that I'd given her too much, she managed to polish off a whole plateful of chicken and roast vegetables.

Mum had calmed down since that morning, but hadn't forgotten Cynthia's email. Out of the blue, she asked Richard if he had children.

'Yes, two daughters,' he said. 'But they're not children. One is twenty-five and the other twenty-seven. I've got a granddaughter too, little Izzy.'

'My word!' said Mum. 'What a handful! And are they both married?'

'Neither of them is married. The youngest lives with Izzy's father but won't marry him. And the eldest prefers girls, if you know what I mean?'

Mum's face went from confusion to wide-eyed wonder about Leanda (or 'Lea' as she was known). That would certainly make a couple of juicy titbits to share over dominoes on Sunday afternoon.

'Well, it's a different world these days, isn't it?' she said, smiling.

'It is indeed. But we love them, don't we? I love the bones of mine.'

'Mmm. Except until they start fighting over what you've got before you've even kicked the bucket,' she said, darkly.

Richard looked at me, confused. 'Kids!' he said, breaking the awkward silence. 'I love kids. I just couldn't eat a whole one.'

***

Later, Richard and I went out for a drink or two at the Wirral Hundreds. It was a big pub, full of a younger crowd and very noisy. When the karaoke started up, we left to go to the White Horse, a tiny old pub tucked away off the road, which was just a short walk away from Mum's. It had become our regular stop-off point for that last drink. It was a low, whitewashed, stone building, which had once been farm cottages and which could, at a push, hold about thirty people between the two rooms inside, with a few more on the little patio hung with fairy lights. It had an old stone fireplace and low-beamed ceiling. The door was so low that taller patrons had to duck.

There were about twenty people in that evening, a few of them nodded in greeting. Jim, the publican (and avid golfer), had struck up a friendship with Richard on our first night there. He looked up from behind the bar.

'Good evening, young man, and how are we this evening?' he said to Richard while throwing a wink to me.

I sat at our usual table at the end of the bar while Richard ordered drinks and discussed golf. A woman stood up close by and, catching my eye, she smiled as if she knew me. Her face was familiar.

'Hello, dear. How are you? Dotty!' she offered. 'From the chemist down the village. I gave you Mrs Sefton's pills.'

I recognised her then. 'Oh, of course. Hello!'

'Are you Mrs Sefton's daughter?'

'Yes, I've come to look after her.'

'Ah! From South Africa?'

I nodded.

'How is your mum?'

'She's well,' I said. 'But her back hurts her, I think.'

'Shame, she used to walk down into the village every day with that old dog of hers. I was just saying the other day that we don't see her anymore.'

'She can't walk very well now. Just potters round the house.'

'Well, please give her my love, won't you?'

'I will,' I said. 'Thank you.'

She nodded and made her way towards the ladies'.

Eventually, Richard came over with our drinks and sat down, exchanging pleasantries with the couple next to us.

After a while, he asked me what Mum had meant by 'till they start fighting over what you've got'. He knew I had two sisters and I had told him all about them, but I hadn't mentioned Mum's will, or their interest in it. So, I told him the whole sorry story.

'Your poor old mum,' he said. 'Can't be nice having your own kids fight over things like that.'

'I'm not fighting over anything. If it gets nasty, I'll just walk away and leave them all to it!'

'I don't think that's the answer. I mean, it's none of my business, but your mum needs you, doesn't she? The other two won't look after her.'

I thought it was nice that he cared about her.

When we got home, I peeped in on Mum. She was fast asleep with Emma at her side, on her back with paws in the air, as they snored in harmony. I closed the door quietly and found Richard in the kitchen, pouring us a glass of wine.

'Go sit yourself down,' he said. 'I'm coming now.'

A few moments later he brought the wine and came to sit beside me on the sofa, where we chatted a while before going, very quietly, into my room.

***

We were already busy making sausage, egg and bacon the next morning when Mum shuffled into the kitchen with her hot-water bottle and looked surprised to see Richard.

'Hello there,' she said. 'You're here bright and early!'

He quickly realised she'd forgotten he was staying over.

'Hello, darlin',' he said. 'Would you like a cup of tea?'

'Oh, yes please, Richard. Thank you. That would be lovely!'

'Have a seat,' he said, pulling out a chair for her.

'No, I don't want to get in the way. I'll go and sit in the lounge, if that's all right. It's more comfortable.'

'Is your back bad, Mum? Can I fill your hot-water bottle?' I asked. 'Would you like some toast?'

She handed me the water bottle and shook her head without answering, before shuffling back out the door.

'I'll take that as a *No* to the toast then, shall I?' I muttered to myself.

Richard caught my expression.

'What?' he asked.

'Nothing.'

'No. Go on. What is it?'

'Nothing. Well, a please or a thank you, or even saying my name now and again would be nice.'

'She does say please and thank you.'

'No, no, not to me, she doesn't.'

'Well, I told you she likes me!'

***

On Saturday night we went out for a meal at what used to be the Whalebone pub just outside of Runeham, now a restaurant called the Wayfarer. The old whitewashed pub had given way to a more modern place with big windows and soft yellow light flooding out to welcome guests in from the early autumn gloom.

As we sat, I told Richard some of the history of the place.

'Do you know why it was called the Whalebone?' I asked, knowing he didn't, of course.

'No, but you're going to tell me, aren't you?'

'It's because when they were digging the original foundations, they found a whale bone here.'

He nodded, but didn't look overly interested.

'There's so much history here,' I said. 'Runeham and Pembie were originally Viking settlements. There's lots of Viking history here. And Roman history also, obviously, with Chester being so close. Can't you just see Viking long boats gliding up the Dee, with oarsmen pulling to the beat of a drum? Wood creaking on wood and the slap of the oars on the water as they row?'

'Not really,' he said, looking at the wine list. 'I'm not really into that kind of thing, I must admit. What wine do you fancy? They've got rather a nice Merlot here.'

'Yes? Okay, you choose.'

We studied the menu and Richard ordered.

'I guess Lancashire's history is more about the Industrial Revolution, isn't it?' I asked, and obviously struck on something he *was* interested in. He told me that his father had worked in the local coal mine in Leigh.

'And my granny,' he said. 'Now she was a scary lady! She had a china bulldog in her lounge window, which scowled at anyone standing at the front door. *That* scared me. And then I'd knock on the door and hear, "What d'you want?" screeched from somewhere inside, and I'd want to run away. But then she'd see it was me, pick me up and kiss me stupid, and give me an apple.'

The waiter came and poured a little wine into Richard's glass. He tasted it, nodded approval and carried on.

'I'll never forget when my granddad died,' he said. 'He also worked down the mine, and he'd collapsed down there. They'd brought him up above ground and took him to the hospital, and there he lay on his death bed for a couple of days. And of course, all the family was gathered. My mum and all the aunties were with my gran at home, and the men took turns to be with my granddad at the hospital. The women took it in turn to go down the street to the phone box to phone the hospital now and again. But by the end of the third day my gran had had enough of waiting, and she took herself off on the bus down to the hospital to see what the problem was. And when she found my granddad, she gave him a piece of her mind, all right! She said, "Aven't thee gone yet? Why's thee keepin' these young lads from the work? Get thee gone now and be dead!" And turned and walked out again. And the poor old bugger died that afternoon! He was only fifty-three.'

It being a Friday evening, the Wayfarer was quite busy, and there was a good atmosphere. Several tables filled and emptied again as we sat there chatting away. But I couldn't help notice the couple sitting behind Richard. They were not a young couple. Probably in their seventies. The odd thing was, they hardly said a word to each other. The man looked down at his meal and the woman stared over his left shoulder as if each sat alone. I mentioned it to Richard, and he casually turned to look.

'Maybe they had a fight,' he said, turning back.

'They don't look angry. They look as if they're well used to it.'

'Maybe they've been married so long, they don't talk anymore.'

'How sad. You'd think they would have split up years ago.'

'You would indeed,' he agreed.

'What about your parents?' I asked. 'Are they still around?'

'No, both gone, I'm afraid.'

'What were they like? Who are you more like?'

'Oh, my mum. No doubt about that. She was a big woman. And my dad was only a little bloke. I've got a photo in my wallet. I'll show you.'

He fished his wallet out of his back pocket and produced a worn, old photo, cracked at the folds. It was, indeed, of a large, grim-faced woman, and a small, Charlie Chaplin-type man.

'She looks a bit fierce!' I said.

'She was that! But not with me. I was the apple of her eye. My sisters didn't get away with half of what I did. They had to pay for their keep. I didn't. Even my dad had to hand over his wage packet to her – but she never asked a penny off me. In fact, she'd spoil me.'

'Your poor sisters!'

He just grinned.

'But she didn't want me to leave home. Vicky had already had Lea and was pregnant with Chrissy before I moved out to go and live with her. Vicky had to arrange a surprise wedding for us, or I'd probably still be at home.'

'Wow, she really didn't want you to leave, did she!'

'She did not. Shall we have another bottle of wine?'

Eventually, the waiter brought the bill and I went to the loo while Richard paid it. When I came back, he was standing by the door with his back to me, talking to a man I didn't recognise. As I approached, I heard Richard talking.

'Yes, we run a little logistics operation out of Leigh…' Then noticing me, he turned and said, 'Ah, there you are!'

The man and I smiled at each other, waiting to be introduced, but it didn't happen.

'Right! Are we ready to go then?' asked Richard.

I nodded, and he turned back to the man.

'Nice to see you again, Roger. It's a small world, isn't it? We must get together again sometime.'

'Yes, we must,' said Roger. 'But I'd better get back to the missus.'

And with an understanding smile, Richard put a hand firmly on the small of my back and propelled me out of the door.

'Who was that?' I asked, intrigued.

'Oh, it's a guy I used to know years ago. He worked for one of our clients. I handled their portfolio.'

'I see,' I said. 'I was waiting for an introduction.'

'Oh, sorry! I suppose I should have, hey? Right, where to now? D'you fancy an Irish coffee? The White Horse?'

I wondered what Richard had meant when he said, 'We run a little logistics operation.' Really? I supposed that sounded better than admitting to an old acquaintance from the world of financial services that he was now just a lorry driver for a logistics company. But he had nothing to do with the running of it, so why lie? Was he that embarrassed? He was a proud man, I knew that much about him already. But I didn't say anything. Maybe I had misheard or misunderstood, anyway.

***

We didn't do much on the Sunday. It was a bit of a grey day and I gave Mum her breakfast in bed and crawled back into bed with Richard again. We had our breakfast late, when Mum had gone over to Barbara's, and then took a ride in the afternoon to Parkgate for an ice cream, after which we ended up in a rather nice pub overlooking the marshes out towards the Dee estuary.

We talked about our childhoods, our siblings and our marriages and I pulled his leg about him being a mummy's boy, or as he put it, 'the apple of my mother's eye'. And he told me again about Vicky, how she had been a married woman when he first met her, and it was Richard getting her pregnant that had ended her marriage – as you can imagine it would! And how Richard had remained living with his mum.

I'd heard most of this story before, and the thought had crossed my mind that Richard must have had major commitment issues. Or was it more to do with his mother not wanting to let go of him, even threatening suicide? Richard seemed to think it all a big joke.

He was still quite friendly with his ex-wife and said I would probably meet her one of these days. Apparently, she was a very forceful woman, with the nickname Dragon Lady. *Can't wait*, I thought.

The afternoon grew late and we became increasingly aware that Richard needed to go home as he had to be up in the early hours of the morning. I didn't want the weekend to end, but eventually he dropped me back at Mum's and left, phoning later to say how much he already missed me.

'Me too!' I said, thinking of the lonely week ahead.

***

Next morning the letterbox rattled, Emma barked and Mum said, 'That's the post. D'you want to fetch it?'

There were a couple of small envelopes addressed to Mum and a big, thick brown envelope addressed to Mrs M Sefton and Ms N Sefton, in large, very black, very angry letters. I hadn't been 'Ms N Sefton' for over thirty-five years, and I couldn't imagine who this could be from. But Mum knew immediately.

'That's from Brigit,' she said. 'That's her hand-writing.'

Inside there was a letter in the same angry script, pretty much echoing the sentiments expressed in Cynthia's email of the previous week. But Brigit's was written with far more flourish and far more acid resentment. It spoke of Mum's 'psychopathic tendencies' and of my 'pathetic need', which stemmed, basically, from me being such a loser in life. It also went on to accuse me not only of brainwashing Mum into changing her will, but of stealing her money in the meantime!

She enclosed a letter from her solicitor that also hinted at 'mis-appropriation of funds', and stated that Brigit would be contesting the will and would be requesting a certificate of mental competency.

I was shocked. Could this be the same woman I shared a bottle of wine with a few weeks before? The little girl in me wanted to cry because big sister Brigit was angry with her. But then I realised that I didn't have a big sister anymore and thought, *To hell with that!*

Mum took her glasses off to look at the letter more closely, and quietly, intently, read every word. Her mouth took on the same tight, straight line it had when reading Cynthia's email, and I was waiting for the same anger to erupt. But it didn't.

When she'd finished reading, she contemptuously threw the papers down beside her, and replaced her glasses.

Calmly, she asked, 'Who's stirred up that wasps' nest, then? Did you say something to her?'

'No, but I think Cynthia must have.'

'The times she's told me I mustn't leave her anything – that she'd give it to the local dogs' home!'

'I know,' I agreed, thinking to myself that Cynthia obviously hadn't told Brigit that she wasn't in the will.

'When do we see the solicitor?'

'Mum, are you sure you want to? Really? Do we need all this nonsense? I didn't come over here to get involved in a big family bun fight.'

'I will *not* be dictated to by those two!' she said. 'When is it we go? Was it Tuesday? Tomorrow?'

'Yes.'

'Right. Well let's go and get this sorted out then,' she said, picking up the TV remote. She started watching *Judge Judy*, letting me know that the subject was closed. Her face remained stony and inscrutable.

And I must say, as it dawned on me that Mum might actually leave the bungalow to me alone, there was some little girl part of me that liked the idea very much. I wasn't proud of it, or of feeling as smug as I did. I felt sad to think I had lost Brigit. Realistically though, we were never really going to be friends.

Half an hour later, Mum had forgotten the whole thing and sat chuckling at a cleverly animated advert in which a small dog was apparently dancing a Highland fling with its owner. But Mum had never heard of animation.

'Isn't it marvellous how they've taught that little dog to dance like that.'

I tried to explain to her that it wasn't real, but she didn't understand. She could see the dog dancing, so what was I trying to tell her?

***

The next day we went down to see Mr Browning, and I took Brigit's letter. He didn't say much about it, but was clearly disgusted. He advised that before Mum went any further, she should get a certificate of competency from her doctor.

We popped into the surgery on the way home, but they were fully booked. Mum's old doctor, Dr Griffiths, was going to be in the next day, however, so we made an appointment with him.

When we walked into his surgery, he greeted Mum warmly, and smiled at me, recognising me from years ago. I'd been to him most winters with tonsillitis.

Mum had asked me to go into his surgery with her, but when Dr Griffiths understood why we were there, he asked if I wouldn't mind stepping outside. I didn't mind at all.

Mum was in there a good thirty minutes or so. Dr Griffiths came out holding Mum on his arm and smiling, and told her he would post his report on to her.

It arrived a week later and stated that Mum was fully alert, aware and capable of acting on her own behalf. And she read it with great satisfaction.

'So, do you still want to change your will?' I asked.

'Of course!' she said. 'Make the appointment.'

***

The next time I went to see Maggie I took both Cynthia's email and Brigit's letter to show her. She was absolutely appalled but not, apparently, surprised. When she'd finished telling me, in no uncertain terms, what she felt about each of them, she turned her attention to Richard.

'I hope you're not telling this Richard fella all your business,' she said, holding up the papers.

'I wasn't going to, but Mum said something that made him curious. So yes, I ended up telling him about it.'

'You never learn, do you?' she said, shaking her head. 'D'you still want us to meet him?'

'Yes, of course. I'd love you to.'

'Well, Softlad's asked me to ask you if you want to come to his golf club's annual dinner. It's not for a while yet, but he has to book tickets now, if you want to come.'

'That's very nice of him. Tell him, thank you. We'd love to go! How much are the tickets?'

'You know he won't let you pay – you know him! But I'll tell him. It's quite a nice do actually.'

'Sounds good. I'll look forward to that.'

***

And that was not the only invitation forthcoming that week, either. Richard asked me if I would like to go to the annual concert at Tatton Park. I knew Tatton Park was one of these old stately homes that opened to visitors, but not that they held outdoor concerts. This one was to be given by the Liverpool Philharmonic Orchestra. Apparently, people took wine, spread their picnic blankets and ate *al fresco* while they listened to the music. That brought back memories of 'Concert in the Park' events held at the Johannesburg

Botanical Gardens, which I used to really enjoy. So, of course, I said I would love to go.

***

Richard came over on Friday and we went to the Stamford Bridge restaurant, which had become one of our regular haunts. I had told him, in the week, all about Brigit's letter and going to the doctor, and as the subject came up again, he told me what an absolute disgrace he thought it all was.

'How's your mum doing?' he asked.

'She's okay. Her mind doesn't dwell on things too long. She lives in the moment, mostly. Now and again, she'll ask when we're going to the solicitors, and that's it.'

He looked very serious for a moment. 'And the competency test at the doctors'? Do you think she'll be declared competent?'

'Why? Don't you think she is?'

'Oh yes, definitely. But would she want to be *seen* so? More wine?'

'Yes please. Why wouldn't she want to be seen so?'

'Oh, I don't know.' He smiled a sheepish little smile as he poured.

'If she failed the competency test,' I said. 'Then she wouldn't be able to change her will.'

'Well, exactly.'

I wasn't quite sure what he was trying to say, so I just carried on. 'Well, we received the report today and Mum is fully aware and capable of making a will.'

At that moment he was pouring himself a glass of wine, but instead he somehow managed to knock it over. He stood up quickly, and a waiter came across with a cloth to mop it up.

Settling himself down again, he smiled across the table. 'That's great news!' He poured himself a new glass of wine. 'Great news!' he repeated.

Chapter Ten

The night of the concert rolled around. It being a Saturday, Richard had also arranged to play golf over in Leigh in the early morning. So, the plan was that he would come over to Little Rutford on the Friday evening and leave early for golf on Saturday, and I would follow him over there at about lunchtime to get ready for the concert. He would provide the drink and me the food, which, as he had a proper picnic basket, I would make up at his place.

I managed to leave at about one o'clock, and once on the motorway, as always, I had that wonderful sense of freedom – like the outside world and the future were waiting for me. And the future was bright.

He came out of his door as I arrived.

'You're late!' he said. I thought he was cross at first, but then he kissed me hello and smiled.

'What do you mean, "late"?' I checked my watch. 'It's two o'clock.'

'Exactly! That's not lunchtime.'

'Course it is,' I said, smiling back at him.

He shook his head in a resigned sort of way, gave me another little kiss and took the bags out of the boot.

'What have you got here? There's enough food to feed the five thousand.'

'A veritable feast,' I said, following him inside.

We had coffee and he told me all about his golf that morning, which had ended up with a few beers at the nineteenth hole. That was probably why he started yawning and asked if I would mind if he went for a nap.

'Not at all,' I said, quite happy to have him out of the way while I made the picnic basket. And when I had made the sandwiches, cut up the chicken, packed crackers and crisps and put brie and cheddar, grapes and pork pies (and a pickled onion that I knew he particularly liked) into Tupperware, then I crawled into bed with him.

***

As the concert sounded quite a smart occasion, I thought I would put on some smart black pants. But as it turned out, I could have worn anything. The audience gathering there wore everything from denim jeans to long, silver-lurex dresses. What wasn't appropriate were the two-inch heels I'd chosen, as from the car park there was a half-mile hike up a rough, dirt road to the field where the concert was to be held. We joined the stream of pilgrims making the trek, all weighed down with picnic gear. Richard looked like a packhorse with fold-up chairs, blanket and cooler box, while I picked my way with my handbag and picnic hamper.

The track eventually opened up onto a small rise at the top of a field. The grass sloped gently down into a flat bowl shape at the bottom, through which meandered a little river; and within the bends of the river, the stage, looking like a big, open clam shell, had been set up.

We claimed our spot near the top of the slope and made ourselves comfortable. I bought a programme from a wandering vendor and sat down to read it while Richard poured me a glass of wine.

It was just gone six o'clock and the sun was well on its downwards path as we looked down over the undulating meadows around. A warm stillness lay in a golden haze over the slopes. People opened up their airlocked, easy-seal containers, popped their beers, poured their wine, and tucked into their picnics with chatty anticipation. As did Richard and I. It reminded me of the old hippy concerts back in the day! Except there were no picnics involved back then. And it seemed strange that after all the years in between, here I was, now, with my egg butties, my just-in-case cardigan – and a new romance. *How strange is life?*

Somewhere in the shadows at the bottom of the slope the orchestra went on stage, and very quietly started tuning their instruments. Eventually, the MC tapped the microphone and the crowd went quiet.

'Good evening,' he said, and introduced the conductor and the orchestra, and told us that we were in for a 'musical delight of light opera and popular classics, with a spectacular surprise at the end'.

The orchestra started up with 'Morning Mood' from *Peer Gynt*, which happened to be one of my favourites. The melody swelled to its grand crescendo, which filled the whole valley with sound, and the crowd sat in rapt silence as the volume receded again to the last, peaceful cuckoo call. And after a second or two of silence, the audience exploded into rapturous applause.

And so, the evening progressed. We sat side by side in our camping chairs, Richard holding my hand and keeping my wine glass topped up as he worked his way through a cooler box full of beer. In no time at all we were all clapping along to the *William Tell Overture*, at the end of which the MC, raising his arms for quiet, announced a fifteen-minute interlude.

Piped music filled the air as Richard made his way to the mobile toilets. When he came back, he turned his chair to face me.

'So, what do you think of it so far?' he asked.

'I think it's wonderful,' I said. 'Thank you so much for bringing me.'

He smiled, broadly. 'I thought you would enjoy it.'

He leaned forwards and took my hands in his.

'You know,' he said, with a goofy, lopsided smile, 'I don't know how you feel, but I've really enjoyed the time we've had together. I know we've not known each other very long, but I've come to think an awful lot of you, you know. I'm not good with w... words,' he said, stuttering slightly, 'but... well, I've... come to think a lot of you.'

I squeezed his hands a little. 'I feel the same,' I said.

'I know we got off to a bit of a rocky start,' he went on. 'Because you didn't even want to *talk* to me. But I think we've come a long way since then. And, and... I really...'

'I get it!' I smiled. 'Me too. I feel the same.'

But he was on a roll now. It was as if he was willing himself to get the words out, and his voice was getting louder with the urgency of it.

'And I know we've not known each other very long, but I want you to know that I think you're lovely, and I don't know where this, this... "us"... is going,' he said, his voice getting louder, 'but I really hope... *really* hope... I think... I've got a really good feeling about us.'

'I'm so happy to hear that,' I whispered, noticing the people around us looking in our direction.

'I think you're a really, really nice lady,' he said, really loudly now. 'And I never thought, at this stage of my life, I would meet anybody like you.

'I'm so happy that I have.'

People were staring now, some snickering, so I put my

finger to my lips to say, 'Ssshh!' But he totally ignored me and carried on.

'I just wanted to say, that I really, really think the world of you. And you've changed my life so much. And…'

At this point he was almost shouting, and the guy on the nearest blanket to ours got up and came over, leaned over Richard and said quietly, 'Steady on, mate. You know the whole world can hear you, hey?'

And it was as if Richard clicked back into reality. He looked at the man and he looked at me and he muttered an apology to us both. I smiled thanks to the man as he walked away and, squeezing Richard's hand, mouthed, 'Thank you.'

He gave me a sheepish look but didn't speak for a while. I thought what a tremendous effort it had taken for him to say those words, and embarrassing as it was, it was one of the sweetest things any man had ever done for me. I was thankful, though, when the master of ceremonies spoke again, and we were off down 'The Blue Danube'.

It was very pleasant to sit out in the fields like that, sipping wine and listening to the music. But as the sun sank lower and the air became a little chillier, I eventually began to feel tired and ready to go home. I was just considering putting my cardigan on when the MC announced that before going into their last medley, he would like to thank us for coming, and he hoped we'd had a good evening and that he would see us all again next year.

The sun had sunk into a dusky, red sunset, which reflected in the little river as the orchestra started up again to the quiet, dramatic strains of Ravel's *Bolero*. And then a black silhouette, as mysterious as the music itself, drifted silently into sight around the bend of the river – a smaller version of a Viking boat, complete with carved prow and single, square sail. The hair went up on the back of my neck at the sight of it. I knew it could not be real, but the effect was stunning.

As the boat drifted, slowly meandering along the course of the river, the music melted into the 'Ride of the Valkyries' and gained momentum. Then suddenly, the boat burst into flames; a floating fire ball reflecting in the water all around and burning steadily into the night, it drifted. And as the flames started to subside the music changed again, into the *1812 Overture*, to which, in time with the cannon fire, the sky above us was lit up with the most spectacular firework display. Along with the rest of the crowd, we could do nothing but 'Oooh!' and 'Aaahh!' with each new blossoming of light.

The music and fireworks finished simultaneously as the boat slipped silently out of sight around the bend, and there was an eerie moment of silence before another explosion of applause. Everyone stood up and clapped and whistled for what seemed ages, and at least until my hands were sore.

'Wow,' I said. 'That was absolutely stunning.'

'It was, wasn't it?' he replied.

'Did you know about the Viking boat?'

'No idea,' he said, and started packing up.

Marshals with torches lit the way back to the car park. I was tired, but Richard seemed more so, and very quiet. We hardly spoke on the journey home.

***

The next morning Richard was up bright and early and brought me a cup of coffee in bed, as usual.

'I've got something for you,' he said, with a sheepish grin. 'Your own mug!'

He placed it where I could read the words written on the side: 'Good Morning Gorgeous'.

'Aaah! Thank you, dear,' I said, touched, and he grinned like a happy little boy.

That was not the only surprise that day. While I was showering (or else he would have asked me if it was okay first), his younger daughter, Chrissy, had phoned to see if she and her sister could come over. He hoped that would be okay. If not, he could phone her back and put them off.

'It's fine,' I said. 'I'd like to meet them.'

We met them for lunch at the Moorings, the pub where Richard and I had eaten the last time I stayed over, and at twelve on the dot we walked in there. The girls were already there, in a booth at the bottom end of the dining room. They saw us and waved, and as we walked over, a little girl ran up and threw herself at Richard's legs.

'Grandpa Richard! Grandpa Richard!' she cried, lifting her arms to be picked up.

He picked her up and kissed her. 'Hello, my sweetheart,' he said, and turned so that I could see her face. She was a pretty little girl, chunky for her three years.

'And I've brought a friend with me,' he said. 'This is…'

'Natalie,' I interjected quickly, in case I suddenly became a 'Granny' or 'Nana'. *Nana Nat? I don't think so!*

The little girl gave me a long, serious look.

'Hello,' I said.

'And what's your name?' prompted Grandpa.

'Izzy,' she said, and wriggled to be put down again.

'Grandpa, Grandpa, I can whistle! Look!' she said, holding him back at the knees with both hands, so that he had to stand still and watch. She puckered up and made a strange sound, which was not a whistle.

'Very good!' he said, smiling at her. I smiled and nodded, too. Then she dashed off back to her mother as quickly as she had arrived. We reached the table and exchanged hellos.

'Natalie, these are my daughters,' Richard said. 'Leanne, or Lea as we call her. And this is Chrissy.'

I nodded to them in turn. 'Hello, how are you doing?'

'Hi!' said Lea, giving me a big, open smile and moving to let me slide into the booth. Chrissy leaned back against the wall, her expression unsmiling and inscrutable, and Richard sat on a chair at the open side of the booth, facing us.

'Right!' he said. 'What are we all having to drink?'

He ordered, while we all pored over the menus.

'How's your mum?' he asked.

'She's okay,' said Chrissy. 'She says to say hello.'

He nodded acknowledgement as the drinks arrived.

I liked Lea. She looked exactly like her dad, but a slightly smaller, prettier version, and with more hair; a tousled, mannish, mane of it. She had a clear, direct gaze, and there was no question about it – she was a bloke. In a T-shirt and low-slung denims (the crotch of which hung nearly to her knees), she moved and spoke like a man; far more *blokey*, in fact, than her dad!

Chrissy, although she was obviously from the same chunky mould, seemed very different. Even though she wore a dress and had long hair she was not a great deal more feminine than her sister, but she didn't have her sister's open face and didn't look me in the eye. Her hobby in life, apparently, was to find bargains online, and to do so before other buyers beat her to it.

The conversation centred mainly around the two girls, who both spoke in short, sharp bursts, which, together with their accent, I had trouble in understanding. I picked up that Lea had just had 'yet another' breakup with a partner, which had turned nasty, and she was quite happy to let her sister spill all the sordid details onto the table for us.

But when Chrissy spoke about *herself*, she spoke of how well she was doing in her job as stand-in assistant manager at a pub, how pleased the manager was with her and how well she controlled the staff, 'not taking any shit' from anyone! In fact, she hoped the actual assistant manager didn't come back off maternity leave, as she believed the job would be hers if she didn't. I couldn't help thinking that if she was as unsmiling at work as she was here, the other staff were eagerly awaiting the return of the regular assistant manager.

Mixed grills arrived for the girls, which they attacked immediately. They put the toast in the middle, chopped up everything else and piled it all on top of the bread, then doused everything in tomato sauce.

Lea smiled across at me. 'This is how we eat it at home,' she explained.

I just smiled back, noticing how Richard's eyes glowed with pride and love as he watched them.

Izzy, who had already downed half a strawberry milkshake, didn't want her fish fingers, but *did* want the ice cream that Mum had promised when the fish fingers were eaten. She sat, with chin on chest and an angry pout. The adults had decided to ignore her, but she was not going to be ignored.

'Grandpa, can I have an ice cream?' she asked Richard.

'If you eat your fish fingers,' he said.

Her pout deepened as the grownups carried on with a different conversation, and the little girl slid off her seat and under the table to come and stand next to Richard. She was eye level with the table top, and spied Richard's car keys lying there. She looked at him, and then back at the keys, then at each of us in turn as her hand came up slowly and rested on them. She looked around to see who'd noticed.

Without skipping a beat, Richard removed her sticky fingers from the *Saab*-logoed keys. 'No. Don't touch my keys, please,' he said.

The little girl sidled away around the edge of the table and the conversation continued.

Two minutes later she was back homing in on the keys again, and Richard raised his eyebrows at her. 'If you touch my keys, I *will* smack you,' he warned.

She pouted, and looked to her mum for support, but seeing none offered, she sidled away again. Two minutes later she was back, and all eyes were secretly watching as she made contact with the keys, and Richard's hand came out of nowhere and slapped hers.

She dropped the keys immediately, scrambled under the table to her mum and buried her face in her lap, howling blue murder.

'Mum! Mum!' she cried. 'Grandpa Richard smack me!'

Chrissy coolly said, 'He told you he would.'

Aunty (or uncle) Lea said, 'Come on, Izzy. That didn't hurt!'

'Yes, it did!' she wailed. 'I need ice cream!'

Her mother placed her on the seat beside her, facing again the plate of untouched fish fingers. 'Eat!' she said.

Izzy stopped crying instantly, mid-sob, and went back to pouting. She was *not* going to eat fish fingers. Eventually, Richard took a mouthful of them, saying, 'Yum! I'm going to eat them all up if you don't.'

And the whole table had to hide their laughter at the little girl's wide-eyed expression, which said, loud and clear, *Go ahead! See if I care! I hope you choke!*

Sensing that Izzy was getting tired, we felt the need to finish up then. Nobody wanted dessert and Chrissy and her dad seemed keen to get out of there. Time for me to be heading home too.

As we drove back to his place, Richard asked what I thought of them.

'I think they're very like you,' I said, laughing. 'Lea's like your clone!'

'Yes, poor child.' He laughed. 'Unfortunately.'

'And I can see you're all there for each other.'

He was pleased with that.

'*They've* been there for each other since they were tiny. Yes, they fight like cat and dog sometimes, but if anybody else starts – well, I'd feel sorry for them.'

'I can see that.'

'And they like you,' he said. 'I can tell.'

'That's nice. I like them, too.'

He smiled. 'Yes, give Vicky her due, she did a good job with the girls.'

I didn't have a response to that, so changed tack.

'So, tell me again why you and Vicky split up?'

'God! It's so long ago, I can hardly remember. I think we just drifted apart, as you do.'

'So, who divorced who?'

'It was by mutual agreement, I think. We both knew it was over.'

'Was it an amicable divorce, then?'

'Not at the time, no. But we're okay now,' he said.

'And her husband. Tom? What's Tom like?'

'Tom? He's all right, I suppose. Bit of a wimp. But he worships the ground she walks on and will do anything for her, and I guess that's what she needs. She's hard work to live with – a slave driver! The poor old bugger was supposed to retire two years ago, and she won't let him.'

'So, she's the boss?' I asked.

'Oh. Most definitely. They don't call her Dragon Lady for nothing.'

'Who was the boss when you two were married?'

He had to think about that one.

'I don't know really – too long ago.'

I didn't believe him for one minute.

When we got to his place, we had a quick cup of coffee and I left in time to get back home before Mum, who was playing Dominoes with Barbara-next-door.

Driving home, I wondered why he had avoided the question of who was the boss in his marriage. Why was he so vague with me? Was he always going to be a man who kept his emotions secret? But then, I thought, he was probably still nursing hurt pride and a bruised ego, if (as I suspected) it was her that had asked for a divorce.

***

A few days later Mum had her appointment with the solicitor. I took her in and waited in the waiting room while she went with him into his office. It didn't take long for Mum to check over and sign her new will, and I was called in to witness it, and also to be told that I had been made the executor, instead of Cynthia. I could just imagine her face when she heard that.

In the car going home again, Mum seemed very pleased with herself.

'I'm glad that's done and out of the way at last,' she said.

And she wasn't the only one.

Chapter Eleven

The following Thursday evening, I was round at Maggie's again. Alan had gone out and left a lasagne in the oven for us, which we dished up and ate off trays in the lounge. I told her all my news and about meeting Richard's daughters, and that started us on a conversation about kids.

'It just made me think,' I said. 'Watching Richard with Izzy when he told her he would smack her if she did it again. Nobody jumped in and said, *You can't do that!* They were all of one mind. It was like, one family, one set of rules, and they all stick to them. And Izzy learned something more than just not to touch his keys. She knows she's part of something. She has a family and structure and rules to stick by. You know what I'm saying?'

Maggie just frowned at me. 'It's a big no-no to smack your kids these days.'

'What?'

'It's just not done anymore.'

'I'm not talking about giving them a hiding,' I said. And with a sigh, I tried to explain. 'Bringing my three up, there was only me and Hennie. No one else. We both came from crap childhoods and must have brought all sorts of baggage with us; but not much in the way of family, or family values, for the kids. There were no set-in-stone family rules. Not much consistency. It was Hennie being too strict and me not being strict enough. We were just feeling our way in the dark all the time. And kids need consistency, don't they? I just wish I'd been a bit stronger for them, and paid more attention after Hennie and I split up. I think I dropped the ball a bit then, while we were getting divorced.'

'You had your Cynthia, didn't you? She was there.'

'Fat lot of good she was. I never saw her. And she was never interested in my kids, anyway. Yours had family in the background, didn't they?'

'Alan's gang? Yeah, if you can call them a family. More like a bloody shoal of piranhas,' she said. 'But it didn't matter because I was the perfect mother, anyway.'

'Pfft!' I replied.

She gave me the I-don't-know-what-you-mean! look.

'There's probably things I could have done better,' she conceded. 'But too late now, isn't it! Nothing to be done about it now. So why worry? And they just better remember to buy me a birthday card, and a Mother's Day card or they're dead. And they know it!'

'Yes, your two had stability, hey? One home, with Mum and Dad in it. The same school. I look back and see what my kids were dragged through: bankruptcy, divorce, moving house so many times, different schools. You think they're kids and don't know what's going on. But they feel it. *And* they had their own problems at school, with bullies. I should have been more aware. And you know what, I always felt that the kids were "mine" – part of me. And that meant I gave them as much loyalty and respect as I gave myself – which unfortunately was precious little. I learned too late that kids need respect – and loyalty. Those things are so important.'

'Yes,' she said. 'And hindsight's a marvellous bird, isn't it? It's the same for everyone. When you're in the thick of it, you don't realise what's happening till it's too late. That's life, isn't it? You get some things wrong, you get some things right. You try your best and that's all you can do.'

'I suppose,' I said.

'They survived, didn't they? And they've turned out surprisingly well, considering.'

'Considering what?' I asked.

'Considering they had you for a mother.'

'Thank you very much!' I said, indignantly.

'And they're okay, aren't they?' she asked.

'Ja, they are. Well, they're as mixed up as anyone else, I guess. And sometimes there's those little underlying resentments, you know?'

'There's always those,' she said, whichever way you try to bring them up. Nobody gets it all right.'

'I wonder what I did get right? What did I teach my kids?'

'One thing, at least – that you don't have to accept crap and that you can walk away from it.'

'I never thought of that,' I said. 'I hope so.'

'But they're all adult now, aren't they? And kids have got their own lives, too, you know. They're out there doing their own thing, living life. They're not worried about you. They don't want to be thinking about bathing you when you shit yourself 'cos you can't get to the loo in time.'

'Oh, God forbid! I don't want any of my kids doing that for me. And both the boys have told me not to expect it. They'll put me in a home first.'

'There you go!' she said. 'At least they're honest. And their wives certainly won't want to know, either.'

'And you know, it only seems like a few years since they were toddlers. I can still remember the day each one of them was born, can you?'

'Not yours, I can't, no. I can mine.'

I tutted at her. 'Remember that feeling,' I went on, 'when

they put that little wrinkled person into your arms and it's like, like the universe itself is patting you on the back and telling you you're worthy to be entrusted with this little life.'

'You're worth it!' She grinned, mimicking a women's hair dye advert off the TV.

'You know what I mean!'

'Yeah,' she said. 'And you just think, yes, I am worthy. I've got this, and then they go and turn into teenagers on you. I swear our Debbie went to bed like a Labrador one night, and woke up the next morning like a rottweiler.'

'I was going to say that after twenty-odd years of trying, that little face, now with a beard, tells you that actually, no, you fucked that up too.'

'Well, we all do. Why should you be any different?' she said. 'Why should you get to be Super-mum? *Something* was going to be wrong, wasn't it? Especially if that's the way they *want* to see it! It's about their choices, too, you know.'

'I don't want to be Super-mum, I just…'

'D'you know what?' she interrupted. 'When the old ladies come into the hospice, the first thing they want to tell you about is their kids; how clever they are, what a good job they have or what a fuckin' fantastic house they live in – how great people think they are, or how rich and important. Their kids are like jewels in their crowns. Like their kids are these wonderful people, and that's because of them, because they were such perfect parents. Or that they inherited their parents' good genes or something. But they're not, are they? Kids *don't* belong to the parents. They're themselves. They're just ordinary people with their own lives to live. And most of those old ladies, good mothers or not, have got one thing in common – their kids don't visit very often. Not after a while, anyway.'

'Well, there's a happy little thought! No wonder you come home and drink yourself silly on the sofa.'

'Exactly!' she said. 'So, get over yourself, shut up about it and let it go. They are who they are – and it's their choice to be, and you're a very small, unimportant part of it.'

She took a slug of vodka. 'We love them, don't we,' she said, 'but we don't always have to like them. And it's the same for them; they don't have to like us. They decide whether they want to or not. So, you just have to believe that whether they like you or not, they still love you – because they do, you know.'

'Yes, I know they do.' I smiled. 'Don't you like your kids, then?'

'Not always. But I still love them. And don't tell me you're not the same.'

'Yeah, I guess,' I said.

'So, say after me...'

'After me,' I repeated.

'Fuck it all!'

'Fuck it all!'

And we downed our drinks.

'Give me your glass!' she said, standing up.

I handed it to her and followed her through to the kitchen with the dirty plates.

'D'you want more lasagne?' she asked, lifting the lid.

'No, ta,' I said, putting the plug in the sink.

'I read a book once,' I told her. 'And the author reckoned that it's our genes that rule our lives – not our intellect or our social conscience, or our ability to paint or write poetry, or build pyramids – just simply our genes telling us to make babies and protect our young so that the species will survive. Just that. That's all we're here for. To make babies, and die!'

She frowned. 'What's that got to do with anything?' she asked, handing me a new drink.

I put the last plate on the stand and dried my hands.

'It's like that poem, *The Prophet* by thingy Gibran, isn't it? "*You are bows from which your children as living arrows are sent forth"*... er... then something about being shot into a future that you can be no part of. Do you remember that one?'

'No,' she said. 'But sounds about right.'

I smiled, and followed her back to the lounge.

'I can believe that, you know,' she said. 'About genes. I think it's all about sex, and not so much about love. Do you think there is such a thing? Or are we just kidding ourselves? Women do, don't they – because they want to believe in love. I'm not so sure many men believe in it. Not really.'

'Or else they stop believing in it somewhere down the line,' I replied. 'But that doesn't mean it doesn't exist, does it? You look at any young couple in love, and tell me it doesn't exist. I think of it like... something like a bubble. You can see it, but you can't touch it or it will burst. Something beautiful but fragile; it might not last forever, but it makes us feel joy, and sadness. Reminds us we're alive, and connected to the rest.'

'And if you've got two bubbles stuck together with that flat bit in between – that's the compromises you have to make. That's marriage. Two are stronger than one and last longer.'

'What? No, that isn't it! The bubble is the love, not the people.'

'What?' she said, frowning.

'Oh, never mind! But you know what I reckon? I think if human beings weren't so arrogant, they'd make a much better job of being in love. They think they're something so special – better than animals because *animals* don't know how to love, and *we* supposedly do? And then we get cynical and far too clever for our own good, because we think we *are* so clever. But we're not. We're just animals. Just lesser spotted, bald monkeys really, aren't we?' I laughed.

'Yeah!' she agreed. 'And don't tell me that animals can't love. D'you remember George?'

'Ah, I do remember George,' I said sadly, remembering her female, Heinz-57 terrier who had died of old age a couple of years before. I knew she'd died when I received a new Christmas card without her name on it.

'They say animals don't even get to heaven because they don't have a soul,' she went on. 'What's that about? Most animals are much nicer than people anyway, except for spiders, of course. They're evil little bastards. But all the others, they deserve to go to heaven. Don't you think?'

'Definitely!' I agreed. 'I think they deserve to go more than we do.'

'Well, if I was God,' said Maggie, 'I would let the animals into heaven first. Can you imagine what a miserable place it would be without them? And if God is all about love, then he's got to have a dog, hasn't he? And if he hasn't – well, what does that say about him, hey? If you got to the pearly gates and there was a sign there that said, "No dogs allowed", well, would *you* want to go in?'

'I don't think there is a heaven, really. D'you think?' I asked. 'I think that's something we'd just like to believe in too, because we think we're so special we deserve to go to a special place. I wonder if we even do have a soul? Or whether it's just an ego we have, telling us that we're so wonderful. Telling us that we are clever and special and capable of love. While all the time our brains are just flesh and blood like the rest of us, just giving out a non-stop chatter, like an algorithm we've set up for ourselves.'

'A what?'

'An algorithm; something that just keeps throwing information at you, but mostly the information you want to hear.'

She looked confused. 'I don't think that's what an algorithm is.'

'Go on then. What is it?'

'I don't know. And I don't want to, so shut up about it! But yeah,' she went on. 'We're not really making a very good job of it all, are we – when you look at the state of things?'

'We're not,' I said. 'I bet we're nothing but a virus or something, smothering the planet. If we didn't think ourselves so special, and showed a bit more respect, we'd probably make a much better job of it.'

'Yes, well, men run the world, so what d'you expect? Although having said that – Alan's not a bad lad in his way. He does the recycling and doesn't leave the tap running, and he's stayed loyal and faithful through the years, I have to give him that.'

'He wouldn't dare to be otherwise!' I laughed.

But she didn't laugh.

'Do you think he loves me?'

'I don't know. Ask him.'

'You know when you first get married?' she went on. 'When you're in love, and it's *real*. And then *real* hits *reality*, doesn't it? When you first start out, you love each other, don't you? So, what happens? Why do men want to go off with other women? Why can't they just keep it in their pants?'

'Why? Do you think Alan's cheated on you?'

'No. Don't be daft. No, I don't think so. But why do they?'

'I don't know. The usual excuse is that the wife doesn't understand them, isn't it? Which means *won't-give-me-sex-anymore*. I reckon a man doesn't feel loved unless he's getting sex. And if he gets it, he may love you back, or he may go off with another woman anyway. But if you start saying no, the love dies. For him, it's no sex – no love. For her, it's no love – no sex. It's a vicious circle. Sex is what it's all about, for most of them anyway. It's what Mother Nature made them for.'

'Yeah, but it's not "giving" them sex, is it, it's "allowing" it. It's like allowing them to rape you. Why would you allow them to do that? Like, violate you like that?'

'But if you love each other, it's not him violating you, is it? It's not a case of "allowing" it. It's not rape.'

'But if you feel obliged to have sex but it's not really what you want, then you're allowing it. You're submitting to it, aren't you? And that's something else… it's… giving more than sex. It's giving your whole self away… your dignity… your sense of self. It gives away your power.'

'But it's not supposed to be about power, is it? Do you think at this stage in your marriage, Alan is still trying to get on top? No pun intended.'

'Not anymore, he's not!' She shrugged. 'So why do women get an off switch and not a man?'

'I don't know. Probably because once the babies are there, Mother Nature wants the woman to look after the babies, not be wasting all her energy on sex anymore. You think how you were before you got married, and before the kids. When you were all loved-up. Weren't you just as eager for the rompy-pompy as he was?'

Maggie pulled a face of alarm, but I ignored her and carried on.

'And then somehow things change. What was the smell of his manliness suddenly starts to smell more like his dirty socks. And maybe we start to think he's not quite as wonderful as we dreamed he was going to be, or what the romcoms and the aftershave adverts tell us he *should* be like. And then all the nitty gritty of life creeps in – and sex creeps out, doesn't it – and it's just not the happy ever after.'

Maggie nodded in agreement. 'Half the time it's sheer exhaustion. You know what it's like with kids, and running round after a family. It's hard to feel sexy and in the mood for it when you're at that stage. But the man's always up and ready for it.'

'Of course!' I agreed. 'If he's not getting any and he's just left wondering what happened to his loved-up little soulmate, and where did this whingy-whiny always-tired person come from, who gives far more time and attention to the kids than to him. He probably starts wondering where did the love go, too. Mother Nature dupes both sides, I think.'

'So how did you feel when Hennie told you he'd been screwing around?'

'Sad… obviously! Disappointed. At first, I thought it must be my fault. That I must be lacking in some way. You know – what was it they had that I didn't? But over the years I've come to the conclusion that some men are just like that. That some have other women, and some stay faithful, and it's nothing about their marriage partner. It's who *they* are. How they see themselves and what they're entitled to do. If they cheat on one, they're probably going to cheat on all. Mostly, anyway, unless they were in a bad marriage that was going to come to an end anyway.'

'Yeah. They think they've got the right to screw around, don't they? But the wife must stay home and stay faithful. Fuck that!'

'And some men stay at home and stay faithful to one wife.'

'And women?' she asked. 'Why do you think women cheat?'

'You tell me.' I grinned. 'I stayed faithful! Too busy playing *happily-married-with-kids* to think about having an affair. *You tell me* why?'

'I think because they get so fuckin' bored with the monotony of it all. And of a husband who doesn't even see his wife as a human being anymore.'

'And then?'

'Then they have an affair. They realise it's not going anywhere and that they have too much to lose – so they say goodbye!'

She looked away from me, to the silent, flickering images on the TV and we didn't speak for a minute.

'I'm coming back as a swan,' she said. 'They mate for life.'

'What? You and Alan drifting along the river of life together?'

'Oh, God, no! One lifetime is enough! I wish somebody would just switch his "off" switch! He still thinks he's up for it, even now.'

'So, what's wrong with that? Don't you ever… you know?'

'No, we don't.'

'I thought you said you did, "occasionally".'

'Very, very fuckin' occasionally!'

'But you're lonely. And he's probably lonely, too. Why don't you just give him a hug and a kind word now and again?'

'Because it would never stay a hug. He'd think his luck had changed and he'd be pestering me for more, and more! That's not going to happen!'

I didn't know what to say to that. I knew exactly what she meant, because I'd been there too.

Eventually, more thinking out loud, I said, 'It's very true what they say, isn't it, "the whole world's a stage". But we're really all alone. It's so sad. We seem to live our lives playing out our own play, expecting other people to play their part in it. And the truth of it is, we're all just alone. If we could see beyond the foot lights, we'd see there's no audience either. There's nobody watching. We're just alone.'

'Yeah, well, normal people don't live like that. It's all this social media crap that's changing things. Facebook – *look what a wonderful life I'm living!* And that online dating and stuff. Whatever happened to falling in love with a guy? Now you just swipe right or left, or whatever.'

'I think you're right,' I agreed, but she hadn't finished.

'And everybody's so scared about just being themselves, nobody's being *real*. How can people fall in love if they won't be themselves?'

'Probably scared of showing how vulnerable they are,' I said.

'But that's what you've got to be, isn't it, to fall in love. Isn't it? Both have to be. It's about trusting the other person with that?'

'And did you ever?' I asked, genuinely surprised that she'd said that.

'Once.'

I didn't think she was talking about Alan, and it was clear she didn't want to say any more, so we were quiet again.

'I'm coming back as a blue-footed booby,' I said.

She squinted at me over her glass. 'Of course you are! What else would you be!' she said sarcastically.

'You don't even know what they are, do you?'

'No. And I don't want to, thank you!'

'They're birds. With bright blue feet. And the male does this little mating dance to show off his blue feet, hoping she will fancy him.'

'Does the female have blue feet, too?' she asked.

'Yes.'

'Well, yes, that would be an improvement on what you've got now. I suppose!'

It was my turn to squint at her.

'You are sooooo fuckin' weird, d'you know that?' she said. 'Here, take my glass. It's your turn.'

When I came back she took the glass from me, and resting it on her boobs she blinked slowly, fixing her gaze on the TV again.

'I watched a movie once,' she said. 'Was it a movie, or was it a doccie? A movie, I think. Not sure. Anyway, it was about a tribe of Red Indians…'

'Native Americans,' I corrected.

She glared at me for interrupting. 'Red fuckin' Indians' she went on. 'And they would spend a whole year travelling in a big circle following a herd of buffalo, as you do! And once a year they would come to this fast-flowing river and a high cliff with a waterfall going down over it, and anybody who was too old or ill to get across the river, they just left behind to die.'

'Charming!'

'No, everybody was okay with it. It was just accepted that you didn't slow the rest of the tribe down. They had to keep up with the buffalo. No tears and sad goodbyes; just a little wave as the tribe pulled up sticks and moved off. Then the old ones would just sit there and choose their own time, with dignity. No catheters and tubes and life support machines and all that shit,' she said.

'So, what happened to them? They just sit there and die of starvation?'

'No, they sit round the bonfire chatting for a while, chant, have a bit of a sing song, y'know; maybe chew a few magic mushrooms. Then chuck themselves off the waterfall.'

'Mmm. Might tell my mum about that… or not!'

'Knowing your mum, she'd probably still be sat there waiting for you the next year when you all came back again.'

'She would, too!' I said, and we laughed.

'Don't you think it's a good idea, though?' she said. 'No hospice rooms for the dying, or sad relatives waiting for you to kick the bucket. Just a bit of a party, and off you go.'

'Weren't they sad, leaving their loved ones behind?' I asked.

'No. 'Cos the next year the tribe would come around to the same place again and dance around the fire, chew a few magic mushrooms themselves and talk to the ancestors. Have a little chat with them, you know?'

'Much more dignified,' I agreed. 'Elephants do that.'

'What? Dance around the camp fire or jump off waterfalls?'

'No! They go off to a secret place to die.'

'Yeah? Very civilised. And you have to be glad we don't have to follow herds of buffalo round in circles, hey? Fuck that!'

I laughed. 'But we do go round in circles, don't we? Everyone in their own little hamster wheel. Must have been nicer when people were a tribe and did things together.'

'Yes,' she said. 'Nowadays, everyone's in their own bedroom with their own telly – or sitting on computers talking to strangers – putting their false lives all over that Facepage thing. It's just sad! It's so fucking sad!'

'It's Facebook, for fuck's sake!'

'Whatever.'

She went quiet, and I was sorry I'd interrupted her.

'Yeah,' I said. 'And there's not even a communal waterfall to chuck yourself off these days, either.'

'Oh, you can always improvise. I know a perfect little bridge over the River Dee in Chester.'

'Oh, yes?' I asked, catching the implication. 'And have you ever stood on it?'

'I have, actually. Yes.'

'And what stopped you jumping?'

'Julia,' she said, that being explanation enough. 'And you?'

'Yes,' I sighed. 'I've been there once or twice.'

'So why are you still here?'

'I guess, in the end, I thought I could still cross the river one more time.'

She considered that and nodded slightly.

'I'm going to the loo,' I said. 'All this talk about water!'

'Well, if you're getting up – may as well top us up!' She handed over her glass.

I came back from the kitchen with a brilliant idea.

'You know what,' I said. 'Sitting by the waterfall could be a beautiful time. Just imagine; you wouldn't be bumped along on the back of a horse anymore, you wouldn't have to be constantly chasing buffalo in all the dust and noise, or be too hot or too cold, or have to share a tepee with ten other folks. You could just rest and enjoy the beautiful scenery. You could build yourself a little shelter. You've got fresh water – catch a few fish, trap a few rabbits – what a beautiful life! You could even set up a little hot-dog stand for those who weren't ready to jump off the waterfall just yet.'

She narrowed her eyes at me, trying to focus. 'And when did you last trap a few rabbits?' she asked. 'A hot-dog stand? Where are you going to get hot dogs from in the middle of the desert?'

'Well, buffalo biltong then! You could buy buffalo meat from the various tribes as they pass through, and make biltong.

Biltong and spring water. You'd make a bomb! Collect a few magic mushrooms, as well – trade for a bit of "fire water", for you. Perfect!'

She looked at me through half-closed eyes. 'You really are so, so… fuckin' weird,' she said.

And we laughed.

Chapter Twelve

That Friday I was doing a bit of housework before Mum got up. I was vacuuming the sofa, and took the head off the vacuum so that I could get into all the little nooks and crannies. I had just started on the backrest when the vacuum cleaner made the most alarming '*shchluuuuuk*' noise, as if it had sucked up something it shouldn't have.

Opening up the vacuum I found, lying in the dust, half a roll of chewy mints. A little cavity had opened up in the puffy part of the sofa padding, and slipping my hand into a hole in the lining, I came upon... Mum's stash! Used tissues, toothpicks, hair clips, coins, half a bag of treacle toffee (now congealed into one, dust-covered lump), and five pairs of tweezers; one of which (not counting the pair I had given her) was mine. I smiled to myself, vacuumed out the cavity and put it all back, minus my tweezers. And then I realised that to find them, she must have been rummaging around in my bedroom. That was quite a disconcerting thought.

***

Richard came over that evening (with sweeties for Mum), and we went out for dinner at the Stamford Bridge. I told him about my find that morning and he laughed.

'Old ladies do strange things,' he said. 'My granny was convinced that the man next door was pinching her knickers off the wash line.'

'He might have been,' I said, in her defence.

'Trust me! No one would nick *them*!'

We laughed.

'Hey! I've got something to ask you,' he said. 'You know you said you'd never been to Spain?'

'Yes?'

'Well, how would you like to go?'

'Really?' I asked, getting excited. 'Where to?'

'How about Malaga?'

'I've never been, but if you reckon it's nice – I'm in. And I'm sure Barbara-next-door would keep an eye on Mum.'

***

So, it was at the end of October that Richard and I drove through the rain to Manchester airport to board a flight to Malaga.

We weren't staying in Malaga, however. I had available points in a holiday club, so we agreed that I would pay for the accommodation (with my points) and Richard would pay for our flights. The holiday club didn't have any resorts available in Malaga, so we were staying in a little town close by called Benalmadena. We caught a train from Malaga to Benalmadena, where the hotel courtesy bus collected us from the station and delivered us to the Southern Star Hotel. It was a tall, white building, more imposing than those around it, and had wide steps leading up to a pillared veranda. However, at the top of the steps, a billboard advised of renovations being carried out, and pointed the way to reception through a dark, plaster-board corridor. This opened up into an open-air, central space filled mainly by a swimming pool (packed with people), a deck with dining tables, and a pub-restaurant. Positioned in an arch around this, the guest rooms rose in tiers of gleaming white balconies and red-tiled roofs.

Richard wanted a room on the ground floor close to the pool, and a balcony within hailing distance of a bar waiter. What we were actually given was a third-floor room at the back of the hotel, which I actually preferred. It was quieter, caught the late afternoon sun and overlooked a picture-perfect Spanish street.

Richard was not impressed. He moaned about the place being 'only half finished', the shower being too small, the temperature and pressure of the water, the lack of coat hangers, the noisy air conditioner, the stairs and the distance to walk to the pool.

I tried to make a joke of it all, and reminded him of the lazy, sunny days we had ahead of us. He carried on, and eventually I was starting to get a little annoyed. I took the complimentary bottle of wine and one glass out onto the balcony and ignored him. In a while he came to join me. He'd brightened up some and suggested we go down to the hotel pool. So off we went.

After a quick swim we lay refreshed on a couple of sun beds. Richard took out his e-reader. Trying to strike up a conversation, I told him I didn't know why he liked that thing so much and that I much preferred a real book. He put it away and dozed. It was so good to feel the warmth of the sun again as I lay watching the glint of water through the brim of my straw hat and listening to the splashing and voices of happy people. We were both a little pink as we went back to the room for some warm-skinned sex, and a nap.

Later, we took a stroll down along the quayside to find somewhere to eat. This one road pretty much offered the entire nightlife of Benalmadena. It stretched alongside the inky dark waterfront on one side, and a row of eating establishments on the other. Pizzerias, seafood restaurants and pavement cafés sat side by side, competing for customers and filling the air with intoxicating aromas. We sat at a little pavement café and shared a seafood platter and a jug of sangria, before sauntering back to the hotel, arm in arm, feeling warm, well fed and lazy.

The next day we wandered around Benalmadena and strolled back to the hotel looking at what the street vendors had to offer. Richard showed interest in a pair of cufflinks, but didn't buy them. I thought I might slip back before the end of the week to buy them as a little surprise memento for him.

We tried out the hotel restaurant that evening: a cosy, candlelit room with would-be starlight swirling around the little dance floor. They advertised a different type of entertainment each night, which on this particular occasion happened to be a pub quiz. And how Richard loved a pub quiz! He was all smiles as he put his hand up for the blank sheet, then passed it to me to fill in the answers because, he said, he wrote 'like a doctor'.

'What subjects are you good at?' he asked.

'Art?' I offered. 'I'm not bad on biology – body parts and all that. History maybe – natural history definitely, and maybe religion.'

'How about sport?'

'Not a chance!'

'Movies?'

'I'm awful at remembering names!'

He looked unimpressed. 'Pity Jos isn't here,' he said. 'She really knows her stuff.'

'Sorry to disappoint!' I said, jokingly. But apparently a pub quiz was no joking matter.

'No, I wasn't saying you're stupid, my dear. Heaven forbid!' he said, a little too patronizingly.

I frowned at him. 'I didn't use the word "stupid".'

'It's just that Jos is a very clever lady. She has three degrees and is studying for her fourth, and let's just say that she and I together make a formidable team.'

'So you keep telling me,' I said, sceptically. 'And what subjects are *you* good at?'

'I'm pretty much a good all-rounder when it comes to general knowledge, I think. Sport and history definitely.'

He went up to the bar for fresh drinks so that he wouldn't have to get up during the proceedings, and on his return, told me there were quite a few people with quiz sheets on their table, including a group of eight over in the corner. He'd been scouting out the competition. This was serious stuff!

The MC tapped the mic and welcomed everybody, invited those at the bar to grab a sheet and join in if they wished, and after a couple of feeble jokes he turned his attention to the questions.

'Question one! Are we ready?' he asked. 'What is the largest bone in the human body?'

'Damn!' said Richard. 'It's on the tip of my tongue.'

Unconsciously I put my hand on my thigh trying to give him a clue.

'Femur!' I whispered.

He rolled his eyes towards the ceiling and whispered back.

'Take your hand off your leg! Just write it down!'

I did so, even though I was sure there was nobody looking at us.

There were ten questions in all and we both knew the answers to about half of them, but unfortunately the same half. I gave him *Pluto*, and I would have been right about *Freddy Mercury* if he hadn't insisted on *Mick Jagger*. But he was right about *Catherine Parr* when I thought it was *Catherine Howard*, and we were wrong again. So, the whole thing was a bit of a disaster really. At the end of the quiz, the party of eight won with three more points than we had and were rewarded with a bottle of wine. The MC thanked everybody for participating, and reminded us that there would be more fun the following night.

'Can't wait!' sneered Richard, screwing up the paper.

'I think we did very well, considering there are only two of us,' I said, smiling.

'We threw at least two points away,' he said, looking at me as if that was my fault.

'We wouldn't have won even if we hadn't.'

'Jos and I would have!' And with a disdainful sniff, he looked away.

I didn't know what to say to that without causing a fight, so I just kept quiet and sipped my drink, wondering why it was so important to him anyway. It was only a bar quiz, for heaven's sake. It was supposed to be *fun*. And why was it my fault we lost?

'I'm just going to the gents',' he said, and left.

I sat there with all those happy people around me, but felt quite miserable. I'd never seen this side of him. I thought he was being pretty childish and felt like saying, You know what? Next time, just take Jos on holiday! But I knew that would be equally as childish and I didn't want to spoil things. But was this how our holiday was going to be? Why had he changed so suddenly?

He was gone an awfully long time. Eventually he came and sat down again with a new pint of beer for himself, but nothing for me, which was unusually inconsiderate of him. I had only one mouthful of wine left, which I drank, and looked pointedly at the empty glass as I set it down. He seemed not to notice, and minutes passed in awkward silence while I considered whether to fetch myself another drink or just go back to the room. I was just about to leave when he spoke.

'Oh. Sorry! Do you need another drink?' and he was up and on his way to the bar before I could answer.

When he came back, I said, 'Thank you,' without even glancing at him. But he sat opposite, and waited for me to look at him before reaching out to place his hand on mine.

'I'm sorry,' he said. 'I tend to get a bit carried away, sometimes.'

'And you don't suffer fools gladly?' I asked, coldly. *Where did that come from?* I thought. *That's not what I wanted to say.*

His face relaxed and he closed his eyes for a second, then looked directly into mine. 'I don't think you're a fool,' he said. 'Believe me, I wouldn't be here with you if I did!'

He smiled his funny, crooked smile, and I smiled back.

***

The next day we took a bus ride to Malaga and wandered round the old Spanish town and down to the harbour. For tourists like us there was a sixteenth-century Spanish galleon moored there, which, although a replica, was still very impressive. I thought so, anyway. We marvelled at the mass of rigging, the cannons and the tiny, wood-panelled rooms below deck. Everything in them was so beautifully carved – so much more exquisitely worked and fragile than in today's throw-away style. It spoke of a world so different to ours.

In what was probably the captain's cabin, the whole back wall was one huge window of small diamond-shaped, leaded panes. It sloped down into the room at an angle and looked out of the stern of the ship. It appeared to be so fragile, I wondered how such a thing could have survived a storm at sea and I imagined the captain standing there, watching the waves thrash and crash down. It must have been terrifying. I said so to Richard, but he was getting bored at this point, and jumping up out of the captain's chair, he suggested we go.

So, we went, instead, to walk around the Picasso art gallery. And that didn't exactly grab his attention, either. But I wanted to see it. I know art speaks in a language both profound and provocative, but unfortunately Picasso's message was entirely lost on us two philistines that day. And by this time, Richard just wanted to get back to the hotel for a beer.

***

You really get to know someone when you're with them twenty-four-seven, and I was beginning to see a different side of Richard. Sometimes he just needed his own space, and I could almost see him withdrawing into himself. At such times he would take out his e-reader, and I and the rest of the world would cease to exist for him.

There wasn't an awful lot to do in Benalmadena and he may well have been just thoroughly bored. With me, too, for that matter. Or maybe he was just sick of having to think of things to do. Sometimes he'd ask me what I wanted to do, and he would seem slightly annoyed if I said I didn't mind. But I *didn't* mind. I always enjoyed his company whatever we did. But maybe he didn't feel the same.

I thought about Vicky, and what a strong person – wife – she had been to him. Maybe he liked a strong woman: someone to take the lead and make the decisions? To take the initiative and be proactive and all that crap. Well, that wasn't me.

At such times I would just leave him alone to stew, and think of it as a good opportunity to find out such things about each other. At our age, neither of us was going to change, so we just had to find out if we were compatible, warts 'n' all.

***

The next day, the last full day of our holiday, was just such an occasion. We slept late and had brunch by the pool and without him even asking what I wanted to do, he took out his e-reader and ignored me. I had a book with me also, but decided to take myself for a walk. He asked if I wanted company, but didn't argue when I told him to stay and read.

I walked along the quayside feeling quite sad and not knowing why, and spent an hour or so in a street café looking out over the sea. Then a couple of cappuccinos later, I strolled back past the street vendors and their wares. The cufflinks were still there. I thought about buying them for him but decided not to, and treated myself to a pretty, yellow silk scarf instead. How, in one week, our relationship seemed to have changed.

When I returned to the hotel, I found Richard in our room just waking up from an afternoon nap.

'I was just about to send a search party out for you,' he said, smiling.

Looks like it! I thought, giving my best shot at a smile.

He asked where I would like to go for supper, and I told him that I really didn't feel like going out. He suggested a pizza takeaway, and I said I fancied cheese and biscuits. So, he ordered pizza and I went down to the hotel shop for crackers, brie, olives and a nice ripe mango, and an hour later we were sitting out on the balcony with a bottle of wine, sharing an *al fresco* picnic.

We were on the same level with the top floor of the three-storeyed, terraced houses opposite. So starkly white in the day, they were now varying shades of blue against a navy sky. They had pillars, arches, intricate wrought-iron balustrades and twisting staircases. Below us, the soft-yellow street lamps lit the narrow, cobbled street, and the blues and yellows made it a very Van Gogh-esque evening.

Richard noticed two seagulls perched on the apex of the red-tiled roof opposite, their white plumage looking almost translucent against the inky sky. It seemed as if they wanted to roost there for the night but couldn't, as one bird wanted to cuddle up and the other one didn't. Each time the amorous bird came near, the other would move slightly away along the roof, eventually reaching the end, when it would flutter into the air and settle once more at the opposite end of the roof again. The other would follow, and the whole process would start over.

Richard said, 'Forget it, mate, you're getting none tonight!'

'Maybe she's got a headache!'

'Maybe he's come home drunk and she's pissed off with him.'

The female bird flew up again, and I spoke for her. 'Don't you come near me, you drunken bum.'

'Ah, come on. Come on,' cooed Richard. 'I'm not drunk. I only had a couple. Come give me a little peck on the beak!'

'A couple! Look at the state of you. Get away! Go on! You're up the other end of the roof tonight!'

'Ah, my little chickadee, don't be like that!' He laughed. And so it carried on until we were both in stitches.

That was probably the most pleasant evening of the whole holiday. We talked about life, marriage and kids, where we'd like to travel or retire to, and he told me long-winded jokes with silly endings. Eventually, the birds cuddled up together for the night, and so did we. We made love in a lazy, tender way until, lying back on the pillows, he half turned towards me and took my hand, opened it and gently laid a kiss in my palm. Then closing my hand again, he held it against his heart while he fell asleep. I know it sounds silly, but it felt as if he was trusting me to take care of his heart – and I silently promised I would, feeling my own would burst with love.

***

The following morning it was time to pack the bags and leave. Richard was in a happy mood over breakfast and I had the feeling he was glad to be headed home. A few hours later we landed back at Manchester airport and picked up the car (in the rain), and very shortly we were back in Greenfield Crescent.

Mum was pleased with the chocolates and bottle of orange liqueur we'd brought her and said she'd been well looked after while we were away. I think she'd enjoyed having the place to herself again, to be honest.

Richard went straight to bed as he had to get up early, but I felt I should sit and watch TV with Mum for a while. I doubted very much that she could follow the plot of the who-done-it she was watching, but she smiled when the advert with the little dog dancing the Highland fling came on.

'Isn't it marvellous,' she said, 'the way they've taught him to dance like that!'

'It is, isn't it!' I agreed. I didn't have the heart for getting into that discussion again. I felt deflated, sad, and wasn't sure if it was just because the holiday was over. There was a gnawing little anxiety that spoke of something else.

***

I didn't see Richard until the following weekend, when I was due to drive over to his place. I'd had a few days to think over our holiday, and although he sounded fine on our nightly phone calls, something was niggling in the back of my mind. A question, I guess, about whether our relationship was going to last. Friday morning was dark and cold, typical for mid-November. I had to scratch frost off the windscreen and it took ages for the car to warm up. As I drove, wispy white mist drifted across the motorway to lie in flat shrouds over the fields. I had come to love this journey, seeing the countryside change with the seasons. Would this be my last time?

Again, my thoughts went back to our holiday. Spending a week with Richard was certainly different from grabbing a few hours here and there over a weekend. It had changed things. I wasn't sure how it would go with him this coming weekend, if he'd dump me. Or if I should be dumping him?

By the time I left the motorway, the sky was pale grey streaked with pink, and threw a pinkish glow across frosty fields of brittle, winter stubble. At one point on the road, I could see a little river running like a trickle of ink between bare, black trees and it reminded me of when I arrived back in the country, nearly a year ago now. And what a year it had been!

He was waiting by the door when I pulled up, and judging by his smile, my fears had been totally unfounded. He took my bag while quickly ushering me in, and shut the door on the cold. He gave me a big hug and a kiss and said he'd missed me, and in an instant all thoughts that there was something amiss between us were forgotten. His little flat was warm and cosy and smelled like toast, and it felt so good to be there with him again. Because he was back to being *him* again.

Chapter Thirteen

Two weeks later, we were putting on our finery for Alan's golf club dinner. It was a formal affair. Richard looked very smart in his black waistcoat and dicky-bow tie, and I felt rather elegant myself, in a strappy, long, black dress.

We arrived at the car park at the same time as Maggie and Alan, which was not the plan, but still. Maggie had had her hair done, and was looking good in a long cream dress. Alan was wearing a smart dinner jacket and pants, but looked very uncomfortable in it.

I did the introductions and Alan led us to the function room where a dozen or so eight-seater tables glittered festively around a small dance floor. People were gathering at a bar up at one end of the room, and we made our way over in that direction.

'I believe you're a golfer, Richard?' said Alan.

'I am indeed,' he answered, and the conversation inevitably turned to golf.

As Alan started introducing Richard to other club members, Maggie rolled her eyes towards the tables and I followed her over.

'So, what's *your* handicap then?' I asked her.

'Softlad, there!' she said.

We found our table and our place cards, which Maggie quickly swopped around so that we two could sit together.

'So, what do you think of him?' I asked.

'Didn't you say he was shy?' She frowned.

'Yes, I think he is underneath.'

'Well, he keeps it very well hidden,' she said, nodding towards the bar where Richard, in the middle of a group of guys, was holding court.

'He's probably telling them his rabbit-on-the-golf-course joke.'

As the tables slowly started to fill, Alan and Richard came to sit down. Eventually, the MC took the microphone and welcomed everybody, thanked Meryl and team for 'doing the honours again this year', and asked us to please welcome the mayor of Chester, who would award the prizes. He noted that Gerald's 'posh gear' was as eye-wateringly bright as his golf gear, and as people laughed, he wished us a good evening. Shrimp cocktail was served amid lively chatter, followed by a carvery, and halfway through the trifle the prize giving began. The winners started going up, each one to a man thanking his wife for her support and patience, as if they'd all agreed that to be the prudent thing to do. Alan was eventually called up, had his photo taken shaking hands with the mayor, and took the mic to say 'thank you' to certain people.

'For Christ sakes! Get on with it!' whispered Maggie. 'You'd think it was the fekkin' Oscars, wouldn't you?'

'What was his prize for?' I asked, having missed it.

'I don't know! For hitting the ball?'

'You don't play golf, Maggie?' asked Richard.

'No! No!' She smiled, then frowned. 'I work!'

'Ahh!' he said, with a sniff of disdain.

'Yes,' she said. 'I'm a cook in a hospice. And you? Oh. Right! You drive a truck. Don't you?'

He smiled around the table, checking that nobody else had heard. 'I suppose you could say that,' he said, quietly.

She was about to say something else, but I gave her a swift kick on the ankle. She glared at me, but it worked.

Then Alan came back with his prize and Maggie gave him a kiss, took the little trophy and smiled with pride.

'Well done, you!' she said, and handed it to Richard to look at. Alan beamed. With the ceremonies over, the MC told us to enjoy the rest of the evening, and to feel free to take to the dance floor, where strobe lights now flashed around and a DJ started playing old sixties hits. As the opening notes of 'My Guy' played, Maggie looked over at me.

'Remember dancing to this at Chester Jazz Club?'

'I do! Those were the days. Remember how we used to get all dolled up to go out, hey? Long dresses, high heels, the lot.'

'Yeah. And it would take you forever to get ready.'

'It would seem that some things never change,' put in Richard, wryly.

Alan smiled, but Maggie and I both ignored the remark.

'But we had some good nights out, hey,' I said. 'Remember the night Long John Baldry was there, and he pulled us up on stage to dance while they played?'

'Yeah. I remember!' she said. 'And the night you won the Miss Hotpants competition?'

'I remember. And I can remember you in that off-the-shoulder blouse with lace-up bodice thing over the top!'

The two men looked at each other, no doubt thinking that some things *do* change.

'Who's going to dance?' I asked, hopefully.

'Alan doesn't,' said Maggie, straight out.

'What? Haven't you seen your wife dance?'

'I'm not stopping her,' said Alan apologetically. 'But I can't. Two left feet!'

'And you?' I asked Richard.

'I have been known to,' he said.

So, taking him by the hand I led him onto the floor and was

surprised to find he was a pretty good dancer. As we walked back, I suggested that he might ask Maggie for a dance.

'That's not going to happen,' he said, smiling, but meaning it.

Shortly after, Alan went to fetch drinks and Richard went to the loo and they met up at the bar, where they seemed to get stuck. Meanwhile, the DJ played 'I Heard It Through the Grapevine', and I just couldn't sit any longer.

'Come, let's dance!' I said to Maggie.

'No ways! It looks pathetic when two women get up to dance.'

'I know. But it beats sitting here like stuffed prunes.'

'No!' she insisted.

'Come on! There's nobody here that's going to mind, or even notice.'

I dragged her on to the floor where two or three couples had already taken the plunge. Maggie stood there awkwardly for a moment, but then, with a grin, started dancing. After the first track we had to take our high heels off; we just couldn't dance in them, and within minutes other shoeless women came to join us. Maggie was letting her hair down by now, and it was so good to see. The DJ kept the music coming – and we kept dancing!

A good while later, when people started leaving, we squeezed our feet back into our shoes and made our way back to the table. Richard and Alan were still at the bar talking, although their drinking buddies were beginning to thin out. Richard noticed us sitting down, and said something to Alan that made him laugh as they came back to join us.

'Looks like you two had a good time,' said Richard.

'We did indeed,' I said. 'You too?'

'Did you enjoy that, my dear?' Alan asked Maggie.

'I'm knackered!' she replied. 'And I'm going to have blisters on my feet tomorrow.'

'Yes, I did,' said Richard. 'I was just telling Alan what a nice group of guys he has here.'

'Well,' replied Alan, 'I'll give you a call and you can come and have a round with us.'

'I'll look forward to that,' he replied.

Maggie gave me a look that said she wasn't quite sure about that idea.

'Shall we have a last round?' asked Alan.

'Why not?' I said. 'Do they make Irish coffee here?'

'I'm sure they would,' he said. 'But I'll stick to beer.'

'Yeah,' said Maggie, 'I've not had an Irish for years. I'll have one of those.'

The two men went off to get them.

'So, do you like him any better yet?' I asked.

'Oh, stop asking me.'

'That much, hey?'

She just looked at me. 'I'm off to the loo.'

As I sat on my own, swaying to the strains of 'Unchained Melody', Richard came and took my hand and led me onto the dancefloor. It felt so good to be held in his arms, gently rocking together to the music. We had a second dance, too, and I noticed Maggie sitting watching us. She had such a sad expression on her face. Then Alan signalled that he'd brought the Irish coffees, so we went to join them.

Maggie and I were too tired to chat much anymore, leaving Alan and Richard to discuss the merits of diesel engines versus petrol, and the prospect of electric. The room was emptying out quite quickly now though, and eventually, with very few people still hanging about, we also left.

We stood in the car park, white breath on the cold night air, shivering as we said our good nights, then hurried off to find our cars. As Richard and I climbed in, he looked up, his eyes searching the sky. I asked him what he was looking at.

'Just checking for broomsticks!' he said, which was a jab at

Maggie poorly disguised as a joke. It wasn't funny, and I was just too tired to laugh at that stage, anyway.

***

The following Thursday I was back at Maggie's.

'Yes, it was a great do,' I answered her. 'We really enjoyed it. I can't remember when I last danced like that.'

'Yeah, it was good, wasn't it? Better than last year, sitting there on my own. And Alan's made up with his trophy.'

'I saw. So, what do you think of Richard?'

'Oh. God! Here we go again. It doesn't matter what I think. He's your boyfriend. All that matters is that *you* like him, isn't it?'

'You don't like him then?'

'Not particularly.'

She sat down on the sofa and sipped her vodka. 'But it doesn't matter what I think,' she repeated. 'And I know you love him, or think you do. So, I don't want to say anything bad about the bloke. And I know you wouldn't listen anyway.'

'But what *do* you think of him?'

'Really?' she asked, with a sigh. 'I think he's a prat! I think he's arrogant, pompous, and stuck so far up his own arse he's almost lost himself. *And*, I think he's up to no good.'

'I see. Is that all?'

'Yeah. I think that covers it,' she said, looking at me with a serious look on her face. 'You did ask.'

'Why do you think that?'

'Because that's what I see. Maybe I'm wrong. But I'm not often wrong, am I?'

'I *do* love him,' I said.

'I know you do – or *think* you do. But you don't know him really. Do you?'

'I think I know him better than you do!' I retorted.

'Well don't ask me what I think then!' she snapped. 'Because you're such a crappy judge of men and you don't want to hear different.'

I didn't know what to say.

'I'm not trying to be shitty,' she said, gently. 'But I can't tell you I like the bloke. I'm worried for you – and I have to say it – he's a wrong'un. So please, just be careful.'

'I think you're wrong.'

She looked at me sadly. 'Well, I hope for your sake I am.'

Chapter Fourteen

The following weekend saw Mum's eighty-ninth birthday. We spoiled her with chocolates and flowers and were also going to take her out for afternoon tea at the Crooked Spout tea shop, which I'd heard served lovely fresh-baked scones with jam and cream.

Barbara-next-door phoned to ask if she and Arthur could pop round to give Mum a present, so I invited them to come along with us. Arthur, a retired gentleman farmer in his mid-eighties, with ruddy cheeks and white hair, carried a silver-handled walking cane, which he used as a cattle prod on anyone not paying him attention. Half deaf, he refused to wear a hearing aid and consequently spoke far too loudly. This was fine over a game of dominoes in Barbara's kitchen, as the ladies were also quite deaf. But not so much in a tea shop, especially as he was fond of telling corny and crude old jokes.

The tea shop was quite full and obviously popular, but they found us a table for five.

'So, what are you young ladies going to have?' asked Arthur, looking at the menu.

'Tea and scones,' said Barbara, looking through the top of her bifocals. 'They do a nice cream tea here.'

'What?' said Arthur. 'Ice cream? No, I don't want ice cream. It's too cold for that! These cakes look good. I think I might have a scone. What'd you say, Richard?'

'Yes, that sounds good to me,' answered Richard, hailing a waitress. 'So, it's scones all round, is it?'

A young waitress came to stand by Richard, order pad ready, but jumped with surprise when Arthur prodded her with his cane.

'We'd like scones with cream and jam for three, please,' said Arthur. 'Just a minute, don't go,' he said. 'What about you two? Are you having scones, too?'

'Yes.' Richard and I nodded.

'Okay,' he said, turning back to the waitress. 'That's scones with jam and cream for five. And what's everybody having to drink? Barbara, are you having tea?'

'Yes, tea please,' said Barbara.

'Margaret?'

'Scone with jam and cream, please,' said Mum.

'Yes,' said Arthur, 'but what d'you want to *drink*?'

'Er… oh, er… let me look,' said Mum, even though we all knew she only ever drank tea.

'Mum, would you like a cup of tea?' I asked.

'She'll have tea!' instructed Barbara, ending all debate.

Arthur gave Barbara a little dig in the ribs. 'They've got French horns here, Barbara,' he said, pointing to the menu. He smiled wickedly. 'Do you fancy a little French horn? Hey? Hey?'

Frowning, she smacked away the walking cane. 'She'll have tea,' she repeated. 'What about you two?'

'Cappuccino, please,' I said.

'Me too,' said Richard, smiling reassuringly to the poor waitress, who looked ready to run.

'That's scones with jam and cream for five, three teas and two cappuccinos. Okay?' he said to her.

'Oh, yes please,' said Mum. 'I'd like a cappuccino.'

Richard repeated the order again and the waitress dodged another prod from Arthur as she scurried away nearly in tears.

Richard leaned over to me and whispered, 'I think we'll be needing something a little stronger than tea.' But then he seemed to enjoy their company for the next couple of hours. And the scones were *really* good.

I arranged for a huge iced muffin with a candle in the middle to be brought over, and we sang 'Happy Birthday' to Mum as she blew out the candle. She was delighted.

As we drove home, Mum asked me once again how old she was.

'You're eighty-nine,' I told her.

'Still a spring chicken, my dear,' said Arthur, putting a hand on her knee. 'What's this about you taking a test to see if you can make your own will? What utter nonsense! Ruddy solicitors! They must play dominoes with you, what! You don't miss a trick. Can't get away with anything with you. You tell 'em that.'

Mum giggled. But the outing had tired her and as soon as we arrived home she headed for the sofa where she dozed for a couple of hours.

***

The first one happened a couple of weeks later, in late November. I didn't realise what it was at first. Mum and I had just had our tea. I finished the dishes and went back to watch TV with her, when I noticed she'd slumped to one side a little. I thought she'd fallen asleep. But her eyes were open.

'What do you want to watch, Mum?' I asked, picking up the remote, but she didn't answer. I saw then, her fixed, vacant stare, and immediately knew something was wrong. She was watching the TV, but wasn't seeing a thing.

'Mum?' I asked, bending down. 'Are you all right?'

Her eyes slowly came to rest on me, but they were strangely distant.

'Yes, I'm fine,' she said, in a weak, dreamy voice.

'Can I straighten your cushion for you?'

She didn't answer. I tried to straighten her up and her head rolled forwards for a moment, like a rag doll's.

'Mum, can you raise your arms? Up. Like this?' I demonstrated. She watched and slowly, with difficulty, tried to copy me. I knew I had to get her to hospital.

Mum was very proud of the fact that she had never been in hospital. Her normal self would tell me not to fuss, might even refuse to go – but there was no resistance now. I wrapped her coat around her and loaded her into the car as she was, old slippers and all, and drove as fast as I could the three miles to hospital.

Pulling up outside the A&E, I grabbed the first hospital uniform I saw, pointed to Mum and told him I thought she was having a stroke.

Within seconds, two other staff were wheeling Mum off down a corridor, but they made *me* go and move my car.

Back in A&E, I was told to wait. And wait. Until at last, a nurse told me where I could find Mum, sitting up on a gurney now in a hospital gown and watching everything that was happening around her in total amazement. But she looked much better. We were in a small room with several curtained cubicles, most of which were occupied.

'There you are,' she said, as I approached her. 'Where am I? What's going on?'

'You're in the Cottage Hospital, Mum. You had a funny turn. But you're looking much better now.'

'There's nothing wrong with me! Why am I in hospital?'

'You went very pale and you just didn't look right.'

'There's nothing wrong with me,' she repeated with disgust. 'Where's my clothes? Let's get home.'

'Well, we just need to hear what the doctor has to say. We just need to wait till he comes.'

'Oh. What a waste of time,' she moaned.

Just then a uniformed man with grey hair and a pleasant smile came over. 'Everything all right here?' he asked.

'Yes, we're fine, thanks,' I said. He looked at the board hung on the end of the gurney.

'Mrs Sefton?' he asked.

'Yes, that's me, and there's absolutely nothing wrong with me. I'd like to go home now please.'

'Is this your daughter?' he asked.

'Yes,' I replied.

'Oh, yes. That's nice,' he said. 'Would either of you ladies like a cup of tea? Or coffee?'

'Yes, please,' said Mum. 'Tea please. I'm parched.'

'I'm fine, thanks,' I added, thinking he must be a nurses' aide or something.

'Are you warm enough there, dear?' he asked Mum. 'I can fetch you an extra blanket if you like?'

'No, thank you,' said Mum. 'I won't be here for long.'

'Well let me know if you change your mind. It's a cold night, isn't it? What's it like outside? Is it still raining?'

'I don't know,' I said.

'I think we're going to have snow before too long. I think it will come early this year. It's just right for it.'

'I wouldn't be surprised,' I said, not really interested in chit chat at this time.

'Do you know when I can go home?' asked Mum.

'They'll be looking at your results, dear. Don't worry, they'll be around soon. I'll just get you that tea.'

Soon after, a small, serious-faced young doctor in a white coat came by. I think he was Pakistani, maybe.

'Good evening, Mrs Sefton?' he asked, picking up Mum's chart. He wrote something on it, clicked his pen closed and returned it to his top pocket.

Mum looked at him, but said nothing.

'Yes,' I said, for her.

'Hi,' he said, with a pleasant smile. 'I'm Dr Nadire. And you are...?'

'I'm Natalie, her daughter.'

'Okay,' he said. 'Well, we're going to keep Mum in overnight just to keep an eye on her, and you should be able to take her home in the morning.'

'Okay,' I said. 'What seems to be the problem?'

'Mrs Sefton,' he said, looking at Mum. 'You've had what we call a mini-stroke. But you're stable now.'

'There's nothing wrong with me,' insisted Mum. 'I need to go home. I'm not staying here for the night. I can't leave Emma alone. I have to go home.'

'It's important that you relax, Mrs Sefton, and we need to monitor you for a while. Just a precaution.'

'No, I can't stay...'

'Yes, you can, Mum. I'll look after Emma. She can sleep on my bed tonight. But you need to stay here.'

Mum glared at the doctor, who gestured for me to follow him out of earshot. He asked about her medication and I told him.

'And will she be okay?' I asked.

'Your mum is eighty-nine years old,' he smiled, 'and this is not her first stroke. She's doing very well except for the blood pressure, and we will help her to manage that.'

'Not the first stroke?' I asked, surprised.

'No,' he said. 'Didn't you know? The results of the MRI show signs of scarring from a previous stroke, possibly more. She probably wasn't aware she'd even had one.'

'No, neither was I.'

'We will send a report through to her doctor so that he knows what's going on, and if you have any questions, please don't hesitate to ask.' He smiled and moved on to the next bed.

When I went back to Mum, she was not happy.

'Where's that other doctor? We need to talk to him. This one isn't a doctor. He doesn't know what he's doing!'

'What other doctor?' I asked.

'That nice one that brought us tea.'

'He wasn't a doctor, Mum. I think he was just a nurses' aide or something like that.'

And on cue, the same nurses' aide came to take Mum up to the ward. And all the way there she cajoled the poor man to intervene on her behalf so that she could go home.

Thankfully, within a half hour she was safely tucked up in bed. A nurse told me that she would sort Mum out with anything she might need. So, promising to return in the morning, I left her there on the verge of sleep.

***

The bungalow felt strange that night. Emma was happy to see me back but sat on the sofa, looking very sad.

'It's okay, old girl,' I assured her. 'She won't be long.'

Richard phoned as usual, and I told him all about it. He very sweetly offered to come over, but I told him it was fine. Everything would be back to normal by the next day.

'How will this affect you coming over here?' he asked. 'Will you still be able to?'

'I hadn't even thought about that.'

'Well maybe we should,' he said. 'We can talk about it at the weekend.'

***

I was back at the hospital early the next morning. Mum had to wait for the doctors to make their rounds before she was allowed to go, and it was nearly lunchtime when we arrived back home. As we did, Barbara-next-door popped her head out of her front door.

'Oh, hi! How are you today? Everything all right?'

'Yes,' I said. 'Everything's fine. Mum had a funny turn yesterday and she was in hospital overnight, but she's fine.'

'Oh dear! I am sorry to hear that. What was it?'

'It was nothing,' said Mum. 'I am perfectly all right. They were just fussing over nothing.'

Barbara looked at me for more details.

'They said it was a mini-stroke.'

'I have *not* had a stroke!' Mum insisted. 'There was only that Indian chappie said anything about a stroke, and what does he know? There's nothing wrong with me!'

'And are you feeling all right now?' asked Barbara.

'Of course I am!' she said. 'I'm fine!'

'Come on, let's get you in out of the cold,' I said. 'Barbara, would you like to come in for a cup of tea?'

'Thank you, but I can't right now. I need to get these books back to the library before it closes.'

Mum settled back onto the sofa with an ecstatic Emma by her side. She had soup and toast, watched TV and dozed, and all seemed pretty much back to normal.

I phoned Brigit. The call went to voicemail, so I left a short message telling her what had happened, and then I sent an email to Cynthia telling her all about it.

That evening, Mum asked, 'Natalie, where did I go today?'

'You didn't go anywhere, Mum,' I said. 'You came out of hospital this morning, and we came home, here.'

'In hospital? What was I doing in hospital?'

'You had a little stroke. You were in the Cottage Hospital overnight. Don't you remember?'

Her eyes went wide with surprise. 'Stroke! I haven't had a stroke! I would remember that. Who said that?'

'The doctor,' I said. But she just looked at me as if I was crazy, and then started watching the TV again.

The following morning the phone rang. It was Cynthia, speaking in her would-be voice of authority.

'Natalie? Is that you?'

'Yes, Cynthia, it's me,' I said. 'How are you?'

'I got your message. How's Mum?'

'She's okay. She's back home and okay.'

'So, what did the hospital say?'

'They said it was a mini-stroke, not the first, and they have changed her blood pressure tablets. I don't think there's a lot else they can do.'

'Not the first?'

'Apparently not.'

There was a short silence while she digested that.

'Well, I'm coming over. I've booked a flight for next Monday, so I'll arrive there Tuesday. I know you're in the spare room, so I'll be staying with Ma Rawlings.'

'Oh. Okay. Is Doug not coming?'

'No, he's working.'

'Do you want me to pick you up at the airport?'

'No. Doug's brother is picking me up, and he's lending me his car, so I'll be over next Wednesday morning.'

'Okay. See you then,' I said, thinking, *Oh, God. No!*

'See you then!' she said, and cut me off.

I went through to collect Mum's breakfast dishes and found her happily propped up on her pillows, looking out at the frosty, foggy morning.

'Did I hear the phone?' she asked. 'Who was it?'

'You will never guess.'

Her face brightened with expectation. 'Who?'

'Cynthia!'

Her expression dulled instantly. 'Oh. Really? How is she?' she asked.

'She's coming to see you,' I said. 'Next week.'

'Oh, Lordy!' said Mum. 'Why? What's the matter? Is there something wrong?'

'No,' I said. 'I told her you'd had a bad turn and she's coming to see that you're all right.'

'No,' she said. 'You shouldn't have said that. There's nothing wrong with me and it's such a long way for her to come. And you're in the spare room. You'll have to come in with me, and give her that room.'

'She's staying with her mother-in-law. But she'll be over to see you on Wednesday morning.'

Her face darkened. 'And no doubt she'll be wanting to know about the will, won't she?'

I smiled that Mum had so quickly made the connection, stroke or no stroke.

'Oh. I'm sure! There's no doubt about that.'

'I don't want any fighting or nastiness. Tell her I'm fine, and she needn't come. Does she know you're in the spare room? Tell her you're in the spare room.'

'She's staying with Ma Rawlings,' I repeated. 'She'll come to visit you on Wednesday, but she won't be staying here. And it's *your* will, Mum. You don't have to discuss it with her if you don't want to. But there'll be no fighting, I promise you that. Don't you worry.'

'That's what *you* say!' she said, unconvinced.

***

I told Maggie all about it when I went round that Thursday.

'What's she coming over for?' she asked.

'To see that Mum's okay after the stroke.'

'Right! Of course!' she answered, with a cynical smile. 'You know what she's really coming over for, don't you?'

'Yes, of course. She wants to check the will hasn't been changed.'

'Yes. And good luck with that one!'

***

Richard arrived on Friday night, with liquorice all-sorts and kind words for Mum.

'Hello, darlin',' he said, taking her hand. 'I hear you've not been feeling so bright this week?'

'Haven't I?' she asked, eyes wide with surprise.

'Didn't you have to go to the hospital?'

'Oh, that!' she said, disgustedly. 'A lot of fuss and bother over nothing. There's nothing wrong with me.'

'I see,' he said, gently laying her hand on her lap. 'Well, that's good then.'

Later, I told him about Cynthia's intended visit.

'I wonder why she's really coming?' he said.

'I wonder!' I replied, cynically.

'Bad timing, isn't it?' he said. 'Your mum doesn't need any upset right now. I'd tell her not to come, if I were you.'

'She's booked the ticket. And besides, she'd never listen to me. But there'll be no upset, I'll see to that!'

'Do you want me to come over on Wednesday? A bit of moral support? I could change shift with somebody?'

'No. That's kind of you, thank you – but I'll be fine.'

We had a lovely weekend together, and on Sunday evening, as we sat in front of the fire at the White Horse, Richard cleared his throat ready to say something that he'd probably been thinking about all weekend.

'I've been thinking,' he said.

'Did it hurt?'

'No,' he answered, smiling. 'I'm used to it!'

'Pffft!' I said.

'No, seriously though,' he said. 'With your Mum having this stroke, will you still be able to come over to my place?'

'Yes. Why not? Well, I think for the next couple of weeks I'll stay home. But if she's okay then, it will be back to normal. Barbara-next-door has already offered to help whenever I need it. She'd keep an eye on her for me.'

'Okay,' he said, 'but if you think about it… one day… if we're going to carry on with this relationship… logically, one of us must move in with the other. Either I must come and move in with you or you must come and live with me.'

'One day, I guess. And I hate this place.'

I laughed. But he didn't laugh; he didn't even answer at first.

'Can you see yourself living in *Leigh*?' he eventually asked.

'Mmm, not really.'

'The thing is, we don't exactly have time on our side, do we? And it's not as if we don't know what we want?'

'I guess not.'

He took my hand. 'I hate leaving you on a Monday morning knowing I won't see you again till the weekend.'

'Yes, I know,' I said. 'I hate that, too.'

'Good! So, all we have to do is decide who is moving in with who!'

'What? Now, you mean?'

'Why not? What are we waiting for?'

'Well, I can't move in with you right now, can I?'

'No, I suppose not,' he replied. 'But…'

'What? Do you want to move in with me and Mum?'

'Makes sense, doesn't it?'

'Yes. I guess so.' I agreed. 'But what about your work?'

'No problem. I'm basically self-employed, so I'd just be working out of this side instead of from Leigh. So, what do you reckon?' he asked, giving his goofy grin.

'I suppose so, if you want to, that is.'

'Do *you* want me to?' He smiled broadly.

'Yes, of course. But we'll have to ask Mum first. It is her house, after all.'

'Of course! But I doubt she would object.'

'What will you do with your place?'

'Probably sell it,' he said, without even thinking about it. I had the feeling he had done all the thinking already.

'And all your stuff? What if we split up?' I asked.

'I'm prepared to take that chance, if you are.'

He squeezed my hand. I was dumbstruck!

'When will you move in?'

'Well, probably not this side of Christmas. New Year would be a good time to put my place on the market, I suppose. So how about the New Year?'

'So soon!' I gasped. 'That's only weeks away.'

'Do you want to wait longer?'

'No, no. That's fine.' I smiled. 'Exciting! But can we not tell Mum just yet? Wait till Cynthia's been and gone and things get back to normal again?'

'Yes, of course. I thought that too.'

I had the feeling that he'd planned the whole thing already.

The bell rang for last orders and he gave my hand another little squeeze before taking our glasses up to the bar. I sat reeling, asking myself what had just happened. But I was happy. Very, very happy.

Chapter Fifteen

I was up early the next Wednesday morning. I hadn't slept well, anticipating Cynthia's arrival. After taking my coffee through to the lounge, I sat watching the grey morning light gradually seep into the dark crevices of the garden outside, until I heard Mum going into the bathroom.

I made her a cup of tea and took it to her bedroom.

'Morning, Mum,' I said. 'How are you feeling today? Are you going to have a lie-in?'

'No, I must get up! What day is it today?'

'It's Wednesday.'

'Oh, I thought it was Thursday. What's happening today, then? Was there something?'

'Yes, Cynthia's coming to visit you.'

'Cynthia?' she asked, surprised. 'Where is she?'

'She's staying with Ma Rawlings.'

'Oh. That's right. I remember now. No, then I must get up. What time is she coming?'

'Mum, you don't have to get up if you don't feel like it, you know. It's Cynthia – not the queen mother!'

'No, I must get up,' she insisted. 'Will you just tidy my hair up at the back a bit?'

'Yes, sure. Call me when you're ready.'

At just gone ten o'clock a little blue car pulled up at the gate. Cynthia climbed out awkwardly, hampered by a heavy coat and scarf, and stomped her way to the front door.

'Hi!' she said, a thin smile on her lips. 'How are you?' And she offered her cheek to be kissed.

'I'm well, and you?' I said, kissing the air somewhere around her right ear.

'I'm bladdy cold! You forget how cold it gets here, don't you!' The South African accent sounded strangely incongruous in Mum's hallway.

'It is cold this morning, yes. Come through. Mum's in the lounge.'

Mum tried to struggle to her feet as we entered. Cynthia leaned over and gave her a kiss.

'Don't get up, Mum. Stay where you are.' She patted Emma and went to stand in front of the fire.

'Are you cold?' asked Mum. 'Will you have a cup of tea? Natalie, go put the kettle on. Let's have a nice hot cup of tea. That'll warm you.'

While making the brew, I heard Cynthia ask Mum about her night in the hospital, and Mum flatly denying that she'd had any such thing as a stroke. Then Cynthia's voice went low and I couldn't catch what she said, but Mum's reply was plain enough.

'No, we're getting along fine. She looks after Emma and me very well.'

As I went back into the lounge, I heard Cynthia apologise for not phoning on Mum's birthday. She'd tried to, but there had been no answer. Mum told her not to worry, she knew how busy she was, and she'd probably phoned while we were out for her birthday tea. What a pity it was that Cynthia had missed that!

Cynthia took her coat off and sat down. She looked pretty much the same as when I had last seen her, her doughy face and (as Brigit put it) her 'Queen Mother hairstyle'. But she did look older, the creases deeper, especially at her mouth; they gave her a sour expression without her even trying. She had quite a good figure, although still round-shouldered; even more so, in fact. She wore straight-legged pants, a thick, cream jersey and sensible navy shoes. Nothing too bright, nothing too sexy! Always sensible.

'Sorry about that email I sent you, through Barbara. Remember?' said Cynthia. 'I didn't mean it to upset you. It just came as a bit of a shock to me. It's just that I was worried that you might not, er… or might… do things that you don't want to do.'

'Like what?' said Mum.

'What came as a shock to you?' I asked.

'Well, like change your will,' she said to Mum, ignoring me. 'You did seem happy with the way it was when you first made it, and I just wondered whatever could make you want to change it now?'

Good-naturedly, I said, 'I think what she means, Mum, is am I brainwashing you into changing your will?'

Cynthia frowned at me.

'I see,' said Mum. 'Well, you don't have to worry, Cynthia. Everything's all right. I'm not the decrepit old fool you think I am, and I can't be brainwashed that easily!'

I smiled broadly as Cynthia patted the back of her hair in that little way she had. This was obviously not the situation she was expecting, and she was at a loss for words.

'I don't know what you mean, Natalie, but I've not come here to argue with you,' she said.

Mum saw her chance to change the subject. 'Oh, good! That's settled then. So how are the children? And the grandchildren? How many of them are there now? I lose track! Amelia had two, didn't she, a boy and a girl. And Danny?'

Cynthia had no option than to answer Mum's questions and be side-tracked away from the subject she'd come to discuss, and her face showed her frustration.

Soon, after a second cup of tea, Mum started to nod off.

'Are you tired, Mum?' I asked. 'Would you like to lie down for a bit?'

'Yes, I think I would, Natalie, if you don't mind. Cynthia, will you still be here a bit later?'

'Yes, yes... you go,' said Cynthia. 'I'll go and say hello to Barbara-next-door.'

I went to help Mum up and, for once, she allowed me to. It felt odd touching her; like a frail little bird that's dropped out of the nest. And cold. When I came back, Cynthia was in the kitchen putting the kettle on. She glanced up at me.

'We need to talk!' she said.

'Okay,' I answered, sitting at the kitchen table.

'Has Mum changed her will or not?'

'Why do you ask? And why ask *me*?'

'Because I want to know, obviously!'

'But if you didn't know what was in Mum's will in the first place, what difference would it make now?'

She looked at me wide-eyed and annoyed. 'I didn't actually *see* the will,' she said. 'But Mum *did* tell me that she had left the bungalow to you and me – not Brigit, because Brigit had said she didn't want anything.'

'I see! So why didn't you tell me that when I last saw you in South Africa? I told you then that Mum had promised to leave the bungalow to me if I came to live here with her? You had no objection then, so why now?'

'Because it's just not fair, is it? Why should you get everything and Brigit and I nothing?'

'But if I hadn't come over, you'd have put her in a home anyway, and the bungalow would have been sold to pay for it. So, you wouldn't have got anything anyway.'

'Whichever way you want to put it across, the fact is you're being greedy! Selfish and greedy! You just want everything for yourself and don't give a damn about me and Brigit.'

'Brigit wasn't going to get anything anyway, as you well know. I bet you haven't even told her that, have you?'

I could tell from her face that she hadn't.

'It wasn't for me to go discussing Mum's will with Brigit or anybody else,' she said. 'What she told me was said in confidence. And anyway, Brigit was left very well off when Peter died. She'll never want for anything.'

'So, it only became unfair when you thought *you* were going to miss out, too? Mmm? You're not so badly off yourself, are you – not to mention a granny flat Mum paid for, which you're still getting rent on!'

She looked ready to explode.

'That's got nothing to do with it. It's nothing to do with what Brigit or I have or haven't got – it's the principle of it all. Daddy would turn in his grave! And the fact that you've got nothing is down to the choices *you've* made in life. Like marrying a… a… Hennie.'

Breathe. Just breathe. Cynthia's red-faced anger could, even now, trigger the scared little girl in me. I was shaky and close to tears, but determined not to let her see it.

'And it's Mum's choice to leave the bungalow to me,' I said, very calmly.

'Is it?' she spat. 'That, I very much doubt!'

She stood up, slung her bag across her shoulder and pushed past me. 'Why would she ever?' she sneered.

'Because I'm the one willing to live in it with her and allow her to end her days here. You were probably hoping she'd keep quiet about the will, weren't you? Well, she didn't. And it's *her* choice to change it. Not mine.'

'Mum knows she can come and live with me anytime she wants…'

'Ja, that works!' I interrupted.

Our eyes locked, and then with a look of sheer disgust she made for the back door.

'I'm going to see Barbara,' she said. 'This is *not* over!'

Shaking, I made myself coffee and sat in the lounge trying to compose myself. About an hour later, I heard the back door open again and a cold blast of air brought Cynthia in its wake. Calmly, she asked if Mum was awake.

'No, not yet,' I said, though I really had no idea. 'She'll be asleep for a couple of hours now.'

'Well, I'm not going to wait then. Tell her I'll be back to see her again on Friday,' she said, pulling her gloves on. 'Right! Now listen, Natalie, we're having a family meeting tomorrow up at Brigit's at ten o'clock to sort this nonsense out. I'll pick you up on my way.'

'To sort what nonsense out?'

'Mum's will!' she said, anger flashing again.

'But I thought you said it's not for us to discuss!'

She just raised her eyebrows but didn't answer.

'It's *Mum's will*,' I continued. 'Don't you think she should at least be present?'

'It's best not to upset Mum with all of this. So, I'll pick you up at about quarter to ten. Okay?'

'No,' I said. 'I have nothing else to say about it. I've said everything I want to. You and Brigit can discuss all you like… but I won't be there!'

Her face lost its smug self-righteousness and she looked aghast at the sheer insubordination of it.

'You *have* to be! We need to clear this up.'

'If I change my mind, I'll meet you there at Brigit's. But don't wait for me.'

'Well, there's no point in meeting if you're not going to be there, is there?' she spluttered.

'That's up to you.' I shrugged.

"Ugh!' she said, disgustedly. 'I'll phone you in the morning.' And with that, she turned on her heel and left.

I went into Mum's bedroom in time to watch Cynthia

climb back into the little blue car and drive away. As it turned the corner of the crescent, Mum opened one eye and looked around, then opened the other also.

'Has she gone?' she asked.

'Yes. For now.'

'Oh, Lordy! Is she coming back?'

'She's coming to see you again on Friday morning,' I told her.

Mum rolled her eyes and muttered something to herself.

***

Cynthia phoned the next morning and got straight to it.

'Well, are you coming?' she asked.

'No,' I answered. 'I've decided not to.'

'Well, this isn't going to be the end of it,' she went on. 'Brigit and I just want to settle this in a fair and amicable way. We're all mature women, now, for God's sake. We should be able to settle this without all this bickering!'

'I'm not bickering with anyone!'

'So, come and discuss it properly with us, like an adult.'

'I have nothing to say to you, Cynthia.'

'Well, you haven't heard the last of it! Both Brigit and I are absolutely appalled by your attitude. So much for being the big Christian, hey! When it comes down to it, you're just greedy and selfish! You don't want to listen to reason or be fair about this. If you did, then you'd come and talk to us.'

'It's you I don't want to listen to, Cynthia. You are *not* the voice of reason, or fairness. And you never were!'

'Ugh!' she said, and hung up.

I hung up too, feeling remarkably calm, considering.

***

I told Richard all about it when he phoned that evening, and he was very supportive, bless him.

'I'm just sick of the whole thing,' I finished. 'I hate this nastiness and animosity.'

'Well, from what you've told me, that's all you're going to get from them anyway. You've never got on, have you?'

'No,' I admitted. 'But at least we're not usually trying to rip each other's throats out.'

'Look. It's nothing to do with either of them. It's your mum's decision, not theirs. And I know for a fact that your mum wants to help you.'

'What d'you mean? Why d'you think that?'

'She as much as said so. I was having a little chat with her. She even asked me to look after you, too.'

'Did she really?' I could hardly believe that.

'She did. And whatever you do, don't let them bully you into going against your mum's wishes. They have absolutely no right to do that. And you mustn't let them.'

'I hadn't thought of it like that,' I said.

'Well, that's what it is. They're bullies. That's why they're ganging up two against one on you.'

'According to Cynthia, they just want to be fair.'

'My backside they do!' he said. 'I don't know about the other one, but that Cynthia's just in it for herself. She's the greedy one! When is she coming back to see your mum?'

'Friday morning.'

'Well just let me know if you change your mind about me being there, okay? I don't mind at all coming over. Let me know.'

***

When Cynthia came back on Friday morning she was as different again. Cool, calm and aloof, she talked to Mum about anything *but* the will.

At one point, when Cynthia had gone to the loo, Mum sent me to her bedroom to fetch her other glasses, and Cynthia, coming out of the bathroom and seeing me in Mum's room, followed me in there.

She looked up at the big oil painting on Mum's bedroom wall: a bowl of pale pink flowers.

'This is mine,' she said. 'I bought this for Mum.'

'Then take it!'

'Not now!' She frowned. 'And the Royal Albert tea-set in the kitchen cupboard? That's Brigit's.'

'You're welcome to them,' I said, looking at the picture. She was glaring at me, her face red and her eyes shiny with anger, and I wondered why I had ever let this person intimidate me, and for all those years. Well, she wasn't going to anymore.

She turned on her heel and went back to Mum. After about an hour she said she must be leaving as she had things to do, and told us that she was flying home the next day. Mum and I exchanged a glance.

I left her to say goodbye to Mum and went to open the front door.

'Stay in touch,' she said, as she caught up with me. 'I want to know what's happening. Okay?'

'Of course.'

With that she again offered me the side of her cheek but I made no effort to oblige. She straightened up stiffly.

'Goodbye, then!' She turned and walked to the car giving a little wave over her shoulder (more of a gesture of dismissal, really).

When I returned to the lounge, Mum was sitting looking out of the window, her face expressionless.

'You okay, Mum?' I asked, for a second thinking she maybe having another stroke.

'Yes, I'm fine. Has Cynthia gone?'

'Yes. Thank goodness!'

'So, what was it she was asking about before?'

'When?'

'When you were in my bedroom?'

'Oh. Well, apparently that's her painting in your bedroom, and she wants it back some day.'

'Cheek! She sent me the picture all rolled up. *I* had it framed. The frame's mine,' she said, punching the cushion before putting her head down. She closed her eyes.

Richard arrived later and Mum was happy to see him and as talkative as ever, telling him that Cynthia had been to visit her and what a pity it was that he hadn't met her.

Later, he and I went to the Wayfarer for dinner and he wanted to know all about the events of the day. I told him, and he smiled approvingly.

'You're not half as daft as you look, are you!' he said and I jokingly went to slap the back of his head.

'Do you think I'm being a greedy, selfish bitch?'

'No, you're not. Don't think like that. Your mum's a strong-minded woman – she knows what she wants and it's up to her, not your sisters.'

I smiled at him, and he raised his glass to me.

***

Every time we went to the Wayfarer on a Friday night, we would see the same old couple we saw the first time we ate there. They always sat on the same table, in silence.

Again, I said to Richard that I couldn't understand why they would even want to come out together. He said maybe she refused to cook on a Friday. Or maybe they just enjoyed the food in this restaurant.

'Well, if we ever get to that point,' I said, 'we'll know it's time to go our separate ways. Don't you think?'

'That's for sure!' he agreed, laughing.

Over Irish coffees, Richard asked, 'So has your Cynthia always been like this?'

'Pretty much. But not usually so openly.'

'I didn't think I was particularly close with *my* big sister, but we'd never carry on like that.'

'Well, Cynthia's never been any kind of a sister to me. You don't know the half of it.'

He raised his eyebrows at me as he slurped some of the cream off his Irish, waiting for me to continue.

'Well, for instance,' I started. 'When I told her I'd given in my notice at work, I joked that my boss had probably replaced me already. But she must have taken that as meaning I might actually have been fired. So, just in case that might be so, the following week – and for the first time in the ten years I'd worked there – she phoned me and said she was in Jo'burg that day and how about she popped over to my work and had lunch with me.' I paused to see if he had understood what I was saying. 'She just wanted to see what was going on, see if I'd been sacked!' I said. 'Then as soon as I said yes, it would be fine for her to come, she suddenly didn't have time after all.'

'Mmm,' he said. 'Are you sure you're not being a little paranoid there?'

'No,' I said. 'I don't think so. Another time, when I told her I was divorcing Hennie, all she said was that she'd never thought it would work, anyway. But then she went behind my back and had coffee with Hennie's *ex-wife*, who she'd met just *once* before, to find out what was *really* happening; to dig up a little dirt, like if one of us had cheated, or was Hennie perhaps the one divorcing me.'

'So, how did you find *that* out?'

'Marianna, his ex, phoned me and told me. We were quite friendly with each other at that stage.'

'Good God! Why would Cynthia do that?'

'Just in case there was a bit of dirt to dig up!'

Richard seemed lost in thought, quietly taking a sip of his Irish and placing it carefully in front of him again.

'Penny for them?' I said.

But he just shook his head and smiled. 'Sorry. I was just miles away for the minute.'

He patted my hand in a fatherly way. 'But let's talk about happier things. Did I tell you I was accosted by Arthur as I pulled up outside tonight?'

'No, really? What did he want?'

'I think he was going to invite us to play dominoes with them on Sunday, but I skirted around it and told him we had plans.'

'Oh, thank goodness for that!'

Chapter Sixteen

Richard left early Monday morning again. When I got up a couple of hours later, the sun was shining and it felt a little milder than usual, making me want to get out of the house and fill my lungs with fresh air. So, after giving Mum her breakfast, I put on a couple of pairs of socks, boots, and padded jacket and took myself off for a walk. I needed to take Mum's new prescription down to the chemist in the village anyway, so I headed down in that direction.

I enjoyed the sun on my face, even though there was little warmth in it and my nose still felt cold. I walked down past the library and the bowling green, crossed the road at the junction and on into the village. There were Christmas lights strung up along the road and on the lampposts, but they didn't look very impressive in the daylight.

An old-fashioned bell chimed above the door as I entered the chemist shop and Dotty came through from the back to serve me.

'Hello!' She smiled. 'How are you? How's your mum?'

'Not so good, I'm afraid. She had a mini-stroke last week and was in hospital overnight. They gave her a bag full of pills and a new prescription,' I said, handing it over.

'Oh dear. I'm sorry to hear that.'

After catching her glasses on the end of a necklace chain, she put them on her nose and frowned down at the script.

'So how is she now? Is she back at home again?'

'Yes. She seems to be back to normal.'

Dotty smiled, sadly. 'Will you wait for this, or can Bill drop it off for you?'

Bill was the pharmacist and he lived in Greenfield Crescent and was used to dropping off Mum's medication.

'Would he mind?'

'Not at all. He'll pop it in tonight.'

'Thank you,' I said with a smile.

'Give your mum my love, won't you.'

After leaving the chemist shop, I walked over the little bridge that overlooked Little Rutford Station. The station was quiet except for three young boys skateboarding along the platform, and a gardener sweeping around the flower beds. The boys 'whooped' as their boards clattered up onto an oblong block of a seat and back down again, the sound echoing up to me together with the sooty smell of the place.

The silver track disappeared into the horizon between banks of dried brambles, and in that moment, I wished I was on a train, leaving this place forever.

I carried on into the centre of the village, which was just a dozen shops or so on either side of the road, linked by a zebra crossing in the middle. Where the shops petered out, there was a car show room and then the local primary school. It must have been morning break as the playground was full of noisy, red-cheeked kids running round.

Further up, I would have come to the Red Lion and the Black Bull facing each other on opposite sides of the road, marking the end of the village. I decided not to go that far and, after crossing over, walked back up on the other side. I couldn't help notice the number of shops that were boarded up, advertised for sale or for rent. I tried to remember what they had been in the past, and I remembered a green-grocer's, a butcher, a wool shop and a betting shop. The bank had gone. I guessed the big supermarket chains were putting local shops out of business these days. And who knits anymore?

I went into the local supermarket for a loaf. It was dismal and virtually empty; strip lights cast ghostly white light over sparsely stocked metal shelves, and strands of threadbare tinsel. The one, sour-faced, assistant, took my money without even looking up.

I walked on up the village. As I passed the undertakers, there was a hearse outside being hosed down by two young lads. An older man, dressed in scruffy-looking funeral clothes, leaned against a doorjamb and nodded his head to me as I passed. I nodded back hoping he wasn't sizing me up. I'd obviously been watching too many old westerns. I smiled, remembering how Dad and I used to watch *Rawhide* together when I was still a kid. It felt like hundreds of years ago now.

I was feeling pretty depressed at this stage, and when I smelled the fish and chip shop, I went in as much for the warmth and comfort as for the fish and chips. But I knew Mum would like some for lunch.

The woman behind the counter was perhaps in her early fifties with thin, henna-coloured hair trying to escape a messy bun, dangly earrings, and a greasy apron. Her bare arms were covered in tattoos and the saggy boobs were not confined by any bra. But she gave me a brilliant smile as I walked into the warm shop.

'Hello, luv,' she said. 'What'll you 'ave?'

I didn't much like being called 'luv'.

'Fish and chips for two, please.'

'Okay. The fish has just gone in,' she said. 'It'll take a few minutes. Is that all right?'

'Yes, that's fine,' I said, sitting down in a sunny spot on a window bench.

'You're not local, are you? Is that an Australian accent?'

'No,' I said. 'Probably South African. But most people remark on the lack of an accent.'

'Ah! I see. South Africa, hey. Over on holiday, are you?'

'No. I've come over to look after my mum, actually.'

'I see,' she said again, shaking sizzling chips in the deep fryer and squinting her eyes against the steam and heat. She dropped the basket roughly back into place.

'So, your mum lives in the village, then?'

'Yes,' I said, not really wanting to chat.

'What's your mum's name then?'

'Her name is Sefton, Margaret Sefton.'

The name didn't seem to mean much to her as she lifted the fish out of the fat to inspect their progress. I noticed her earrings again, dark red and marble-like, and realised they matched a link of beads that Mum had adorning her bedhead.

'Sefton,' she repeated. Then she looked at me and asked, 'Does she 'ave a little dog? A cocker spaniel?'

'Yes, she does.' I smiled. 'Emma.'

'That's right. She used to walk down into the village with Emma every single day. I *thought* I hadn't seen her in a while. She used to come in 'ere and ask for scallops. They're not on the menu anymore.' She whispered, 'But I'd make her a few anyway.'

I smiled. 'That's good of you.'

'Yes, I'd take her fish and chips to the door to her, because she'd wait outside with the dog. Is she all right, then?'

'Well, she had a bit of a bad turn last week. But she's fine again now. She'll be turning ninety next birthday.'

'Ah, God bless her,' she said. 'Tell her Rose says hello, would you?'

She went to busy herself at the back of the shop. Within a couple of minutes, she was back at the counter again, shaking the chips.

'So, do you think you'll settle 'ere now?' she asked.

'I doubt it.'

'Yeah, that's what I said.' She laughed. 'And I've been 'ere nearly twenty years now.'

She told me she had originally come from London, and had hated the village at first. Then she'd come to love the quiet, village life. She had a daughter, who relied on Rose as granny, to look after her little girl while she went to work.

In the end I decided there was something very likeable about Rose, and by the time I left the shop we'd had a good chat and a laugh, too. Funny how a complete stranger can cheer you up.

When I got home, I asked Mum if she'd like some fish and chips for lunch.

'Oooh! Yes,' she said. 'That sounds nice.'

I warmed the plates and unwrapped the packets and out came fish and chips, and something else.

'Scallops!' exclaimed Mum, smiling. 'You've seen Rose, haven't you?'

'Yes. She said to say hello.'

Mum grunted as she stuffed a scallop into her mouth.

'And Dotty in the chemist shop – she sends her love.'

But Mum, with eyes closed, was enjoying her scallops. I don't think she even heard me.

***

Maggie phoned me one afternoon. She had just officiated over the burial of Archie the hamster, who died of old age and was buried in style in a pebble-covered grave out in the back garden. And her granddaughter, Julia, happily convinced it had now gone on to hamster heaven, was fast asleep on the sofa.

'Don't know why her mother couldn't bury it in their own back garden, or why she's got to send it over here to be buried,' she complained. 'Always in a rush. Never any time for anything.'

Eventually, she asked if I wanted to go with her to the Black Friday sales at the retail park. I'd never heard of such a thing, but she quickly explained what they were, telling me that you could pick up some good bargains, big brand names, through their outlets there if you were there early enough. She sounded eager enough about it, so I agreed.

'Okay,' she said. 'The shops open at eight o'clock but we need to be there at least by six to get into the queue.'

'You *are* joking, aren't you? Six in the morning?'

'Definitely!' she said. 'If you don't get there early it will all be gone by the time you do.'

So, on the appointed Friday morning I gave Mum her tea and toast early, although I don't think she was aware that it was, and after chipping ice off the windscreen in the dark, I drove round to Maggie's.

Several houses already had their Christmas lights up, even in the gardens. There were reindeer, elves and a Santa or two. It was beginning to feel a bit Christmassy.

Maggie came running out as soon as I drew up at the kerb and jumped into the car.

'Good morning,' I said.

'Shit!' she said. 'It's cold.'

'I know! I could have been wrapped up warm in bed still. I hope this is worth it.'

'So do I. I brought us some coffee and a roll,' she said, showing me the bag before putting it down on the floor at her feet and settling herself in.

It was just on six o'clock when we found parking and made our way to the nearest shops. I just followed her blindly and found myself at the end of a queue that already reached quite a distance from the door. But within minutes there were far more people behind us, pulling woollen hats over their ears, rubbing gloved hands together and stamping their feet. Out came the flasks of tea and breakfasts of choice, and I realised this was a ritual.

By the time the doors opened at eight o'clock I was so cold I thought my nose would snap off, and my feet would not move fast enough for the stampede that carried me forwards through the doors of the store, into bright lights and warmth, at least.

What absolute chaos and madness! Maggie hung on to my arm as people grabbed trolleys and started dashing about as if their lives depended upon it.

'Let's go see the handbags,' she said. 'Sometimes they have Ralph Lauren or Louis Vuitton going half price.'

'Who?' I said, trying to look enthusiastic.

There wasn't much of interest at all for me, but we dragged ourselves around various shops for about two hours before finally making it to the last till queue. Maggie had an armful of clothes, shoes and a handbag. I had two jumpers and a long winter nightie.

As we stood waiting, Maggie took the pale pink nightie with the pretty little flower design off my arm and held it up by one lace-cuffed sleeve. She looked at it in dismay.

'Really?' she asked, as if she could not believe that even I would buy such an item.

'It's for Mum,' I said, laughing. 'She'll love it!'

'Don't worry. It'll be our little secret!'

She dropped it back onto my arm as if it was contaminated.

When we at last left the shop by mutual consent, we made for the nearest pub, the Three Owls, and over an Irish coffee and toasted cheese sandwich we thawed out a little.

'So, what happened with your Cynthia?' she asked. 'Did she come back again?'

I brought her up to date with what had transpired. She laughed at the tale of Mum disappearing off to bed during Cynthia's first visit.

'She's as sharp as a pin, isn't she?' she said. 'There's nothing missing there!'

I laughed with her. 'Definitely not!'

'And is the lovely Richard coming over tonight?'

'No, it's my turn to go over there this weekend.'

'How about your mum? Is she going to be all right? She knows she can phone us, doesn't she?'

'Yes, she does. Thanks. And she seems to be back to normal. Or as normal as possible. You know?'

'Yeah, I know.'

'In fact,' I said, seeing my chance, 'Richard and I are toying with the idea of moving in together.'

She screwed her face up. 'How would that work?' she asked.

'Well, I suppose, at the moment, it would mean Richard moving in with me and Mum.'

'I see,' she said, shocked. 'And whose idea is this?'

'I think it was mutual,' I lied. 'It just came up when we were talking about Mum and her stroke, and our future. It seemed to be a good idea all round.'

'I think it's a bloody awful idea!'

'You would!'

'And when does he want to move in?'

'We've not decided yet. No fixed date.'

'How does your mum feel about it?'

'We haven't asked her yet.'

She just gave me one of her looks – her serious, stern, Grandma-is-not-happy looks, and I felt myself blush.

'I know,' I said. 'I must be careful!' I knew that was what she was thinking.

'I'm not even going to say it. But I hope he's going to pay rent?'

I hadn't even thought about that.

We had another Irish coffee and the mood lightened again, and she showed me the clothes she'd bought in the sale.

'So, what did you think of the sales?' she asked.

I told her it was a nightmare and no wonder Alan wouldn't take her. But yes, I was happy with my plunder. She eyed the bag that held Mum's nightie, giving me a funny sideways look.

'They take stuff back within a few days if you change your mind, you know,' she said. And we laughed.

***

That Friday evening, I was supposed to arrive at Richard's no later than six o'clock because he had arranged for us to go out for supper with some good friends of his, Dermot and Cathy. Dermot used to live in the flat above him, but had moved out to go and live with Cathy. Richard didn't see so much of them anymore, but they had arranged to meet up this evening.

I was going to leave Mum's at five o'clock to be there on time, but at four o'clock Richard phoned and asked if I could come a little earlier, as it was a long drive back to Manchester for them and they didn't want to leave too late. I told him that I still needed to give Mum her supper, but I would try. As it happened, it was five o'clock anyway before I'd done everything I had to do, and could leave.

When I arrived there, the door was open but there was no Richard to greet me. I went inside and found two strangers standing around in his lounge, a slightly built, blond-haired man with an easy smile, and a slim, very pretty girl with long black hair and blue eyes. They smiled broadly.

'Hello,' said Dermot, in a beautiful Irish accent. 'You must be Nat'lie?'

'I am indeed,' I said, 'and you must be Dermot.'

He held a hand out to the girl. 'And Cathy.'

She came forwards and gave me a little hug. 'Hello,' she said. 'It's so nice to meet you.'

'Thank you, and you too.'

And at that moment, Richard came rushing in like a whirlwind, coming to an abrupt halt right in front of me, his face red and angry like I'd never seen it before.

'What time do you call this?' he demanded. But before

I could answer he continued, 'I thought you were going to come early?'

'Well, I tried, but there were certain things I had to do first. Sorry.'

'What things? What was so important? Why couldn't you just leave earlier like you said you were going to do, just for once?'

'Listen, I said I would try, okay?' With Dermot and Cathy standing there, this was becoming embarrassing.

'But you didn't, did you? You said you would be here early, and you weren't, and to tell you the truth I'm getting more than a little sick of your tardiness.'

'My *what*?' I said, wanting to burst out laughing at the ridiculousness of this, and I could see out of the corner of my eye that both Dermot and Cathy were actually trying to smother smiles.

'*Really* sick of it! You're never on time. You're always late and you've always got some silly excuse.'

'I think you're overreacting a little, perhaps?' I said, trying to defuse the situation.

'Pffft!' he said, and turned and scuttled away back into his bedroom like an old woman with wet knickers. There was something actually comical about him – almost feminine – like a pantomime dame in drag, and the three of us looked at each other trying not to laugh.

'I'm sorry about that,' I said, not knowing quite what to say to these people. They were, after all, *his* friends.

They both smiled broadly and Dermot said, 'Don't you worry, Nat'lie. We know Richard, don't we, Cathy?'

Cathy raised her eyebrows and nodded in agreement.

'Well, I'm glad you do,' I said. 'Because I've never seen *that* before.'

'Have you not?' said Dermot, pouring me a glass of wine. 'Don't worry, you'll get used to his little moods, so you shall.' He smiled.

I smiled back, but thought, *Do I want to?*

After about ten minutes or so, and after Dermot had called to ask Richard if he was ready to go, he came out of the room again. He'd calmed down, but didn't want to meet my eyes. He was just going to sulk.

As they put their coats on, I quickly went to put my overnight bag away – inside the door of the spare room. As we left, Cathy linked her arm through mine in a friendly, supportive way. They were nice people.

We were going in Dermot's car, and he climbed into the driver's seat. On the other side, Richard pulled the passenger seat forwards, and instead of waiting for me to climb into the back first, he stuck his bum in my face and rather awkwardly climbed in himself. Cathy held the front seat forwards and waited for me to climb in beside him, and as I did so, I caught the tail end of a conversation between Dermot and Richard. I just heard Dermot's soft persuasive tone, and over the squish of leather as I sat, I heard some of Richard's reply.

'Huh!... had one more brain cell, it would still be lonely!'

I saw Dermot's eyes looking at me through the rear-view mirror and I knew that comment was about me. If Cathy had not already clicked the front seat back into place, I would have climbed straight out of the car again. *Breathe*, I thought. *Just breathe.*

I turned in my seat to look him straight in the eye.

'You'd just better hope that I never do grow another brain cell!' I said.

Just for a second his expression changed. It wasn't quite shock, but near enough to make me feel good, whatever it was!

'Well said, Nat'lie!' said Dermot, laughing out loud, and Cathy turned round to wink at me. Richard laughed too, as if I'd made a joke. I just smiled.

And from that moment on, it was as if somebody had thrown the 'Mr Happy' switch on Richard. In the restaurant he was jovial as ever, ordering a steak, 'so rare that a good vet could bring it back to life again!' I sat there wondering, *Who is this man?*

Dermot and Cathy proved to be a lovely couple and very pleasant company. After we'd eaten, we moved over to the sofas in the bar for a last drink. But eventually, Dermot looked at his watch and said they really should be getting back now. We finished our drinks and drove back to the flat, them apologising for not coming in. We understood, said goodnight and waved to them from the kerb.

'D'you fancy one at the Brewer?' asked Richard.

That would have been the usual thing to do.

'Not really. You go ahead, if you like. I'm a bit tired. Think I'll go straight to bed.'

I was, in fact, still angry. If I'd have been fit to drive, I would probably have climbed into my own car and gone home.

He unlocked the flat door and came in with me. 'So, what do you think of them?' he asked.

'Nice people! I like them very much.'

'They are, aren't they?' he said. 'I've known Dermot for about ten years. Always the same, always a smile.'

'Cathy's nice, too.'

'Yes, she suits him very well. Will you have a glass of wine with me?' he said, opening a bottle.

I didn't feel like being social with him. I wanted to disappear into the spare room, but it seemed churlish to start sulking now. As I hesitated, he poured the wine and, with a smile, handed me a glass.

I took the wine and sat down, but I just didn't have a smile in me at that moment. He came to sit by me.

'Look,' he said. 'I'm sorry if I seemed to overreact earlier, but I *was very*... angry with you.'

'You made that *very* apparent!'

'It just seemed selfish of you that we were all here waiting. And you just pitch up when you feel like it. After having said you would get here early.'

'I didn't say I *would* come earlier, I said I would *try* to come earlier. And I did try, but I had things to do first. I can't just rush Mum. It was already four o'clock when you phoned. I couldn't just drop everything to come over here.'

'Well, that's part of it, isn't it? If you gave yourself more time and were more organised, you wouldn't be in this spin every time you're trying to go out somewhere.'

'I wasn't in a "spin"! And I did get here on time. But I couldn't get here early, as you wanted me to.'

'You were actually thirty-five minutes late, but don't let's argue about it again. Can we forget it?'

He wanted the last word and I wasn't going to let him have it. 'Yes, as we're obviously not going to agree on it, we might as well forget it. But there's something I need to say.'

'What's that?'

'I don't like being embarrassed in front of other people. That's not acceptable.'

For a second, I thought he was going to start arguing again. And I was ready to! But he obviously had second thoughts, and a sour little smile turned into a more friendly one.

'Okay,' he said. 'Tell you what, do you fancy some buttered toast?'

The truth was, I did, even after the big meal we'd had a few hours before.

'Yes, please.' I smiled.

Chapter Seventeen

It was time to drag the Christmas tree and decorations out from the 'gloryhole' (Mum's hall cupboard), and put them up. Mum watched from the sofa, handing me individual baubles and telling me where and when they came into her possession. When it was all finished, I turned the lounge lights off and the tree lights on, and we had a quiet glass of sherry together, watching the flickering colours reflecting in the tinsel.

She told me once again about the Christmas her father had given her an orange, a rare sight to see in those days. She had been seven years old, and that was pretty much her only memory of him before he'd disappeared into the wide blue yonder, never to be seen again; and never to be forgiven by her mother. Granny's first husband had died young, but he had been a pillar of virtue and respectability, as were his two children. But the second husband (Mum's father) had run away without a word, leaving six children for Granny to bring up on her own. So, he was a 'drunkard', a 'waster' and a 'scoundrel', and his four children had constantly been reminded of the fact.

***

The weekend before Christmas, Richard and I went present shopping around the wet and shiny, brightly lit streets of Chester. All the Christmas lights were up and there was a huge tree in front of the town hall. It all looked very festive, and busy, as people did their last-minute shopping.

I'd actually already done all mine. I'd bought Richard a bottle of Paco Rabanne cologne. The one he had was virtually empty and I knew how much he liked it… me too. But I helped him choose presents for his daughters and granddaughter, and cards for various people. It was so cold we bought a pie off a street vendor to warm us up. I bought an extra one for an old man sitting on the pavement playing an accordion. I don't know how he kept playing, because his fingers must have been so cold. But Richard frowned his disapproval at me, and already cold and fed up, I just wanted to go home then.

***

A few days later I popped in to see Maggie. She had Debbie and little Julia with her, and the little one was running around excitedly, telling me all the things she'd asked Father Christmas for.

The tree was up, with a stack of presents beneath it, and enough food, sweets and chocolate to last till next Christmas, I'm sure! And for someone who didn't like this time of year, Maggie had a smile from ear to ear.

We exchanged the gifts we'd bought for each other; a pair of thick, winter sock-slippers for Maggie, and a box of golf balls for Alan. I knew she already had a pair of sock-slippers because she always seemed to be wearing them when I went to visit – so I bought her another pair for when those wore out.

I wanted to save the wrapped gift she gave me, for Christmas morning, but she made me open it there and then. It was a pair of soft, grey leather gloves, something I didn't possess, and I truthfully told her I loved them.

She didn't, at first anyway, seem so enthusiastic about her sock-slippers, frowning at the zigzagged pattern.

'Turquoise?' she asked. 'Why turquoise?'

'To go with your dressing gown. Don't you like them?'

Her face broke into a smile again. 'I do, actually!'

Then Julia wanted to start opening her presents, too, but Maggie wouldn't let her and told her that grandmas were allowed to open presents early but little children were not. She was amazingly patient with the little girl, and never, I noticed, swore in front of her.

Julia's face was serious. 'Are you *very* old, Grandma?'

'Well, yes. I am,' replied Maggie, thinking, I'm sure, that her old age was in some way gaining her brownie points as far as early present-opening went.

'Are you as old as Archie was?'

'Yes, I am. I think I might be older. Why?'

'So, are you opening your presents in case you die before Christmas?' Julia asked.

I was battling to keep a straight face at this point, but a warning glare from Maggie told me I'd better, as she answered, casually.

'Well, I probably won't, you know – die! But just in case – yes!'

I rolled my eyes at her and she gave me her innocent *What?* face.

Julia heard her mum's voice in the hall, and ran out of the room.

'How can you tell her that?' I laughed.

'Excuse me. Have you got grandchildren?' she asked.

'No.'

'Well, shut up then!'

***

Christmas fell on a Sunday that year. I wanted to spend it with Mum at home, but as this was going to be Richard's last Christmas in Leigh, he wanted to invite his pub-friends and his daughters for Christmas dinner at his place. So, we agreed to do that on the Friday, the night before Christmas Eve.

I arrived at his place, as I said I would, 'at about two-ish', to find him busy in the kitchen with the turkey and a leg of lamb soaked in red wine and garlic, all of which smelled divine.

He had put a little Christmas tree up, which I decorated for him, and we pulled the table out to its full size, which I then set with a crisp white table cloth and four place-settings on each side, with Richard's at the head. I placed two little centre pieces with red candles, holly and fir cones, tucked red serviettes into the wine glasses, and placed red and gold crackers on to each side-plate. It all looked very Christmassy.

First to arrive were Jos, Estee and David, followed by Belle and Mike, and a few minutes later, the girls. It was a cosy fit in the small flat with little room to manoeuvre, but everyone was in a good mood and there was much hugging and sharing of season's greetings. We had drinks while we waited for the food, which took longer than Richard had anticipated. His face was red from working in the hot little kitchen, but he tried to stay calm and cope. He would not accept any help, but under supervision I was allowed to make the gravy. When he opened the oven door and blue smoke and a burning smell billowed out, I offered my help again, but he ignored me. He actually turned his back on me so I couldn't see what he was doing. But I could see it was only the bottoms of the roast potatoes that were singed slightly. If it had been me, I would have made light of it and said, 'Oh. Shit!', and would have told the whole room what had happened. But not Richard. He arranged the potatoes in a serving dish, singed bottoms down, and didn't say a word! And nobody noticed.

We chatted, ate, laughed and poured more wine. The loudest voice at the table was Belle, of course, with her paper hat on, reading aloud the corny jokes out of the crackers. Her husband, Mike, sat quietly alongside hardly saying a word, but even he had a little smile on his face. I sat by Jos, whose dry sense of humour had me in stitches. But it wasn't long before Belle singled me out.

'So, Natalie,' she said. 'We 'ear you're takin' our Richard away from us. Is that right?'

'I'm not taking him anywhere,' I said, laughing.

'You've asked him to move in with you, 'aven't you?'

'Well, it was a joint decision really. I can't move here; I have to look after Mum. So, it just makes sense, really.'

Richard smiled blandly.

'Well, I must say,' said Jos, 'you do bring the best out in him, and you're a hell of an improvement on his last girlfriends. So don't cock it up this time, Richard!'

I realised this was an opportunity not to be missed.

'Oh, do tell!' I said. 'What were they like?'

'The last one,' said Jos, 'was as rough as a bear's arse. The mouth on her!'

'Not the widow Rochelle, who had her own horse? I thought she was posh?' I said, looking over at Richard. He was not enjoying this at all.

'It wasn't *her* horse, she just rode it,' said David. 'And she knew words that I've never even heard before.'

'Stuff that would make your eyes water,' said Jos.

'And temper!' said Lea. 'Talk about a short fuse!'

'Ah, c'mon! She wasn't that bad,' said Belle.

I might have known that *she* would like her. I looked over at Richard, who was not going to meet my gaze but who looked uncomfortable.

'And before her?' I asked.

'Oh, what was *her* name?' Estee asked Richard.

'I forget,' he said, without even thinking about it.

'Tina!' said Jos. 'She was a strange, timid little thing.'

'Talk about from one extreme to the other,' said Lea.

'Did you tell Nat about the Paco Rabanne?' asked Jos.

'I can't remember,' he said. 'Possibly not.'

'That was Tina, wasn't it?' said Jos.

'So, tell me!' I said.

Richard smiled; he obviously enjoyed this story. 'I was still going out with Tina,' he said. 'But I'd been chatting with Rochelle online and she wanted to meet me. I don't cheat – I'm not like that. So I had to finish with Tina quickly so I could meet Rochelle.'

'Isn't chatting online with another woman cheating?' I asked.

Jos nodded her agreement that it was.

'No,' he said, frowning at the interruption. 'But going out with her would have been. That's why I had to finish with Tina first. Anyway, it was the day before my birthday and Tina came round to mine, unannounced, to give me a bottle of Paco Rabanne cologne. I had been going to text her that night anyway, so I just told her it was over – and I thought it only right to give her the cologne back. But she told me to keep it. So I did!'

Everybody laughed and obviously thought that very funny. I couldn't see the funny side myself. I think I would have thrown it at him. And I couldn't help wishing that I hadn't bought him the same stuff for Christmas. *Damn it!*

'But Jos is right,' Estee said. 'You're certainly having a good effect on him. I've never seen him so well behaved.'

'Really?' I asked.

'Oh yes,' she said. 'He's a different person!'

'Right!' said Richard. 'Who's for pudding?'

'You sit, Dad,' said Chrissy. 'Me and Lea will dish it up. Did you make the custard already?'

'Of course. My special brandy custard!'

***

Next morning, we said goodbye to the girls as they went home to spend Christmas with their mum, and Richard and I headed to Little Rutford.

Richard was tired that evening and we just went out for an hour to the White Horse, where a very loud and drunken crew was celebrating Christmas Eve.

Mum had already taken herself off to bed when we came home, and Richard followed suit. I said I would just clean the kitchen up and would join him shortly. Just as I'd finished, the laptop announced an incoming Skype call. I knew immediately it must be one of the kids. It was late for them to be calling. But then it *was* Christmas.

It was Erin, and she looked anything but merry.

'Hello there!' I said, with happy surprise.

Tears immediately welled up in her eyes.

'Hello, Mom,' she said, trying for a brave smile.

'What's the matter? Are you crying? What is it?'

'No, I've just got a bit of a cold, that's all. I'm a bit snuffily, I'm afraid,' she said, wiping her nose with a tissue.

'Oh, shame. There's nothing worse than a summer cold, especially at Christmas.'

'I know. And it's been so hot here today.'

'But otherwise? How are you? Where's Sean tonight? Is he there with you?'

'No, he's out with his mates tonight. And ja, I'm fine,' she said, unconvincingly. 'And you? How are you?'

'I didn't know he had mates?'

'Mom!' she exclaimed. 'Of course he has mates.'

'Well, you've never mentioned them before. And why is he out with them on Christmas Eve and not taking you out?'

'Oh, it's just a boys-only do. It doesn't happen often. And anyway, how are *you*?'

I brought her up to date with my news, but didn't mention that Richard was going to move in. She told me about her job and about the things she'd been doing. Nothing much about her plans for the future.

'Are you still set on going to Australia?' I asked.

'Supposedly.' She smiled.

'Supposedly? What does that mean? Are you having second thoughts?'

'No, we're still going. Sean's all excited to go.'

'And you?' I asked.

'Ja,' she answered, but very half-heartedly.

'You don't want to go, do you?'

'No, it's not that. I do. It's just... nothing. Of course I want to go.'

'Come on, Erin, spit it out. What's the matter?'

She sighed and her whole body seemed to slump. 'It's nothing, really, Mom, I'm just feeling grotty and tired and sorry for myself and I need my mom to make me some egg-in-a-cup,' she said, her eyes welling up again.

'Shame, my darling. If I could, I would. I'd wrap you in a duvet, give you a big hug and make egg-in-a-cup.'

She looked at me and smiled, but so sadly.

'Are you sure everything's okay?' I asked. 'You would tell me if there was something, wouldn't you?'

'Yes, of course,' she said, trying for a brighter smile. 'I'm fine, Mom, don't worry! And I must let you go now. I know it's late there. I just wanted to hear your voice, and to wish you merry Christmas.'

'That's fine. You know I'm always here, sweetheart. Have you got anything you can take for your cold?'

'Yes, I'm going to dose myself up and go to bed.'

'Okay. And don't forget the Vicks on your chest!'

'Yes, Mom,' she said, rolling her eyes. 'Okay, Mom, I'm going to go now. Love you lots, and I miss you so much,' she said. 'Merry Christmas!' A tear escaped and ran down her cheek.

'Erin, I'm in no rush. We can talk as long as you like, really! I know there's something the matter.'

'No, I must go now, Mom. There's nothing, really. Don't worry. I'll talk to you again soon. Promise.'

'Okay, my sweetheart. I love you.' I blew her a kiss. She blew one back and the screen went blank.

In the sudden silence, I knew something was wrong. The boys would be phoning me the next day. I would ask them to check on her.

***

Richard woke me up on Christmas morning with coffee and toast, and gave me my present: an e-reader! Which bit of 'I don't like e-readers, and much prefer books' didn't he understand? He'd either forgotten I said that, or thought he would convert me. And both options were annoying.

It already had hundreds of books on it, which he said he'd downloaded for me, and he presented it in a bright pink cover – not in its original box or wrapping. And then a third possibility occurred to me. Maybe Chrissy had 'sourced' this, second-hand, online for him?

But I smiled and said thank you.

His card more than made up for it. It was absolutely gorgeous. Thick card embossed with gold lettering, it bore the picture of a single red rose, and inside there were three pages of beautiful, oh-so-soppy verse. And it was just him! It spoke of being too shy to say the words, but hoping I understood how much I meant to him, how much he loved me. It was signed, *With all my love, now and forever, Richard*. How could I not love this man!

When he opened his Paco Rabanne, he looked at me questioningly.

'I'd already bought it before I heard the story of Tina and the last bottle,' I said, laughing. 'Hope you like it!'

'I wouldn't wear it if I didn't, would I?' he said, smiling.

***

The boys Skyped to say merry Christmas and I mentioned my phone call with Erin the night before. Josh told me that they were all going round for a Boxing Day braai (barbecue), at Mark and Jen's, so he would chat with Erin then. The day after Boxing Day, however, I phoned Josh back to see how the braai went, only to be told that Erin and Sean hadn't pitched up as Erin still had a cold. But either he or Mark would go round there later.

A few days later Josh reported that he and Mark had been out for a drink with Erin and Sean and she seemed okay. Sean had not been particularly welcoming, which was not surprising as he must have realised by now that neither of the boys liked him very much. Otherwise, all seemed well. At least Erin was over her cold and feeling better.

***

The new year rolled in, snow fell, white and silent, transforming the landscape. Driving to Leigh (the last bit, anyway) was like driving through an old-fashioned Christmas card of winter-white fields and little cottages with smoke coming out of the chimneys.

By the end of the month the snow was still thick on the ground. Richard, Lea, Chrissy and I wrapped and packed Richard's belongings, cleaned his flat, and moved him and his stuff (which there really wasn't much of) to Mum's bungalow. I gave him half of my wardrobe and two drawers, into which his clothes fitted, and there were a few boxes and his bike to go into the garage.

The sale of his place had apparently gone very smoothly, but I was surprised that there was no paperwork involved. He said that his flat was in 'negative equity', but he'd sold it back to the guy he'd originally bought it from, for the same price he bought it for, although it didn't seem as if any monies had changed hands. I thought it all a bit odd, but I didn't pry. Maybe I didn't properly understand what was going on there.

He gave his old computer to Chrissy, as I'd told him he could use my laptop if he wanted to, until such time as he treated himself to a 'tablet'. And when he did buy himself a new tablet, he still used my laptop for his emails because he had already set up his email account on mine. I didn't understand the logic of that either because I'm sure you can access your email from anywhere if you have the passwords. But no matter.

Checking his emails became part of his morning routine. He would bring me coffee in bed and then sit in the kitchen dealing with his inbox. I didn't mind that his account was hidden from me. Well, truthfully, I was a bit miffed that he didn't trust me. I wouldn't have read them.

It did intrigue me, though, that once or twice he'd casually closed the laptop lid when I walked into the kitchen, as if he was just about to close it anyway. Maybe he was, or maybe he thought it was just good manners to do so. Besides which, everybody needs their privacy, don't they?

Mum was delighted to have him come live with us.

'It will be nice to have a man around the house again, won't it!' She chuckled.

For me it meant having him to snuggle up to on those cold winter nights, and somebody to bring me coffee in bed each morning. He would leave before six and come home just after four in the afternoon, which gave Mum and I the day to ourselves, and his company in the evenings. The subject of rent never came up, but we shared the bills down the middle, saving us both money. It was the perfect set-up.

I started cooking proper evening meals, buying in the things that he liked to eat, and even made his lunchboxes for him, complete with little treats.

And I started driving his car more, which he actively encouraged because at weekends, I would drop him at the pub to watch the rugby while I went shopping in it, picking him up again after the game was over. Most times the rugby was not quite finished when I got there, and I'd sit and have a quick drink with him while he would explain the game. I was starting to understand it a little when he suggested, one day, that he take me to an actual match.

'Yes, sure!' I said, thinking *that* would never happen.

He supported 'The Saints', and just a couple of weeks later, he suggested we go to see them play.

It was a cold afternoon and we stood waiting in a long barn of a place to buy beer in plastic beakers and lukewarm hot chocolate, then sat on cold plastic bucket seats in the stands. I tried to warm my hands around my cup, and willed the next couple of hours to go quickly. I was not having fun.

The game started and excitement ran around the crowd like a wildfire. We were close to the field and could hear every thump, crunch and thud, and I found myself standing up with the rest of them when the ball came close to the posts. Even when it snowed, the players carried on like ghosts in the blizzard. The old man next to me opened a crumpled tin-foil wrapper and took out an egg and bacon toasted sandwich. It smelled wonderful, and lifting up the other half he offered it to me. I smiled and declined, but was warmed by his friendliness.

When the game was over, Richard took us to the club shop to buy a T-shirt, which Lea had asked for. I was just grateful for the warmth in there. He picked up a Saints scarf, which he put around my neck, saying that now I was a Saints fan, I would need a scarf. I was so cold I didn't care what the colours were, as long as I could keep it round my neck. I wouldn't be wearing it again.

***

The weeks passed and eventually the days started to lengthen and the last of the snow melted in grubby piles along the roadsides, in between the first patches of bright yellow daffodils.

March was wild and windy, but on one Saturday afternoon, with glimpses of pale blue sky here and there, Richard and I took the bikes out for a ride up the Wirral Way, following the old disused rail track to Parkgate.

We rode through fields, between steep walls cut through natural rock, and through overgrown, dripping culverts, and despite a couple of stiff slopes it was a very pleasant ride. Richard mostly stayed with me, but every now and again would 'stretch his legs', which meant him taking off at high speed for a while, then stopping to wait for me. I didn't mind, but I did not like the way he'd take off again just as I caught up. It was a long ride and I arrived back home hot and tired, but proud of myself.

Richard went for a shower, and I was sitting at the kitchen table, recovering, when the phone rang. It was Josh.

'Mom?' he said, his tone instantly chilling.

'What is it?'

'Mom, sit down and brace yourself.'

I felt the blood drain from me. 'Why? Josh? What's happened?'

'Erin's in hospital. But she's okay. She's going to be okay. She tried to overdose on sleeping tablets, but we got her in time. She's going to be okay.'

'Oh God, no! Why? What happened?' I said, the guilt immediately flowing through me. I should have known. *I should have known!*

'I don't know all the details yet. I only had a few minutes with her and she was very groggy. She's sleeping now. But I'm going to stay here with her.'

'What happened?'

'I was just driving up Republic by hers, and thought I'd give her a call – go and have a coffee with her maybe. She didn't answer, so I just went round there anyway. When I got there the door was open and she was unconscious on the bed, empty bottle of sleeping pills by her. So, I picked her up, got her in the car and brought her to Wavelhey Clinic. They've pumped her stomach or whatever and she's asleep now. She's okay.'

'Oh. Thank God for that. Thank God you were there, Josh. And the boyfriend? Sean? Where's he?'

'Sean? No idea!' he said. 'I called Mark. He was here just now, and he's coming back now-now to take over. We'll take it in turns, me, him and Jen, to be with her.'

'Good. That's good. And I'll come over. I'll get the first flight I can and come over there.'

'Mom, just wait. Okay. Let's just see what's happening here before you jump on a plane.'

'Why? I need to come over!'

'Mom, please, just listen to me. Just wait.'

'What for? I need to be there.'

'Mom, she doesn't want you here, okay? In the couple of minutes I had with her, she said, "Don't let Mom come." So just let's go with that for now. Okay?'

Those words were like a kick in the stomach. 'Why?' I whispered.

'I don't know, Mom. She's not herself right now. Let me talk to her and see what's going on. Okay?'

'I can't bear to be here and not know what's happening, Josh. I have to come over.'

'I will keep in touch. And Mark. We'll let you know what's happening all the time. Okay?'

'Okay,' I heard myself say.

I found myself at the kitchen table, shaking like a leaf with legs of jelly that wouldn't let me stand. So, I sat.

Even then, I knew in my gut that what had happened was

something to do with Sean, and that Josh wasn't telling me the whole story. If Josh had said then, *'by the way, Mom, Erin also has a black eye, a swollen and bruised cheek, split lip and cracked rib'*, then I would have known exactly what had happened. And I would have been over there on the next plane to kill the little bastard myself.

Richard found me in the kitchen a couple of minutes later and asked what was wrong, and I told him what had happened. He was very sorry to hear it, said he was there for me, whatever I wanted to do. And I was grateful for that.

The next day, Erin was put into the psych ward for a few days for evaluation. Josh, Mark, Jen, and even Hennie (who came down from Tzaneen to help out) were taking turns to sit with her. I was jealous as hell that her father was there when I was not allowed to be.

They did phone to give me updates, but for those few days I tortured myself with all sorts of scenarios. They pleaded with me to stay put, however, saying that maybe Erin should come over to me, so I should wait in the UK for her.

Josh told me that when he found her lying across the bed unconscious, her lips blue, he had thought she was dead. That image stayed in my mind and drove me crazy with anxiety, and guilt. Guilt that I hadn't seen the signs of depression; guilt that I'd left South Africa and hadn't been there for her when she needed me, guilt over a million things.

And then Maggie would put me back together again with reason and common sense, telling me (kindly, for her) that this wasn't about me but about Erin, and I needed to be there for her. And I was going to be.

Bits and pieces of the story filtered through. Apparently, Erin had told Sean that she didn't want to go to Australia with him, and they had had a huge fight.

'I knew it!' I said. 'I knew she didn't want to go.'

'Do you know why she didn't want to go?' Mark asked me.

'No, why?'

There was a pause before he said, 'She doesn't want us to tell you. But in the circumstances…'

'Tell me what?' I asked. 'C'mon, Mark, spit it out. Is it something to do with Sean? Where is he?'

'He's trying to find her. He keeps messaging her phone and asking where she is, and we keep telling him to stay the fuck away from her.'

'Why? Mark, what's going on?'

'They had a fight, Mom. A big fight, and he beat her up – good and proper. Then next minute she's trying to kill herself.'

'Was he there? Didn't he try to stop her?'

'No, he'd done his dirty work and left by then. And if that bastard comes anywhere near her, Josh or me will break his fuckin' knee caps for him. In fact, if we knew where to find him, I think we just might do that.'

My mind went to the Skype call I'd had with Erin when I'd asked her if she had a black eye, and I knew immediately then that that's exactly what it had been, even though she had denied it. Another thing I'd missed!

'And it's not the first time he's hit her, is it?'

'No. Apparently not. And that's why she didn't want to go to Australia with him.'

'Well, thank God for that! What on earth did she stay with him for? Why didn't she get out?'

'Because he kept giving her the same old story. "I'm sorry." "I didn't mean it." "Please don't leave me, I love you." "Please don't tell anyone." "I'll never do it again." You know what these guys are like, Mom.'

'I can't believe it! After everything we've ever said.'

'Ja, well, she's not herself at the minute. She's skin and bone 'cos he told her she was fat, and how she's lucky he's even sticking around. She's having panic attacks, depression, can't sleep. Mom, she's a mess. That's why she didn't want you to see her right now.'

'How has she managed to do her job?' I asked.

'I honestly don't know. And she's in no fit state to go back to it. She's coming out of hospital tomorrow and will come and stay with Jen and me. Jen's taking a week off.'

'That's good,' I said. 'You mustn't leave her on her own. I think I must come over now.'

'Well, we've been talking, Jos, Dad, Jen and me, and we think she needs to get away from Sean. Like, well away – out of his reach. We think it might be good for her to come over to you and Granny for a while.'

'Oh, yes. I agree. Do you think she would? That would be wonderful. Have you asked her? That would be for the best. Yes, she needs to come over here.'

'But what about this Richard bloke there with you?'

'We can make a plan. There won't be a problem.'

'Well, you can ask her. We will phone you. How about tomorrow when she's home with us?'

'How about Skype?'

'She won't Skype you, Mom. You can't see her.'

Those words stabbed my heart. All I wanted to do was hold my daughter, hold her close and protect her.

My heart broke when I heard her frail little voice the next evening. We didn't say a great deal. She cried a lot and kept saying, 'I'm sorry, Mom.'

I kept telling her she didn't have to be, that everything was going to be all right. I asked her about coming over.

'But you've got Richard there now?' she said.

'That's not a problem. It would be so good to have you here, sweetheart. What do you say? Granny would love you to be here, you know that.'

'But where would I sleep?' she asked.

'We can put a sofa bed in the lounge. It won't be forever; it would do for now. We'll manage and it would be so good to have you here, Erin. Please say you'll come?'

'I don't want to be in anyone's way, Mom,' she said.
'You won't be, sweetheart. Just come. Please?'
'Are you sure?'
'Oh, Erin, I want nothing more!'
'Thank you, Mom,' she said. 'Yes, please.'

***

I explained the situation to Mum.

'Tell her to come, we can look after her,' said Mum. 'Silly girl, what is she getting herself in such a state over a man for? Men! My mother used to say they all want tying up at the bottom of the garden with the family pig!'

'Would you mind if I swopped this sofa for a sleeper couch for her?'

'No. Do whatever you want. Or she can come and sleep in with me if she likes?'

'No. Mum,' I said. 'That's your room. She doesn't want to be any bother. She'll be fine on a sleeper couch. I'll get one that matches the room. It won't be for long.'

'She can stay as long as she likes, tell her.'

Richard was not so enthusiastic. He was very serious and quiet as I explained what was happening.

'You've asked her to come and live *here*,' he said.

'Yes,' I said. 'If that's all right with you?'

'Well, it's a bit late now to ask *me*, don't you think?'

'Well, you did say you would support anything I decided, and what else could I do? I am her mother.'

He didn't answer. I was surprised by his attitude – it was hardly the support he'd promised.

'It won't be forever,' I said. 'It's just for a while.'

He remained serious. 'It just would have been nice of you to ask me first,' he said. 'I know this isn't my house, but I do live here, too.'

I thought about it a moment. 'I'm sorry,' I said. 'You're quite right. Yes, I should have asked you first. But you know what it's like with your kids. You'd do anything for them, wouldn't you? I know you would for your girls.'

'My girls would never behave in such a way,' he said to the wall, and then turned his attention to a news item on the television. The conversation was over.

By Saturday morning he was back to his usual self again and came with me to choose a sofa: a comfortable, slouchy-armed one in cream corduroy-type fabric, and we put Mum's old two-seater in the bay window of her room. I also bought a pretty, floral duvet cover. We had a nest for Erin.

Chapter Eighteen

It was a week later that Josh, Mark and Jen put her on a direct flight from Jo'burg. She was feeling stronger, not suicidal, and despite Mark's offer to escort her over, she promised she would be fine on her own. She arrived at Manchester Airport at six o'clock the next evening and Richard and I were there to meet her.

I couldn't speak when I saw her. She was just a rag-taggled little bag of bones in a purple knitted hat, hardly able to push her trolley. As soon as I could reach her, I held her close and we both burst into tears. She still had greenish marks around her face and her lip had not completely healed. Richard stood silently by, waiting for us to eventually break apart.

'Erin, this is Richard. Richard, Erin.'

He held out his hand for what must have been the shortest handshake in history.

'Hello, Erin. It's nice to meet you,' he said. 'It's a pity it's in such circumstances.' *Richard being a pompous arse.*

Erin muttered that she was pleased to meet him, too, but looked at me with a question in her eyes. I smiled reassurance, and hugged her again.

'Shall we make a start then?' said Richard.

He took her trolley and pushed ahead towards the car park. I put my arm around her and we followed him.

'Mom, you sure this is going to be okay?' she asked.

'I'm definitely, very, very sure. And your granny's so looking forward to seeing you again.'

'And Richard?' she asked.

'Don't you worry about Richard. He's a man – he doesn't like change much. But he'll get used to it.'

'I don't want to upset things between you and him,' she said. 'I know how important he is to you.'

'Nothing could be more important to me at this moment than you. So please, don't forget that.'

She gave a weak little smile and we went home.

Mum was all smiles when she saw Erin and sat with her arms around her. Erin hugged her back. Mum and I had never been that close, but I was glad that she could find it in herself to be that way with Erin.

'Silly girl,' she scolded. 'What are you? You don't let a man do this to you.'

Erin was crying again, and Mum fished out a few used tissues from her stash in the sofa, and after inspection, offered her one.

I said I'd put the kettle on, but Richard said he'd do it. I think he was glad to get out of there. He went to bed shortly after tea, saying he would 'leave you girls to it!'

Erin looked absolutely exhausted, and despite her smile, sadness hung around her like a black shadow. It was not my bubbly, happy Erin. This was somebody else.

When Mum went to bed, I pulled the sofa couch out and soon enough she was tucked up snug in her bed.

'Are you glad to be away from him? Sean?' I asked her.

'I don't know,' she said. 'I guess so. Right now, I just don't know how I feel. Numb? Like I'm not really here. I…'

She couldn't finish as tears overwhelmed her again. I put

my arms around her and rocked her as I had when she was a little girl.

'Do you remember when Smokey got run over?' she said. 'You sat me on your knee and rocked me and hummed "You Are My Sunshine". I've never forgotten that.'

'I do,' I said. 'And like I told you then, things will get better.'

She didn't answer, but closed her eyes, and I started to hum the same tune to her. After a few minutes, I lay her back on the pillows, fast asleep, and pulled the duvet up under her chin.

The next day, when Richard had already left for work but before Mum was up, when Erin's bed had been turned into a sofa again and she sat cross-legged on one end of it, we chatted. She was looking a little chirpier, and over hot chocolate, started to tell me about her life with Sean.

They had been together for two years, and for the first year he had been lovely, caring and considerate. But then he'd changed. Once, when she had prepared a full Sunday roast and was helping herself to a couple of potatoes, he had said something like, 'Do you really need all those?'

Then he'd started questioning the clothes she wore for work, or for going out with the girls on a Friday night. He questioned why she even wanted to go out with the girls anyway. Was she hooking up with other guys? Consequently, she'd given up her Friday nights with the girls.

Then more and more he'd wanted to know where she was and what time she would be home. One time she was going to visit and console a friend who had just broken up with her boyfriend. He asked what time she'd be home, and getting fed up of being asked, she replied that she would be home when she was ready to be. That's the first time he'd struck her.

He'd thought the friend, Yvette, just wanted Erin to go out clubbing with her, so they could both find new boyfriends. So consequently, she stopped seeing Yvette anymore.

After he hit her, he'd been sorry, and cried, and said things like, 'I'm sorry, but you make me so angry!' So, she tried not to say things that might make him angry.

Then he'd started finding fault with everything she did. Whatever she did, it was wrong. Was she *stupid*? She'd told him that she did happen to have a degree – and that was the second time he hit her.

Her boss had noticed the bruises, and also that her timekeeping had become erratic, and had told her to sort her life out. She didn't feel she could tell either Mark or Josh because she knew they didn't like him (I guessed the same went for me, too). But she'd finally begun to see the light and knew she mustn't go to Australia with him.

The night she told him, he'd gone crazy, smacking and punching, pulling her down onto the floor by her hair and kicking her. He'd stamped her phone to pieces. Then screaming that it was all her fault, slammed out the door, leaving her physically and mentally in a crumpled mess on the floor.

And she had believed him. Over the past year she'd withdrawn from her friends and family, and didn't believe anybody loved, or even liked, her. There was nobody to turn to. And even if she'd wanted to phone her brothers, she had no phone. But it didn't matter anyway, because she was tired; tired of trying to please everyone and in the end pleasing no one. She'd had enough. And hence the sleeping pills.

'But to kill yourself, Erin?' I asked. 'Why would you want to die? You're young, intelligent and beautiful, with your whole life ahead of you. Why would you want to die?'

'It's not that I wanted to die, Mom,' she said, trying to hold back the tears again. 'It's just too hard to live. Life is too hard, and I'm so tired.'

'And now? You're not going to try it again, are you? Will you try and live?'

She smiled wearily. 'No, I won't do it again.'

'Why did you stay with him? You should have said. Why didn't you tell me?'

'You'd just met Richard and were so happy. I didn't want to spoil that. And Sean begged me not to say anything. The boys would have half killed him! And he's not a bad man, Mom. He can be sweet and loving and funny, too. And he has nobody. Just me. And he really does love me. When he says sorry, I know he means it. He just can't help himself,' she said.

'No! Get that idea out of your head, Erin. He *can* help himself. But he doesn't want to because it makes him feel good to hurt you. Does he lose it in front of anyone else – does he hit anyone else? No. He controls himself. It's just with you, behind closed doors, because he knows he can. That's not love, Erin. You deserve so much better than that.'

'Do I, Mom? Look at me. I'm a mess.'

'Sweetheart, I know that right now you feel you're in that dark place that you'll never be able to climb out of. But you can. You will. And you'll come out stronger and more beautiful than ever. Like a butterfly coming out of a chrysalis. I'm here. We've got this, yes? I promise, okay?'

I wanted to brush her tears away, but couldn't. But through them, I saw a tiny smile flicker.

Chapter Nineteen

A few days later I walked into the kitchen and found Erin having a full-blown panic attack. She was slumped on the floor by the kitchen cupboards, shaking like a leaf and wide-eyed with fright, and it took some time to calm her down.

The same thing nearly happened again when she came shopping with me. The noise and the people in the superstore turned her into a shivering wreck again, and we had to drop everything and get out of there.

The next few weeks were hell. She couldn't go anywhere on her own, or handle a phone conversation, or even fall asleep at night. But then totally exhausted, she would sleep most of the day. As soon as Richard left, she would crawl into my bed and I would pack the sofa bed up and make the lounge look normal again before Mum got up.

I realised that she was going to need more help than just her granny and I could give her, and so took her down to Dr Griffiths. He referred her to a psychologist, and within a couple of weeks she had a regular weekly session booked.

At home, there was a certain tension with Richard. He was *tolerating* the situation and avoided discussing Erin as much as possible. When the two of us went out alone, he was his usual happy self and things were fine. But an expressionless mask would be put back in place the moment he stepped back inside the bungalow.

Slowly, he began to accept her, eventually to the point that he even agreed to her coming out for a drink with us. In the end, I think he *preferred* having her with us so that he could give his full attention to the rugby while Erin and I chatted.

And considering we were four living in the bungalow, we slotted in together rather well. Richard was more polite with Erin than friendly, but he would occasionally ask me how she was doing. When I told him she was seeing a psychologist, he rolled his eyes to the ceiling and asked if I really thought that was necessary. I did. And I told him so.

Erin felt his prickliness, and asked me more than once if everything was okay between him and me, apologising for the strain she was putting on us. I told her not to even think about it, that he was a big boy now and he must get over himself. She must just ignore him.

The boys phoned now and again to ask about her, and during one conversation, Mark asked if I thought she was bulimic.

'Bulimic?' I asked, shocked. 'Why ever would you think that? She's got a good appetite.'

'Not anorexia, Mom,' he said. 'Bulimia. It's binge eating and then making yourself sick. I don't know, it's just a thought Jen had a while back.'

'Why ever would she think that?'

'Erin and Sean came to our place for a braai, and Jen was waiting for Erin to come out of the loo, and she's sure she heard Erin being sick in there. She called to ask if she was all right and Erin called back that she was fine. Then when she came out she just walked past Jen and just smiled.'

'Is that it?' I asked.

'Well, ja. It's just something she mentioned. Not something to get all worked up about. But she's so rake thin, isn't she? Maybe just keep an eye on her.'

So, I started watching her at mealtimes. For the first few days I didn't notice anything at all. Then one evening, straight after tea, she went to the bathroom and was gone for some time. I thought I would go listen at the bathroom door, but as soon as I reached the door, it opened, and Erin came out, her eyes red and watery.

'Are you all right?' I asked.

'Yes,' she said, with a slight frown. 'Why wouldn't I be?'

'Your eyes look red. You're not crying, are you?'

'No,' she said, smiling. 'I'm just a bit tired, that's all.'

I could smell mouthwash on her breath. 'Okay,' I said, going into the bathroom as if that had been my intention all along.

I didn't say anything to her then because maybe the red eyes *were* just from tiredness. Maybe she *had* just felt like using mouthwash halfway through the evening.

But then one evening when Richard and Mum had gone to bed, Erin and I decided to watch a girlie movie. We raided Richard's snack cupboard, and found some crisps and chocolate, and with some ice cream from the freezer we had ourselves a little feast. When the movie ended, we had one last cup of hot chocolate, then I kissed her good night and went to bed.

As I lay there in the stillness, I heard her go into the bathroom. I wasn't even thinking about what she might be doing in there, until I heard a quiet but definite retching sound. If the house had not been so still, I would not have heard a thing.

I got out of bed and went to the bathroom door. The toilet flushed and nearly, but not quite, drowned out the sound of more retching. I heard her cleaning her teeth and gargling and I knew that door would open any second now, and I hadn't a clue what I was going to say. But I couldn't run away. I had to deal with it.

The door flew open and Erin stopped dead in her tracks as she saw me standing there.

'Mom! I thought you'd gone to bed?'

'I had. But I heard you being sick.'

'Me? Nah! You probably heard me gargling.'

'I know what I heard, Erin,' I said, leading the way back into the lounge because I didn't want to wake up Richard or Mum.

She followed me, her face a little defiant.

'So, tell me? What is it? Are you bulimic?'

'No, I'm not bulimic!' She frowned, like, *Der!!!*

'Well, something's not right,' I said. 'That's not the first time I've seen you come out of the bathroom with red eyes and smelling of mouthwash.'

'What?' she said, shocked. 'Are you spying on me?'

'No, but I have the feeling I should be.'

She relaxed and looked at me with tired eyes. 'I'm not bulimic, Mom, trust me!'

'You were retching, Erin. I heard you. And I've heard you do that before, also,' I lied.

She blinked. 'Sometimes, when I've had all the wrong things to eat and I feel bloated and uncomfortable, I just bring it back up. It's no biggie. All the girls do it. It's not bulimia!'

'Erin, that's an eating disorder and I don't care who else does it. How often do you do it?'

'I don't know.' She shrugged, impatiently.

'How long have you been doing it?'

She just shook her head and shrugged again.

'Have you told your psychologist, Alice?'

'No,' she said. Again, the slight defiance.

'I think you should,' I said.

'It's nothing, Mom, really. You're making a mountain out of a molehill.'

'Well, if it's nothing, you won't mind mentioning it to her, will you? Just to hear what she thinks about it. Okay?'

'What the psychologist and I discuss is between her and me, Mom. You can't get involved.'

'I'm not getting involved, but you need to tell her about this. Okay?'

No response.

'Erin, if you don't, then I'm sorry, but I will.'

She glared at me. 'You can't!' she said, angrily. 'It's none of your business.'

'Oh, yes. I think it is.'

I kissed her goodnight again and said, 'I love you, Erin, but you have to play the game. No secrets. I don't know how bad it is, but we sort it out now before it gets worse.'

She glared at me, but didn't answer.

'For your own sake, sweetheart, you have to get healthy and strong now, okay?'

Her eyes dropped to the floor and she nodded.

'Goodnight,' I said. I gave her a quick hug and made to go back to bed.

'Goodnight, Mom,' she whispered.

***

Richard was not impressed that his snack cupboard was suddenly virtually empty. Or that nobody knew anything about it. He sat with a stony face over tea, aware, I think, of the little smile exchanged between Erin and me. When the table had been cleared, I made out a shopping list, asking Richard what snacks he would like on it. He put in his order and I made a note of the items.

'Can we have some Ben and Jerry's ice cream?' asked Erin. 'Have you tasted it, Mom? It's gorgeous. They have all these different, weird and wonderful flavours, like…'

'Those who don't contribute, don't get to choose!' interrupted Richard in an irritated voice. He glared at Erin.

Erin blushed and looked like she'd been slapped.

I looked at Richard ready to say something, but he just put his head down and checked for messages on his phone.

'What's your favourite flavour?' I asked her.

She just shook her head, so I asked her again.

'*Phish Food* or *Chunky Monkey*,' she whispered.

'Right,' I said. 'I'll see what they've got.'

Richard got up from the table and walked out of the room, and Erin looked at me in wide-eyed disbelief. 'What was *that?*' she asked.

'That was Richard being an arsehole!' I said, crossly. 'It's nothing! Don't worry. Everything's fine.'

But, of course, it wasn't.

***

The crunch came a few nights later. Richard and I went out for a meal, and Erin stayed home with Mum, as she did on a Saturday night, giving us some time alone. It was about eleven o'clock when we got in. As we came in through the front door, we heard snoring coming from Mum's room. I peeped into the lounge, because if Erin had already gone to bed, then we would just go to bed and not disturb her. But the lounge was empty.

'Erin,' I called, softly. The bathroom door was open. She wasn't in there, nor the kitchen. Richard was already standing by the kitchen table reading something when I walked in. He handed me a note, his face grave.

It read:

Dear Mom, I'm so, so sorry. I can't do this anymore – it's too hard. I'm too tired. Sorry. I love you. Erin.

My knees buckled beneath me and I felt I was going to fall, but there wasn't time for that. 'We need to call the police,' I said.

'Now don't be too hasty,' said Richard. 'She's probably fine. She can't be far. Just give her a little space. She'll come back, believe me. Just give her some time.'

I couldn't believe what I was hearing. I wanted to scream at him, but couldn't. On shaky legs, I went to the phone and dialled the police. I was panicking. I couldn't get the words out in a calm, logical way and I knew this was wasting time, which made me panic more. But eventually I managed to tell them what was going on and they said they'd send a car.

They arrived four minutes later, blue lights flashing. Two police officers jumped out and I opened the front door and ushered them in. They listened to the details, read her note and took a description of her. Then one of them spoke into a radio, spreading the word to patrol cars in the area.

They asked if they could check the other rooms in the bungalow. I explained that Mum was asleep in one room, but they insisted it was necessary to check.

Thankfully, Mum was not asleep. In fact, she was sitting up in bed looking at the flashing police car outside. Her eyes went wide when she saw the policemen coming into her room in the middle of the night, all uniforms, weapons and urgency.

'What's going on, Natalie? What's happened?'

'Sorry to bother you, luv,' said the one officer.

'Don't worry, Mum,' I said. 'It's just that we can't find Erin, so we need to look everywhere.'

'Oh. No, she's not in here,' she said, not knowing quite what to make of all this, but bright-eyed and excited at having two burly officers search behind her curtains.

'Okay, thanks, luv,' said the same policeman, and they moved on to search the other rooms.

'Shall I get up?' asked Mum.

'No,' I said. 'Don't worry. Would you like some tea?'

She said not, so I turned off the light and closed the door.

There were more conversations over the police radio and the two officers came to settle in the lounge. It was only then that I noticed Richard sitting in the corner chair, still as a statue, just staring but not saying a word. He obviously wanted no part of this.

'And you are, sir?' the first policeman asked.

'I'm Richard, Natalie's partner,' he said. And that is pretty much all he did say for their entire visit.

Soon enough the radios were crackling into life again, and from the police-speak used, I realised they'd found her. He clicked off the radio and stood up.

'Right, then. Your daughter has been found safe, but they've sectioned her, so you won't be seeing her tonight.'

'Sectioned her? What does that mean?'

'It means she's been taken into custody for her own safety, for psychiatric evaluation.'

'Why? What happened?' I asked, horrified.

'She fought them. Didn't want to get in the police van.'

'She's from South Africa. You *don't* get into a police van in South Africa.'

It was his turn to look horrified. 'Well, she's there for the night,' he said. 'They'll no doubt review the situation in the morning.'

They had found her about a mile away walking up the main road.

I thanked them and walked them to the gate.

When I went back in, Richard had gone to bed.

***

They brought her back home the following morning. As she came in through the door, her eyes flashed such anger and disgust at me that I was taken aback, and I was glad Richard wasn't there to see it. He'd gone to golf.

The first thing she wanted to do was take a shower, which took her about an hour. But when she finally came out, I asked her to come and talk to me in the kitchen.

'Erin,' I said. 'What's going on with you?'

'Nothing's going on, Mom. Why on earth did you have to call the police?' she said, angrily.

'*Why?* I thought you were going to kill yourself, that's why!' I answered, just as angrily.

'Mom, I was walking to the garage to buy cigarettes. That's all. How could you embarrass me like that?'

'Cigarettes! That's not what your note said, Erin!' I said, throwing the note down in front of her. I think she'd forgotten the note. She looked down at it, half-heartedly reading it as if she'd never seen it before.

'It doesn't say I'm going to kill myself, Mom.'

I picked the note up and read it to her out loud. She just shrugged and looked at the floor.

'Talk to me, Erin. Please! Tell me what's going on with you. You know you scared the living daylights out of me last night?'

She gave a little sigh. 'I'm sorry I scared you, Mom, really. I didn't mean to do that. There's nothing going on. I just went to buy ciggies, that's all.'

'And what was I supposed to think when I read this?'

'I don't know,' she said, pausing. 'Maybe I was feeling a bit sorry for myself. I was just sat here alone on a Saturday night, just me and Granny – no friends – nowhere to go – no job – no money – no cigarettes – no nothing. I've got no life, Mom. I don't know where to go from here.'

'So, *were* you suicidal?'

She hung her head and shook it. 'No. Just sad.'

I went to her and hugged her. There was no way I could be angry.

'Erin, I want you to make me a promise. Okay?'

'What?'

'That you will talk to me. Let me know what's going on with you. I would never have gone out last night if I thought you felt like that. Will you tell me next time?'

'I didn't feel like that till you'd gone. I didn't want you to *not* go out because of me. I feel guilty enough around here as it is! I don't want to be any more of a nuisance. I don't want to be a problem between you and Richard.'

'And you weren't a problem last night?' I asked, angrily. 'How often is that going to happen?'

She didn't answer.

'I'm sorry, Erin. I didn't mean that.'

'I'm sorry,' she said. 'It won't happen again, I promise.'

'Erin, you are the most important, precious person in my life right now. There is nothing and no one more important. Do you understand that?'

She looked down at the floor, and nodded.

'So, talk to me,' I repeated. 'Okay?'

'Okay,' she said. 'How's Richard? Is he pissed off?'

'He's literally not said a word. But I'd just keep out of his way for a while. Okay?'

'It will be my pleasure!'

***

'So what's her story?' asked Richard.

'I'm not sure that she was actually suicidal,' I replied. 'But it was definitely a cry for help.'

'Where was she?' he asked, and I told him that she said she was just going to buy cigarettes at the garage.

'Well in that case you would expect the note to read, *Just popped out for cigarettes*, then, wouldn't you?' he said, giving me a disgusted look. He started taking his work shoes off and I couldn't see his face then, but he said no more, so maybe that was going to be the end of the subject? Or not.

At about half past two the next day, Richard phoned to say he was taking his truck back to the depot and would be travelling along the A54. He would be at-the-gap-in-the-hedge by Mum's in about one hour's time. Would I please meet him there as he needed to talk to me.

'Okay,' I said. 'But you'll be home anyway soon after that, can't it wait till then?'

'No,' he said. 'We need to talk. Privately.'

My heart sank. 'Right! I'll see you there then.'

I felt as if I'd been summoned to the head master's office.

I made sure I wasn't late, but before I even passed through the-gap-in-the-hedge, I saw the great, dark shape of his truck looming above it. Close up, it was a monster of a thing. The passenger side door opened slightly as I came near, and reaching up I pushed it open, wondering how on earth I was supposed to climb up into the cab.

'Hi,' I said.

From his perch in the driver's seat, he gave instructions on where to step and where to hold for me to clamber my way up. When I finally made it into the passenger seat, I looked around the cab, a whole different little world in itself. His world.

'Wow, it's like a cockpit in here,' I said, cheerfully.

He didn't answer me. He looked strange in blue overalls as he busily filled in forms on a clip board, reading gauges above his head and scribbling numbers down. I felt I was deliberately being made to wait, his terribly official looking paperwork obviously being far more important than me. I wondered why he couldn't wait till he got back to the depot to do that. After two minutes I'd had enough.

'So, what is it you want to talk about?' I asked.

He waited a few seconds before replying, calmly, coldly, and without even looking up.

'Your daughter.'

He'd been calling her 'your daughter' a little too often lately, and I didn't like it.

'She has a name, you know.'

He finally put his board down and looked at me.

'What happened the other night? What?' he said.

'You know what happened. You were there. What are you asking me?'

'I knew when I read that note that if you'd just given her some time and let her cool off, she would have come back home. But no, you knew better. Totally ignored me – phoned the police – blue lights flashing everywhere in the middle of the night – the whole neighbourhood awake! And why? Because *your daughter* wants to make trouble?'

'The whole neighbourhood was *not* awake!' I retorted. 'And Erin was walking the streets at midnight, alone, despondent and possibly suicidal. Anything could have happened to her. She was vulnerable. You don't know what could have happened. And you don't just ignore a note like that and say, "Give her time." What if she *had* killed herself? You didn't know that she wouldn't.'

'Believe me,' he said. 'That was never going to happen.'

'How do you know? You've only known her for two minutes. You don't know her.'

'Sometimes when you're not directly involved in a situation, you can see it for what it is, and more so than the people involved.'

'Is that so? So, what d'you see in this situation?'

He hesitated. 'Why do you think she wrote that note and then went walkabout? She clearly had no intention of killing herself, did she? She clearly just wanted to cause trouble.'

'It wasn't to cause trouble. I think because we were out, and she was alone and suddenly realised that she had no life of her own, she despaired. She's lost everything. She has to build a whole new life and she doesn't know where to start.'

'"Because we were out",' he repeated.

'What are you saying?'

'She wants to cause trouble between us.'

'Oh, Richard. Don't be ridiculous. It's not about *you*! She doesn't *want* to cause trouble. It was a spur of the moment thing. Her head is all over the place at the moment.'

He didn't answer immediately, and when he did, he changed tack.

'You know,' he said. 'When we first started dating, we both agreed that what we wanted was to start a new life, not fit into one or the other's. And that's not happening, is it?' He paused. 'I'm not used to police running around the house in the middle of the night. It's not the kind of home I come from, and I must tell you, I was not impressed. I didn't sign up for this.'

'I understand,' I said. 'And it's not what I wanted to happen either. I didn't see this coming. I would never have expected it. But when one of your kids needs you, you're there for them, aren't you? Wouldn't you have reacted the same way if it was one of your girls?'

'My girls would never have carried on like that. They might not have been to university, but they know how to get on with life and take responsibility for themselves. Give Vicky her due, she did that for them. You treat Erin like a child, but she's twenty-four years old for God's sake! And we need to sort this situation out.'

'Well, what do you expect me to do about it, Richard? She's come unstuck and she needs family around her while she gets herself together again. So, what do you expect?'

'She needs to stand on her own two feet. The more you mollycoddle her, the longer this will go on,' he replied.

'That's not fair.'

'Life isn't, is it? And as I said, I didn't sign up for this. Your daughter is a problem, and clearly your priority now – and I'm not sure if I can see myself in this picture.'

I thought then that he was dumping me, and I was sad.

'It won't be forever,' I said. 'She'll be back on her feet soon enough.'

'When?' he asked. 'You can't say, can you? It could go on for years.'

'No, it won't,' I assured him.

'You don't know that, do you?' he said. 'Can you put a time limit on it? You can't, can you!'

I couldn't, so didn't reply immediately.

'So, what now?' I asked.

'I don't know. I would never try to come between you and your daughter, but I need to think about my life, too, you know.'

We sat in silence for a couple more minutes. I felt sad and confused and wondered whether that was how he genuinely felt, or if he really *was* trying to make me choose between him and Erin. Did he really think there could ever be any contest?

Eventually I answered. 'Okay, I get it. I love you Richard, and I thought we could have a wonderful life together. I still think we can, and I would be very sad if you felt you needed to walk away from all this. But I would understand.'

He didn't answer, just looked straight ahead as if he was driving, his face like stone. After another minute of silence, I climbed back out of the cab and went home without looking back.

At that moment I thought our relationship was over. I was pretty sure that he was going to dump me and all I wanted was for him to put his arms around me and say everything was okay. I loved this guy, and losing him would mean losing my last chance of that happy ending. How sad would that be.

When I went in the front door, Erin called to me from Mum's bedroom and I went in to see her, stretched along the two-seater, reading a book.

'Have you just come in?' she asked.

'Yes,' I said. As I watched from the window I saw the bulk of Richard's truck above the hedge, as it pulled away from the kerb.

Erin saw and asked, 'Is that Richard's truck?'

'Yes. He wanted to talk, *privately*.'

'Oh, shit. Mom. What's going on?' she said.

'I don't know,' I said honestly. 'He's throwing his toys out of the cot, but he must just get over himself.'

'Is it because of the other night?' she asked.

'Yes, mostly.'

'What does he say?'

'He thinks you're trying to cause trouble.'

She looked horrified. 'I'm not, Mom. I mean, I know I am, but I'm not trying to. Oh, Mom. I'm so sorry. You're not going to split up because of me, are you?'

'If we do, it won't be because of you. Don't be thinking it's your fault. If that's the kind of man he is, then rather I find out now rather than later. Yes?'

'Can I make you a cup of coffee?' she asked.

'No, thanks, sweetheart. I'm going to get the tea on now; he'll be home in half an hour.'

He was very quiet when he came in. Not angry, not sad, just very serious and quiet. Erin, too, didn't have much to say and there was an awful tension as we all sat watching TV for a short while – broken only by Mum, laughing at the little dog doing the Highland fling on the TV advert. Then Richard went to bed.

***

After our little chat in his truck, the subject was not raised again. He wasn't particularly happy, and I thought any day he would tell me it was over. But it didn't happen. And as the days passed, things started to get better. Erin was referred to a doctor specialising in eating disorders and she was getting stronger, and happier.

She didn't like Richard, but she apologised to him for the upset she had caused, which, although acknowledged with little more than a grunt, was, I think, appreciated.

The real breakthrough came one Friday night when Erin came up to the White Horse with us for the pub quiz, which Richard and I, as a twosome, never won. There were always about five or six teams of at least three, and the prize of a bottle of wine was usually awarded to either 'The Old Biddies' or 'Colin's Corner'. But on this particular evening the gods were with us. The Old Biddies and Colin's Corner were both a man down.

Erin has a good general knowledge, and during the quiz, she and Richard started talking to each other. In the end, we were right on thirteen out of fifteen questions, one more correct answer than any other team – and we won! Richard was ecstatic and went up to collect the bottle of wine with the biggest smile I had seen in weeks. It put him in a good mood for days.

After that, he couldn't go back to being grumpy with her, although he tried once or twice. He started calling her 'Erin' again, and the Friday quiz became a regular thing. We never did win again, but came close once or twice.

Chapter Twenty

Spring was coming and there was a new mildness in the air. The daffodils were taking over in every garden, roadside and traffic island. The bare hawthorn bushes around the gap-in-the-hedge were covered in clusters of tiny, bright leaves, which within a week made the hedge thick and green again – and soon after, it was covered in clusters of heavily scented white blossom.

And it was the season of birthdays. Erin's was a month before mine, and Richard's ten days after.

On Erin's, Mum gave her some money, so she and I spent the day in Chester buying her some new clothes and spending a fortune in The Body Shop. But it was worth it to see her so happy. She'd always loved the smelly stuff! We had lunch at the Boathouse, looking out over the river, and chatted and giggled away together just as we had in the old days.

Richard asked me what I would like for my birthday, and as it happened, there was something I had seen, in (of all places) the post office. A pendant, with a large, teardrop-shaped lump of amber set in silver.

'I love amber,' I said.

He listened carefully as I told him exactly why it intrigued me, and then he suggested something totally different.

'Or, what I was thinking, was that I might buy us both a new bike. What do you think of that?' he said.

So much for asking me what I wanted was what I thought of that. But then on the other hand, I did quite like the idea of a new bike.

'But you have a good bike,' I said.

'Lea wants it,' he said. 'And they've got a scheme going at work where they'll subsidise employees quite a hefty chunk, so I thought I would treat myself to a good one.'

As usual, he had the whole thing planned already.

'Okay,' I said. 'Yes, that would be nice.'

***

That year it would be Richard's sixtieth birthday, which I thought deserved something special. And I had come up with an idea.

Richard had mentioned a few times the way Vicky had arranged a surprise wedding for him, and the way he loved to tell the story told me that it had meant a great deal to him that she had. So, why not a surprise sixtieth birthday party?

I phoned Jos and Lea and asked them who to invite and Jos had a few ideas about a venue also. Lea said she had some banners we could use. She and Chrissy would go early and put them up, blow some balloons up and make the place look like a celebration. And so a plan came together.

The following Saturday morning Richard and I went down to the local bike shop to buy me a new bike. The choice was narrowed down by Richard pointing out the various advantages of this one over that one, and I chose a pretty blue one with a comfortable saddle, which, admittedly, did look a good deal smarter than Maggie's trusty old steed.

'This is the one,' I said, patting the saddle. 'Thank you. I love it.'

He added a little seat pouch, a pump and a puncture kit and paid nearly four hundred pounds. I felt really spoiled. So, while

I went to help them load it in the boot of my car, Richard went to look at the men's bikes. I went back to join him there.

'See, this is the kind of thing I want. Feel how light it is.'

I felt, and it was feather-light, sleek and slim – and pricey. That one was nearly two thousand pounds.

'Wow! Have you seen the price?'

'Yes, but the company is paying most of it.'

'Right,' I said, feeling not quite so spoiled anymore.

***

Erin gave me a birthday card she had made herself, in which she had written a little poem for me, which even now brings tears to my eyes. She had raided her granny's sewing box, which was like Aladdin's cave to her, and dug out little beads and sequins and threaded together the most delicate little butterfly, which when hung in the sun, sent out coloured shafts of light in all directions. It was beautiful, and so precious. I gave her a hug and a thank-you kiss.

Then Mum handed me a small, square box – a jewellery box – and I thought, *Here comes another charity-shop special!* But it contained the amber pendant I had seen in the post office. Mum had seen Erin making the butterfly, and asked what she could give me. So, Erin told her about the pendant and Mum, bless her, told her to go and buy it for me. I was so touched. I felt the urge to give her a hug too, but I hesitated, and then the moment was gone.

Richard had gone to work, leaving me a card behind. Again, a lovely big, embossed card (very similar to the first one), with wonderfully romantic words written in the two or three centre pages. And again signed, 'Yours forever and always, Richard.' It was beautiful.

The boys phoned, and a couple of close friends, too, and in the afternoon (Mum being out with Barbara), Erin and

I went to the local nursery and sat in the tea garden. I was reminded of the girls' nights out we used to have, and on a whim, suggested that she, Maggie and I might go out. The regular Thursday evening routine of going round to Maggie's had fallen off a little since Richard had moved in, but we did get together now and again. I phoned her to thank her for her card, and the following evening the three of us went out for 'pub grub' and a few drinks. Maggie and Erin got on well, both into the quick, witty banter.

***

And Richard's birthday party also went well. He sat at the head of the table holding court to sixteen people, old friends who he hadn't seen in a while, old neighbours and family. He was king for the night – and virtually ignored me.

When the éclair stack came out with a single lighted candle stuck in the top (in lieu of a birthday cake), he had a smile from ear to ear as we all sang 'Happy Birthday'.

I was definitely miffed when Richard pulled Jos in close to him for a group photo. It was as if I wasn't there! I think Jos picked up on it too, grabbed my hand and put me in her place, asking Lea to take another photo. But Richard was seemingly oblivious.

Erin enjoyed herself, too. She sat on my left next to Lea, and the two of them hit it off immediately. The party got very noisy in the end though, and I was quite relieved when people started to leave.

As we drove home, Richard said what a wonderful surprise it had been, how much he'd enjoyed being with all his friends like that, and that he'd had a really good night. I took that as his 'thank you'.

A couple of days later he came home with his new bike. It was the expensive one he'd been admiring in the bike shop, and he invited Lea and Chrissy to come over the following weekend to pick up the old one. But mainly to show off the new.

They had tea with us, and Mum was pleased to meet them. Later, she said that Lea looked 'just like his dad, didn't he?' To which it was easiest to just nod.

***

Spring turned into a long, hot summer and pleasant days were spent with the French windows thrown open, and Mum sitting at the little table outside, supervising Erin and me with the gardening.

Erin grew stronger and happier by the day, and more restless to get on with her life. She was sitting reading the local paper one afternoon when she looked up and read out an advert for shop assistants required at a little supermarket a couple of miles away.

'What do you think, Mom?' she said. 'I could do that.'

In South Africa, Erin had worked as a PA to the owner of quite a big property management company. She was capable of more than this. She must have read my mind.

'I've got to start somewhere, Mom,' she said. 'I'm not sure I'm ready for too much pressure just yet. I think this would be ideal; and I could even walk there.'

When I thought about it, I realised that it would get her out of the house and talking to people again, and that would help her self-confidence. It was exactly what she needed. And she smiled when I said I thought it was.

So, she phoned and arranged an interview, and a couple of days later she had a job at the local Spar. She was very pleased with herself, and could even laugh at the oversized overall she was given to wear, which was definitely not a 'Small'!

Richard was pleased about her taking a job.

'There's nothing wrong with doing an honest day's work, whatever it is!' he said.

And she blossomed. Within a couple of weeks, she'd made friends with the girls and was going out, and had her own money to do so. She liked the contact with the people who came into the store, especially the regulars, the old ladies who enjoyed a chat while waiting for their change. There was no pressure or deadlines, and for the first time in ages, she slept at night.

***

In July, Richard and I had our first anniversary, so we went out to celebrate at the Boathouse. We sat in a cosy little corner by the window watching the boats being tied up to their moorings and ducks busily diving after anything thrown overboard. Richard ordered a bottle of sparkling wine, and we enjoyed the relaxed atmosphere of the place. After the crème brûlée, he reached over and took my hand.

'Thank you for a wonderful year, my dear. It has certainly been an interesting one,' he said with raised brows, 'and I am very, very glad to have you in my life.'

'Well, thank you,' I said. 'And I feel the same.' I raised my glass. 'Happy anniversary!'

'Happy anniversary!' he repeated. 'In fact, considering what we've come through in recent months, I think we could get through anything together. Don't you?'

'Very possibly!' I said, smiling.

He took another sip of his wine. 'So maybe we should make it more permanent? What do you think?'

Good grief! Was this a proposal?

He rubbed the back of my hand with his thumb and gave me that crooked smile. He was waiting for me to say something, but I didn't know what to say.

'What do you mean?' I asked.

'I mean if *you'd* like to, I wouldn't be opposed to the idea of getting married.'

Was that it? Was that his idea of a proposal?

'If it's what *I* want?' I asked, slightly puzzled.

'Yes. I know it's not been at the top of the agenda so far, but I just wanted you to know that, well, if you did feel inclined to, I wouldn't mind giving it a go.'

'Okay, I'll keep it in mind!'

'I mean, that's why we got together in the first place, isn't it? For a committed relationship?'

'I guess so,' I said. 'It's not really the piece of paper that makes it *committed* though, is it? And at our age? I mean, it's not as if we're going to have kids or anything.'

His face fell in disappointment.

'I'm not against marriage,' I added. 'I don't really mind one way or another. I don't mind. Do *you* want to?'

'No! No! Do *you* want to?' he repeated, the crooked smile back in place.

'I guess! If you want to?'

He kissed the back of my hand and raised his glass for another toast.

'Let's do it, then,' he said. 'To us!'

'To us!' I repeated.

Putting our glasses down, he took my hand again.

'Would you like to go and look at some rings tomorrow?' he asked.

'Wow! You don't waste time, do you!'

'Not like some,' he said – jokingly, I hoped.

'Okay. There's a shop in Chester that has nice stuff – I'm sure we'll find a nice engagement ring in there,' I said, smiling like a Cheshire cat now.

His face clouded suddenly.

'That's what you meant, isn't it?' I asked.

'Yes, of course,' he said, smiling. 'I just had a touch of indigestion then, sorry.'

I knew I loved this guy, so why not make it official?

Nothing to do with the idea of flashing an engagement ring on my finger, of course!

He picked up my hand and traced a finger over my palm. 'I see a wonderful, wonderful future ahead,' he said. Then lifting it to his lips, he very gently placed a kiss in my palm, folded my fingers over it to keep it safe, and placed it back on the table.

***

The next morning we went back into Chester. I saw the ring I wanted in the shop I'd mentioned, and would have been quite happy to buy it there and then. It was a very simple, square-cut diamond set on elegant, gold shoulders. Richard liked it too, but just to make sure, suggested that we look around some more. It was a hot, sunny day and we traipsed all over Chester looking at just about every jewellery shop there was, until my head buzzed and my feet hurt and I needed to sit down.

We took a break and went down into 'The Cellars' for a late pub lunch. The old Roman vault was as cool as a cave under the curved, sandstone ceiling. I flopped down onto the padded bench greatly relieved.

Richard asked if I had made up my mind about which ring I wanted, or did I need more time to think. We could always leave it for another day?

'I know exactly which one. The one in Barratt and Jones, the first shop we went in.'

He nodded and licked beer off his top lip. 'Okay. If that's the one.'

'Are you happy with the price?'

'Well, put it this way, I wasn't expecting anything less.' He smiled. Then noticing my look of concern, he said, 'It's fine, really. It's a nice ring.'

The assistant in Barratt and Jones remembered us and smiled when we entered the shop again.

'So, have we decided?' he asked.

'It would seem so,' said Richard. 'Can we look at that tray again?' he asked, pointing to the one. The assistant brought it forth and I pointed to the ring. The assistant took it out and put it on my finger.

'Is that *the* one?' asked Richard, yet again.

I nodded. 'It's beautiful!'

'I'll buy it for you if you want me to,' he said.

'Well, isn't that why we're here?' I asked, flippantly.

He just shrugged.

What? I thought. *If I* want *you to! What on earth is that supposed to mean?*

'If I *want* you to?' I asked, hoping he would rephrase it into something like '*Yes, I would love to buy it for you as a token of my undying love!*'

But he didn't.

'Yes. If that's what you want,' he said, with wide-eyed innocence.

And suddenly there was something very wrong. I couldn't put my finger on it, but wrong none the less. I just stood there wondering what to do. What to say. The shop assistant was smiling at me expectantly, but I couldn't do this. After slipping the ring off my finger, I handed it back to him.

'Thank you,' I said. 'It's lovely, but maybe I must think about it a little more.'

He bowed his head gracefully acknowledging my decision and put the ring back on the tray.

'Thank you,' I said to him, and walked out of the shop without even looking at Richard, who followed me out. We walked back to the car in silence, no longer holding hands, and apart from polite little comments here and there, the drive home was pretty much the same. I was expecting him to ask me what that was all about, or what had just happened, but he didn't. That was just as well, because I didn't know myself. But he drove, calmly, in silence. It was as if he knew exactly what had happened – and he was fine with it. So, I sat there, trying to figure it all out for myself.

By the time we reached home, I had a little speech prepared in my mind, questions I wanted answering. But as soon as he walked into the kitchen he said he was tired and went for a nap. And stayed there till tea time. I sat out in the garden with Mum and Erin.

After some time, Erin asked, 'You okay, Mom?'

'Not really,' I said, but smiled at her.

'D'you want to tell me?'

'Not now. Later.' And she nodded.

***

Erin came out with Richard and I for a drink at the White Horse that night, and the atmosphere was a little easier with her around. The first time she went outside for a cigarette, though, the silence between us was palpable.

When I couldn't stand it any longer, I said. 'Do you know why I didn't take the ring today?'

'Okay?' he said, inviting me to tell him.

'It's because you said you'd *buy it for me if I wanted you to.*'

'So?' he asked, as if he didn't understand.

'I didn't want you to buy it because *I* wanted you to,' I said. 'I wanted you to buy it because *you* wanted to.'

'What's the difference?'

'There's a world of difference!'

He shrugged. 'I don't see it!' he said shortly. I felt the subject was closed to him now and he didn't really want to discuss it anymore. So, I said no more, and within a couple of minutes Erin was back with us. Richard perked up then and the rest of the evening was pleasant enough. By the next morning it was as if nothing had been said, and nothing needed to be, either. So, I decided to leave it.

As time passed, I started to wonder whether I had been irrational or paranoid even, and what did Richard think about it? Had I hurt his feelings? Did he think I'd rejected him?

I tried to ask Erin in a purely hypothetical, 'for instance' kind of way, what she would think in a similar situation, but ended up telling her all about it. I knew she would give a straight answer if she had one, but on this occasion she didn't. She just thought him strange.

***

Richard and I managed a few bike rides that summer, usually along the old rail track to Parkgate, stopping for an ice cream before riding home. Sometimes, just Erin and I would go for a bike ride, a much more leisurely affair. She and I rode all the pretty country lanes in the area, taking our time and sometimes stopping by a farm gate or field just to relax and take in the view, or say hello to a horse.

And towards the end of that summer, Mum gave up her Thursday afternoon shopping trips with Barbara-next-door. They were getting too much for her, especially on rainy days when her back hurt, and she would rather stay in bed with a hot-water bottle. But on her 'good' days, I (and Erin, if she wasn't working) would take her out for a walk around the local nursery, and have tea and scones.

Erin enjoyed her job at Spar and her self-confidence grew by the day. So much so that she was beginning to feel she could take on something more demanding, and she started looking online for jobs.

It was September when Maggie asked me if I (and Erin if she was interested) wanted to go and look at the end-of-summer sales in Chester. I groaned at the prospect, remembering the Black Friday mayhem, but she assured me it wouldn't be like that. We could go at any time and just take a casual wander around the shops. Erin seemed quite keen, so I agreed.

We were walking up Eastgate Street and past Barratt and Jones and my mind immediately went back to the engagement ring incident. I pretended to look at the watches just to see if *my* ring was still in the window. It was, and Erin caught me looking, so I surreptitiously pointed it out to her. She looked at the ring, and then sadly at me.

'It's fine,' I whispered.

Luckily Maggie was looking at something else further down the window and didn't appear to have noticed. I hadn't told her anything about the non-buying of the ring.

Then after about three hours of shopping, and me being mercilessly 'got at' by the two of them about my taste in clothes, Maggie announced that she was ready for a drink anytime we were. Within ten minutes we were sitting comfortably on a sofa in the Slug and Lettuce, with wine in hand and having a second look at the things we'd bought.

'You're not seriously going to wear that, are you?' asked Maggie as I pulled out a burnt-orange jersey.

'I am! I like it, and I don't care if you don't.'

'You'll look like a walking pumpkin in that,' she went on. 'It's bloody awful!'

Erin burst out laughing, obviously in agreement.

'I don't care what either of you say,' I said. 'I like it!'

'And do you know, Maggie,' started Erin. 'When Mom buys shoes, she buys two pairs of the same, just in a different colour, but the same shoes!'

Maggie looked suitably shocked. 'I know! She always did do that. Crazy, hey? I mean, why would you?'

'Makes perfect sense to me,' I said. 'Having the second pair means I still have a pair of shoes I like, and I can still wear them when the first pair fall to bits.'

'But you could go out and buy a perfectly nice, *different* pair to wear?' said Erin, not understanding my reasoning. She shook her head and looked at Maggie, for backup. Which was immediately forthcoming.

'And her taste in shoes is just about as good as her taste in men – feckin' awful!' She rolled her eyes to the ceiling.

Then she inspected a pair of bottle-green pants she had bought, and frowned.

'And those?' I asked. 'I guarantee you'll be taking them back to the shop within the week!'

'Might be even sooner than that!' she said, screwing her face up at them. 'Or I could always give them to Slapper-bitch for Christmas!' She smiled, wickedly, and shoving the pants back in the bag, she sat back and relaxed.

'Cheers!' she said, and we raised our glasses.

Putting her glass back down, Maggie said, 'So, why were we whispering about engagement rings outside Barratt and Jones, then?'

How does she do that?

I looked at her, not knowing where to start.

'How is *Dick*?' she asked, provocatively.

'He's fine, thank you.'

'So, has he asked you to marry him?'

'I'm not sure,' I answered.

'Er…' she said, confused. 'I think you'd know if he had!' She looked at Erin hoping for an answer there.

'We had a conversation about making our relationship more permanent,' I said. 'And I think we were talking about marriage, because he asked me if I wanted to go and look at rings. We actually came into Chester to look, but it all went pear-shaped somehow – not sure what happened. But we didn't buy one.'

'Engagement ring, or wedding rings?' she asked.

And a sudden realisation dawned on me. 'It wouldn't be

wedding rings, would it?' I asked. 'You only buy them when you're about to get married?'

Maggie just shrugged but said nothing.

'I don't really know,' I said, honestly. 'I had actually chosen an engagement ring – in Barratt and Jones – and we went back there to buy it. Then Richard said, "I'll buy it for you *if you want me to*?", and that just sounded such a weird thing to say. Don't you think? I just said I needed to think about it some more, and walked out of the shop, and we haven't really spoken about it since. It's as if it never happened.'

She looked at me as if she was in pain. 'Do you seriously want to marry him?'

'It doesn't bother me one way or another. It was him who brought it up. I thought that's what he wanted.'

'Do *you* like him, Erin?' she asked.

With an apologetic little glance over to me, Erin shook her head. 'Not really,' she said.

'You see! Even Erin can see he's horrible. Why do you always go for complete tossers?' she asked.

'They're all tossers to you. You don't like anybody,' I said.

'Because you always find them! You have the worst choice in men that I've ever come across. Look at that knobhead in Manchester that you were so crazy over. I told you what he was like, but you didn't want to listen, did you? And was I right?'

'As it happens, yes. But you didn't know him. You could just as easily have been wrong.'

'No,' she said. 'There are some men you can just see are bad news. You can just see that they're… bad… and you stay away from them. Or at least any sane, normal person would. But not you!'

I sighed. I didn't have the energy to argue with her.

'Look, I'm sorry if that sounds harsh,' she said. 'But you know I'm only saying it for your own good, don't you?'

'You must admit, he is a bit weird, isn't he?' said Erin more gently. 'Don't you think, Mom? Look how he was about this ring. What's going on with him?'

I just bit my lip, feeling more than a bit defensive.

'He's up to no good,' said Maggie. 'I'm telling you, Nat, don't marry him. Really, I'm serious.'

'Well, it looks like it's not going to happen now, anyway,' I said.

We changed the subject and a couple of minutes later were laughing again. I knew she had my best interests at heart. And Erin. But they didn't know him like I knew him.

However, maybe I wouldn't be marrying him any time soon.

Chapter Twenty-One

Richard had his annual leave coming up in October, and he was ready for a holiday.

'So d'you fancy going away somewhere?' he asked.

'For sure,' I said, thinking Greece or Italy perhaps. 'Have you got anywhere in particular in mind?'

'How about a cruise?' he asked, grinning.

'A cruise?' I was stunned. 'Where?'

'I was thinking Barbados. Have you ever been?'

'No!' I gasped. 'Have you?'

'Years ago, with Vicky and the girls. So, what do you think? Would you like to go?'

'Wow! I would love to go! But it must cost a fortune. I have a few savings stashed away, but not much.'

'These "all-in" deals are not bad,' he said. 'And there just so happens to be a good one coming up in October.'

'A cruise! How absolutely amazing would that be!'

I tried to imagine myself doing such a thing, which was not very hard at all, really.

'Okay,' he said. 'Well, I'll look at the figures. I can pay up front for the tickets and you can pay me back later, if you like.'

'But what about Mum? I can't ask Erin to look after her on her own while we go swanning off around the Caribbean.'

'Well,' he said, smugly, 'Lea's stuck at home for all of October while the pub gets renovated. I'd bet she'd be glad to stay with them for a couple of weeks.'

'Two weeks! We're going for two weeks?'

He nodded and smiled. 'One week in a hotel on Barbados, and the second week cruising around the islands. How does that sound?'

It sounded pretty good to me. In fact, it sounded like heaven.

I needed a new stamp on my passport to enter the USA, which meant applying for a visa. I bought new clothes, packed and repacked my suitcase several times, and spent my days drooling over the brochure until it was finally time to wave Mum and the girls goodbye and drive to Manchester airport.

After checking in, Richard looked around for the closest bar.

'I'm having a beer. What'll you have?'

'It's not even lunchtime yet!'

'That doesn't count. I'm on holiday!'

So, I sat with a white wine, looking at our tickets. Manchester to Barbados – it seemed inconceivable that those two words could be on the same piece of paper. I just couldn't believe it!

***

The plane flew in low over a sparkling blue sea to land at Barbados airport. Looking down, the airport itself looked like one big hangar. It had only one runway, and was surrounded not by a sprawling city, but by a green, rural landscape. When we had landed and actually walked into the airport, it was very basic, hot, and nearly empty – and it didn't take long at all before we were in the minibus driving along potholed roads with cracked pavements to our hotel.

The Hibiscus Grove Hotel had a very colonial look about it, with a pillared, semi-circular front porch and a fountain of white marble, around which traffic moved in an orderly, clockwise direction. We parked at the door where a bell-boy loaded our bags onto a trolley, and after check-in, showed us to our room on the first floor.

Richard started moaning again but I tuned him out, and stood on the balcony looking out on... paradise. Just to the left, we had our own palm tree, and beyond, white sand and a glistening turquoise sea stretched out to a hazy, mauve horizon. We were right above the beach. A little further up, closer to the reception, bronzed bodies lay on beach loungers under more palms.

So what if there was a strange noise in the pipes when the hot water tap was turned on!

The first morning when I opened my eyes, I thought I must have died and gone to heaven. I wanted to get out there and take a look around, but Richard just rolled over and grunted that it was too early.

I made myself a coffee while debating what to wear to go exploring. Then deciding on cargo pants and T-shirt, I told a snoring Richard I was going for a walk, and made my way down through the hotel to the beach. All was quiet as I passed the now empty sun loungers, except for the rustling of palm trees; their long fronds cast gently swaying shadows on the cool white sand. I walked down to the water's edge and dipped my toes in the crystal-clear water, the reflected sunlight glinting up into my eyes, then on, following the shoreline away from the hotel.

There must have been a storm in the night as the whole length of the beach had a tide line etched in strands of sea weed, driftwood, shells, and hundreds of tiny, silver fish, some still flapping. Two long-legged plovers ran by my side at the water's edge, and tiny sand crabs eyed me suspiciously before scuttling away down into their burrows.

I'd gone a fair way and was walking along a deserted stretch of shoreline when I was startled by a rough, raggedy-looking man coming out of the scrub at the edge of the beach. He was skinny, wearing just a pair of old cotton shorts, and waving a skinny, dark-skinned arm trying to catch my attention. As he came closer, I could see he was not a young man; tufts of greyish white hair stuck out from his head and chin. With there being nobody else around I was keen to keep my distance, but he beckoned, and came trotting towards me. He stopped a couple of metres away, trying to explain something in a strange tongue and holding outstretched hands towards me, and in his hands, a tiny baby turtle. He pointed up towards the edge of the beach, signalling for me to follow. Maybe he wanted to show me the nest, I thought. But that wasn't going to happen. I gestured to him, asking if I could hold the little creature and he gently gave it to me. Even so small, it had the forlorn expression that turtles have, and I instantly felt sorry for it.

So, smiling at the man, I took the little fellow and placed him at the water's edge, taking photos and putting myself between it and the man while it made its escape. He protested, but too late; the little turtle scuttled away and instantly disappeared into the pristine shallows.

The man was not happy. I don't know what he was saying, but it wasn't nice; neither were the hand gestures. I just shrugged, smiled innocently, and turned, nervously, homewards. When I looked back, he was walking up to the trees again and I breathed a sigh of relief.

When I got back to our room, Richard was up and showered and we went down to the dining room. He had a good old moan about how long we had to wait for the full English breakfast, but when it did finally arrive, it was good. As we ate, I told Richard all about the baby turtle. He viewed the photos with mild interest, saying it was probably not a good idea for me to wander up the beach on my own.

Another English couple came to share our table, Jim and Eileen. He was a quiet type who let Eileen do most of the talking, and she was happy to oblige in a lovely, Geordie accent. They were celebrating their thirty-fifth wedding anniversary and she asked how long *we* had been married.

I smiled and said, 'We're not, actually.'

'Oh. I'm sorry,' she said. 'I just thought…'

'Don't worry, it's fine,' I said.

'And besides,' said Richard, taking my hand. 'We're working on it, aren't we?'

I just smiled and thought, *Are we?* First I'd heard!

***

Barbados was such a beautiful place, and in such a relaxed, holiday mood we connected all over again. For most of our week there we just soaked up the sun, sea and sand, crayfish, rum punch, and each other.

We were both very red for the first couple of days but by mid-week had turned a deep golden brown and began to look a little more local than the whiter-than-white new arrivals. Richard was relaxed and smiling and we spent romantic evenings walking hand in hand and sitting on the beach to watch the sunset.

We walked around Bridgetown one day, browsing our way through the shops with the rest of the tourists. In one, a jewellery shop, I stopped to look at a display of turquoise-blue stones set in necklaces, rings, pendants and such. It was so striking, and reminded me of the creamy, turquoise colour of the ocean. The shop lady told me it was called *Larimar*, and of its origins and rarity.

I wanted to buy something, but spoiled for choice, I didn't know what. I think I was hoping that Richard might help choose, and maybe even treat me to something to commemorate our holiday. That would have been so romantic and would have meant so much to me. But it didn't happen. He stood by watching with a bemused smile, and was no help at all. Eventually I bought myself a little pendant.

Another day, we took a day cruise around the island in a thirty-foot, shiny white catamaran with billowing sails. It was wonderful to be out on the open water with the breeze in our faces, and to look up through the rigging at an impossibly deep blue sky. The Bajan crew handled the boat with taught muscles and agile expertise, as the double hull cut swiftly through the white surf.

We sailed up the west coast, and after a short stop for those who wanted to snorkel, we sailed on to the next stop where hawksbill and green sea turtles glided and flapped around the boat, inviting us out to play. What a feeling, coming eye to eye with these amazing creatures, or being aware of their sheer bulk as they nudged gently by.

Lunch was a tapas buffet of Caribbean delights washed down with something from the bar, which was open for the duration of the cruise, and which was probably more to blame for the way we all eventually wobbled off the boat, 'trying to find our land legs' again.

One evening we went with Jim and Eileen and Sandy and Mike (another couple at the hotel) to visit Oissens Fish Market. Eileen had told us that it was a very different sort of place, and the restaurant was 'not to be missed'.

When the hotel minibus dropped us off, we just followed the sound of reggae music and the smell of fish, booze and dagga into the fish market. Once inside, we melted into a throng of people that moved like a river, eating, drinking, dancing, in a happy, relaxed oneness. Wooden stalls stood on bare earth and offered touristy knick-knacks for sale under strings of bare lightbulbs. The music was mesmerising, the vibe infectious as we were carried along on the rhythm (nearly tripping over a ring of men sat cross-legged, playing a game of dice), until we came upon our restaurant.

Open along the front terrace and softly lit with round, red lanterns, it welcomed us in. There were long trestle tables each seating twelve or more people, and candles in glass jars casting a warm glow on happy, chatty faces as the reggae music played. As one party of people vacated their end of a table, we quickly claimed it for our own.

Of course, there was fish on the menu – an amazing variety, cooked whichever way you liked it, and served with either beer or red house wine. Richard and I shared a seafood platter, which would have easily fed a family of five, served with savoury rice and a rough kind of bread to be dipped into the fishy juices. It was divine. We ate the lot, and sat back licking garlicy fingers.

After a while the music became irresistible and the six of us went to dance on the bare-earth dancefloor, which I am not too sure was even part of the restaurant. The men soon deserted us, but we women carried on dancing on our own, with each other, or with anybody who drifted in front of us. Such was the mood. Everybody was smiling – singing – feeling the love!

Richard eventually came back and we slow-danced together and I was reminded again of how good that felt. But all too soon, the hotel combi came to pick us up and we headed home tired, and more than a little drunk. But what a night!

***

On our last day on Barbados, we hired a little yellow car and drove around the island. The rain in the night had made everything fresh and shiny and a warm trade wind blew as we drove up the coastline.

We soon found ourselves on dirt roads closed in by sugar cane and banana plantations. We were just about the only vehicle in sight that day (not counting a couple of donkey carts). We stopped here and there along the way to admire beautiful, picture-perfect coves, or settlements of neat little houses painted in different shades of pastel pinks, blues and yellows. The people in these places all seemed so laid-back and happy. They waved or smiled to us from their stoeps or as they walked, leisurely, down the dirt roads, or tended their front gardens, where flowers and mielies and pumpkins all grew together. Everywhere there were telephone poles and wires, thick and thin, strung haphazardly all over the place. But they were not ugly – somehow, they added to the charm of the place.

Sometimes the little houses (or sometimes shacks) would be more scattered, dotted here and there down green hillsides, with sheep and goats wandering freely among them. At the bottom of one hillside, a line of colourful little boats pulled up onto the shale down at the water's edge, looking shiny and bright in the sun.

Life seemed so easy and simple in this place. Time seemed totally irrelevant. People had all the time in the world to say 'Hello'. Nobody rushed (which annoyed Richard tremendously when he was waiting for service).

At one point I asked Richard to stop the car so that I could take a photo of the view: a single palm tree silhouetted against a perfect sea and sky in varying shades of blue and mauve. Richard obliged, and I went to stand under the tree. Then a young Barbadian man with a big white smile came over, and put an arm around me, posing for the camera.

'I come in your picture with you, Mommy. You can't take picture on your own!' he announced. That picture always makes me laugh.

It is the people I will remember most about Barbados; the people, and the colours.

We stopped at a beach bar in Pebbles for lunch and, over crab salad, talked about joining the ship the next day. I was excited as much about the ship as the cruise.

'This is a beautiful place, isn't it?' Richard said.

'It's paradise,' I agreed.

'I could easily live in a place like this, away from the rat race, the rain and cold. Can you imagine?'

'I can indeed,' I said. 'South Africa is very much the same. Well, not so different, anyway.'

Richard sat quaffing his beer in a pink T-shirt that, on the front, read *To Have and To Hold*, above a picture of a pint of beer.

'How appropriate!' I said, giving it a nod.

'What?' He looked down at his shirt as if he'd just noticed which one he'd put on that morning.

'To have and to hold!' I said.

'Appropriate?'

'Yes. You having a beer in your hand, as you very often do! And indeed, do have at this very moment.'

'Oh! I see! To have and to hold a beer. I thought you were talking about something else.'

'Like what?'

'To have and to hold. It's usually about marriage, isn't it?'

'Usually, yes. So?'

'Nothing!' he said, giving his best lopsided smile.

I looked at him quizzically.

'Did you know that captains can marry people?' he asked.

'Yes, I believe so,' I answered.

He just kept smiling at me till it was getting a bit weird, and then he turned serious again.

'So what's South Africa like? Is it as nice as here?'

What was that about? I wondered.

'Very similar,' I said. 'Down on the coast it's sub-tropical like here. It's always warm, and very beautiful.'

'Maybe we must go and take a look sometime.'

'Now that is an excellent idea!'

'Maybe make it our next holiday?'

'Definitely! You would absolutely love it.'

'Would you go back there permanently?' he asked.

'I don't know, I guess that depends on *us*.'

'Well, I meant *with* me!' He laughed.

'Yes, I'd go back tomorrow.'

'Well, we know where to go for our next holiday then, don't we!'

The following day we packed our bags and went to join the ship. We saw the huge, white shape of it long before we were anywhere near, but I had no idea just how huge until we were on the quayside, where it loomed above us like a massive iceberg. I'd never been on anything bigger than the Mersey ferry before.

There was a steel band playing calypso music and much hustle and bustle as excited people found their way to the entrance, which was like a square cut-out low down on the side of the ship. We were allowed through the checkpoint two by two, like the animals entering the Ark!

We sat around in a kind of lounge for about an hour while they processed incoming passengers, but eventually we were allowed into the labyrinth of the ship to find our cabin. We went through the door into our private little space, which was modern and filled with light from the picture window overlooking the harbour; a beautiful, strange and exotic new world. There was a sliding glass door onto a little balcony outside, which was just big enough for a table and two chairs. The king-size bed was against the window (I guess privacy is not an issue at sea), and Richard sat on it, his glasses halfway down his nose, reading out information on the ship's facilities while I hung up our clothes.

The first thing we did, of course, was explore the ship, which we soon realised was like a floating city with everything from swimming pools to exclusive spas. There were several eateries above and below deck – everything from small restaurants to a huge open-air dining area. Below deck there was a full-size theatre, pubs and coffee shops, and lots of brightly lit, glitzy shops. Escalators and glass-tube lifts slid up and down the various levels with clockwork precision as people milled everywhere.

It was late afternoon. We were sitting out on our little balcony as we realised the ship was moving and we jumped up to see the furrow of white foam churn away from the prow. Then sitting down again, he held my hand as we watched the sun sink into the unbroken horizon. Was this real? Was it really happening? I looked at Richard and found him already smiling back at me.

'Not bad, hey?' he said.

But I didn't have words. I just nodded.

***

Richard and I were comfortable with each other by this time. I'd learned the difference between an easy, contented silence (which this was) and one of his *quiet* moods, which I ignored. I'd come to realise that the latter were about him, not me, and he was best left alone in them.

He wasn't one for showing his feelings much at all really, or for sharing his innermost thoughts. They were his – private – like his email account! Sometimes he would just withdraw into himself, into his own inner world, where I knew, instinctively, he wanted to be alone. He was a very private person.

Suddenly I remembered Richard burning the roast potatoes at Christmas and how he had turned his back on me so I wouldn't see. He wanted to keep it a secret. And then, for some reason, remembered him sitting with that blank stare when the police had been searching the house for Erin. Also keeping a secret? Where did that thought come from?

Sometimes, when he was off in his own little world, I would wonder if we were ever really *together* at all. And I would think, *Who is this man? What are we doing together?* But then maybe I was overthinking things again. Two old fogies like us were mature enough not to expect perfection in each other. We both understood that everybody has their little foibles, and part of accepting another person into your life is accepting their funny little ways, too. If he was willing to live with mine, then I could respect his. Give and take. Wasn't that what it was about?

Then there were other times when he made me feel loved. Maybe he didn't have the words to say it, but when we were close, I felt it. As I sat there, feeling my hand resting in his, watching the sun set on this exquisite world that we were sharing together, I felt at peace, that everything was right, and that we were meant to be together.

***

As I woke the next morning, I had an eye-level view of dark green, forest-covered hills encircling a sparkling blue harbour, where a fleet of white yachts and sailing boats bobbed at anchor. The mauve sky told me I was still in the Caribbean and a snore in the bed beside me brought me fully back to reality.

We were anchored at St Lucia: our first port of call. I didn't move, but just lay in the sunshine among the white sheets, taking in the view as if it were the continuance of some dream. That's what it felt like; Richard, this holiday – everything felt like a dream.

After breakfast we left the ship and took a water taxi over to the other side of the harbour into Castries, and wandered around sight-seeing the hustle bustle of the harbour. The minicab drivers offered various trips and tours, and we chose to take an all-round trip to the mud flats, sulphur springs and waterfall.

To be honest, I wasn't overly impressed with the mud or sulphur, but the tropical waterfall was beautiful. It cascaded down from a dizzy height, sending little splashes of light around the misty, forest vegetation surrounding it, before exploding noisily into a tumultuous pool of sunshine and rainbows at the bottom. A few people, locals I think, laughed and played around in the water.

We hit the road again, climbing higher up around the hairpin bends and stopping at various viewing points where we could look down on the harbour below and, a little further out, chains of small green islands scattered upon the endless blue ocean.

We stopped for a lunch of snapper fish, yams and crunchy salad and then our driver took us to see the Two Pitons, cones of bare volcanic rock which rise dramatically out of the forest-green hillside. But then it was time to return to the harbour and catch a water taxi back to the ship, passing under its huge bows as we did.

At dinner that evening we were joined by a young couple who had also spent their day on the island. They had obviously had a far more exciting time than we had, and were determined to share it with us. Where we had driven, they had hiked, and rather than our 'genuine Cajun lunch', they had shared a meal of chicken backs and pigs' tails. Richard rolled his eyes towards the door, and we escaped from them into the cosy piano bar.

Later, when we were sitting out on the balcony for a nightcap (which became routine), we realised that the ship was underway again, churning through the dark waters.

The next morning, we woke up at St Maarten (or St Martin, depending which side of the island you're on). And it was just as breath-taking as St Lucia. We took a day tour, and as the minibus climbed higher and higher, we watched the sun twinkling over the flat expanse of the sea, way out to the distant blue horizon. Along this coastline, too, lay the chains of little islands that perhaps had once formed one mass, but of which now only the highest peaks showed above water level. They lay like a necklace of green emeralds casually thrown upon the turquoise sea; each fringed with silver surf and the space between them dotted with little boats and yachts.

We spent the afternoon on the beach, under thatch, being served cool, rum-based drinks with fruit in them. I'd picked up an information booklet along the way, and it seemed a good time to read it. It gave some history of the Caribbean, the various nations that had invaded and enslaved the native Caribs to work the sugar plantations, and the wars those nations fought between themselves for the sugar – during which the native Caribs were nearly wiped out by the foreign diseases brought in by their marauders.

I generously tried sharing some of this information with Richard, who lay with a towel over his eyes showing little more interest than the occasional grunt. I read him some facts about the island of Martinique, and checking the map, realised we must have sailed past that island during the previous night, and I pointed this out to him.

'No shit, Sherlock!' came the lazy response.

'Did you know,' I asked, 'that on the island of Martinique in 1902, Mount Peleé erupted and killed the whole population of St Pierre – within minutes?'

Another grunt.

'And did you know,' I continued, 'that just off the end of Martinique there is a tiny island called Diamond Rock, where the British built an outpost and caused havoc by firing cannon balls at passing French ships, until a clever French admiral sent a boatload of rum to the British soldiers, who got so pissed they allowed the French to take the island!'

He sat up and swung sideways to face me. 'That sounds a very civilised way of doing things,' he said. 'Speaking of which, d'you want another drink?'

On Tuesday we woke up anchored at the island of St Thomas, and after breakfast left the ship to join another minibus island tour. Again, we climbed steep, winding roads to various viewing spots, and Richard craned his neck to see what he could of a very exclusive-looking golf club. Indeed, this island had a decidedly affluent feel about it.

At the summit, we all climbed out onto a gravel car park to stretch our legs and look down at our cruise ship, looking like a child's toy, docked below. There was a ramshackle little store/café up there, which sold a variety of weird and wonderful things, including five-litre plastic containers of rum with hand-written labels marked '*Confusion*' and '*Wipeout*', and colourful Rastafarian hats complete with their own attached dreadlocks.

We walked through the shop to a small wooden balcony overgrown with greenery and bright red bougainvillea, and sat at one of the rough wooden tables there. A movement in the foliage caught my eye, and another, and realising what it was we began a game of 'spot the iguana', which were camouflaged among the leaves. For their part, they just turned beady, unimpressed eyes upon us.

Outside, in the car park, there was a man with a rather handsome donkey wearing a bonnet of brightly coloured flowers, and for a small price you could have your photo taken with him (the donkey, not the man). I went over and stroked the animal and he immediately pushed his big head against me, and (I swear!) smiled for the camera. So of course, I had to have a photo of him. His owner, a tall, thin Carib man (with a smile not unlike his flower-hatted friend), had trained him well.

The next morning, we woke up to cool, grey skies and the skyline of what could have been any European city. It was San Juan in Puerto Rico, and again, we took a tour; this time of bustling, busy streets that ran like narrow canyons between tall rows of tightly packed buildings on either side, each painted in its own bright colour. They seemed to be a mix and match of styles, with ornate cornicing and lots of balconies and arches. The streets were lined with trees and haphazard telephone poles – and wires everywhere. It was all very picturesque, and the winding, cobble-stoned side streets running up off the main thoroughfare had me imagining conquistadors marching down them, and the clatter and spectacle they would have made.

We stopped for coffee in a little café, but during this welcome break it started to rain and Richard started to feel ill. I would have loved to have seen more, but the minibus windows steamed up and I don't think Richard, who had turned rather pale, was very interested anyway.

By the time we got back to the ship, Richard was experiencing quite severe stomach cramps. He was given electrolytes at the ship's medical suites and told to lie down and rest, and to stay in his cabin. He slept, while I had a little 'me' time out on the balcony as the ship got underway once more.

The next morning he felt fine again, and was sure he would be well enough for the Captain's Table Dinner that evening. We spent the morning strolling around the island of St Kitts, had a nap in the afternoon, then got ready for the dinner. I had bought a dress especially for the occasion and was looking forward to the evening ahead, and Richard was looking very dapper in a cream dinner jacket and dickie bow tie.

A waiter greeted us and we were shown to a table where two other couples already sat. The men stood as I was seated. They looked like two retired colonels, both with moustaches, and one with badges on his jacket. Their wives were bejewelled, besequinned and neatly coiffed.

However, no sooner had we introduced ourselves and sat down than Richard suddenly felt ill again, and within minutes we were on our way back to the cabin. He went to bed. I was starving, so went to get myself a pizza. I took it out onto the balcony, where Richard joined me and ate half of it. I was disappointed; and I couldn't help wonder at Richard's remarkable recovery. I wondered whether he was really ill at all that evening. He said he was, but later also said he hadn't felt like chatting with the people we'd been sat with. Thinking about it, I wondered if he'd just not wanted to tell them he was a lorry driver?

Richard went back to bed as the ship made way again and I felt sad as I watched the lights of St Kitts fade into the distance behind us. It felt like it was not only St Kitts fading away, but our whole holiday, which was nearly at an end now.

We spent the whole of Friday at sea as we sailed back to Barbados and it was actually very pleasant to stroll around deck, sunbathe, and generally do very little for the day. Richard was feeling absolutely fine again, and that evening we had dinner watching a comedian in one of the little bars.

Back at the cabin, sitting out on the balcony for the last time, we talked about our holiday. I said how much I loved this place, and how sad I'd be to leave.

'For now,' he said, smiling and taking my hand. 'But we'll find our own place in the sun, don't you worry.'

That sounded like a wonderful idea to me.

He turned his chair towards me a little more. 'What do you think?' he asked. 'I know we were talking of marriage a while back, and I still don't quite know what went wrong then. But I know how I feel now. And I wondered how you do?'

'Yes. I'm not quite sure what happened in the jewellers that day either, but…'

'Well, it's you who walked out!' he cut in, then quickly smiled.

'I know. It just didn't feel right. It just felt like you were buying the ring because you felt pressurised to, because *I wanted* you to, when *you* didn't necessarily want to. I didn't want you to feel pressured. I wanted it to be what you wanted, too.'

'That's nonsense! Of course it was what I wanted. It still is,' he said, squeezing my hand.

'So, what? Do you want to get engaged?'

He hesitated. 'Or we could just get hitched?'

'Married? Just like that?' The idea seemed a bit drastic to me.

He shrugged. 'Why not?'

I realised then that that's what he had in mind to do before: buy wedding rings, not an engagement ring.

But I wasn't ready to marry him. And I think the little voice in the back of my head was telling me I might never be.

'We might, one day,' I said, 'but not just yet. It's a bit soon. We've only known each other a year.'

'A year and three months, actually,' he said. 'But it's okay. I didn't mean right away. To be honest, I can't afford it right now. But soon, maybe?'

Struck with sudden inspiration, I said, 'We could get engaged, if you like? How about we buy each other an engagement ring for our birthdays? How about that? You know the sort of thing I like and I know what you like, but it would still be a surprise. Better than traipsing all around Chester again, hey?'

Permanently engaged, I thought, *could be the solution.*

He gave me a look of resignation. 'We could. Just don't expect me to go down on one knee! I'd never get up again!'

***

We arrived back in Barbados the following day and on leaving the ship went straight to the airport. Within twenty-four hours we had touched down in Mordor, er, sorry… Manchester, and I stood shivering under the overhang of an office roof, with the luggage, while Richard trotted through the rain to find the car.

Things at home were fine. The girls had looked after Mum very well, and she was looking very chipper.

There was a new face also. Erin introduced us to Dylan with a smug little smile on her face. He greeted us with an open, friendly face and I immediately liked him. Tall, slim and blond, maybe a little older than Erin, there was a calmness and intelligence in the bright, grey eyes, which he could hardly take off her.

They had met at the Red Lion when she and Lea had gone for a drink one night and, sitting next to each other in the crowded pub, they'd chatted. They'd seen each other since, and there was no mistaking the sparkle in her eye.

Chapter Twenty-Two

I went for tea at Maggie's house that Thursday. She was in a mood; I could see it the minute she opened the door. She didn't say a word, just glared at me before she turned and went down to the kitchen. Alan grabbed his coat off the stair banister and, giving me a look like a startled rabbit, escaped without a word through the open door. I followed Maggie down to the kitchen where she was making us a vodka and coke each – and her mood was, indeed, dark.

She handed me my drink. 'So, you're back, are you? How was it? And I hope you haven't brought any soddin' holiday snaps because I don't want to see them!'

'Holiday snaps?' I said, incredulously. 'What's that?'

'They're what people who have just come off holiday bore the tits off other people with.'

'Well, no. I haven't. Unless you want to look at them on my phone.'

Her deadpan glare answered that one. I couldn't help but laugh as I followed her back down to the lounge.

'I brought you a little present back.'

From over her shoulder, I heard her mutter something like, 'It better not be a tea towel or fuckin' fridge magnet!'

Sitting down in our usual places, I handed her two

wrapped gifts. One was a striped, Rastafarian hat complete with dreadlocks, and the other a bottle of rum. The shape of the bottle was a bit of a giveaway, so she unwrapped the other parcel first and, holding up the hat, regarded it as she might a dead cat. She was slightly more gracious about the rum.

'If you don't like the hat,' I said, 'give it back, because Lea fancies it. I'll give it to her.'

'Who?'

'Lea, Richard's daughter.'

'No, she's not having it,' she said. 'Softlad will like that.' And she put it up on the mantlepiece.

'So, what's up?' I asked, as she sat down again.

She gave a big sigh and took a slug of vodka. 'They're putting me on a three-day week at work.'

'So? That's not so bad, is it?'

'Course it is! That's a big dent in my pay cheque that I can't afford. And my pension is worked out on my last earnings.'

'Shit! Can they do that?'

'Apparently, yes! They're *restructuring*. It's that, or early retirement,'

'Is it just you?'

'No, there's three of us. The three oldest ones there. We've all been there for twenty years or more, all near retirement age. They're just trying to get rid of us.'

'That's crap,' I said, stuck for words.

'And worse,' she went on, 'I'm going to be stuck here with Softlad going stir crazy.'

'But that was going to happen anyway when you retire, wasn't it? I thought you wanted to retire?'

'No, that's not what I said. I said I'd love to give up work if I could afford to. But I don't want to be stuck here with *him*! I'll end up killing one of us!'

'No, you won't.' I laughed. 'You'll be fine! And maybe going on a three-day week might ease you into it?'

'I can't imagine it. What d'you do if you don't go to work? Why would you get up in the morning?' she asked.

'For yourself instead of for a boss,' I told her.

'And what do you do with *yourself*?'

'Whatever you want to. You can do nothing at all if you like. Or you can do all those things you haven't got time to do at weekends. Hobbies and interests.'

'I haven't got any hobbies and interests,' she said, with a disdainful scowl.

'Well, now you'll have time to get some.'

Disregarding the suggestion, she pulled a face and carried on.

'I hate work. Well, no, I don't hate the work, I hate the people. I don't even like being there anymore. But I can't imagine just being stuck here, either. I need to get out. D'you know what I mean?'

I nodded. 'Of course. That's why I wanted to look for a job when I first came over here. I thought I'd go crazy stuck at home with Mum. But you know what, I don't know about you, but I've always felt that there's something more to life than having to sit at a desk for eight hours a day with a smile on your face, pretending you just can't wait for your boss to give you something else to do.'

'Mmm. Well, I hope it doesn't say "proactive" or "self-starter" on *your* CV,' she said, raising her eyebrows at me.

'Oh, don't you hate those employment agency ads that use those words. It's the hamster wheel, isn't it? Get a job to earn money, so that you can eat; work for eight hours a day for most of your life so that you can have a few hours left to "live". I would like to have lived back in the day when people bartered a sheep for a bag of flour, or let you keep your sheep in their meadow in exchange for a few lambs.'

'And when you got married to the shepherd, the lord of the manor came and raped you the night before your wedding just because he could.'

'That's not true. That's only in the movies,' I said.

'Well even if it's not, the boss men always had the power, didn't they? In fact, not necessarily boss ones. *Men* have always had the power. Even back then. You would have just been the property of the shepherd. Thank God things have changed now.'

'Not much though, really, hey? You know when I left Hennie, my bible-study group tried to tell me that a good wife stays with her husband. Basically, we were only put on this earth to be our husbands' little helpers.'

'Is that why you knocked the Jesus thing on the head?'

'No, but it's one of the things that irked me. I got out because it all felt so fake. Like, let's be one of the *good* people so we won't burn in hell, and while we're still here on earth we can feel superior to everyone else. But really, they were no better than anyone else. And I just couldn't believe that any god worth his salt could be so judgemental and petty as the one they believed in, or said they believed in.'

'D'you remember our old boss at the paper mill, Tom Hughes?'

'I do,' I said. 'Lovely guy.'

'He died in the hospice, you know. About ten years ago now. He was very religious at the end.'

'Shame. Really?'

'Yes. Who'd have thought? It was good working at the mill, wasn't it? My first job was in a shoe shop and that was the pits. The mill was so much better. It wasn't your first job either, was it? You worked somewhere else first, in Chester somewhere?'

'Yes. At the insurance brokers. I still remember my first day there!'

'Yeah?' she said, encouraging me to tell her.

'It was in a row of little old houses in Grosvenor Street, you know, down by the racecourse? I went up these rickety old stairs into what had once probably been a bedroom, which was now an office with three desks; two women sat at the two desks by each window and the third desk faced the wall – and guess which one was mine!'

Maggie smiled. 'You and your windows.'

'And we all three smoked, so it was like a blue fog in there. I sat down in front of the old manual type-writer, you know the old Hermes? And I looked up at this dirty great damp stain coming through this awful old wallpaper, and they plonked a pile of files by me and said, "That's yours!"

'I had to type the same short letter, one for each file, just to enclose a renewal note, say. But each letter needed three copies, and three sheets of carbon paper, so that was seven pieces of paper going in each time. If you made a mistake, you had to rub out all the copies, neatly, making sure the carbon paper didn't smudge. So each mistake would take forever to correct. And we were only allowed to make three mistakes per letter – a fourth meant you had to rip it up and start again.'

'Oh, God!' said Maggie. 'I can just imagine *you*!'

'Well, I sat down at my desk, looked at the big damp stain and the pile of files, and thought, *Is this the rest of my life?* And I just wanted to burst into tears. And at the end of that first day, I'd filled the waste paper basket and had only about three letters for the post girl to collect. She was younger than the others, about my age, and gave me such a dirty look that I very nearly did burst into tears.'

'And then?'

'I think Pam, the senior typist, told me not to worry, that I'd get into it. And I did, I suppose, but I hated it. I always had that feeling that I wasn't good enough, and that someday the boss would realise it and sack me.'

'And did he?'

'No. I cottoned on quite quickly that as long as I kept smiling, they would like me and my job was safe. I think I was there more as eye-candy than to be useful.'

'Yes,' said Maggie. 'And you wonder why women don't dress up more for work these days?'

I just smiled. I had to give her that one!

'I know what you mean though,' she went on. 'That's one reason I was grateful for my big boobs; until the Christmas party, that is! Some men think that just because they've given you the job, you owe them something in return – like sex, for instance.'

'Ja, or at least to be able to pinch your bottom when they want to. I've had a few like that. I just used to ask them how their wife was.'

'I just used to tell them to fuck off!' she said.

And I could just imagine her doing that. I had to laugh at her.

'So, what are you going to do?' I asked. 'If I were you, I think I'd take early retirement and get out. Another six months isn't going to make much difference, is it?'

'I would love to. But I can't afford to. And that doesn't answer the question of what I do with myself then? You think about that a minute!' And she took my glass and disappeared off to the kitchen.

After bringing back new drinks, she settled on the sofa again.

'I always had that *not good enough* feeling, too,' she said. 'I came out of school feeling that way. In fact, I think I always felt that way! And at least you got to go to secretarial college. I was working in a bakery down the Port when I was fifteen – Saturday mornings included – and even that was better than school.'

'Well, anything was better than school, hey!'

'I bet you weren't the "Mickey-no-friends", *were* you? You know, that one smelly kid who comes to school with nits in her hair and the same dirty little dress every day?'

'You?' I said, shocked. 'You never told me that. You're kidding me? How come?'

'That's what happened when my mum started going weird; when she started losing it. She didn't know or she didn't care; I don't know which. I had to look after myself anyway, and it's hard at nine years old. I remember the teacher taking pity on me and making me a dress to wear. She took me into the store cupboard to try it on away from the nosey little buggers in class, but they all knew it.

'Then Dad died about then, and after a couple of years, social services sent me to live with our Linda. I cleaned up then, but I was always *that* girl.'

'I thought your dad died when you were thirteen, like me?'

'No. I was nine,' she said. 'So anyway, why did *you* hate school?'

'Well, I *was* "Mickey-no-friends" at junior school. At break, I would go outside and hug a big pipe that ran up the wall outside the canteen. It was always nice and warm, and I'd stand there hoping the other kids wouldn't see me. And I'd hate going inside again, because there'd be some teacher asking questions I didn't know the answers to, when it seemed like everybody else did. They all lived locally and played together after school and I just didn't feel part of anything. We came from Pembie, a fifteen-minute bus ride away, and couldn't hang around to play with them after school because we had to catch the bus home again. I never fitted in. And I always felt like a bit of a weirdo, or that they thought I was, anyway.'

'Well, that goes without saying, doesn't it?' she said. 'But why did you feel that? Why did *you* feel you were a weirdo?'

'For one thing, I used to rock back and to, or from side to side like a pendulum, and the teachers would tell me to sit still. The other kids would giggle and give me weird looks. But I wasn't even aware I was doing it.'

Maggie bit her lip, but the twinkle in her eyes gave away the fact that she was dying to burst out laughing.

'It might sound funny now,' I said, 'but it was hell.'

'Yeah, I know. And the teachers themselves didn't exactly make you feel good about yourself back then, either. Did they? If you weren't one of the few clever ones, you were rubbish.'

'Oh, yes,' I said, remembering. 'We had a Miss Dreyer. At home time, she would randomly call out the times-tables – six nines? Four tens? Like that. First one with their hand up and the right answer could go home. And I knew my tables, but I was so scared of being the last one out, I froze. And there was always someone quicker than me to get their hand up, so I always *was* the last one out.'

'We had one like that,' said Maggie. 'She'd go round asking us to spell words like "gnome". Sadistic bitch! When are you ever going to need to spell a word like gnome?'

'You might if you worked in a hardware shop, or a garden centre?' I offered.

She just pulled a face at me. 'You still wouldn't need to spell it even then, would you!'

'School is like a sausage machine, isn't it? They take innocent little kids and brainwash them into fitting into the system. Doesn't actually teach you much that you're going to need to know, does it? Just how to sit and behave and do what you're told for seven or eight hours a day. Then if you're clever you'll get a "good job", which doesn't matter much if you're a girl, because you're going to marry and have kids and nobody's going to take you very seriously anyway.'

'Yes, that's about how it *was*, hey?' said Maggie. 'I married the publican's son and you married a travelling salesman and we had kids.'

'He wasn't a travelling salesman!' I protested.

'Well, what was he then?'

'He was a sales engineer. He was in engineering.'

'He was a travelling salesman!' she insisted.

I couldn't be bothered arguing with her. I thought back to the time I'd met him, and then married him.

'When I married Hennie, I thought the search for "the one" was over. He was my knight in shining armour come to rescue me from the drudgery of being single and working in an office. He was so full of enthusiasm and optimism, he could take on the whole world for both of us. I felt like a tumble weed just blowing around in the wind, and that he caught me and held me steady so that I could grow roots.'

'And how did that work out?'

'Well, he didn't want me to go out to work, and I was quite happy to stay home and look after the kids – so quite nicely, really. It was like he was the one who went off into the world with a smile on his face to conquer the competition and win the contract, and I was the comfort provider when he came back home. And he needed that: to come home and recharge his batteries.'

'Yeah, just plug into the old charger!' She gave a resigned little grin.

I laughed. 'Less of the *old*, thank you! But well put! Couldn't have put it better myself!'

'Cheers!' we said, and drank.

'Do you think he loved you?' she asked.

'I don't know,' I said. 'I'd like to think he did, in his own way; for most of our marriage, anyway. But I don't think it was my idea of love.'

'Do you think men and women ever really do get on the same page on that?' she asked. 'Do they actually think they love women, or do they just say that because they'd be lonely without one?'

'No, it's 'cos they'd never find their socks,' I said.

'Well, yeah, that too. But seriously?'

'Yes, I'm sure they think they love their women. Some of the time, anyway. Why wouldn't they? They're not a different breed, you know. And "love" is just a stupid word anyway, isn't it? It doesn't mean anything. It's how you are together that counts. And that changes all the time.'

'Yeah, I know, but how often do you hear of a couple being married for donkeys' years and then *she* dies, and he finds another wife within a couple of months? How much did he love the first one if she's so easy to replace?'

'A lot, I should think, to want another one! And women do that, too. We all need somebody, don't we? Everybody needs a friend.'

'I've told Softlad that I'll come back and haunt him if he does that to me!' she said.

'Not "till death do us part" then?'

'Just let him try it!'

We were quiet for a moment.

'And what is Dicky Boy?' she asked.

'I'd like to think he's a friend, and a lover.'

'I can't imagine him being *romantic*,' she said, then, 'Oh, God! I don't even want to imagine it! He's hardly Mr Personality, is he!'

'Excuse me!' I said, trying to look shocked.

She just raised her eyebrows. 'Well, is he?'

'Is he what?'

'Romantic? Sexy?'

'Well, there's no firework display, but we manage a few sparklers!'

'Oh! God! Don't tell me. I don't want to know!'

'Well, don't ask then! And how about you and Alan?'

She shook her head. 'He's neither,' she said, flatly. She gave me her glass. 'Here. Your turn!'

I went to the kitchen and came back with the drinks.

'At least you had a cushy office job,' she said. 'At least you got to go to grammar school even!'

'Ja, by the skin of my teeth,' I said. 'I actually failed my eleven plus. I felt so awful letting my dad down, 'cos Cynthia and Brigit passed first time and I felt I had to, too. But I took it again at thirteen, and got in. I only found out years later that the first time I took it, when I was eleven, there were too many kids and not enough places that year. So, to choose who would go, they took the names of all who'd passed and allocated scholarships alphabetically, so anybody up the wrong end of the alphabet didn't get in.'

'How could you know that?'

'From Michael Wright's mum. He was the cleverest kid in the class and he also failed, so his mum queried it and that's what she was told. My mum only told me about it years later.'

'So what did you do in the meantime? Oh, was that when you went to that posh girls' school?'

'Yes. Dad sent me to Erindale Private School for Girls, where we learned to walk with a book on our head, talk with a plumb in our mouth, and how to cross our legs in a ladylike manner!'

'Of course you did!' she said, disgustedly. 'Well, you didn't learn the last one very well, did you – to cross your legs!' She smirked.

I shook my head at her. 'Cheeky mare!' But I couldn't resist a smile. 'I hadn't even kissed a boy at that stage,' I said. 'But the girls at grammar certainly taught me a thing or two.'

'I bet they did!' she said.

'Well, there were two types of girls back then, wasn't there? Virgins and sluts, and nothing in between. And both were just trying to catch themselves a husband, one way or another. You were a good little girl, weren't you? How old were you when you lost your virginity?'

She gave me a deadpan look.

'Oh, shit. Sorry,' I said. 'Okay, well how old were you when you had sex with a boy your own age for the first time?'

'The first real one was Colin,' she said.

'You're joking? Love-of-your-life Colin? What d'you mean "real" one?'

'Well, there were some awkward fumbles before that. But he was the first. And then there was Alan.'

'Is that it?' I asked. 'No, come on… there was…'

'Ssshh!' she whispered. 'Don't even say it.' Then in a normal voice, 'Yes. I told you, I was a Billy-no-friends. I went to secondary modern school – and they were rough!' She rolled her eyes to emphasise the point.

'I bet they weren't as rough as Pembie Grammar,' I said. 'It was an overspill school for Liverpool, and believe me, they don't come much rougher!'

'But I thought you had good friends there?'

'I did, they were like family. But they *were* rough.'

'I didn't even want to know about boys,' she said. 'All they wanted to do was look at my boobs, anyway.'

'Really? I would have died for big boobs.'

'No, you wouldn't, really. And besides, I'd been told to be "a good girl" and not to "get into trouble".'

'Ja, we had a few teenage pregnancies at school, too,' I said.

'It was the worst crime you could commit, wasn't it?' she said. 'And today nobody bats an eyelid. Now you've got young girls – and lads – looking at porn and sending each other pictures of their dangly bits on their phones. You've got online bullying and blackmail and teenage suicides. It's horrendous. And swipe-swipe dating sites and all that crap are just as bad.'

'Swipe-swipe dating sites?' I laughed.

'Piss off,' she said. 'You know what I mean.'

'I do,' I said. 'The world is a very different place, these days.'

'You want another?' she said, holding her glass up. 'Your turn!'

'No it's not. I went last time. It's yours!'

'I'm sure it's not, but I want a wee anyway. Give me your glass then.'

In a couple of minutes she came back with refills.

'So, did your dad see you go off to grammar school?' she asked as she came back in.

'Ja. He saw me go off in my bottle-green tunic that came way down past my knees, when the other girls wore theirs as miniskirts. And I know he was proud of me. But then he died about six weeks later.'

I shook my head, remembering something else.

'What?' she asked.

'When he died, I was off school for a few days, and when I went back on the Monday, the teacher wanted to know why I hadn't handed in my homework. There were three of us who hadn't, and we had to stand up to explain. The other two made their excuses and when it was my turn I just said, "My dad died," and there was this horrible, shocked hush 'cos nobody knew what to say. Not even the teacher. I felt like I'd grown two heads or something.'

'Well, yeah! I bet she didn't get that excuse too often! What did she say?'

'Well, I was still the new kid, too, so I don't think she knew what to say. She just told me to sit down again.'

'I remember the day *my* dad died,' Maggie said. 'Two men came to see my mum to tell her he'd had a heart attack at work. Then my aunty Cissy came and there was lots of crying and hugging, and all that crap. I went out into the garden. I was on the rope swing when the old woman next door, Mrs Rigby, came to hang out her washing. She saw me and said hello and asked me how I was. I said, "My dad's dead!" And she looked at me like, horrified, and said, "You wicked girl! How can you say such a thing!", and went back into her house. I'll never forget it! She probably thought I'd killed him or something.'

We laughed.

'Were you sad when your dad died?' I asked.

'No. I don't know what I felt, to be honest,' she said. 'But no, I don't think so.'

'Ja, I know what you mean. I felt the same. People expect you to be sad, but you half expect him to just walk back in again, somehow, hey?'

'Really?' she said. 'I'm pretty sure I didn't want mine to.'

I understood why, and smiled at her.

'Did you ever tell your mum about him?' I asked.

She stared at the floor and took a long time to answer.

'It wouldn't have changed anything if I had.'

'You didn't tell her?' I asked, amazed.

'What for? Dad told me I mustn't because it would upset her and she would be jealous. Because I, after all, was his "special girl". And even if she'd have known, she couldn't have left him. Where would she go? It was his house, his money. He'd never actually married her. He'd never *actually* divorced his first wife,' she said, rolling her eyes. 'That's why *she* got everything and my mum got nothing when he died.' She shook her head. 'It's all in the past now. You have to get on with it, don't you?'

'If that had been you, or me, we would have killed him. You know that.'

She nodded, and we sat quietly a moment.

'So, come on! What am I going to tell Madam Bickerstaff? What am I going to do? You know what, that woman has only been there a few months and it just isn't right that she can just dismiss me like this. I've been doing that job for years, and given it my best, too. Who is she to come in now and say it's not good enough? And what am I going to do all day when I'm stuck here with knobhead?' she asked again.

'Oh, the days will fill up, don't you worry. I bet you'll be seeing a lot more of little Julia!'

She sipped her vodka. 'D'you ever feel that life is passing you by? Like, time's running out and you haven't done anything?' she asked.

'Yes. Of course. What is it you feel *you* haven't done?'

'I don't know,' she said. 'If I knew that, I would have done it, wouldn't I? When you're working you don't even think about such things. You just work.'

'Well, very soon you're going to have all the time in the world to think of those things – and to do them.'

'You know,' she said. 'When you're working, there's always something to look forward to, isn't there? Putting money away for next year's holiday, or to buy something for Christmas. And then what? You give up work and there's nothing. No holidays because you haven't got the cash to splash anyway. So, you sit and watch the telly and then you die! What's that all about? All that do well at school, get a good job, find a good husband. What was all that about? What for?'

'So what are you waiting for? What do you want to happen?' I asked.

'Nothing! That's just the point! Nothing's going to happen now, is it? It's too late! You scrat around all your life working your arse off, hoping that someday things will change and you'll be happy. But it doesn't happen. And then they put you on a three-day week!'

'Life's a bitch, and then you die.'

'Exactly! What will you do when your mum dies?'

'Hopefully start a new life with Richard.'

She gave me a sour look. 'Good luck with that one.'

'You know,' I said. 'It's no good hoping things are just going to happen, or get better, or that somebody else is going to make you happy. You can't *wait* to be happy – it's just something you have to *be*. It's a choice you make when you wake up in the morning. To hell with everything that gets you down, and if you don't like your life, change it!'

'That's easy for you to say, you're a free agent.'

'There's the door!'

'It's too late now,' she answered.

'It's never too late. D'you know that time doesn't even exist? Did you know that? The way we measure time – that only exists on this earth.'

She looked at me as if I'd just gone mad. 'What?' She scowled.

'Time doesn't really exist,' I repeated. 'There's only *right now*.'

'What?'

'Do you think cows in a field ask each other what time it is?'

'What? Well, I know time doesn't exist for you, maybe, but it does for the rest of us. Cows?'

'Time is a man-made thing – a way to measure the schedule – go to school, go to work, get married, have kids, work. And then at the end they tell you you're too old to be of use anymore. And by then you just don't know what to do with yourself anyway.'

She just frowned at me. 'So?'

'Well, now you're off the schedule. You don't have to *do* all the time. You can just *be* instead. Sit on a rock and watch the waves for a whole day if you want, or watch how snow falls, or how a flower turns to the sun. Why don't we get time to just *be*, and know who or what *we* are? We're like robots. But now is your chance to be human again.'

Maggie was frowning now. 'What? I know who I am, thank you very much!'

'If you knew who you were, you would know what you wanted to spend your time on.'

'I do know what I want to spend time on. I want to spend it with my grandchildren.'

'There you go then. That's where your passion is. That's what you love. And that will make you happy.'

'"Happy" is another stupid word like "love", isn't it? Doesn't really mean anything.'

I just looked at her, lost for words for a second or two.

'Doesn't mean it doesn't exist. But you're right,' I said. 'It's just easier to get a Labrador, isn't it?' I laughed.

'Yeah. And at least dogs love you back,' she said. 'Unconditionally!'

'You know,' I said. 'You *have* done something with your life. Your years at the hospice weren't wasted. They've been appreciated by every old lady or man that you've spent time chatting with. But it wasn't so much about the shepherd's pie as about the teaspoon of kindness you gave them when they needed it most in their life. That's no small thing. And Madam Bickerstaff can't take that away from you or from them, not with all the scientifically proven, suitably balanced, nutritious and cost-effective meals under the sun.'

She looked at me with squinty eyes over the top of her glass. *Are those tears?*

'So come on, you still haven't answered me about what I'm going to do stuck at home all day with knobhead.'

I didn't know what to tell her. 'You could always get a dog,' I offered.

She raised her brows in surprise, her eyes piercing into me.

'Is that all you've got?' she said, 'Sit on a fuckin' rock and *be* – or get a fuckin' dog?'

Something about the way she said it just made me burst out laughing.

And she laughed with me. 'You are *so* fuckin' weird, you,' she said. 'Wierdo!'

Chapter Twenty-Three

It was about that time that Chrissy phoned to invite her father and me to Izzy's fourth birthday party. She invited Erin also, but she had a date with Dylan on the day.

So, after breakfast the following Saturday, Richard and I set out on the three-hour drive over the Pennines to Doncaster. It was a frosty morning with fog on the motorway slowing the traffic down, but it was cosy in the Saab. We eventually left the motorway and were travelling (for me) unfamiliar roads, singing along with Meatloaf and sharing a bag of liquorice allsorts. We climbed higher up onto the Pennines on roads that wound through villages of terraced houses and little cottages made of grey granite and slate. Then, leaving civilisation behind, we climbed towards the peak and, through wispy mist, looked down on miles of desolate, dark hills and moorland. Soggy sheep and cows peered at us, and it reminded me of Jasper Carrott's song about sheep and cows. Richard knew it too, which prompted him to sing a selection of his own from his rugby days.

By the time we reached the highest peaks the sun was trying to break through, and sent dramatic shafts of light slanting down to illuminate patches of emerald green hillside and purple heather here and there. We started to descend around hairpin bends and at one point, at the top end of a big lake, we passed over an old stone bridge that sat just inches above the water.

Eventually, we hit civilisation again, and pretty soon found our way to the community hall where the party was to be held, pulling up next to a dark green Jaguar in the car park. The boot was open and a woman was bent into it trying to lift something out. She turned awkwardly to see who had parked next to her, and gave a kind of exasperated smile as she recognised Richard.

'That's Victoria,' he said. 'The dragon lady!'

I'd already guessed.

As Richard got out of the car, I heard her say, 'Here, make yourself useful.' He went to take a bundle of folding chairs out of her arms and she offered her cheek to be kissed at the same time. He obliged.

Her eyes drifted in my direction as I joined them, but without acknowledging me she pointed to an open door.

'Just take them in there, you'll see where they go.'

'And hello to you, too!' said Richard.

'Oh, sorry! It's been one of those days,' she said, wiping her hands on her hips.

Richard smiled indulgently and turned to me. 'Natalie, this is Vicky; Vicky, this is Natalie.'

'Hello,' she said, beaming and holding out her hand.

'Pleased to meet you,' I replied, shaking her hand as firmly as she did mine.

'Me too. It's nice to put a face to a name, isn't it? No doubt you've heard mine? The *dragon lady*?'

'I have, indeed.' I smiled.

She had an open, no-nonsense face, and as per her reputation, I could well imagine her speaking her mind. She was a big woman, tall and sturdily built. More sturdy than feminine, but she obviously took pride in her looks, even if she was a bit Miss Marple-ish.

She turned back into the boot again.

'Do you think you could take this in for me?'

She dumped a cardboard box into my arms, which I caught on reflex.

'Of course,' I said, and followed Richard.

It was a typical village hall and a few mums and small children had already arrived, their voices echoing in its expanse. The girls were there: Chrissy busy putting food out on trestle tables, and Lea sitting cross-legged on the floor, blowing up balloons, which bobbed in a colourful pool around her. They waved when they saw us walk in.

Vicky followed, carrying the birthday cake, and immediately took charge.

'No, wait, Chrissy! Where's those plastic table cloths I bought? They must go on first.'

Richard carried his bundle over to where another man was putting chairs out. They shook hands and started chatting and I presumed that was Tom.

Lea took the box out of my arms. 'Hello, Nat, how're you doing?' she asked. 'What have we got here? Ah! Prizes… and party packs.'

I chatted with her and Chrissy a while, and after being told there was nothing I could do, I walked over to the men.

'Here she is,' announced Richard. 'Natalie, this is Tom. Tom, Natalie.'

Tom, a tall, round-shouldered man with kind eyes and a weak smile, offered his hand. It felt limp and cold compared with his wife's.

Then Izzy came hurtling over and threw herself at Richard's legs, nearly felling him, followed by two or three other highly excited little people in pink party dresses. He picked Izzy up and hugged her, but after a few seconds she wriggled free and ran off up the hall, followed by her screaming entourage. They fell into the balloons, and squealed with delight as Lea chased them away again.

When all the guests had arrived, Chrissy and Lea took over organising the first game of Simon Says, and Vicky came over to join us. She offered us a cup of tea.

'Is there nothing a little stronger?' asked Richard.

Vicky shook her head. 'Afraid not! There's orange juice?'

The two men looked at each other and Richard spoke.

'How about we leave you ladies to it and we go…'

'Don't even think about it!' Vicky interrupted. 'It's your granddaughter's birthday and you're not going to the pub!'

He looked at me for a second opinion.

'Don't even *think* about it!' I repeated, but for totally different reasons.

So, Richard, Tom and I sat on the cold plastic seats for a couple of hours, trying to keep smiles on our faces and now and again exchanging 'aren't they cute' type chit chat. I was just glad I'd put on my denims and boots, and that my jacket was long enough to cover my bum.

Vicky and the girls joined us now and again to take a break from the mayhem. Trouble broke out a couple of times because Izzy, assuming she could do anything she liked on her birthday, became a little tyrant. Firstly, she tried to dictate who was *out* when she said they were, and then demanded that she, and only she, should get to unwrap the layers of paper around the pass the parcel. She threw a major tantrum until Grandma Vicky waded in, and fixed her with 'the look'. Izzy was immediately quiet. Her chin fell to her chest, eyebrows knitted together and bottom lip curled outwards. After a few seconds of that she sneaked a look up at Grandma again, but seeing that the death stare was still upon her, she turned and ran over to Grandpa Richard and climbed up on his knee.

She just wanted to bury her face in his shirt, but she had a bit of a snotty nose at this stage and Richard held her at arm's length until I passed him a tissue. He gently wiped the little girl's nose and explained the rules of pass the parcel to her, after which she was quite happy to give it another go.

I wished Maggie and Erin could see Richard like this, with his family; see his good side.

Eventually, when all the sandwiches and cup-cakes were either eaten or crushed into the floor, all presents opened and balloons popped, and when weariness and tears were replacing hysteria, it was time to call it a day. Thank goodness! It felt so good to get up off the chair that I even helped clear up.

That done, Vicky suggested that we all go for a drink together and Richard gave a hopeful little nod in my direction. It sounded like a good idea to me. Apart from a couple of egg sandwiches and a piece of birthday cake, I hadn't eaten since breakfast, so I suggested we might get some pub grub before heading home. Vicky thought that an excellent idea as she didn't feel like cooking, either.

Tom suggested the Horse and Hounds, just up the road, and Lea, Chrissy and Izzy also came along. As we walked into the pub there was a fire crackling away brightly in an old stone fireplace, and I made a beeline for it, claiming the closest table with its squishy sofas and chairs. It was so nice to be warm again, and I felt even better after having eaten their special of beef stew and dumplings.

It hadn't been our intention to stay long, but after a couple of gin and tonics, Vicky became very chatty. She asked me all about myself, after which the conversation became a two-way 'remember when' session between her and Richard, with the girls adding the odd comment.

Eventually she was telling us how she had been a married woman working as a barmaid when Richard had first walked into the pub and into her life. She told us all about the hot and steamy affair that had followed, and how she had then fallen pregnant.

'Yes. I'm pretty sure that Lea was conceived at that Christmas party, or should I say, on the back seat of the bus that took us there! D'you remember, Richard?'

'How could he forget,' said Tom, 'when you remind him of it every time?' He looked at her with weary eyes.

But she ignored him and carried on. 'And I was having the second one before he left home and married me,' she said, looking at me.

'I believe so,' I answered. 'And you organised a surprise wedding?'

'Yes, I had to,' she said. 'Because if his mother had heard about it, it wouldn't have happened! But there were only a few people there. Not many to surprise, really.'

'I was surprised.' Richard smiled. 'I didn't know!'

'Oh, rubbish!' said Vicky. 'Of course you did. You paid for it.'

'Yes,' he said, 'I ended up paying for it, but I didn't know about it till the last minute, did I?'

Vicky was about to reply, but Richard stood up and asked if anybody was ready for another drink, so she turned her attention to finishing hers.

'I'll help you,' offered Tom, and the two of them went off to the bar.

'So, *was* it a surprise to him?' I asked.

'No, of course not,' she said. 'It was his idea! But he likes to kid himself. His mother was something else again. She tried her best to get shut of me. Has he told you about her?'

'Not much,' I replied.

'I'd go round there to see him and she'd tell me he'd gone out to see some other girl, and he'd be up the stairs in his room. Or I'd phone and she'd tell me he wasn't there, when he was!'

'She sounds very strange,' I said.

Vicky nodded. 'She got me to bake him a chocolate cake once, telling me he loved chocolate cake when she knew he hated it. He doesn't like cake at all.'

'And didn't she spill the beans about you and Dad to your first husband also, Arnie was it?' asked Lea.

'That's right. She did,' said Vicky, nodding again.

'I can only very vaguely remember her,' said Lea. 'Only when she came to us on holiday and died of a heart attack. I remember that.'

'Do you?' asked Vicky in amazement. 'You must have only been about four or five then?'

Without waiting for an answer, Vicky remembered something else and turned to me again. 'Did he tell you about the time she slit her wrists in the bath?'

'No!' I said, shocked.

'Yes. He came home from work to find her passed out in a bath full of bloody water. Didn't cut them deep enough, though, more's the pity.'

'*No!*' I said, my jaw dropping open. 'I knew she'd threatened, but…'

'That was because he told her he was leaving home,' she said. 'She had a weird way with her, very possessive. Something a bit unhealthy about it.'

'Was she naked?' I asked.

'Starkers!' replied Vicky, and mouthed the words, 'Very strange old girl,' as Richard and Tom returned.

Eventually Izzy fell asleep and Chrissy said she was going to take her home to bed. Lea was driving them, so she was leaving as well, and Richard carried the little girl out to the car for them. Two minutes later, Vicky realised that the snuggle blanket had been left behind, so quickly took it out to them, leaving Tom and me alone at the table.

'So! Natalie!' he said. 'How long have you been going out with Richard?'

'About eighteen months, now.' I smiled.

'You mustn't mind Vicky going on about them in the early days, you know, they're long gone now.'

'Oh, I know. It doesn't bother me, really. I'm fascinated to find out all this stuff about him. And I think it's nice that they can still be friends. I can't understand how they could have just drifted apart?'

His kind eyes studied me closely. 'Is that what he told you?' he asked. 'Is that why they broke up?'

'Apparently. Why, what did you think it was?'

He looked at me for a long moment and I thought he was about to say something. But then he just stood up.

'I'll get another round in,' he said.

'I'll help you,' I offered, starting to get up.

He smiled. 'No, you stay here and keep the table. I can manage.'

He stooped to pick up empty glasses off the table, and with them dangling off each hand, he looked at me again.

'Maybe you should ask him again,' he said.

I looked at him quizzically, but he just raised the glasses in the air a little and said something about his fingers, and turned and walked to the bar.

Sticky fingers? Did he just say 'sticky fingers'? Was he talking about Richard or the glasses? No, surely not. He must have meant the glasses? Theft? Surely that's not what he meant? I must have misheard. Must have misunderstood.

In any case, I would never know, because at that moment Richard and Vicky came shivering back into the bar and sat down again. Tom came back with the drinks and didn't even give me a second look.

Soon it was time to call it a night and Vicky kindly offered us her spare room if we wanted to stay over, but Richard said he would rather get back.

'Are you sure?' I asked.

'I'm fine!'

'I can never tell whether he's had too many,' I said to Vicky and Tom who were watching the exchange.

'Oh, I know!' agreed Vicky. 'The only way I knew was because he would get very soppy and romantic and wanting to declare undying love when he'd had too many. And he snored twice as badly.'

Richard just smiled benignly and I smiled too, but my thoughts went back to how soppy and romantic he'd been at the concert in the park, and the cooler box full of beers he'd had.

I excused myself to go to the ladies' quickly before we left, and Vicky got up to come with me. I was already washing my hands when she came out of the stall and came to wash hers.

'I hope you don't mind me rabbiting on about Richard and me and what we used to get up to on the back seats of busses?' She smiled at me through the mirror.

'"Rabbiting" being the operative word?' I smiled back.

'Oh. Sorry! Was it that bad?'

'I'm joking!' I said, and smiled. 'Don't worry, I understand. I was married for nearly twenty years to my ex, and had three kids with him. I know how it is. They get under your skin, don't they?'

'Yeah! Like a rash!' she laughed. 'Bless them! But as long as you know it was all in the past.'

'Yes, don't worry. I understand.'

'You should have seen him back then,' she said. 'He was so handsome and smart. And so romantic! He used to do this little thing – kiss the palm of my hand. Oh! I just fell head over heels for him, even though I was a married woman.'

I don't know why, but that came like a gut punch. The thought of Richard kissing the palm of her hand was far worse than any other image of them together. I felt sick! I gave her a smile; hopefully, a convincing one. But it probably wasn't.

Ten minutes later we had said our goodbyes and were ready to go. It was seven o'clock and Richard thought we would be home by ten. He buckled his seat belt, then rubbed my knee as if to warm it.

'You okay?' he asked.

'Yes. I'm fine,' I said, surprised that he asked.

'You're very quiet?'

'I'm just tired.'

I snoozed most of the way home. I kept my eyes closed anyway, because I didn't feel like talking to him. I went over again all that had been said, and I felt angry, betrayed almost, and I knew that was ridiculous. And here we were driving home and I couldn't say a word because I *was* being ridiculous. He knew something was wrong, but I could never share that with him.

And 'sticky fingers'? What the hell was that about?

***

The year was rapidly drawing to a close. Mum turned ninety in November and we decided to give her a little party. Well, not so much a party as an open day, when friends and family could just drop in for a while and have a cup of tea and a chat with her.

A couple of weeks before, I went through her phone book and sent out invitations to anybody she agreed to. I ordered a birthday cake, and made all the finger foods.

She put on her pink dress (of which, she told me, the queen had one very similar), pink beads and earrings, and a dab of Blue Grass perfume. Erin brushed her hair, and she sat primly on the sofa ready to hold court, indeed, looking very regal.

Richard was at work but had arranged for a bouquet of roses to be delivered, with which she was delighted. With a wave of dismissal, she sent me to the kitchen to put them in water. I gave her a box of her favourite dark chocolates. Boring, I know, but she said there was nothing she needed.

The first to arrive was the lady from across the road whose name I had forgotten, but I remembered her face because whenever I mowed the front lawn she would come and timidly ask how Mum was, but never wanted to come in and 'disturb her'. They hadn't spoken since Mum had given up walking Emma, so they had a good catch-up session. As she did with someone called Joan, who she used to work with once upon a time.

My cousins Sally and Jane came. They had been to see Mum a couple of times already, and always came huddling together and giggling behind their hands. Their brother Peter came later that day, making sure his sisters had left before he would come in. They had not spoken for over seven years.

Cousin Robert came, looking very old and bent, and cousin Amelia also, her large frame wafting along in a cloud of billowing silk blouse and heavy perfume. Husband Graham tagged along behind looking harassed. And of course, there was Barbara and Arthur. One person conspicuous by her absence was Brigit – but no surprise there.

Even the window cleaner and his son stopped and had a cup of tea and piece of cake with her, as was their usual practice, birthday or not. The father was a lean, rough-looking old guy with tanned, leathery skin, a few missing teeth and sharp, ice-blue eyes that didn't miss a thing. Barbara-next-door called him a gypsy, and certainly wouldn't let them into *her* house. But Mum, perhaps through loneliness, allowed them to sit in the garden for a cuppa and a chat, and in winter at the kitchen table, as was the case today.

Mid-morning, we sang 'Happy Birthday' to her and cut the cake, and with a little help from Arthur, she blew out the candles. In between visitors, she took cat naps. We made far too much food of course, but Richard helped that situation when he came home from work.

Mum was in bed by eight o'clock. It had been a busy day for her. And Richard went off at about nine, leaving Erin and me to sit by the fire and have a chat about the extended family she had met for the first time that day. She told me what she knew about

Dylan's family. She was to meet his mother that weekend and was quite nervous about it.

Soon enough though we were both yawning, and decided to call it a day.

As we took our coffee cups to the kitchen, Erin asked, 'Are you okay, Mom?'

'Course I am. Why?'

'I don't know. You just seem a bit off.'

I gave her a tired smile and said, 'No, I'm fine.'

She looked at me unconvinced. 'You know you can tell me anything, don't you?'

'That's my line. But yes, I know. And I will... would... I'm just a bit tired, that's all.'

And then suddenly there was this strange little silence. An elephant had come into the room, and we both knew its name was Richard. At that moment, I thought it was something she wanted me to tell her. Looking back, I realise it was something she wanted to tell me. But instead, we kissed goodnight and I went to bed.

Chapter Twenty-Four

Erin decided she and I were going to put the Christmas tree up together, which was something we two had done since she was a little girl, discussing each bauble, bought or made at school, and each having its own memory. This year we would have to make do with Mum's baubles, most of which were much posher than our hotch-potch assortment back home.

We had just finished and turned off the lounge lights to admire the tree twinkling in all its glory when the motion sensor light came on in the garden. In the centre of the lawn stood a large red fox with a black and white face, sniffing at some bread.

'Oh, isn't he beautiful!' I said. It wasn't one of the scabby little grey foxes that slink around the bins. This was as big as an Alsatian, strong, muscular and proud as he stood still, alert, watching for danger.

'He's magnificent!'

'Isn't he,' I agreed. 'Richard said he saw a big red fox out by the gate the other night. I bet it's the same one.'

Then in an instant, he trotted off again.

'He's gone,' I said. 'Off on his travels.'

Erin sipped her Baileys thoughtfully. 'I saw a nice job online today.'

'Oh, yes? What was it?'

'It was for a claims administrator.'

'Okay,' I said, happy and surprised. 'You got your mojo back?'

'I'm not sure. I've never done claims administration before, but they do say they give training.'

'Look, after what you were doing at the last place, this would be a doddle. You're intelligent, and you're a people person! Why don't you send your CV in? No harm in giving it a shot.'

'Mmm, I'm not sure if I'm up for that yet, and it's nice working at the shop; no worries, no stress.'

'Well, what does the advert say?'

She found it on the laptop and read it out loud to me.

'So, what do you think?' she asked, when she'd finished.

'I think it sounds made for you. You've got the right skills, and that's a very good salary!'

'D'you think? The skills bit, I mean?'

'Of course!'

'Well, maybe I'll send my CV in, just to see what happens,' she said, with a little sparkle in her eye.

By the following afternoon the agency handling the position had phoned her and asked her to go in for a preliminary interview. She was flustered; it was getting real now.

'But I don't have any work clothes!' she said.

'So? We can soon fix that. Let's go shopping.'

'But they want me to go in tomorrow. I don't know where it is. I don't know Chester.'

'Have you got an address? I've got a satnav.'

'Could you take me?' she asked, shyly.

'Of course! Come, let's go shopping!'

In the past she wouldn't have batted an eyelash at taking herself to an interview, especially one just with an agency. But it would take time to get her back to that place again.

That evening I told Richard all about it and he admitted that it sounded like a good job, especially the salary. But he wasn't impressed when I told him I was driving her there.

'She's a big girl now,' he said. 'She doesn't need babysitting. If she can't even find her own way there, she's not going to be able to do a job like that, is she?'

He did not see her the next day dressed in black pencil skirt, black and white spotted blouse and heels. She looked every bit the part.

She gave me a twirl. 'What do you think?'

'Miss Sandton City is back!' I said, approvingly.

She smiled at the reference to the up-market office block she used to work in.

'Thanks, Mom, for all you've done for me the past few months. I know I've not been the easiest person to live with and I'm sorry for all the hassle.'

'Agh! Erin. Don't worry, my sweetheart. We all hit the wall now and again, and that's what moms are for, to help you pick yourself up again. And just look at you!'

'I love you, Mom,' she said, and gave me a hug.

A while later, she got out of the car, straightened her skirt and walked purposefully towards the agency door. I sat and waited for her, and after an hour she climbed back in the car looking wide-eyed and panicky.

'How'd it go?' I asked.

'They want me to go for the interview *now*! They've phoned the insurance company and I have an interview in an hour and a half's time!'

'Great! They must have liked you.'

'No, Mom. It's not great. I can't do this. I'm not ready for this yet. Can we just go home? Please?'

'Well, tell you what. Let's go for a cup of coffee and you can tell me what happened so far, and then you can decide then what you want to do.'

She agreed to that, and conveniently enough we were already parked outside a little café. After a cappuccino and a toasted tea cake she relaxed and considered the possibility of going to the interview, which was just further up the same street.

'What have you got to lose?' I asked. 'While you've got your corporate clothes on and look fabulous, let's make the most of it. And what's the worst that can happen? You make a total idiot of yourself! So?'

'Will you wait outside for me?'

'The get-away car?'

'Better keep the engine running!'

An hour later she walked back to the car with a long, confident stride and a smile on her face.

'So?' I asked, as she climbed back in.

'Ah, Mom! It was so nice! The people are so friendly. Gorgeous offices, everybody seems chilled and happy. The boss seems lovely. Oh, this is so my job, Mom!'

'Really? How did you do? D'you think you've got it?'

'I do!' she said. 'This is my job, I'm telling you.'

And she went on to tell me all about the interview.

'Well, it all sounds good and very promising. But don't get your hopes up too high. Just in case.'

'I know,' she said. 'And the agency has more jobs for me if this one doesn't work out.'

Then her face broke into a grin again. 'But this is *so* my job!'

***

'How did the interview go?' asked Richard over tea. 'Did you get the job?'

'I hope so,' she said. 'It was such a nice place, and nice people, and I did okay on the tests they gave me.'

Now dressed in her jeans, she no longer looked very corporate, and he gave a little sniff of disdain.

'Well good luck! I hope you get it,' he said, popping a piece of sausage into his mouth and staring out the window.

Erin and I shared a little smile.

Two days later, Erin called me from work, and before I could say a word, I heard her scream, 'I got it! I got it! I got it!', and my heart burst with pride for her.

She told her granny that evening, and Mum was just as pleased for her. She stroked Erin's hair and said, 'See, I told you so, didn't I?'

Richard couldn't keep the look of amazement off his face, but he seemed to mean it when he told her, 'Well done!' And that was nothing to the surprise he had the first time he saw her in her work clothes.

***

It was nearly Christmas. Erin and I spent a day together in Chester, shopping. I didn't seem to see much of her at all, these days, and it was good to have her to myself for the day.

I didn't buy much. Richard and I had agreed to just buy each other little token presents and to save the money towards the next holiday and 'other things', which I took to mean our engagement rings on our birthdays! What an exciting year it was going to be! Boy! If I only I'd known!

We *did* buy each other Christmas cards, and again, Richard gave me a big, embossed card with the double centre page, all four pages filled with wonderfully soppy words. It was beautiful.

Erin gave me a scarf that she had crocheted herself in shades of baby pink and purple. It was like gossamer, soft, light, and warm. So her! It was gorgeous.

She examined the new bike seat that Richard had bought for me, and seemed rather less than impressed.

'And this?' she asked.

I had to laugh at the expression on her face. 'It's a new bike seat; wider. More comfortable for my fat bum!'

'Is that what *he* said?' she asked, angrily.

'No, it's what I said,' I lied. Well, he hadn't actually used the word 'fat'.

She put the bike seat down.

'Where is he?' She looked up at me and there was sadness in her eyes, and the elephant was back in the room. There was something she wasn't saying, and just as I was about to ask her, Mum shuffled her way slowly into the room.

'Merry Christmas, Granny,' said Erin, standing to give her a hug. She gave Mum her present, a lipstick. I would never have thought to buy Mum a lipstick. She only wore it to go next door, these days. But she was absolutely delighted with it. Not so much with the new slippers I had bought her.

***

A few days later Erin and I were alone together, and had the opportunity to talk. We'd just had breakfast and were sat in the kitchen having a second cup of coffee. She'd met Dylan's family and was telling me all about them. They sounded more of a clan, really, which came together at Christmas, and which had welcomed her with open arms.

'And how are things going with Dylan?' I said. 'He seems well and truly smitten with you.'

'Oh, he's lovely, Mom. He really is. He's so kind and *there* for me. Sometimes I think it's all too good to be true.'

She smiled happily and her fingers played with the silver and crystal pendant he'd bought her.

'That's good. He's a nice guy. And I hope he knows how lucky he is!'

She pulled a funny face. 'And you and Richard? How are you two? No more marriage plans?'

'We talked about it on holiday. I think he would have been happy to ask the captain to marry us right there and then.'

'You didn't *actually* consider it, did you?'

'No, he didn't *actually* ask. Just hinted. But I wouldn't do that. I'd never do that. We agreed to buy each other engagement rings for our birthdays this year, though. And I think I'd be happy to stay permanently engaged!'

'Do you love him, Mom?' she asked, sadly.

'Erin, what is it? What is it you need to say?'

She bit her bottom lip, a dead giveaway!

'Come on,' I said. 'Tell me.'

'Mom, I can't. It's something Lea told me while you were away. She told me when she was drunk one night, and the next morning begged me to forget it. If Richard found out, he'd kill her. Or never speak to her again.'

'But you're going to tell me anyway, so spill!'

'It's something you need to know,' she admitted. 'Do you promise never to tell him you know?'

I couldn't promise that. 'I promise never to tell him who told me,' I said, a sick, anxious feeling starting to churn in my stomach.

'Or mention Lea's name?'

'Or mention Lea's name,' I agreed.

She thought about that, then took a deep breath.

'He's been to prison,' she said.

There was silence for a couple of seconds while I processed that.

'What for?'

'He went to prison for eighteen months for fraud. You know when he was a so-called financial adviser? Well, he'd been diddling his clients out of their money in some way and he got caught and sent to prison. He even forged Vicky's signature on something and nearly got her arrested, too! That's why they broke up.'

I was so shocked, I didn't know what to say. But the words 'sticky fingers' came to mind.

'Mom, are you okay? You've gone very pale?'

'I'm fine. It's just that… what? Can you believe that? Surely not?' I was struggling to grasp this information. And yet I didn't doubt it for one minute.

'Mom, the police came when they were all sitting having tea. They put him in handcuffs and took him away.'

'If that were true, there's no way Vicky would still be friendly with him today? She wouldn't even be talking to him.'

'She didn't for years, apparently. But this was, like, fifteen years ago. And I do believe it, Mom. I think it tells you what kind of guy he is. Doesn't it?'

'Sticky fingers,' I said, almost to myself.

'What?'

I told her about the conversation I had with Tom.

'You see!' she said. 'That's why their marriage broke up. And it's also why he went back to being a lorry driver, because he was not allowed to work in financial services anymore.'

'Oh. God!' I said, the whole picture coming together in front of my eyes. 'And he didn't tell me!'

'What do you see in him, Mom?'

I couldn't answer.

'He doesn't respect you. D'you know that? You know the first pub quiz I came to with you, at the White Horse?'

'Yes.'

'He kept rolling his eyes at you behind your back. I smiled at first, thinking he was just joking. But he kept doing it, and it wasn't funny. I gave him a dirty look in the end, to make him stop.'

'Bugger!' I said, offended. 'But, there again, Richard thinks everyone is stupid, doesn't he?'

'And you're okay with that?'

I just shrugged. 'It's his problem, isn't it?'

'You have to be careful of this guy, Mom. He could be a con man. You'll be coming into an inheritance soon.'

'Oh, surely you don't think that? It's only a little bungalow. If that's what he was about, I'm sure he would have gone after someone with more money.'

'It's more than he's got, Mom. I don't think he even owned that flat he was living in. I don't trust him one little bit, and I don't think you should.'

'Well, if he's not been in trouble for the last fifteen years, that says something, doesn't it?'

'Yes, that they did well to keep him out of financial services. I don't know, Mom. I just think you should be very, very careful. And *please* don't marry him!'

'I will be very careful. I promise.'

'And don't say how you heard all this?'

'Of course not. It could've been anyone at the party!'

'Are you going to ask him about it?'

'Oh, yes! Maybe not immediately. But I need to hear what he has to say. And why he didn't tell me.'

She didn't reply, and when I looked at her, I could see there was something else she was holding back.

'Oh, no!' I said. 'What else?'

'No, nothing. Don't worry! But…'

'What, for heaven's sake?'

'What does he do on the laptop every morning?'

'His admin. Answers his emails and things. Why?'

'What admin? What emails? He's a truck driver!'

'I don't know! Why does it bother you?'

'Because a couple of times when I've walked in on him, he's put the lid down pretty quickly.'

'Maybe it's private?' I said. 'What? D'you think he's trying to hide something?'

'Maybe. Is he still on *Soulmates.com*?'

'I hope not,' I said. 'But I'm past playing games. If he's

looking for someone better, then he can; and good luck to him.'

'And it doesn't bother you that he may be looking?'

'You don't know that he is! But yes, I guess it would. But if they're like that, you can't stop them. If you try, they just hide it better. But I don't think he is.'

'Have you ever walked in on him while he's on the laptop in the morning?'

'Not for ages,' I said, shaking my head. 'He brings me coffee in bed. There's no need for me to get up.'

'Maybe you should try it,' she said.

I sighed. 'You know what? You think you know somebody, and then something's said and within a minute, everything changes. Life is suddenly different. I thought he and I had something good going. I hate to think that we haven't. I just can't believe it.'

'I'm sorry to dump this on you, Mom, but better you know. You don't need a flamin' con artist, do you? And if he is? There could be a really nice guy waiting out there for you. And you're wasting time on *him*.'

'No, whatever happens with Richard, there'll be no more after him. I can't go back on that dating site now and start all over again, going on dates and trying to make small talk with strange men. No. Richard's the last.'

***

New Year found Richard and me in the White Horse, which was absolutely heaving, hot and noisy. I wasn't in the mood for it and half wanted to stay at home, but Mum said she'd be going to bed at nine, so I had no excuse.

The whole pub came to a standstill to count down the last ten seconds to midnight, and Richard, with that soppy expression on his face that heralded his 'romantic mood', squeezed my hand and leaned forwards to kiss me. I smiled and kissed him. But it wasn't half as romantic as it should have been. But it *was* New Year, and there was certainly much drunken kissing going on all around us!

'Happy New Year, darlin',' he said. 'This year's going to be the best!'

I smiled and nodded. *I so hope so*, I thought.

***

The house became quiet once the holidays were over and Erin and Richard were at work all day. Once Mum got up, of course, the TV would go on, loud. But Mum had been tired lately, and sometimes didn't get up until midday on these cold mornings.

I sat at the kitchen table next to the radiator, looking at my laptop. There was a shortcut button that took me directly to my email account, but there was no such button for Richard's account. Not that I would look at his emails, anyway.

Immediately, I realised that I was doubting him, and knew that if I allowed doubt to creep in, I would be finding evidence of crimes that didn't exist. I knew me.

I had to talk to him about being in prison. If I could do that, I'd have a better idea of what was going on and my imagination wouldn't try to fill in the gaps.

I'd pick my moment and steer the conversation in that direction. I'd be very calm, matter-of-fact... and subtle. Maybe Friday night in the White Horse would be a good time.

And meanwhile, I would get up and walk into the kitchen one morning, while he was doing his admin. Erin was going out with Dylan that evening, and she told me that she would be staying over at his place that night, going straight to work from there. So, that would be a perfect opportunity for me to walk in on Richard on the laptop.

***

I would never make a spy. I'd be the world's worst.

Richard brought me my coffee as usual, and I lay there thinking about following him back to the kitchen. I gave him a minute, then told myself it was now or never as I nervously fumbled with the belt of my dressing gown. My heart started beating so fast I was sure he would hear it.

I went very quietly through the lounge. The kitchen door was closed, which was unusual. I walked in as nonchalantly as possible, yawning and pretending to be oblivious of what he was doing in there. But he wasn't even sat at the laptop, which stood open on one side of the kitchen table while he sat at the other side, reading something off his cell phone, which was plugged in and recharging on that side. The laptop was sideways on to me and I couldn't see what was open on it.

But his reaction told me he didn't want me to. He froze, but didn't say a word.

'I fancied a biscuit,' I said, rummaging in the cupboard for the biscuits. 'Why's the door closed?'

He was watching me intently, and he was not usually one for holding eye contact for any length of time. Normally, a quick glance is all. But not this time. He didn't take his eyes off me.

'To keep the warmth in. Why?'

'Oh, no reason. I'm just not used to seeing it closed.'

There was definitely something wrong. I could feel it. His face was without expression and yet the tension was palpable, his eyes alert and unblinking. I could feel his awareness of the laptop standing open on the other side of the table from him and he was willing me, like some Jedi knight, not to go near it. And I knew, without a shadow of a doubt, that if I did I would not like what I saw.

Our eyes locked and we had *a moment*. I wanted to look at the laptop, but if I did, he would know I was spying on him.

Did I want that? What would I see? Some other woman's profile – that he would explain away as something innocent while I pretended to believe him? I needed time to think. I couldn't confront him now.

Nonchalantly, he got up and placed himself between me and the laptop.

'Oh, yes. I'll have a biscuit!' he said, still watching me.

I grabbed the biscuits, took one and handed him the packet. He took it from my hands and just smiled at me, and I smiled back, and went back to bed. Ostrich, that's me! I know it.

I lay there with a feeling of total unease knowing that Erin was right; there was definitely something going on. His face, before the smile, had been cold and expressionless; and said it all.

And it suddenly came to me that it was the same stony face he wore the night the police were searching the house for Erin. The same alert watchfulness, like the fox in the garden – expecting danger.

What was it he had said about that night? 'Not used to having police running around the house like that'. *Really? What about the night they came to arrest you then?* I thought.

Oh, here I go! Finding evidence again! All because I knew he'd been in prison. I had to talk to him and get to the bottom of it all. I couldn't live with this doubt.

***

On Friday night we were sitting in our usual spot in front of the fire in the White Horse, feeling warm and relaxed, and with nobody within earshot. *This is it!* I thought. I felt nervous and didn't know where to begin, but I think he sensed there was something in the air.

He went to the bar to replenish our drinks and when he came back he sat opposite me with purpose, giving me his full attention – almost inviting me to say something.

'Cheers,' I said, lifting my drink.

'Cheers,' he said, still waiting.

'What?' I said.

He just shook his head. 'Is everything all right?'

'Yes, fine!'

Relaxing again. He looked at the TV screen over my left shoulder.

'Well, actually,' I said. 'There *is* something we need to talk about.'

His eyes flicked back to mine. 'Yeah?' he asked, picking up his pint again. 'What's that?'

'I heard something about your past that I think we need to discuss.'

'Like what?' he said, his eyes glazing over.

'That you were in prison.' *Oh! Subtle, Natalie!*

He took a long, slow quaff of his beer, placed it back down and looked at me. 'Who told you that?' he asked, calmly.

'Not you!'

'So, what have you been told?'

'That you did eighteen months for fraud? Something about client investments when you were in financial services.'

'Is that it?'

'Pretty much,' I said.

'I did fifteen months, actually, for a mistake that I have regretted ever since.'

'Why didn't you tell me about it?'

'It's hardly the way to impress a new girlfriend, is it? And when I wanted to tell you, it was never the right time. It's not something I'm proud of. It was one stupid mistake and it isn't who I am now. I didn't want you to think less of me. You know I've become very fond of you; you know that. I didn't want anything to spoil what we have.'

'Do you want to tell me about it now?'

He gave a heavy sigh, and then began.

'It was ages ago. I'd had this old client for many years and had made him a shitload of money, and in all the years I had never put my commission rate up at all, when in actual fact I had every right to. I was going to at the next renewal, but then the old man died and his son inherited his portfolio. So rather than try to explain everything to the son, it was just easier to up the commission rate a bit when it transferred into his name.

'It was when the kids were small and we were battling for cash, and as I said, if it had been the old man himself, he would no doubt have agreed to the increase. He was always very grateful for the money I had made for him! But technically, legally, what I did was wrong. The son reported me to the police and they found me guilty. That was the first and last time I've ever been in trouble with the law, and I've never regretted anything so much in all my life.'

'And is that why you and Vicky broke up?'

'Is that what you were told?'

'I'm asking you.'

'Partly, but not entirely. Things were far more complicated than that. She was very angry with me over it, and I think it was a convenient time for her to get out of the marriage. If she'd have told the court I had a home to go to, they wouldn't have even locked me up – but she didn't. So what does that tell you? We had a good standard of living and a good circle of friends, but I'd become an embarrassment.'

I sat quietly taking all this in and I knew he was waiting for me to say something, but I didn't know what to think at that moment, or what to say.

'What was prison like?' I asked.

'Not too bad!' he said, with a big sigh. He relaxed. 'I worked in the library and had a little *delivery round* going.'

'Delivery round?'

'Yeah! You know, a bit of wheeling and dealing.'

'You're joking?' I said, incredulously.

'No!' He laughed. 'It was quite lucrative!'

I just shook my head at him.

'So, who told you?' he said, still smiling. 'Vicky?'

'You know I'm not going to tell you that.'

'That's hardly fair…' He started.

'What isn't?' I asked. 'Keeping secrets?'

He took my point and didn't pursue it.

'I just need you to tell me if there's anything else,' I said. 'Anything I need to know or that I should know?'

'No, nothing. I swear!' he said. 'And you have no idea how relieved I am to get this off my chest, believe me!' He picked up my hand and held it.

'Promise?' I asked. 'No more secrets?'

'Promise!' he said, kissing the palm.

***

Of course, Erin wanted to know what had been said, and I told her all about it. 'Mom, please tell me you didn't fall for it?'

'I'm keeping an open mind, Erin; it sounds like the truth to me. He seemed very glad to have it all out in the open and he didn't deny any of it.'

'Well, he couldn't deny it, could he! And his version is not what I heard from Lea. I'm sure she said there were multiple counts of fraud, not just the one.'

'Well, we don't know the facts, do we?'

'Okay, well tell me, in the way he tells it, where could Vicky have been implicated?' she said.

'Maybe she wasn't. Maybe Lea got that wrong.'

'Why would she?' asked Erin. 'And the laptop? Did you ask him about that?'

'No,' I said. 'I didn't know what to ask. I can hardly say, "By the way, Richard, what are you trying to hide when you sit on the laptop every morning?"'

'Yes, you can! You should have, Mom.' She glared at me.

'I did walk in on him the other morning, but he was sat over the other side of the table. I couldn't go look at what was on the laptop; it would have been too obvious.'

'Oh. Mom!' she said, throwing her arms in the air.

'I did sense something,' I said. 'My eyes are open.'

'Please, just be careful, Mom.'

'I will,' I promised.

Chapter Twenty-Five

It was late in March when Mum had another stroke. It was a bright, blustery morning and I was vacuuming the lounge. She and Emma were sitting on the sofa watching TV. I told her I would be quick and then I'd make us a cup of coffee. She smiled and nodded.

As I finished hoovering, I heard the post being shoved through the letterbox and went to collect it, sifting through it as I returned to the lounge.

'Just bills and adverts,' I said to Mum. 'Nothing interesting.' I put it down on the coffee table and started packing the vacuum away. The cable ran under her foot and I asked her to just lift her foot for me. There was no response and when I looked up to see her glazed, deadpan expression, I knew immediately what it meant.

'Mum, can you hear me?'

There was no response.

'Can you get up, Mum?' I said, pulling her arm upwards.

There was no way I could lift her weight out into the car, so I rang for an ambulance, trying to keep calm as I answered their questions. Help arrived within minutes. I drove behind the flashing blue lights to hospital, parked, and found my way back to the A&E. She was receiving treatment and I was asked to please wait in the appropriate area. So, I waited. And waited. Eventually I was allowed to see her in the intensive care unit, fast asleep and looking very small and frail in the hospital bed. I sat beside her and waited for somebody to come and tell me what was going on, and it wasn't long before a young doctor came around and told me that she had indeed had a stroke, but that she was now stable. They were admitting her, and as she would be sleeping for a while it might be best if I came back later that evening.

When I got home, poor old Emma was looking totally forlorn. I sat on the floor next to her and told her what was happening, and she licked the back of my hand as if to say 'thanks for sharing'. Then she actually came back to the lounge with me, climbed up onto the sofa and dozed.

Within minutes, the phone rang and Barbara-next-door, who had seen the ambulance, wanted to know what had happened. I told her, and knowing that would start the jungle drums, I phoned Cynthia to tell her also. We spoke for all of three minutes and only about Mum's present state of health, about which there wasn't much to tell. I phoned Brigit three times but got no further than her answering machine, so I just left a short message.

When Richard came home, I hadn't even thought about tea, so he said he would go and get us fish and chips.

I told Erin when she came in, and after tea, she came with me to the hospital. We had a shock when we saw Mum slumped against pillows, her head tipped back and mouth open. Erin and I looked at each other in alarm, reading each other's thoughts.

Then Mum's eyes fluttered open and she half smiled at us; she was very tired and groggy. Her eyes seemed to have sunk into her pale, gaunt cheeks, and her arms were bruised where drips had pierced the thin skin. Tears welled up in Erin's eyes as she sat and held her granny's hand, and Mum held on to hers all the time we were there.

I gave Mum a drink of water and sat down on the opposite side to Erin. Mum didn't know where she was or why, but she was peaceful and unconcerned. We sat. Erin and I chatting quietly until she nodded off. We thought she was asleep and were making ready to go when she opened her eyes to say good night, and I told her I'd be back in the morning.

She was much perkier the following day, now down at the far end of a ward of ten beds. She was confused and asked me where she was and when she could go home. I asked what the doctors had said and she told me she hadn't seen any doctors. A nurse told me that was not the case, and a doctor was due to come on rounds after visiting hour if I wished to stay. And sure enough, ten minutes after the last visitor had fluffed pillows and kissed goodbye, a doctor came working his way down the ward.

He was a pleasant man in his early thirties, I'd say, but he seemed rather distracted. We introduced ourselves and he told me Mum was doing fine. They were going to keep her in for a few days just to monitor her. He smiled and moved on again.

Throughout the exchange, Mum regarded him coolly, not saying a word. I don't think she understood any of it.

'The doctor says you'll be here for a couple of days and then I can take you home,' I told her.

'Oh, not again!' She frowned. 'When can I go home?'

'Not today. You have to stay for a couple of days.'

'What day is it today?'

'Tuesday.'

'I can't stay in here,' she said, suddenly agitated. 'I have to feed Emma. She'll be wondering where I am.'

'I'm looking after Emma, Mum. You don't have to worry about her; she's sleeping on the end of Erin's bed.'

She relaxed a little, and I told her bits of news from home until eventually she nodded off, and a nurse came over and told me it was time for me to go.

The next day she was looking much better again. The colour had returned to her cheeks and a bright feistiness to her eyes as she sat upright watching visitors arrive.

When I reached her bedside, her first words were 'Who are all these people, Natalie? What are they doing in my lounge? Who said they could come in? Did you let them in?' and we went through the whole explanation thing again. But she was adamant that she had not had a stroke.

She remembered that the doctor had been to see her though and could tell me of a couple of happenings in the ward that day, mostly regarding the woman in the bed opposite her who apparently complained a great deal. The bed next to Mum's had been empty, but during the day an elderly lady had been put in there. With big, dark eyes she smiled a wan little smile at me and I smiled back.

'Don't be smiling at her!' instructed Mum, loud enough for the woman to hear. 'I can't be doin' with her!'

'Ssshh!' I whispered, but she took no notice.

'Look at that bunch of bananas there,' she said, nodding towards the big bunch on the bed table at her neighbour's feet.

'What's she going to do with all those? Wouldn't you think she'd offer them around. But no!'

I had come with grapes and a block of chocolate. 'Look,' I said. 'I brought you some grapes.'

She ignored me.

'It's just plain selfish, if you ask me,' she said. 'But that's how some folk are, I suppose.'

She glared at the woman, who smiled back almost apologetically. I smiled at her and offered her some grapes.

'Don't be giving her my grapes!' said Mum, looking at me crossly.

At that moment a nurse who had been at the sink close by, and most likely had heard what Mum said, came over and pulled closed the curtain between the two women. With a frown and a firm voice, she told Mum that Mrs White needed to eat lots of bananas to get better. Mum sat ruffling her feathers, but soon lost interest. Out of sight, out of mind.

The following morning, I took her a bunch of bananas in, which she regarded with little interest. 'Didn't they have any grapes?' she asked.

I sat and chatted with her, telling her about Emma and Barbara-next-door when, halfway through visiting hour, Brigit floated into the room.

She cast an imperious eye around the ward before recognising us and making her way over. I was absolutely amazed! She swept down the ward and leaned over Mum, giving her a perfunctory little hug, and dropped a bag of goodies on the bed: a magazine, grapes and nartjies.

'Hello, Mummy!' she said. 'How *are* you? What on earth have you been doing to yourself this time?' She didn't acknowledge me.

'Hi, Brigit! This is a nice surprise!' I said.

She regarded me, coldly. 'Natalie,' she said, and returned her attention to Mum.

'Brigit?' Mum asked, in a suddenly weak, frail voice.

'Yes, how *are* you? Are they looking after you in here? You really shouldn't be in this place, you know. Don't you think you would be better in a nice retirement place that has its own frail care facility?'

Mum just looked at her in total amazement. 'I've not seen you for such a long time,' whispered Mum. 'How are you? How is Peter?'

Brigit shot a questioning look at me.

'Peter died, Mummy. Don't you remember?'

'Oh. Yes, that's right,' said Mum. 'I *do* remember.'

There was only one chair, which I was sitting in, and thinking I would leave the two of them to catch up, I started packing Mum's washing to take back with me.

'I'll leave you two to have a chat then.'

'No, really,' said Brigit. 'I can't stay long. Don't go.'

Mum made a gesture, waving a hand up and down at me, telling me to sit down. So, I sat.

'I'm sorry I haven't been round to see you,' drawled Brigit. 'We've just finished a big production; hard work.'

I'm sure Mum didn't understand a word, but Brigit carried on about the amateur dramatics, her arty friends and how busy she was, filling what I think would otherwise have been an embarrassing silence. It turned out to be a bit that way anyway, as Mum closed her eyes and fell asleep halfway through the monologue.

Brigit looked at me in exasperation and I just smiled. She picked up her bag and indicated for me to follow her, obviously not trusting that Mum was really asleep.

She stopped at the door. 'What do the doctors say?' she asked. 'Is she going to be okay?'

'This time, yes, but she is ninety, you know.'

'Well, she's clearly not in her right mind!' said Brigit. 'She doesn't know what's going on around her.'

'She's just had a stroke!' I answered. This was not the time to discuss Mum's mental competence. Pulling herself up to her full height she looked down her nose at me.

'I'll be off now then. Please tell her I said goodbye but that I had to go, okay?'

'I can give you a lift back if you like?'

'No, it's fine. I have a taxi waiting,' she said, and floated away.

Mum was rummaging through her goody-bag when I returned. She pulled out the grapes and looked at her neighbour as she popped one in her mouth.

'Has Brigit gone?' she said, her voice normal again.

'Yes,' I said. 'She said to tell you goodbye, but she had to go, she had a taxi waiting.'

'Oh, that's a shame,' she said, eyeing the nartjies.

She was told she could leave on Friday morning and I had her home by lunchtime. She and a very happy Emma were soon ensconced on the sofa (she didn't want to go to bed) when Barbara-next-door came to see how she was doing. Not long after Barbara left, Richard and then Erin came in and made a big fuss of her. She was pleased to be back with her new-found family again.

***

Just a couple of days later Mum called me to her room to look at Emma, who lay on the floor on her side unable to get up, her eyes rolling. I could see she was having some sort of a fit and I called the vet. He came immediately and tried to help her, then took her to the surgery to see if he could do more there. But he could not, and he phoned to ask permission to put her down.

I knew how the news would affect Mum, and that she wouldn't give the answer that he needed. So, I told him yes, of course. He must do what he thought best.

Very gently, I told Mum what had happened. She was distraught. She cried and simultaneously berated me for giving permission to 'kill' Emma. I can't remember the last time I saw her shed tears and it was terrible to see an old lady cry like that. I tried to tell her there was nothing anyone could do, but she was still angry with me. Who did I think I was to give permission? Was Emma my dog? She might have recovered – how did I know she wouldn't? And now it was my fault that she was gone.

Eventually she calmed down, and when Erin came home, she put her arm around her and they cried together. I couldn't do either. But one thing I knew: Emma was in a better place now.

Chapter Twenty-Six

Spring was in full swing, with blue skies and fresh breezes that spoke of warmer times to come. As we went into April, I started thinking about our birthdays coming up in May.

Richard hadn't brought up the subject of marriage or getting engaged for a long time, but there again, neither had I, because I wanted *him* to remember our agreement, and for us both to surprise each other.

As my birthday came a week or so before his, I thought it best if we exchanged rings at the same time, on my birthday. So, with that in mind, I went back to Barratt and Jones in Chester and bought him the type of ring he'd admired before. I was amazed that the same assistant remembered me, and served me with a knowing little smile. I wondered if perhaps Richard had already been back to the same guy to buy mine.

He helped me choose a ring and packed it in a smart little presentation box. I thanked him and walked out confident that Richard would love it. I was thrilled!

On the Friday morning of my birthday, Richard got up and brought me coffee in bed as usual, gave me a kiss, said happy birthday, and went back to the kitchen.

Erin came in to wish me happy birthday with a box set of

David Attenborough DVDs, which I'd been wanting for ages. But then she had to dash off to work.

I had Richard's ring in my bedside table. Perhaps he would come back to exchange presents before he left for work. He did come back, but just long enough to put on his work boots and say goodbye. He turned as he got to the door.

'So, are we going out to celebrate tonight?' he asked.

'Yes, that would be nice.'

Of course! He was obviously going to wait until then, I thought. That would be far more romantic. I lay visualising how it would be, and what I should wear.

Imagine my surprise then, when I later went to the kitchen and found a large envelope and a small paper bag (from Barratt and Jones), sitting on the kitchen table. Sure enough, inside the bag there was a small, square box. I was thrilled. I sat looking at them, savouring the moment. I even made a cup of coffee before opening the card.

It was the usual big card, *Birthday Wishes to the One I Love*, embossed in gold and with three pages of verse on the inside. I was beginning to wonder if he hadn't bought these cards as a job lot at some time, and had a pile of them stashed away somewhere.

Inside was the usual sentimental verse. I read it through, and then again before I noticed that he had signed it, *Yours forever and always, Richard*, on the wrong page – not at the end of the verse, but in the middle, at the bottom of the page. He had obviously signed it quickly, not worrying about the sentiments expressed therein. I wondered whether he had even read the verse right to the end?

I took the little box out of the bag and just held it in my hand. I was surprised he had left it there for me to open on my own and wished he'd stayed to share the moment. Should I open it now, or wait for him to come home from work?

I turned the box around in my fingers, wondering if he had

chosen the exact same ring that I chose before, and curiosity getting the better of me, I slipped the lid off. If it wasn't the same ring, had he chosen a nice one?

But there was no ring inside the box. It was my amber pendant that Mum had bought for my birthday last year.

Is this a joke? It had to be a joke. *He must, after all, be going to give me the ring in the restaurant later. He's teasing me!* I smiled.

But then I noticed that the pendant looked very shiny, and that there was something different about it. I went to my bedroom to check and, sure enough, *my* amber pendant was in its usual place in my jewellery box. I held the two side by side and they were virtually identical, except in Richard's the amber was slightly greener.

I wasn't smiling now! I felt so let down and sad. There would be no engagement ring this birthday. It hadn't been important enough to him, to remember we were getting engaged. Really? He hadn't even remembered that I already had such a pendant. I'd showed it to him. Hadn't he remembered me ever wearing it? How important *was* I to this guy? I felt like throwing the card and the pendant into the rubbish bin. He couldn't even be bothered to sign the card in the right place.

I felt like phoning him and telling him what I thought of his card and his present, and if he had walked in the door at that moment, I most certainly would have done. I was so ready to tell him to pack his things and get out.

But I knew, really, that I wasn't going to. This was my last relationship; I had to try harder to make it work. I should at least see what he had to say for himself before throwing it away? We got on so well together most of the time. I didn't want to lose him.

In the back of my mind, I knew I was being a bit perverse because I didn't want to *marry* Richard. And with that amount of trust (or lack of), how good a relationship was it really? Yet it was. Wasn't it? Or was I just kidding myself?

Regardless of that, however, at that moment, I was angry.

Just to see if he knew the difference, I wore my original (Mum's) amber pendant that evening, and I tried to put a smile on my face when he came in from work.

He kissed me hello, noticed the pendant and smiled, obviously thinking it was the one he'd bought me. He lifted it slightly to inspect it.

'Suits you!' he said. 'Do you like it?'

'I like it very much,' I said, trying to smile.

'What's the matter?'

'You didn't buy *this* pendant for me.'

'What?' he asked, totally confused. 'Of course I did!'

'This is the one Mum gave me for my birthday last year.'

He looked closely at the pendant again, uncertain now.

'I bought that for you.'

But I could hear the doubt in his voice now.

'No, you bought this one,' I said, holding up his.

'Ah! I see. Oh dear. That's probably why I was drawn to that one. It must have looked familiar. Sorry! I just remembered that's what you said you liked. Amber.' He gave a little laugh.

I didn't laugh, didn't speak. Just stood, unamused.

'We can take it back and change it for something else if you like,' he said, a little defensively now.

'Well, yes. I don't need two of them, do I!'

'I'm sorry. Okay?' he said, a little angrier now, and he went for his shower.

Well that went well, I thought.

I was making Mum's tea when he came back to the kitchen, more relaxed, asking if I wanted coffee.

'Yes, please,' I said.

'Sorry about the necklace. I just remember you saying you'd like an amber pendant. Silly mistake.'

I didn't respond.

He peered at the peas and carrots I was straining at the sink.

'Have you cooked for us all, or is that just for your mum?'

'This is just Mum's.'

'So, do you want to go out tonight? How about I treat you to a meal at the Stamford Bridge?'

'Yes, we can if you like,' I answered, half-heartedly. 'Nothing fancy though. How about some pub grub?'

'Yes, okay,' he said, a little frown crossing his face.

He busied himself with cups and milk in silence, then tried to hand me my coffee, but I was still busy with the vegetables. He just stood waiting, so I asked him to just leave it on the table.

'I'll get out of your way, then,' he said. 'I'll go and say hello to Mum.'

He took his coffee and disappeared.

Later that evening, after we'd had some food and a couple of drinks, he returned to the subject of my birthday and his unfortunate gift.

'So, what do you want to do about the necklace? D'you want to swop it for something else?'

I didn't answer immediately – well I thought I'd answered that question already anyway. But I had to start somewhere.

'You know what?' I said. 'I'm sorry I jumped on you like that as soon as you came through the door, but I'd had all day to stew and I was pretty upset about it.'

'I rather gathered that!' he said.

'And it wasn't entirely about the fact that you couldn't remember me showing you the pendant Mum bought me, or me wearing it.'

'Okay…What then?'

'Do you remember at the end of our holiday, the last night before we got off the ship?'

'Yes. What about it?'

'Do you remember what we talked about?'

'Not offhand. No. Was it something important?'

'*I* thought so.'

'So…?'

'We talked about getting engaged.'

Understanding slowly crept into his eyes. 'Oh, God! You were expecting an engagement ring!'

'I was,' I admitted. 'And when I saw the little box from the jeweller's, I thought… And then I opened it up and found an amber pendant, just like the one I already have.'

'Oh, God!' he repeated, closing his eyes. I waited for him to say something.

'I had no idea,' he said. 'I know we talked about it, but I didn't think it was set in stone. I thought it was just a suggestion. And to be honest, I didn't take it too seriously, because you didn't seem that keen on the idea of marriage at the time, anyway. And you haven't mentioned it since. I'm sorry – I had no idea!'

'But we'd agreed on it. I thought you knew. *We agreed.* You even told me not to expect you to get down on one knee to propose.'

'I obviously wasn't taking it as seriously as you. I thought we were fooling around.'

Then you're an idiot! I thought.

'You must think me a complete idiot,' he said. 'I'm so sorry, really.'

There was an awkward silence between us.

Then with his best lopsided smile: 'Did you buy *me* a ring?'

I nodded, but couldn't look him in the eye.

'Have you got it on you?'

'No,' I said. 'It's back at Mum's.'

Did he honestly think he was going to get that now? Did he think he was off the hook so easily?'

'Thank you for the card,' I said.

'Ah. Did you like that, at least? I hope that told you how I feel about you?'

'Which bit?' I asked.

'What d'you mean?'

'Which bit did you have in mind? Which bit said how you feel about me?'

'I can't remember everything that it said on the card, for heaven-sakes, but all of it! That's how I feel about you.'

'Did you read the verse right to the end?' I asked.

'Yes, of course. But it's a couple of weeks since I bought it; I can't remember it offhand right now. What is this? Why the twenty questions?'

'You signed the card halfway through – not on the last page – halfway through the verse.'

'So?'

'So, you didn't read the verse. You just signed it without reading it and it meant nothing to you.'

He looked at me dumfounded. 'Are you serious?'

'Very serious,' I assured him. 'You gave me a very beautiful, meaningful card and you haven't a clue what it said. So, it's actually meaningless.'

'I read it when I bought it, and I bought it for you. I didn't memorise the words!'

'Where did you buy it?'

'Why?' he snapped back quite loudly, and we were suddenly both aware that other people were looking at us.

We finished our drinks in silence and then he asked, 'Do you want another drink or d'you want to go home?'

'I'd like to go home now please, if you're ready to,' I answered, coldly. We left without another word.

We were halfway home before he spoke again.

'You know, I've done nothing wrong here. I bought you what I thought was a nice present, and card. Okay, it was the wrong thing. That was a mistake, and I've said I'm sorry. But it's not like I forgot your birthday. And I don't know why you're being like this. Am I missing something here? Is there something you want to say?'

'Like what?'

'I don't know. Something that would explain your behaviour tonight.'

'*My* behaviour? *Really?*' I said with utter disgust. 'I have said everything I want to, thank you, and if you don't get it… well, we're in trouble.'

'Oh, yes! We're clearly that! If what I do isn't good enough anymore, then we most definitely are!'

He obviously hadn't heard a word I'd said to him. Either that or he didn't *want* to hear. I didn't reply.

After a couple of minutes, he started again.

'You know, I'm a bloke. I don't get all the touchy-feely "guess what I'm thinking" stuff. But if you don't know how I feel about you by now, then we *are* in trouble, because I don't know how else to show you,' he said.

I suddenly felt awful. He was waiting for a response but I didn't know what to tell him. So he carried on.

'You're trying to read things into what I do, or don't do, and I'm a very simple bloke, really; I don't get all this stuff. Vicky used to go on about men from Mars stuff, and I'm sick of it. I don't need this nonsense anymore. I thought we could have a mature relationship… but maybe we should rethink things.'

So here we were, teetering on the brink. And he wasn't the only one who was sick of it. I could see it from his point of view and I felt ashamed. But I still felt angry.

'Would you like to say something?' he asked.

I felt too tired to really, but felt I had to.

'I'm thinking that maybe you're right,' I said, very calmly. 'Maybe we should *rethink* things.'

When we arrived home, he threw his keys on the kitchen table and went straight to bed. I made myself a cup of coffee and sat in the lounge. Erin was, thankfully, spending the weekend at Dylan's place. I didn't want her to see us like this.

The house was very still. Not wanting to share a bed with Richard, I pulled Erin's sofa bed out. It had been the crappiest birthday ever, and I spent the whole night re-running it all through my mind again and again, to try to make sense of it all.

The next morning, he brought me coffee and I pretended to be asleep. He put it down and left for golf. He didn't come home till after three o'clock and had very obviously stayed for a drink at the nineteenth hole, so he went to sleep it off and only resurfaced at tea time. Then he watched TV for a while with Mum, while I busied myself in the kitchen. When I went in to join them, he went back to bed. I sat with Mum, who'd spent most of the day in bed and now wanted some TV and company.

Sunday was no better. He either played on his tablet or watched TV. We ate in silence and he made no effort to start a conversation. And neither did I.

When he went to work on Monday, I took a drive into Chester and returned his ring to the jeweller's.

The same assistant, smiling kindly, said, 'Sometimes these things are for the best.'

***

Things between us were a little prickly for a while, but as time passed and spring turned into summer, they pretty much got back to normal.

I told Erin what had happened with Richard and why we weren't engaged. She didn't say much, but what she *did* say was that she was glad for my sake that I'd 'swerved that one'.

She and I were sitting together in the lounge one evening, when she spoke.

'Mom, do you think things would be better between you and Richard if I moved out?'

'No,' I said, 'I don't think it would make the slightest bit of difference. Why?'

'Dylan's asked me to move in with him.'

'I see,' I said. 'And how do you feel about that?'

'Excited! A bit nervous. But how would *you* feel about it?'

'I would miss you,' I said. 'Very much.'

'Do you think it's too soon?' she asked.

'How long has it been? A year, almost? Does it feel too soon? If it does, then it probably is. And he's not going anywhere, if you feel you need longer.'

'No, he's not pressurising me. He's just asked me to think about it for now. And I love him to bits.' She smiled. 'And besides, I can't sleep on the sofa forever, can I?'

'You can sleep on it as long as you want to. You know that. And I should think you'll be upgrading to your own room in the not-too-distant future!'

'Mom!' she said. 'That's awful! Poor granny!' But she smiled, none the less.

'She will miss you too, if you go,' I said.

'I know, and I'll miss her. But I'll only be around the corner. I'll come visit often.'

'So, does that mean you've decided?'

She nodded. 'Ja. Pretty much.'

I looked at her sadly. 'You know your sofa's always here waiting.'

'Yes, I know. Thanks, Mom.'

Then, lightening the mood, she said, 'Talking of Granny, she seems to stay in bed a lot these days. Is she okay?'

'Yes, she's okay,' I said. 'But the stroke… and losing Emma. I'll be surprised if she sees her next birthday.'

'Oh, shame, Mom. But I think you could be right.'

Richard was very pleased that Erin was moving in with Dylan, 'For their own sakes, of course'.

A couple of weeks later, Dylan's car was sitting outside piled high with her belongings, the engine idling while we said our goodbyes. Richard smiled broadly and shook Dylan's hand as if he was her father, giving her away.

She assured me yet again that she was just around the corner and would visit often – and that I must visit them – but I missed her before the car had even disappeared around the first bend. I felt that yet another chapter was closing.

***

And joy of joys, we heard from Cynthia that her and the whole family were coming over at the end of July for Doug's mum's one-hundredth birthday. She would be staying with her in-laws, but coming to visit regularly during her stay. Well, it would give Mum something to look forward to. I thought so, anyway, but when I told her of Cynthia's intended visit, she just rolled her eyes and said, 'Oh, Lordy!'

Chapter Twenty-Seven

I wasn't going to tell Maggie the engagement ring story, but one Thursday evening she asked me what Richard had given me for my birthday. We'd had a few vodkas and I ended up telling her the whole sorry saga.

'What were you thinking?' she asked. 'Why on earth get engaged? You're not going to marry him, are you?'

'No, I'm not. But I thought that's what he wanted. But I obviously had that very wrong! I thought maybe he'd be happy with a long engagement, a *very*, long engagement. I don't want to break up with him. I do enjoy being with him.'

'Tell the truth! You just want to swan around with an engagement ring on your finger.'

'That would be nice, but not just that, no. It was just more to say... we were committed. Does that make sense?'

'No. Not if you don't want to marry the guy. But thank God you weren't daft enough to give him the ring. I'm amazed you didn't.'

I just shrugged.

'Nat, how many times have you said you'd never again let a man manipulate you, and here you are, doing it again.'

'But he's not...' I started, and she just put her hand up to stop me and carried on.

'He is,' she said. 'He's doing it with his... I was going to say *charm* – but he doesn't have any of that. So, God knows what he does do it with.'

'He's not manipulating me,' I assured her.

She thought for a moment, putting her words together carefully.

'Do you think he has your best interests at heart?'

'Yes, I think so. I don't know. What does that mean, even? At the end of the day, he could be a genuine person just looking for a friend. And he *is* a good friend to me,' I said.

'Are you very sure about that? You don't think that could be an act?'

'Why would he do that? He's a bloody good actor to have kept it up for two years now!'

'I think his whole life could be a big act; it comes very easily to con men.'

'Why do you think he's a con man? How come you think you know him so well?'

'I just don't like him. There's just something... *off*... about him.' She narrowed her eyes at me. 'And you know it too, don't you? I can see it! Come on – tell me.'

'What? I don't know what you're on about.'

'Oh, yes you do. I can see it in your eyes. Come. Spit it out!'

I drew in a long breath before saying the words. 'Years ago, like fifteen years ago, he went to prison for a few months for fraud.'

'I knew it! I fuckin' knew it! Natalie – what are you doing with this arsehole?'

'It was a long time ago and it was just the one time, one mistake that he learned from and never made again.'

'Or he just learned not to get caught!'

'It was when he was in financial services. He forged a signature to give himself more commission. It ruined his life, broke his marriage, and he was barred from working in financial services anymore. That's why he's back to driving again.'

'Not "it", Natalie. "It" didn't ruin his life, *he* did! He did it to himself. And how unlucky to get caught the very first, once only, once-off time he'd tried it. Bullshit!' she said.

'Or, it genuinely was just a once-off mistake,' I said, in his defence.

'He's all about himself, Nat, can't you see that? He just uses other people to get what he wants.'

'How can you say that? You don't know!'

'No, I don't know. But I do. And I'm telling you, he's lying to you, and he's manipulating you.'

'I believe he loves me,' I said. 'He's not very good at saying it, but I think he does.'

'Does he say it? When was the last time he told you he loves you?'

'In my birthday card.'

'Oh, yeah? The one he signed in the wrong place?' She raised her eyebrows at me. 'When did he last say the words "I love you!"?'

I tried to think. It was a few months earlier. He'd come back from golf obviously a bit drunk and, with that soppy look on his face, kept repeating, 'I *do* love you, Nat. I *really do*!' Until, laughingly, I'd said, 'Who are you trying to convince – me or you!' He'd never said it again after that.

Maggie was waiting for a reply. 'I don't know,' I said. 'But he lets me know in all sorts of little ways.'

'Like how?'

'Well, in our more intimate moments…' I started.

'No! No! Don't want to hear!' she said, showing me the hand again.

'Tsk!' I frowned. 'He does this thing… kisses the palm of my hand, then closes my hand up over the kiss.'

'And what's that supposed to be?'

'Well, it feels *special*. Like he's saying he loves me.'

'It's probably just part of his technique,' she said.

'And would that mean it didn't mean anything?'

'Wouldn't mean that it *did*!' she countered. 'If he did it with all the other women in his life.'

I didn't tell her about Vicky. I knew what she'd say. And I didn't want to hear it.

'So what?' I asked. 'Dump him because he *might* be a con man?'

'Well… *yeah*!' she said, as if it was obvious. 'But if you can't do that, at least keep your eyes open. Don't take anything for granted with that one. Can you do that?'

'I can do that,' I said.

'And please,' she said. 'Just be sure you watch your money. That's all I'm saying. All right?'

'I will,' I said.

'Mmmh!' she said, unconvinced.

I must admit, despite sticking up for him to Maggie, I had some very serious doubts at that time about Richard. I began to think that maybe I *was* in denial, or being very naïve, to say the least. Or just trying too hard to make things fit.

However, Richard's mood lightened considerably from then on and our relationship improved. I'm not sure if this was because of Erin's absence or that he had 'rethought' our relationship and decided it *was* what he wanted after all.

Neither of us mentioned engagement rings or marriage and eventually I agreed with Erin that I was lucky to have 'swerved' that one.

Chapter Twenty-Eight

It was a Wednesday, mid-morning on a beautiful day in the middle of July. I had half mowed the lawn and stood at the kitchen door having a coffee break, watching the bees buzz around the yellow climbing rose again, and the butterflies flitting around the shrubs.

Mum had been ill in the night; she had vomited, and fallen back asleep amid the mess of it. When I took her morning tea, she'd seemed confused and couldn't remember being ill, but the evidence was all over the bed and carpet.

I changed the sheets while she went to bath and wash her hair. I offered to help, as usual. But as usual, I was only allowed into the bathroom once she had her clean pyjamas on, just to rinse her hair over the sink. And once she was back in bed with a cup of tea, I got down on my hands and knees and started to clean the carpet.

She watched me. 'I'm sorry to be such a bother to you,' she said.

'Ah, Mum,' I said, truthfully, 'you're no bother at all.'

As I rubbed the carpet closest to her, she dangled her hand over the edge of the bed and stroked my hair.

'Aye, you're a good lass,' she said, in the Lancashire accent she was born to, but which I hadn't heard her speak in years. I don't have a problem with that accent. In fact, I found Richard's quite charming. But when Mum spoke it, it was somehow repulsive. Maybe it reminded me of Uncle Harry, her brother, who *had* been a pretty repulsive sort of guy.

As a haughty teenager I had told her just how disgusting I found it when she spoke like that, and had told her it was very *Barker* of her. She had laughed and asked who the 'divil' I thought I was. And I had put my nose in the air and said, 'A Sefton!' She had reminded me of that exchange many times since, but not now. Maybe she'd forgotten it at last.

Then after a minute, she spoke normally again. 'You know I love you, really, don't you?' she said.

That shocked me. Just like that. Out of the blue. Our relationship didn't allow for 'I love you'. It never had, except when written on a birthday or Christmas card. And it irritated me that she would say it now. It was embarrassing.

'Yeah, love you, too,' I said, probably a little glibly, keeping my eyes on the carpet.

She clicked her tongue impatiently and withdrew her hand as if I'd bitten it. In my defence, the desire to be done with sick and bleach had priority.

I put down my mug and was walking back to the lawn mower when I heard the clattering of buckets that heralded the window cleaner and his son. I think it was an evacuation warning that he was about to wash bedroom windows. I should imagine that after years of washing bungalow windows, he'd learned to do that. Sure enough, a few minutes later Mum appeared at the open French windows in her dressing gown, and sat down at the little garden table. It was so unlike her to be seen outside in her dressing gown, and it didn't bother her a bit when the window cleaner and his son eventually came around the corner of the bungalow. The older one sat to chat with Mum while his son washed the glass of the French window. I made them a cup of tea and went back to the mower.

When they left, Mum sat watching contentedly as I finished mowing the lawn, giving the odd instruction about not mowing over the cable and how to clean the mower blades. Eventually I went inside. She followed me in and went to lie down on the sofa while I made her some toast and jam. She said that's all she felt like. But by the time I took it through, she was already fast asleep.

Richard came home in the early evening and sat chatting with Mum awhile until she said she was going to bed. She didn't really feel like tea, but asked if I would bring her 'a few of those little mandarin oranges out of the tin – with a blob of cream.'

I took the oranges, and a cup of tea as well, and found her sitting up in bed looking out of the open window. A warm breeze brought in the smell of freshly mown grass.

'Look at that big, fat thrush on the fence out there,' she said. 'He was singing so beautifully a moment ago.'

'Oh, yes. I see him! It's a lovely evening, isn't it?'

'It is,' she agreed. 'Summer's here at last.'

'Are you all right with the window open? Do you want it closed now?'

'No, leave it,' she said. 'It's nice as it is. Is Richard here?'

She must have forgotten her chat with him earlier.

'Yes, he's here. Did you want him?'

'No, no, don't worry. I just wondered,' she said.

'I'm just going to dish tea up. Are you sure you won't have some?'

'No, this is fine, this is all I want,' she said.

'Okay, I'll be back in a minute then.'

***

It must have been about fifteen minutes later when I went in to collect her dishes. She was sitting up in bed as before, but still as a statue and frozen in time, in a moment of sudden pain which had arched her back and contorted her features. And in that moment, death had taken her, instantly, and left her body in this horrific pose.

I stood there transfixed, unable to move or to make a sound for what seemed ages, but which was probably just a few seconds. I went back to Richard in the kitchen and tried to find words, but none came. He jumped up immediately and rushed past me through to Mum's room, and I followed him there to find him standing just inside the door.

'She's gone,' he said, stating the obvious.

He dialled the emergency services and passed the phone over to me. I told them I thought my mother had just died. They must have thought there was still some chance that she hadn't, as within minutes an ambulance came flashing up to the gate and paramedics rushed in with what I supposed was life-saving equipment. I saw them signal to Richard to take me out of the room, and we sat on the sofa waiting for them to do their work.

A few minutes later one of them came into the lounge, asked if it was me who had made the call, what my relationship was to Mum and a couple of other things. He confirmed that she was indeed dead, and that they would be taking her away with them now.

I got up, some instinct not wanting them to take her. He said it would be better if I stayed in the lounge. Indeed, he was blocking my way even if I'd tried to go to her.

They left a few minutes later, and closing the front door, I wandered back into Mum's room trying to grasp what had just happened. She'd been there, talking to me less than an hour ago – and now she was gone; forever. I stared at the empty bed and couldn't believe it. My brain knew what was going on, but some part of it couldn't catch up.

I picked up the empty dish that had fallen to the floor, and also the untouched cup of tea. It was still warm.

Richard put his head around the door. 'Come,' he said, urging me out of there.

I took the dishes to the kitchen, put them into the sink and slumped against it, suddenly feeling very weak. Richard came through with bed sheets in his arms. He'd obviously stripped Mum's bed. He put them in the machine and set them to wash, then found the brandy in the pantry and poured two glasses.

'Here, come and drink this,' he said, leading me through to the lounge. He put the drinks down, turned round and gave me a big bear hug. I felt a bit of a hypocrite because I didn't feel upset; I didn't feel anything, just numb.

Over the top of my head, I heard him say, 'It's happening.'

I thought that a strange thing for him to say. I looked up at his face and saw him gazing out the window with a faraway stare, and I realised he was talking more to himself than to me. I didn't know what he meant, but was just thankful that he was there and thinking more clearly than me.

***

There is something about the finality of death that presses a 'pause' button on the lives of those it affects. It sent me into a no man's land in which all the usual daily routines seemed pointless; all life's little rituals, futile. It created a huge vacuum that begged the question, what's it all about? Why do we worry so much about little things – a lifetime of little things – when in just one, unexpected moment, we are blown out like a candle and it all just comes to an end? Do we just cease to exist?

I couldn't cry. I didn't want to cry. I didn't feel I had the right to cry.

I couldn't face talking to Cynthia, so Richard phoned to tell her what had happened. She said she would let Brigit know.

Barbara and various family members told me how sorry they were, and asked how I was doing. And the truth was I was fine, just a little disorientated because there was nobody to get up to make toast for, or endless cups of tea.

But there were arrangements to be made, things to be done, people to tell, and eventually I got on with it in a 'treading treacle' kind of way.

Mum never spoke about her own death and hadn't left any instructions. I knew she preferred cremation to burial, and the crematorium was 'backed up' as one of their ovens was temporarily not working. It would be at least two weeks before they could take Mum.

This tied in conveniently with Cynthia's impending visit, so I accepted the date they offered and, using the guest list I'd made for Mum's ninetieth birthday, phoned around to give people the details of the service planned, including Brigit and Cynthia. The next day, Cynthia phoned to ask if it could all be postponed for a few days, as 'the kids want to go down to London and have a go on the Big Eye first'.

I explained the situation at the crematorium and that a postponement was liable to be a very long one, and also that everybody had now been notified of that date. She whined and asked if I couldn't at least try, so I told her I would send her the number for the crematorium and all the people already invited, and she could do it herself. She changed her mind quickly then and told me (rather petulantly) not to bother.

I told her that Mum was at the undertakers if she wanted to say her last goodbyes, but neither she nor Brigit went. Cynthia did inform me, however, that she and Brigit (and Doug) would not be using the cars provided by the undertaker for the family of the deceased, as Brigit wanted nothing to do with any plans I had made, and that was the condition of her attending at all. Cynthia's kids wouldn't be coming as they would be in London, so Brigit would go with Cynthia and Doug in their car. And once in the chapel, they would sit on the back pew. Fine!

The best bit of it all was that both Josh and Mark took compassionate leave and flew over (as much for a visit as for the service). They were with us for five days, and slept in the little bed-and-breakfast just a two-minute walk away. It was wonderful to see them again and have all three of them in the same house. Their suntanned faces and happy smiles were like a breath of fresh air.

I don't remember much about the service itself; it went by in a bit of a blur. I remember Brigit walking past me without even acknowledging me, the kids or Richard. Maggie couldn't come as she had her own drama at work that day, but Alan was there, and the family members who had visited Mum on her birthday. I felt very proud introducing my children to them.

The minister went through the requisite order of service in a pretty perfunctory kind of way. I read out a short eulogy and Erin stood up tearfully, to share some lovely memories she had about her granny, and then we dirged painfully through a couple of hymns, to which, it seemed, Erin and I were the only ones who knew the words.

As the casket was about to start its journey towards the little red curtains, Brigit chose this time to say her last goodbye – which she did by draping herself, crying, across the coffin. Cynthia followed and stood by, tearfully dabbing her own eyes. Then, Cynthia taking Brigit by the arm, they returned to their seat on the back pew. I sat dry-eyed.

As we left the crematorium, Cynthia tried to be very cool with me but I think curiosity had the better of her, as she wanted to meet Richard. And then the most bizarre thing happened: Richard and Doug started talking about golf, and promised to have a game together before Doug went back to South Africa. As we walked away, I shook my head in sheer disbelief at his mock innocence.

Nobody came to the tea at the Shell Club. Well, not quite nobody. Barbara-next-door, Arthur and the lady from across the road pitched up, but not a relative in sight. And there was food for thirty people! We made a brave attempt at eating some of it, and in the end had to agree with Arthur that it was a shame to let it go to waste. So, he and Barbara and the lady-from-across-the-road took away what they could in doggie bags, for later.

I was just so very glad it was all over.

Richard was back in work the next day, so I had the kids all to myself for a few days. But then at the weekend it was time for tearful, airport goodbyes again.

***

On the Sunday, Richard played golf with Doug, and Cynthia came round to the bungalow just for one last visit. She wandered around and stared at Mum's empty bed, wanting to know the details of what had happened.

'Just so you know,' she said. 'I won't be contesting the will.'

It was said with the air of *just think yourself lucky that I'm not!*

'Okay,' I said, casually.

'I can't say the same for Brigit,' she carried on. 'She's pretty adamant that she is *not* going to let this go!'

It almost sounded like a threat. I just shrugged at her and saw a quick flash of annoyance in her eyes.

'I just don't get it,' she said. 'Why would Mum leave the place to you? Why would she change her will like that, for no reason? I can't help but think…' She paused. 'She was happy with the way it was, so why did she change it?'

'So, you *did* know what was in the first one, didn't you?'

'Only what she told me.' She blushed.

'Well,' I went on. 'When she realised you might put her in an old age home, she asked me to come and live with her so that wouldn't happen. The bungalow was the carrot. I told you this in South Africa, before I came over here. Why didn't you say then if it was a problem? Or were you betting that she just wouldn't mention her will?'

She gave me a sly little look that told me that was exactly what she'd hoped. She'd assumed she was still number one daughter. And she *would* have been if she hadn't pissed Mum off over the granny flat, then the threat of a home, and then that nasty email!

Cynthia started poking around in the cupboards and drawers so I left her to it and went to the kitchen. After a while she called me to the hall to say she was going, and I should give the pink roses picture to Barbara-next-door. I didn't ask her what was in the black rubbish bag she was now carrying. I didn't care.

At the front door she again told me to keep in touch, and offered a cheek to be kissed. I didn't bother. I closed the door behind her, not waiting to wave goodbye.

***

On Monday morning I had the place to myself – and it was so quiet.

I went into Mum's room and just sat on the sofa in the window awhile, looking around the room. Her worn old slippers shaped to her feet (she'd never bothered with the new ones), her dressing gown hanging on the back of the bedroom door, and her cupboards full to the brim with stuff that I hadn't even begun to think what to do with.

Then I noticed the strand of dark red, marbled beads still strung around the bedhead. And it made me think of the lady in the fish and chip shop with the dangly earrings to match – Rose. She had been kind to Mum, and I wondered if she would like to have the beads.

It had stopped raining and it looked bright and fresh outside, so I decided to take a walk down to the fish and chip shop to give the beads to Rose. I didn't know whether to wrap them or not, but decided just to put them in a little net bag I found in one of the drawers.

When I walked into the shop, Rose looked up and smiled in recognition.

'Hello, luv,' she said. 'How are you? Not seen you for a while?'

'Hi, Rose. Yes, I know. How are you?'

'Oh. Same as ever. You know how it is. How's your mum?'

'She died.'

'Ah,' she said, meeting my eyes. 'I'm sorry to hear that, luv. What was it? Another stroke?'

'I think so, yes.'

'Ah. That's a shame. God bless her. But she had a good long life, didn't she?'

'She did indeed.'

'And her little dog?'

'Emma died before my mum, a few months ago now.'

She smiled sympathetically. 'Well, they're together again now, aren't they? Shame. What can I get you, luv?'

'Nothing today, thanks, Rose. I just wondered if you would like these?' And I handed her the little net bag containing the beads. 'They were Mum's. I'm sure she would like you to have them – if you want them.'

She looked down at the beads in her hand and then up at me, and gave me a big, closed-mouth smile but her eyes were sad.

'Thank you,' she said, nodding. 'I would.'

I nodded back at her, and left the shop.

The sun came out as I walked back home again. I got in and put the kettle on, suddenly feeling exhausted. I took my cup of coffee to the little table outside and immediately I remembered being there just a few weeks earlier with Mum and the window cleaners. It had been a day like this one, warm and sunny, but how different things had been then.

I sat there soaking up the stillness, and crying silent tears. I don't know who they were for. Not for Mum. Not for me. Maybe I was mourning the loss of something she and I had never had.

Chapter Twenty-Nine

The next few months were peaceful. Life ran in smooth routines and Richard was the epitome of a caring, loving partner. He persuaded me that what we needed most was that holiday in South Africa. So, while we waited for Richard's annual leave to come up, we planned our trip and booked the flights. The waiting became excruciating, but at last the day arrived, and bags packed, off we went.

***

I fainted again during the flight, much to Richard's alarm. But I was fine. As I stepped out of the plane door I felt the hot sun on my face, breathed in the scorched air, and thought, *The rains haven't come yet.* And in that instant my heart leapt in my chest realising how much I'd missed this place.

We crossed the concrete shielding our eyes from the bright, merciless heat that bounced up at us, and were glad to make it into the cool terminal building. We snaked our way through customs, collected our bags and passed into the arrivals hall. A hand went up and I recognised the boys and Jen, and someone else: Josh's new girlfriend, I guessed. Smiles, tears and hugs, introductions to 'Liesel', and we were all on our way home to Mark and Jen's place.

That evening, the boys lit a braai fire in the small back garden, which, from its elevated position, overlooked Blackheath sprawling out below – and above, a lavender sky with the first few stars starting to peep through. In the distance, a halo of smog lay above the skyscraper outline of the city, and below us, lights started to flicker on in the gathering dusk. DF Malan Drive ran towards the city like a river of molten gold as rush-hour commenced.

The boys had already taken charge of the braai and were taking it in turns to turn enough steak, chicken and wors (sausage) to feed the five thousand. Little bursts of fat sent sparks and sizzles up into the evening air, bringing to me a smell almost forgotten, along with many associated memories of evenings like this.

The girls were in the kitchen making salads. I offered to help, but was shooed away, so went back outside to chat with the boys and listen to their opinions on the latest conspiracy theories. The atmosphere was relaxed, and even Richard had a smile on his face, due in no small part to the inch-thick, very rare steak coming his way.

The sun went down over suburbia while we ate. Josh put more wood on the fire, making it burst into bright flame, lighting up happy faces. I strolled around the little garden. Underfoot, the kikuyu grass was dry and brittle from lack of rain and the few shrubs looked dusty and tired. At the bottom, I found an old swing hanging in a make-do fashion from a jacaranda tree. First giving the rope a tug, I chanced sitting on it, and looked up through the dark, twisted boughs to a purple velvet sky, now sprinkled lavishly with stars.

The swing and I rocked in time to the rhythmic creak of an old wind pump, silhouetted against the sky at the edge of the garden. It moved lazily and brokenly in the breeze, its creaking the background music to the happy chatter and laughter from the braai fire. Kicking off my flip-flops, I dug my toes into the still-warm sand and felt the untamed heart of Africa beneath my feet. 'Hello,' I whispered. This was peace; it was happiness. It was home.

And it was so good to be with the kids again, and to see them getting along so well with Richard, who was unusually animated and engaged with them.

***

Two days later we were all up early, packed into two cars and on our way to the Kruger Park. Mark and Jen were just coming for the weekend as they had to get back to work. Josh (on his own) was coming for all five days.

We arrived at the Kruger gate just before lunch and drove slowly along the dirt road to the lodge – but even so, the road was so dry that the cars sent up clouds of red dust. We looked through hazy, shimmering heat for any animals that might be braving the noon day sun. There weren't many – just a few springboks, and I was reminded of all those long-ago school holidays when it had been a game to be the first one to spot something.

We climbed out of the cars, hot and sticky, and it was lovely to walk into the low-thatched reception, where huge ceiling fans whirred and glasses of orange and mango juice waited to be poured from ice-misted jugs. A porter put our bags on a trolley, and after booking in we followed him to our chalet: a stone and thatch affair with an open-plan living area, en-suite bedrooms, and sliding glass doors leading onto a stoep at the back.

I flopped on to one of the sofas. 'Oh, just smell the thatch! Don't you just love that smell?'

'Ja! Just watch out though. The baboon spiders just love it.' Josh laughed, and raised his eyebrows at Richard.

Richard had a thing about spiders. He eyed the thatch suspiciously and, without comment, tipped the porter. The barefoot, cheerful little chap with mahogany skin and bright eyes told us his name was '*Goodenough*', and asked if we wanted firewood for a braai. We said yes, and off he went to fetch some. When he returned, Richard told him to just leave the wood on the 'patio' (which made the rest of us smile). But Goodenough packed it away next to the stone braai instead, and explained, with a gappy grin, that 'The rain, she is coming!' And turning his nose towards the bush he inhaled deeply. Then he looked at us, inviting us to do the same – but none of us could smell what he could, and chinking with laughter, he walked away.

But a little later we could smell it. Sure enough, as we sat outside having sundowners, the sky suddenly darkened, the air turned chilly and the bush went very still. In the sickly yellow light, we watched a wall of rain approach across a shallow valley in front of us – and we could smell it – the dank smell of fresh rain on the parched earth.

A couple of big, wobbly drops smashed into the dry red dust off the stoep, and then more, and within minutes it was hammering down relentlessly, drumming a deafening tattoo on the thatch, and interspersed with the odd loud crack of thunder sounding like the crack of doom itself.

Richard was sitting in just the right spot to receive an icy droplet down the back of his collar, making him jump up. (Perhaps he thought it was a spider.) Not impressed, he muttered something and retreated into the lounge.

'Is it nice to be home, Mom?' asked Josh.

'Oh! You have no idea!' I answered.

It rained virtually non-stop all that night and into the next day. We took a misty, early morning drive into the bush but didn't see much other than a couple of warthogs, zebra, a troop of baboons and, of course, the inevitable springbok. Then into Sabi for supplies, stopping at a roadside farm stall on the way back to stock up on bananas, mangoes, pawpaw and avos.

In the now humid heat of the afternoon, we lazed around

the stoep chatting, playing Uno, and drinking wine. Later on, the kids suggested another game drive. Richard said he would take a nap, so I went with the kids. And as so often happens, it was on that unplanned trip that we saw more animals than usual, including elephants, a couple of black rhino, and a leopard up a tree with its kill. I was sorry Richard missed it, but he didn't seem particularly bothered. As the sun sank into a glorious explosion of red and gold we lit the braai fire once again, and once we had eaten, sat in mellow mood singing along while Mark played his guitar.

The next day there was a blue sky, shiny green bush, and clean, rain-washed air to greet us, and in the peaceful morning we breakfasted on the stoep, serenaded by the *bok bok bok* of a purple-crested lourie, and the squabbling of minor birds and shiny black starlings with iridescent, electric-blue wings. They were quite cheeky – coming within a metre of us, to see what we had to offer.

After breakfast, we drove out of the park to do a little sight-seeing of the surrounding area. The Lowveld mountains, no matter how many times you see them, are always spectacular, and intrinsic to the magic of this part of the world. With their deep gorges and strange, rondavel-shaped mountain tops, their waterfalls and vistas of endless bush stretching out into shimmering, blue horizons, they bring a sense of peace that is almost spiritual – a sense of something bigger than us mere mortals, that makes human endeavour seem transient and futile.

And where else in the world would you see a road sign that warns motorists to beware of hippos crossing?

We went back to the chalet for a quick lunch and then it was time for Mark and Jen to head back to Jo'burg. But we would be seeing them again in a few days' time.

The mood changed after they left. We were quieter, and there was no braai that night. Supper consisted of last night's leftovers, soon after which Richard went to bed. Josh and I sat and chatted over a bottle of wine, but as we had agreed to go for an early drive through the park the next morning, we also had quite an early night.

We left at dawn, which is the best time to be in the bush – just as it's beginning to wake up. It doesn't take much time at all for the sun to come up, throw her long, golden rays over the earth and warm it. But during that process there is a glorious disharmony of sound as all creatures, great and small, say good morning to the new day.

And it was amazing to see the difference a little rain could make. What had been dry and faded and half dead was becoming green and shiny and alive again. We saw springbok skitting about with the excitement of it all (some with newly born calves), and hippos wallowing in the swollen Sabi river. At first, I thought the grey lump sticking out above the surface was a rock, until an ear twitched and two beady eyes turned upon me. A second hippo surfaced in a great whoosh, up through the lily pads, which it wore as a hat as it grunted its deep, iconic laugh. The sound echoed across the surface and was answered by another hippo further downstream.

There were a couple of long-dead and blackened trees standing half submerged, their bare boughs making a roost for a handful of egrets. The birds sat motionless, sleek and white – they looked like candles set in a holder – and the whole image was mirrored in the shiny black water below.

Nearer to us at the water's edge were tall reeds and grasses, and the whole area buzzed, chirped, and creaked with life. Quite close to me, a tiny green frog, no bigger than my thumb nail, clung to the top of a reed. His eyes were the biggest thing about him!

And further down, overhanging the water, a colony of weaver birds flapped and squawked as they built and primped their nests, which were noisily criticised and ripped apart by some of the lady weavers. I could have sat and watched all day, but Richard and Josh were keen to move on.

***

The dynamic changed dramatically now it was just the three of us. Richard was more relaxed and quieter – back to his normal self, actually – but Josh didn't quite know how to take the change in him and the chat wasn't as easy-flowing as it had been with the others around.

We spent a lazy day looking around the old gold prospecting town of Pilgrim's Rest, but I don't think Richard was that interested in the history of the place. And he was quite happy to spend the afternoon lazing by the pool at the lodge, beer in hand.

Josh asked if he could use the hire car that evening, to go visit an old friend who also happened to be staying in the Kruger Park. I could see Richard wasn't happy about the idea, but begrudgingly, he agreed. He asked Josh what time he would be home, and Josh said he wasn't sure but probably around eleven o'clock.

Richard and I took a walk up to the lodge's restaurant. It was such a balmy evening I didn't even need the flimsy wrap I'd brought to cover my shoulders.

Springbok were grazing lazily between the chalets and watched us without concern as we passed. We turned off to follow the track along the river, and Richard read the sign warning visitors to beware of foraging hippos and water buffalo. He asked if it was a good idea to take that route and I assured him that as it was still daylight and if we stuck to the path, we should be fine. Unconvinced, he bowed and allowed me to go first.

'Such a gentleman!' I scoffed.

But as he fell in behind me there was the sound of movement in the undergrowth and as we turned to look, something streaked across the path just behind Richard and disappeared into the taller grasses at the water's edge.

Richard nearly jumped out of his skin and ran ahead of me – obviously it was a case of every man for himself!

'Bloody hell!' he said. 'What the hell was that?'

I laughed. 'It was just a little legavaan.'

'Good God!' he said, catching his breath. 'Did you see the size of it? What on earth is a legavaan?'

'A monitor lizard, and more scared of you than you are of him!'

'That I very much doubt!' he said, finally calming himself. Then seeing the funny side, he laughed with me.

Five minutes later we arrived at the restaurant and sat out on the wooden stilted deck above the river. Our table was next to the railing and we looked straight across the water to the opposite bank where a couple of crocodiles lazed, and the sun was setting over the bush. The usual chorus of bugs, frogs and cicadas was in full swing, and the flame of the candle between us burned straight and steady in the warm air. Richard smiled and held my hand – then pulled back quickly to slap a mosquito on his neck.

It was about half past ten when we walked the road back to our chalet and relaxed outside with a glass of wine, but the closer it came to eleven o'clock, the more agitated Richard became. He kept eyeing his watch and frowning, muttering words like 'selfish' and 'inconsiderate'. I was sympathetic at first, reassuring him that Josh was a good driver and he would be home soon. But he seemed to take Josh's 'shabby behaviour' personally.

'What's your problem, Richard? He's twenty-eight years old, not a silly teenager!'

'He said he would have the car back by eleven,' he said, crossly. 'It's now two minutes to eleven and he's not here!'

'He won't crash the car. And he's insured anyway.'

'It's the principle of it. He said eleven o'clock. He could at least have let you know he was running late.'

'*I'm* not worried,' I said. 'It's not even eleven yet! And what does it matter anyway? Josh has got no sense of time, so it was pretty pointless asking him in the first place.'

'Well, no prizes for guessing where he got that from!' he snarled.

I was angry then. I wanted to say something really cutting back, but nothing came to mind quickly enough, so I calmly picked up my jersey and made to go to bed, giving him the death stare as I went. But as I passed the window, I saw car lights and then Josh pulling up outside.

Richard heard it also and looked at his watch. I raised my eyebrows at him.

'It's gone eleven!' he said, triumphantly, yet seemingly even more annoyed that Josh should arrive now.

'By how many seconds?' I asked.

Josh came in happy and relaxed and dropped the car keys down on the table. 'Hi there!' he said. Then he saw Richard's face. 'Is everything okay?'

'Yes, fine!' I said. 'Did you have a good night?'

Josh relaxed again. 'Ja, it was good. Everything's good. Still going out with Carly; looks like they might be getting married pretty soon. You okay, Richard?'

'You said you'd be back by eleven,' he snapped.

Josh looked at me. 'I was, wasn't I?' he said, looking at his watch. 'It's only five past on my watch.'

'Well, that's not eleven then, is it?' said Richard.

Josh looked at me with a *WTF* expression on his face and I responded with a *don't worry about it* look. He opened the fridge door. 'Any leftovers, Mom?'

'I thought you'd just been to a braai?' I laughed.

'Ja, but I could do with a little something,' he answered, pulling out a chicken leg. He stopped short when he noticed Richard's look of disapproval.

He looked from one to the other of us. 'Okay if I have this?' He frowned.

'Of course, go ahead,' I said.

Richard turned and went to bed without a word.

Josh looked amazed. 'What was *that*?'

'That was Richard being an arsehole because you said you'd be home by eleven and you were "late"!'

'But I wasn't! What's his problem?'

'I have no idea. But don't worry about it – it *is* his problem, so just let him get over himself.'

***

We took a drive outside the park the next day to take a look at the local tourist sites. Richard was a little stone-faced and sulky first thing, but was soon smiling again. He enjoyed Bourke's Luck Potholes and the waterfalls, but didn't want to see the caves. I think he'd had enough by then and, having spied a shady spot where he could sit with a beer and look out over the bush, he said he'd wait while Josh and I went in. And that was fine. We did.

That night was a very humid, restless night with Richard moaning about what was worse, the heat or the noise of the air conditioner. And despite being well doused with repellent, he waged war on the mosquitos all night long, complaining that they were 'whining in his ears'. Well, there's karma for you!

After breakfast the following day I think we were all ready to pack up and drive back to Jo'burg.

We took Josh to Mark and Jen's place, where he had left his car. Jen was at work, but Mark took his lunch hour to come and have a quick cup of coffee with us before we said another sad goodbye to the two of them. But maybe not for long if Richard liked the idea of moving to South Africa to live.

Then we headed south towards the coast, turning left just before Durban to go up the north coast to Umhlanga, and the Hawaan Hotel. I'd stayed at this resort many times with

Hennie and the kids and it was like returning to an old friend. On entering our room on the eleventh floor I slid open the balcony doors, breathed in the fresh, sea air and looked out on the blue ocean. Straight below us was a very busy and very noisy swimming pool. I think I half expected to see the kids there, as they had been all those years before. How silly was that! And as appealing as the pool was, we'd been on the road for about ten hours by then, and a nap seemed like an even better idea.

We went out for supper later, and I couldn't help but notice how Umhlanga had changed. It had become more upmarket, more glass and chrome and glitz. The street cafés too had changed, but still served amazing seafood. And Richard was more than impressed with the huge rack of spare ribs he had.

The hotel sat at the edge of the Hawaan Forest, and the next day we took a walk through it, me trying to remember how long it had been since I last did, and how to find our way back. The forest is a strange, mysterious place where the paths and walks form tunnels through the dense bush.

It lies just off the lagoon and beach, yet just a couple of metres in, one is totally unaware of sand and sea – only of the quiet, dark forest, dappled in sunlight and alive with the sound of hidden creatures. We didn't see many – just one little duiker in fact, but were aware of quick movements in the bush now and again.

We picked our way carefully over the hollow-sounding forest paths and rampant tree roots, eventually coming to a clearing where an old, wooden-slatted suspension bridge was slung low across the wetlands. The bridge was probably about three metres wide but had no side ropes to hang on to, and its gentle movement as you walked the planks was quite scary. It was for me, anyway, especially when I looked down between the planks at the water below. But I always did look – and wonder what creatures were lurking among the reeds and water lilies.

I smiled to myself, remembering the last time I had crossed this bridge, a few years earlier, with Erin. I was barefoot, and the wooden planks had been too hot to walk on. So, she gave me one of her flip-flops and with our arms around each other's waist, we did a sort of three-legged hobble across the bridge. Halfway over, we felt the vibration of somebody running up behind us, and a skinny old man wearing nothing but a thong between two, walnut-like buttocks, bid us 'Good morning' as he ran past. We'd looked at each other and burst out laughing, then realising how ridiculous we must have looked to him, laughed even more, and nearly fell over.

Richard asked me what I was smiling about and I told him the story, but I guess it was one of those times when you had to have been there to see the funny side.

After a few nights in Umhlanga we hit the road again, travelling down past Durban and to the South Coast. I'd never been to the South Coast before, but had chosen a nice-looking resort in Uvongo, an hour's drive south of Durban.

And in that hour, the scenery changed from urban city and its suburbs, to the soft rolling hills of Zululand; little khayas on the hilltops, and Nguni cattle and goats grazing (or being herded) alongside the motorway. As we dropped off the N2 South onto the coastal road, we found ourselves driving along with a dark, twinkling sea to our left, and dense sugar cane and banana plantations on our right. And it became very apparent that we had left the glitz and glamour of the north coast behind. The little towns we passed through on the south coast being far more modest and rural.

Uvongo definitely had that feel about it. We found the resort, dumped our luggage, and went into the village to look around. Coming upon an estate agent, and just out of curiosity, we looked at the properties advertised on cards in the window. The agent came out to ask if he could help and we told him we were only vaguely interested at this point. He must have been having a slow afternoon though, because he insisted on driving us to see a couple of properties he had listed.

The more we saw of the area, the more we liked it! In fact, we both fell in love with it: the beautiful beaches, the overgrown, tropical vegetation – even the narrow, banana-palm lined roads with just a centre line to drive by. Margate, the main town, was four kilometres to the south – Shelly Beach, four kilometres to the north, and in both directions, there was from thereon a string of little coastal villages.

Both of the properties he showed us overlooked the sea, and were gorgeous. Richard and I looked at each other, both thinking the same thing, *I could live here!*

We spoke about it that evening, sitting on the high, grassy slopes outside the resort. To our left and at eye level were the Uvongo Falls, where the river flowed out from thick vegetation and tumbled over a rocky cliff into a lagoon on the beach thirty feet below. On each side of the waterfall the ancient cliff face sloped down gently, forming two arms that encircled the beach, and which eventually became rocky outcrops running into the sea. We were sitting on one of these arms. To our right, the Indian Ocean lay like a flat, twinkling disc as far as the eye could see, and straight ahead, on the other side of the beach, the rocky coastline ran like a silver snake winding its way north.

'This is paradise,' I said.

'It is,' he agreed, leaning back on the grass. 'Imagine having this view from your lounge window!'

'Can you imagine!' I repeated. Little did we know!

'So, what do you reckon?' he asked. 'Is this it? The little B&B on the coast?'

'I think it just might be!' I smiled.

The following day it was time to pack up and make our way to Haga Haga, following the road along the Wild Coast into the Eastern Cape.

I have always enjoyed road-trips through rural South Africa, seeing the colourful little rondavels nestling among the hills, herders guiding their long-horned cattle, or the beautiful Brahmans in their pastures – perhaps a family riding along the dirt roads in a donkey cart; the farm stalls, and colourful ladies sitting by the roadside selling oranges, mangoes, avocados, bananas and pineapples, talking loudly to each other in their strange, clicking tongue. It is their custom to speak loudly, so that others within hearing distance will not think they are being whispered about.

We drove through dusty little towns straddling open train tracks where goats and chickens wandered freely. In such a place there was a wedding party spilling out of a tiny church in a glorious splash of colour, the friends and family members resplendent in bold and bright traditional dress, singing, dancing and throwing confetti as they went. 'Nosipho's International Beauty Salon', a corrugated-iron shack a little further down the road, had probably done good business with the ladies of the wedding party.

Richard was keen to make good time, so we just grabbed a Kentucky Fried Chicken takeaway for lunch. Eventually we passed East London and were coming to the end of Kim's directions when, suddenly, there she was, waving to us from a gate. She opened it and we followed the dirt track down to a thatch house that seemed to grow out of the hillside itself, and had a one-eighty-degree view of coastline. There were hugs and introductions, nodding of heads and shaking of hands, and we followed them onto the stoep for a welcome glass of wine.

Kim and Gerald were originally from Somerset. I'd met Kim when our kids had attended the same pre-school together in Jo'burg. Now, thirty-odd years later, she didn't look all that much different. A natural blonde with a big white smile that showed off her beautiful teeth. She was a big girl – not fat, but buxom – and always happy, always smiling; she would throw her head back in the throes of the most contagious belly laughs.

If they announced the end of the world, Kim would be the first one to put the kettle on, and if there was no tea, she would be the one to organise a search party to find some – but always with a smile. Gerald liked to give the impression that he was the long-suffering husband, but nobody fell for it. It was obvious to all that she loved him so much he could wrap her around his little finger.

Gerald asked Richard if he would like a round of golf the next morning and Richard beamed at the prospect. But over breakfast, Kim had a few questions for him first.

'So, Richard!' she started. 'I hear you and Nat are thinking about runnin' a bed-and-breakfast together? How do you feel about that?'

'Yes, I think that's the plan,' he said. 'It appears to be a good way to maintain a sustainable income.'

'So, you'll be investin' in it, yourself then?' she enquired.

'Yes, I expect so,' he answered. 'But early days yet!'

'You've moved in with Nat, haven't you? Did you meet her mum?'

'Ah, yes!' he said. 'She was a sweetheart!'

Kim looked at me in surprise at that. I just shrugged.

'So, did you sell your place, then?' she went on.

'Yes, I did,' said Richard. 'And I've a few other irons in the fire, which I need to sort out before we come over.'

'I see,' she said, and smiled. 'Well, I'm sure, between the two of you, you're going to make a great success of it. I hope you're a good handyman – or at least a good cook. Gerald would be hopeless at both!' She laughed.

'Do I hear my name being taken in vain?' asked Gerald, entering the room.

'Of course not, my dear!' said Kim, smiling sweetly.

'Come on then, Richard. You ready?'

'Ready!' said Richard. He'd never been more so.

They left. Kim made a fresh pot of coffee and brought it to the table.

'Hope you didn't mind me grillin' Richard like that. Gerald says I should mind my own business, but when it's about my friends, it is my business. That's how I feel, anyway!'

'I don't mind at all,' I said. 'I found it interesting.'

'Thank goodness for that, then.' She beamed.

'Thanks,' I said. 'So, what d'you think? Did he pass?'

'I think he's very nice,' she said. 'And it's lovely to see you so happy. I bet you'll make a big success of everythin'.' She poured me more coffee. 'But it doesn't do any harm to keep an eye on things though, does it? Don't let 'em get away with anythin', that's what I say! Even after forty-odd years of marriage!' she said, throwing her head back in laughter.

The two days we had there went too quickly and in no time at all it was time to hit the road again. We took the beautiful Garden Route along the coastline but didn't stop much because Richard was tired of the long drive by then, and wanted to get it over with. Eventually we reached Cape Town and found our hotel. As soon as we walked into our room, Richard threw the car keys on the counter and himself on the bed and was snoring within minutes.

We spent four days at the Dolphin Hotel on the seafront in Greenpoint, which, on the first evening we were there, sponsored a wine-tasting event for a local vineyard. Each course of the meal brought with it two or three different types of wine to sample, at the end of which Richard and I were more than a little worse for wear. I don't think you're supposed to drink them all!

Over the next few days, we walked around the picturesque V&A Waterfront, took a boat ride out around the harbour, ate lobster for lunch and Malay curry for dinner, and took the cable car up Table Mountain. I was very glad to see that they had replaced the rickety little six-seater cable cars that were in use the last time I went up there. The new ones looked like flying saucers and held more people.

We visited the Stellenbosch wineries, and I showed Richard the old slave bell in the beautiful little town. On our last day we drove around the peninsula, visiting the southernmost point of the continent, where the Indian Ocean and Atlantic Ocean meet – a lighthouse on a bleak and rocky place – just a spit of windswept black rock in a wild, inhospitable, and endless sea. I looked out to the horizon, trying to imagine the thousands of miles of water between here and the next land mass – which would be South America to the west or Antarctica to the south and Australia to the east.

Then we visited the penguins enjoying life on the white sands and turquoise waters of Boulders Bay, and for the last time, had lunch overlooking the ocean.

'How long do you think it will take to sort things out so we can come back?' I asked.

'Who knows?' he said with a shrug.

'And what "irons in the fire" do you have to sort out?'

His face clouded a little. Was I being too nosey?

'Well, I have to sell the Saab,' he said. 'And I've got a couple of pensions that need looking at. But if we buy a bed-and-breakfast already up and running, we shouldn't need much capital. That would be the way to go, I think.'

'Oh, I'm getting so excited!'

'Yes, well,' he said. 'One thing at a time!'

Chapter Thirty

The flight back to Manchester was uneventful, and by the next evening we were sitting at our usual table in the White Horse, Richard regaling the locals with stories of legavaans and such. It felt very strange being there, and if we hadn't both been so tanned, I would have found it difficult to believe we'd ever been away. A week after that, it was as if we hadn't.

I saw Maggie and Erin, neither of whom liked the idea of me going back to South Africa with Richard, and the thought of leaving them was the only cloud on my horizon.

But by the end of March things were happening. Mum's will had been processed uncontested, and the bungalow transferred into my name. As soon as that happened, I went down to the estate agents to put it on the market. The only worry was Erin. I think, in the back of my mind, I always thought she would come back with me, but I guessed that wasn't going to happen now.

Two months later we had a good offer on the bungalow. Richard pushed for a little more, got it, and papers were signed. Everything kicked up a notch then, because we had to be out by the end of September. I spent my days getting rid of stuff and getting quotes from removal companies while Richard worked his notice, and found a buyer for the Saab.

The day came when we booked our tickets, and that evening we were sitting in the White Horse. He raised his glass to mine.

'This is it, girl, it's happening!' he said.

'I know. Last chance to back out. Are you sure this is what you want?'

'Of course it is. Why would I back out?'

'Good!' I smiled.

'Why? Do you have doubts?'

'Not at all. But it's easier for me. It's like I'm going home, in a way. But for you it's a risk. We don't even know if we'll stay together, do we?'

'Don't we?' he asked, looking alarmed.

'I don't know. Anything could happen, couldn't it?'

'Well, do you want to get married?'

The question came like a bolt from the blue and took me off guard.

'No, that's not what I'm saying. I'm just saying you're taking a risk, and I hope you're sure about it.'

'So, you *don't* want to get married then?'

'It isn't about getting married,' I said. 'It's about whether you're ready to give up your life here.'

'I don't have a problem with that. That was always on the cards. But if we *were* thinking of getting married, we should consider doing it now, before we go.'

'Do *you* want to get married?' I asked.

'I wouldn't have a problem with it. And here we'd be among friends and family.'

'We're leaving in a few weeks' time!' I said, astounded.

'Well, I'd like the girls to be there, and the gang in Leigh. The people at my sixtieth birthday. Now that was a lovely surprise, just walking in and seeing everyone there like that. That was wonderful! Like when Vicky organised a surprise wedding.'

'I've got more friends and family in South Africa,' I said.

'Well, you know my friends. They're yours too, now. The folk at my sixtieth. You know them all. That surprise sixtieth was something else, wasn't it?'

'Well, I'm sorry, Richard, but I'm not going to organise you a quick, surprise wedding, if that's what you're asking.'

I saw a quick flash of anger in his eyes, gone in a second, and it occurred to me that that was exactly what he wanted. Gone, too, was the smile.

'Well,' he said, very calmly, coldly. 'It's not going to happen at all then, is it!' He finished his drink. 'Are you ready for another?'

I wasn't. But he went up to the bar to get himself one.

I was left feeling we'd had a row, but wasn't sure what about. It was so silly. We were leaving in a few weeks. There was no question of a wedding (even if I'd wanted one). We were arguing over nothing. And he must have come to that conclusion also, because he came back smiling again.

'Seriously,' I said. 'Do you honestly think we could pull a wedding off at such short notice?' Surely he could see the impossibility of it.

He unhurriedly took the first quaff of his beer, very deliberately set it down and looked me in the eye, the smile gone again. 'Oh, I think that ship has sailed, don't you?'

I felt like I'd been slapped in the face.

***

And then suddenly we were in our final week. The removal people took the boxes and bikes and the place looked very empty.

Erin and I decided that we couldn't do the goodbye at the airport thing, so instead she took the last Wednesday off, and we spent it together, sitting out in the garden at Dylan's place. And we didn't say goodbye – just 'See you soon'.

I had my last Thursday evening visit with Maggie, who told me not to expect any teary goodbyes from *her* because she didn't do them. And besides, she knew I'd be back anyway because I was making a huge mistake going in the first place.

Alan dished up some chicken casserole for us, and then departed to fix Debbie's leaking fish tank.

Then the conversation went back to old times together, and then to our childhoods and inevitably to the abuse she had suffered back then.

'I can't believe you never told your mum,' I said.

'I couldn't tell anyone – especially not Mum.'

'So how *did* you deal with it? Did you tell anyone else? Did you ever go for therapy, or something?'

She gave me a bored face. 'To be told it wasn't my fault, he was the adult, I was a child. I wasn't to blame?'

'Yes!'

'No.'

'Why not?'

'What for? I knew all that. Alan knows. I told *him*.'

We sat quietly as I imagined how it was for her, and it prompted me to tell her about something in my life.

'When I was little, my dad would drive us kids to Runeham every Saturday morning to pick up the groceries at Collinsons, then cross over to the pet shop, then down to the sweet shop for Saturday night sweets. When we came out of the grocers, Dad would always take my hand to cross the road, and we'd hold hands off and on until we got back to the car. He didn't hold my sisters' hands, and it was *special* for me, somehow. Until I got to about eleven or twelve – and suddenly he didn't want to hold my hand anymore. He said I was "too big" for that now. I was gutted! I didn't know what "too big" meant.'

Maggie looked at me blankly and I felt silly, wondering why I'd even told her that. So, I tried to back pedal.

'I mean, I know that has nothing to do with sexual abuse. I can't imagine what that must feel like.'

'No, I get it,' she said, still without expression. 'You felt a bit betrayed?'

'Yes. Well, a bit rejected, anyway.'

'Well, imagine you have that special connection with him, and you hold his hand even though you feel there's something a bit wrong with it, sometimes he hurts you and you're a bit frightened of him. And then you find out one day that other people find it absolutely disgusting, filthy, and totally unnatural that he holds your hand – and *he* knew it; your dad knew it and never told you.'

'Oh, my God!'

'Yeah,' she answered. 'I knew what my dad did was strange. I knew there was something not right about it – that it was *our little secret*. But I didn't know why. It was only when there was gossip about Angela Roberts, that she'd been "interfered with" by her dad – only then, when the other girls were talking, I found out just how fuckin' disgusting everybody thought it was.'

'Oh, my God.'

'I was his "special little girl" and he'd lied to me – or not told me the truth. So how could the lying bastard love me? He didn't! Not on any level. The bastard. I was his daughter, his little girl, and I meant nothing to him!'

I shook my head. 'So, what happened?'

'After I found out about Angela Roberts, I was waiting for the next time. I was ready for him. I was going to tell him not to dare touch me. But something changed. He didn't come near me for weeks. And then suddenly he had a bloody heart attack!'

'And you never told anybody?'

She shook her head. 'Not back then. They said Angela Roberts was "spoiled goods". That no man would ever want to marry her now. I didn't want that to be me.'

I shook my head, speechless.

She carried on. 'When I found out that there was such things as "sex" and "abuse", I just felt so… ashamed! There was nothing I wanted to tell Mum about. If I was going to, it should have been at the time. Or at least before he died. But I never did.'

'Why? It wasn't your fault!'

'I never tried to stop him.'

'You were a little girl! You weren't going to say no to your dad, were you? And you didn't know it was wrong!'

'Not that simple,' she said, shaking her head. 'It wouldn't have stopped him even if I had said no… but…'

'But what?'

'I did sort of know there was something wrong with it. It didn't feel right and I think I was always a bit scared of him. But sometimes… it's weird… sometimes, my body… reacted?'

I nodded that I understood.

'So how disgusting is that?' she said. 'How dirty was I? Are nice little girls *sexual*? I don't think so!'

I took a deep breath. 'I was,' I said slowly, knowing I was about to tell her something I'd never shared with anyone before.

She looked at me wide-eyed. 'Spill!'

'When I was little… little, little… like in infant school, I used to go to my granny's after school every day, then Mum would come and take me home.'

She raised her eyebrows, winding the air with one finger to tell me to get on with it.

'We'd leave to catch the bus home and invariably, but *every* single time, we'd bump into Mrs Bell coming home from work, and her and Mum would stand under the street lamp, gossiping for hours.'

Maggie was winding the air again.

'And after a while, I would want to pee. Every time. Mum would tell me to just wait a minute, she wanted a quick word with Mrs Bell, and why did I have to be such a damn nuisance? And I would dance around, cross my legs, and do all the things that little girls who need to pee do, hoping no one would notice.'

Maggie looked at me with her 'getting bored' face.

'Sometimes I would wet myself and have to go home on the bus with cold, wet knickers. I'd sit looking at the floor, not daring to look at the other passengers in case they knew I'd wet myself and knew what a disgusting girl I was. I would want to cry, but I wouldn't, because Mum would say, "Stop crying! Everybody's looking at you – they know what a naughty girl you are," or "Stop crying! You're so ugly when you cry! Your face will stick like that!" And stuff like that.'

Maggie gave a deep frown. 'What are you talking about, Natalie? Is that it? Is that all you've got? Wet knickers?'

'No. There's more. Just wait!'

'Well, feckin' get on with it! I've never known anybody spin a story out like you can. It's like pulling hens' teeth!'

I didn't know how to say it. 'From a very young age, I was in touch with my *sexuality*,' I said. 'Although, I didn't know it was that. Let's just say in crossing my legs, I found a new way to comfort myself!'

She looked nonplussed, then understanding dawned. 'You were a little wanker!' She laughed. I rolled my eyes to the ceiling and felt myself blush.

'You were a little wanker, weren't you?' she repeated, enjoying the conversation now. 'So what? What's so terrible about that?'

'That's what I couldn't work out – but my mum was absolutely horrified. She called it "the dirty trick" and she obviously thought it was the most disgusting, depraved thing that anybody could do. I was some sort of freak. I knew I was absolutely the only person in the world who did this. I didn't know it had anything to do with sex. I didn't know there was any such thing as sex! And I didn't know why, but it was something I was supposed to feel guilty about. And boy! Did she make sure that I did!'

'Didn't stop you though, did it!' said Maggie, smirking. 'The dirty trick,' she repeated with a wicked smile.

'Yes. And I didn't know what "dirty" was in that sense. Why was it *dirty*? And worse – I think she told all my aunties, too, because they started to look at me like I was some little weirdo.'

'Yeah, and that was back in the fifties, hey. Even being left-handed was weird in those days. D'you reckon that's why your mum never liked you?' she asked.

'No, she'd already decided that at birth.'

'Why?'

I shook my head. 'I think I was her last try for a little boy – and I wasn't! And she didn't want another girl. I can remember rocking myself to sleep at night chanting, "Mum… my, Mum… my," until our Brigit threw teddies at me, or anything else she had, to shut me up, because Mum was never coming.

'And when the other two started school, she would leave me with granny, a semi-invalid who used to hook us round the neck with her walking stick if you were being "a little divil", and who would send me "down yonder" to find balls of wool and stuff – and I don't, to this day, know where "down yonder" was.'

'Why? Was your mum working, then?'

'No, she didn't work. She would take the three of us on the bus to Runeham, drop Cynthia and Brigit at a school close to my gran's, then leave me with Gran and go home to Pembie. It would have been much easier to put us in school in Pembie, within walking distance of home.

'But the worst bit of it was that she would take me to my gran's and then just disappear without saying goodbye. She'd just wait till I wasn't watching, and slip away. I used to hate that. When she shouted at us kids, she would say, "One of these days I'm going to walk out of this house and never come back!" And each time she disappeared and left me with Gran, I thought she'd gone forever.'

Maggie sat sipping her vodka, watching me and waiting for more.

'You know, I can still remember my first day at infant school. Can you?'

She shook her head.

'All the new kids were crying because their mums were going to leave them behind, but I didn't cry because I knew the drill; I knew she was going to leave, and that was fine. But that first morning, she kneeled down in front of me, put her hands on my shoulders, and *kissed* me! On the lips! And I was so happy I could have cried! I could taste the lipstick for hours afterwards. Still can, now, actually.'

'Why? Was it the first time she'd ever kissed you, or something?'

'I don't know. Probably. It's a very vivid memory.'

'So, what did she do with herself all day while you three were at school?'

'Don't know!' I shrugged. 'Housework, probably. It seemed to be her mission to keep the place in pristine condition and she seemed to be permanently cross because she couldn't keep it that way. When we got home from school, it would be, "Oh. You're home, are you? Don't walk on the kitchen floor, I've just washed it!" And we'd have to walk on newspaper pathways while it dried. And then it would be, "Go change out of your uniform and go play outside. And don't forget to hang it up." And I don't know why the house was so important; we never had any visitors ever come.'

'What? Nobody?'

'Dad's family now and again. Mum's eldest brother sometimes. That was about it!'

'You know, it's a wonder we turned out as sane and normal as we did! Well, as I did, anyway!' She chortled. 'I'm not so sure about you!'

'It is, isn't it?' I agreed. 'Have you ever forgiven your dad?'

'No! Would you? How do you even start to forgive something like that? Forgiveness is something you have to feel, and I *don't*. And I don't *want* to forgive him. I'm quite happy to keep on thinking he was a load of shite.'

'They say it's very healing to forgive. For you, I mean. Your dad doesn't give a damn either way whether you forgive him or not, does he?'

'Well, no!' she interrupted. 'That's 'cos he's *dead!*'

'So, there's only you. And they say it's good for you to forgive.'

'If you can,' she replied.

'If you can,' I agreed.

'And I don't think you've forgiven your mum, have you?'

'No, not really. But I don't hate her anymore. I guess you'd say I've accepted her rather than forgiven her. When I do think about it, I just think, oh well, I was born to a selfish woman who should never have had kids. I won't be the first and I won't be the last. So like you say – you just get on with it, don't you?'

'Do you believe you choose your parents?'

'What?'

'You remember daft Isobel at the hospice?'

'Yeah.'

'She believed in reincarnation, and that you choose your next life, and the people who will be in it. I can't get my head around that though, can you?'

'No. No I can't,' I answered. 'I mean – why would you choose anything but good things? Doesn't make sense, does it?'

'And to believe that, you would have to believe there was some God or some super-power organising everything. And I don't believe that.'

'No, me neither,' I agreed. 'But I don't believe we just die. I think our energy goes on – or we just get absorbed back into the universe again and get regenerated somewhere else.'

'What, as another human being?'

'I don't know. I don't know if you'd keep your own particular energy, like a soul?'

'Well, that would be a human being then. And that would be reincarnation, wouldn't it! Silly bat!'

'Well maybe you don't then. Maybe there is no soul, no "*I*". Maybe humans are like blossoms – they just flower for a season on the same bush – the bush of humanity. And we can't remember flowering the previous year because that was a different blossom. I think it's something like that. Or maybe we don't even come back as a human. Maybe we come back as a rock on the seashore, or on some distant planet – could be anywhere in the universe! We're all made of the same stardust. Dust to dust and all that.'

'And that's a load of bullshite, too,' she said.

I couldn't be bothered to argue with her, so we were quiet then.

'Are you afraid of dying?' she asked.

'No, as long as it doesn't hurt too much! I think it's a new beginning. Cast off the achy, old body and start a new adventure. What do you think?'

'I think you just die, and that's it. And I'm not scared to, because I've had enough of this fekkin' place, anyway. And if I have to come back, I'm coming back as a rich bitch so I can buy myself a desert island and not have to deal with people.'

'Could I come to visit?'

'Maybe… maybe not.'

And then, with a rueful little smile, she carried on. '*You* can come back as a rock and just sit there on the beach saying nothing – and I'll come and talk to you now and again, like in *Shirley Valentine*!'

'That would be absolutely perfect!' I laughed.

'I'd get as much sense out of you then as I do now, anyway,' she added, raising one eyebrow, and her glass. 'Here's to sane and normal!' she said.

'To sane and normal!' I echoed, and raised my glass to hers.

Chapter Thirty-One

Friday came – our last day in England as we were flying on the Saturday. Richard had some things to do, as well as delivering the Saab to its new owner. I didn't fancy sitting around in an empty bungalow, so on a whim, I thought I'd take a drive to Pembie and take one last look at the place I grew up in.

Richard came into the hall just as I came out of the bathroom, and just as some post came rattling through the letter box onto the hall floor virtually at my feet. I picked it up. There wasn't supposed to be any more mail, and here were four, virtually identical brown envelopes addressed to Richard. He stopped dead when he saw me with the envelopes in my hand.

'Why are we still getting mail?' I asked.

He shrugged in a casual, expressionless way, but there was an alertness about him. Despite the casualness, I sensed that he really wanted those envelopes off me; as if he knew they were for him.

He put his hand out for them and I gave them to him. He didn't even look at them, just at his watch.

'Probably junk mail or something. Damn, is that the time? I must get moving!'

'Aren't you going to see who they're from?'

'I will later. Right now, I have to move.'

'Okay,' I said. 'Well, I'm off now, too. See you later.'

'Where did you say you were going, again?'

'Down Memory Lane,' I said, and was about to explain what I meant by that when he interrupted.

'Oh. Yes. That's right. Well, have fun! See you later.'

I had the feeling once again, that something strange had just happened. How had he known the letters were for him anyway? And if he knew they were for him, did he know who they were from? Was it another secret?

By the time I'd driven to Pembie, I'd forgotten all about the envelopes. Here was the village of my childhood, sprawled as ever around the foot of Pembie Hill and reaching as far as it could up the rocky cliff known as 'The Ridge', which loomed over the village and faced out over flat marshes to the Manchester Ship Canal and River Mersey. The road wound through the half mile of shops, pubs, and houses, and for that half mile, it became the main street. It looked pretty much as it always had, except I noticed a couple of pubs had their windows boarded up. I didn't stop, but carried on out of the village until I came to the grammar school on my left, halfway down a straight slope of road. Its oblong, red-brick buildings (left for the boys, right for the girls) looked as stark and characterless as ever.

On the other side of the road, opposite the school, there was a narrow pavement and the bus stop, and a hedge separating them from the fields beyond. A little further up was the entrance to the dirt track, which was Providence Lane. I indicated right, waited for an oncoming truck to go past, and turned into it.

The narrow, puddled lane wound round for about a quarter of a mile, boarded mostly by fields, and big old oak trees on either side made a tunnel for about half of it. At the other end of the lane, the trees on my left gave way to one or two houses, and the valley could be seen, exactly as I remembered it. A patchwork of greens and faded browns stretched to the foot of

Runeham Hill, its heavily wooded slopes forming a long, dark wedge shape across the horizon. On the other side, a field rose sharply to the foot of Pembie Hill.

I parked, locked the car and looked around me. Everything looked about the same – except that Mr and Mrs Jones' house was no longer there.

Old Brocky's bungalow was still there, although he and his wife obviously wouldn't be. Old Brocky had been a friend of my dad's. They would sometimes sit out on a summer evening on garden chairs. Dad would smoke his pipe and they would each have a shandy made with Mackeson Stout, and talk about Mr McMillan and Mr Wilson, how to graft an apple tree, or how to get rid of greenfly. I was allowed sometimes to be with them, if it wasn't a school night, and if I didn't interrupt; which I never would because it was lovely just to be around them.

I crossed to the public footpath and followed it down the valley, passing beside my old home. The double-storey red-brick house and garage looked pretty much the same, but smaller somehow. At the back, the French windows of the front room reminded me of the times my dad's family visited us. Then the front room, which was normally off limits to us kids, was opened up and either a fire was lit in the hearth or the windows were thrown open; a crisp white table cloth would be laid on the table (as opposed to a plastic one in the kitchen), and the best knives and forks brought out. We would have salmon salad and Brigit would be told not to ask in front of our guests, again, what the 'funny knives' were for.

Mum would be very nervous while Dad's family were around and I couldn't understand why she went to so much trouble for people she didn't even like, because as soon as they left she didn't have a good word to say about them. She would tell us the tale about when she and Dad were newly married and had lived for a year with Dad's parents. His sister Rose and her husband, Stan, had lived just a few houses up, and both Mum and she fell pregnant with their firstborns within three months of each other. (As had his brother's wife, Veronica, over in Borneo the previous year.) It was the baby-boom years just after the Second World War when the country needed to replace its fallen sons. Granddad, apparently, had no qualms about saying that baby girls were basically a waste of space. Both Rose and Veronica had produced sons, of course, while Mum had Cynthia, and subsequently Brigit, and then me. I could imagine her waiting the whole nine months of her pregnancy, praying for a little boy – and the disappointment on the day, of having yet another girl.

Because Rose and Stan had lived so close, it had been very handy for them to 'use' Mum as a babysitter while they went 'partying'. It made Mum feel like Cinderella, and she resented the way they had all 'looked down their noses' at her.

I quite liked my aunties Veronica and Rose. Their husbands were nice too, but the ladies were like bright, exotic butterflies that occasionally flitted through my life – happy, and friendly and kind. And so elegant in their fitted suits and fur stoles.

Veronica had cigarettes that she kept in a little silver box. She called me 'darling' once, when I fetched her an ashtray. On another occasion she said I was pretty.

Veronica and Rose would chat and laugh as much as the men did, and they would say clever things that made everybody else laugh – even me, and I didn't even know what they were talking about.

I walked down the path just as far as the end of the property, where the path carried on over a ditch into the muddy field beyond, and I stood a moment, remembering that field in its golden, summer glory; the smell of freshly cut hay, and childhood games of leap-frog, and hide 'n' seek among the bales with our cousins. Going by age, there was Sally, who was the same age as Cynthia; Jane, who was the same age as Brigit; Peter, who was a year older than I was; and then a four-year age gap between Peter and the twins.

Peter didn't play with the girls anyway, so it was mostly just the five girls who played together and, to be honest, it wasn't much fun being the youngest one. I was dragged along under sufferance because Mum wouldn't let them go unless they took me along too. But it meant that whatever they were doing, I was never fast enough, tall enough or strong enough to keep up with them. So, it was usually me who, during a game of cowboys and Indians, would be left tied to a tree until nearly dark, and me who was locked in the dark, under the stairs, with the ghost of a dead tortoise!

I know that sounds ridiculous now, but it was not funny at the time. The tortoise had been put into a box of straw under the stairs to hibernate for the winter. But the following spring, he was just a gungy mess hanging like cobwebs within the shell. I don't know what I thought a tortoise was going to do to me dead or alive, but it wasn't good!

Sometimes, I would get so het up that I would forget how to breathe, literally; I couldn't draw breath, or release it. Mum thought I did it deliberately, but I didn't. I was scared because I always thought I was dying. Mum called them temper tantrums and threw a bucket of water over me once. Well, I guess it got me breathing again!

We didn't play with our cousins very often, and the parents socialised even less; just at Christmas really, when they would come for a glass of sherry and a mince pie.

One Christmas Eve, Uncle Harry was so drunk he'd driven his truck into the ditch along the lane and Dad and Old Brocky had to go and tow him out, and get him home to a very displeased Aunty Eida. He'd been sick all over the freshly plucked turkey sitting in a bowl on the seat next to him. The vomit pooled in the bottom of the bowl like some pale, lumpy gravy. But luckily (I guess), he wasn't hurt at all. And Aunt Eida washed off the turkey and cooked it for Christmas dinner the next day.

A cold wind had come up, and with a shiver I turned back up the path. This little path was still so familiar to me. So many times had I trodden it on my way to or from the ponds. 'Ponding' was my favourite pastime. I would go off for hours at a time, taking my jam jar with string tied around the top to fish for tadpoles, newts and sticklebacks, and all sorts of weird and wonderful things. Old Brocky had been a retired head master, and whatever I brought to him, he would tell me its Latin name, and about its life in the hedgerow or pond – which were facts I would proudly amaze my dad with as soon as he came home from work.

I caught the weirdest-looking thing in my jar one day. It looked like a small scorpion, but Old Brocky told me that it was a caddis fly larva. He said that in the pond it ate tadpoles, and I would have to keep catching them for it to eat. But if I put it in my tadpole tank, with a stick for it to climb up one day when it was ready, it would climb up onto the stick, shed its skin, and a beautiful winged insect like a dragonfly would emerge, and fly away.

This was such exciting stuff for me! I couldn't wait for Dad to come home so I could show him my prize! I did as Old Brocky said, and put it in my tadpole tank. I was dying to see this creature evolve. I'd check it every day. Dad, too, would come to see how it was doing now and again.

But Mum came to look one day, and she was absolutely horrified. She said it was 'plain evil!' A blood-sucking monster that sucked the life blood out of other poor creatures – and I was just as bad to want to have anything to do with it. It became 'that *thing* in a jar', and through subsequent years, I would be likened to it.

I never did get to see the caddis fly emerge, not even its skin left behind on the stick. It just disappeared without trace one day.

***

When I got back to the car, I realised I had parked it under the oak tree nearest to our old front door. How could I have not noticed my old friend! I had spent many hours sat in the cleft where the trunk forked into two, waiting for Dad's car to come up the lane.

Putting my hand on the rough bark, I closed my eyes for a moment and listened to it rustle and creak in the wind. It reminded me of the many times I had stood here, eyes closed, counting to a hundred while the others went to hide.

'Hello, my old friend,' I whispered.

When I opened my eyes I was looking directly at our house, now looming as large as it ever had in childhood. I recalled the shouting, the anger, the fights, the slamming of doors, and a horrible sense of sadness came over me.

When I was eleven, I came home from Sunday school one day, to find two fire engines outside, firemen running around the garden, and flames and black smoke pouring from the window of the bedroom Bridget and I had shared. Dad was running round, blue eyes big with fright in a dirty face, his pants ripped and red with blood. He saw me and shouted for me to go to Mrs Jones' next door.

Mum, Cynthia and Brigit were already there, sitting at the kitchen table looking shocked. Mum was crying and Mrs Jones was trying to get her to drink a cup of tea while Mr Jones stood outside the back door giving regular updates on the fire.

I think that was the first time any of us had been inside Mrs Jones' house. She was a strange, unsmiling lady (Dad said it was because she usually didn't have her teeth in) and was almost always in a headscarf, apron and slippers. It was a strange friendship she had with Mum, if friendship it was. They never called each other by their first names; it was 'Mrs Jones' and 'Mrs Sefton', and every day Mum would stand chatting for hours at her back door, never to be invited in. I just wanted Mum to come home, but if I went near them, they would start spelling words out and using hand signals. And Mum would say, 'Are you here again? What do you want now? Can't you see I'm busy? Can't you leave me alone for five minutes? You're nothing but a damn nuisance!'

Eventually, darkness fell, the fire engines left, and Mum and Cynthia went back home. Brigit and I were left with Mrs Jones, and she gave us sardines on toast for tea.

Our bedroom was so badly burned that Brigit and I had to move in with Mr and Mrs Jones for three months while the damage was repaired. Their kids had long since flown the nest, so Brigit and I shared a double bed in her daughter's old room. Mrs Jones' house was colder and darker than ours and had lino instead of carpets. But it was very peaceful, and she turned out to be quite a kind lady. I liked her cat, Sally-Ann, a friendly little tabby. From then on, I looked after Sally-Ann when the Joneses went on holiday.

The fire department said the fire had probably been caused by an electrical short behind the skirting board. I'd always believed that – until Brigit had told me otherwise.

Two years later it was a hearse that came to our door, bringing my father home. He lay in an open casket in the front room, in the semi-darkness of closed curtains. I thought I wasn't allowed to go in there, but Mum told me to go in to 'Say your goodbyes'.

I remember wondering why he was dressed in a long white dress. Why did they do that to him? I took his hand. Mine looked just like his, just a smaller, paler version. I wanted to feel the warmth and strength of his grip just one last time – its reassurance. But although it was the same hand that used to hold mine, still suntanned and soft-skinned, it was now cold and heavy, and wanted to fall back to his side. This was not Dad. Not now. I walked out the room, making Mum jump at the door jamb where she'd stood watching.

He had died on the Wednesday a few days before, during a heart operation. As I'd walked home from school that day along the lane, I'd been wondering how his operation had gone. I had been to see him the previous evening and thought how out of place he looked, tanned and smiling, amid the stark whiteness of the hospital. Maybe we would be able to visit him that evening, or maybe he would still be too groggy.

As I turned the sharp corner of the lane something stopped me; compelled me to stop. I turned to my left and went to stand by the gate into the field, looking out over the barley field. I had no idea why. Then a feeling of such utter, utter peace came over me; it was like a warm blanket put around me and I just stood there knowing that everything was all right, everything was going to be okay. I felt held there a couple of minutes and I didn't want to move. But eventually I turned my reluctant feet towards home.

A few minutes later I walked into the kitchen and saw Mum sat crying, Cynthia with her arms around her and Brigit just standing there. My heart beat wildly because I knew, even before my mind could process it, what this meant.

Brigit took me by the wrist and whispered, 'Daddy's dead.'

I just stood there with her, trying to breathe, not knowing what to do or say; what to feel, even.

'We heard just now,' she said. 'They phoned her from the hospital a few minutes ago.'

Cynthia left Mum's side and went to make tea or something, and Brigit and I went and sat either side of Mum and tried to put our arms around her. She shrugged us off immediately, stood up and returned to the job of washing the sheets, feeding them through the roller on the top of the tub, stony-faced and silent. It was totally bizarre.

Dad lay in his coffin in the front room for a couple of days, and then one day some men arrived at the house, and the front door was opened wide to accommodate the coffin being taken out again. Veronica and Wilfred, Rose and Stan were suddenly there, all dressed in black. Mum and Cynthia came downstairs also dressed in black and ready to go somewhere. Apparently, it was to the funeral – to which Brigit and I had obviously not been invited. We stayed home with Mrs Jones.

About a year later, it was an ambulance that stopped outside our front door; this time for Brigit, to take her to the hospital to have her stomach pumped empty of the bottle of sleeping pills she'd taken.

It was me who found her, raised the alarm and sat holding her hand, waiting the longest time for somebody to come. The doctor arrived first and soon after, an ambulance. Then Mum came, crying and fussing. But while the doctor was out of the room, she took a soapy flannel to wash the make-up off Brigit's eyes so that the hospital staff wouldn't think her a 'slut'. I thought the soap might sting her eyes but she didn't move; she lay pale and limp and I thought she had died already.

But she survived, as she did the many other crises that followed. And I was usually the one there to hold her hand, which I gladly did on the occasions she allowed me to – if she allowed *anybody* to.

Within the next couple of years Cynthia married Doug and emigrated to South Africa. Mum took a job as a secretary for an engineering firm in Ellesmere Port. Brigit got into as much trouble and mayhem as she could, and I made friends with the wrong crowd (according to Mum, anyway), at grammar school. But they were the closest thing to family I had, even if they *did* teach me how to smoke, drink, bunk off school, shoplift lipsticks from Boots, and, of course, all about the opposite sex.

Mum decided the house was too big for us and wanted to go and live in Little Rutford, close to her sister Eileen, and just up the road from her job. I was taken out of school a year early because she didn't like my friends (not to mention how difficult the journey to school would have been from Little Rutford), and was put into secretarial college in Chester. Brigit was put into a hair dressing college in Liverpool.

The wind was getting stronger and chillier. The old oak rustled and rattled above me and a black cloud passed overhead, foretelling rain. I'd had enough of Memory Lane, anyway, so I jumped into the car, reversed into our old gateway, and headed home again.

Chapter Thirty-Two

We arrived back in South Africa on 3 October 2013, just as England was heading towards winter, and South Africa into summer.

We had information on various properties, a couple of which sounded really nice, and had already arranged to meet the estate agents involved, to view them. Our friendly neighbourhood estate agent, Max, had found us a little garden cottage to rent on a month-to-month basis while we looked.

And we needed to buy a car. I wanted something higher off the ground than an ordinary car, and sitting on the showroom floor of the Hyundai dealership was a grey/blue, eight-year-old Tucson in beautiful condition, which the sales guy told us had very low mileage. Richard agreed, and after a test drive, he gave it the thumbs up. So, I bought it.

We'd told Max that we were looking for a bed-and-breakfast, but the two he'd shown us just lacked that something special; so we decided to wait and look at everything else available. The next couple of days were spent dragging around various places with Max, and I was beginning to wonder why there were so many bed-and-breakfasts and guesthouses for sale. The fact didn't seem of concern to Max though. He just shrugged and told us that there usually were because it was a seaside town.

One thing was very apparent, and that was that, thanks to the exchange rate, we could buy a large property. I was amazed at the size of the houses in our price range. At the end of the second, hot and sticky day, I was fed up climbing in and out of Max's car and walking for miles up and down steps and stairs. I was tired, and just wanted to go home. We had just looked at the last property on his list and were driving back to his office, when he had an afterthought.

'There is another place. In fact, it's not a bed-and-breakfast as such, but it does lend itself to being one. And it does have the sea view you're looking for. If you want, I can pick the keys up at the office and we can go take a look. It's right there in Uvongo.'

Richard and I looked at each other wearily.

'How about in the morning?' I asked.

'Well, we have to go back to the office anyway to pick up the car, and that's in Uvongo,' Richard pointed out.

'Okay,' I reluctantly agreed.

I immediately recognised the road we turned into, and the Lagoon Hotel where we had stayed previously. We pulled up in a wide gateway at right angles to, and just a stone's throw away from, the hotel's entrance, and waited while Max found the remote control and opened the gate.

From the gate, all we could see were the garage doors and a smaller wooden door to the right. But once inside that door, we entered into a pillared colonnade, which ran from the garage, along the single-storey L-shape of the house and formed one side of a private courtyard. The double-storey section of the house formed the L-shape and another side, a high, ivy-covered brick wall formed the third side, and the garage completed the enclosure. Under the wall was a shrubbery, a strip of lawn, and then basically the whole of the central area was taken up with a swimming pool and patio area.

The house was all bright white against the blue sky; and a pillared balcony on the two-storey main house looked down on the swimming pool. The owner had already moved out and we looked around the empty rooms of what was advertised as a five-bedroom, family home. Three of the bedrooms were downstairs in the single-storey L-shape part, and I immediately saw the potential for guest bedrooms. The house had big rooms and big windows, which I loved. But it was when we went upstairs to the master bedroom that I was blown away. Richard too.

As we walked into the master bedroom, we faced a picture window filling the whole wall, which framed the great expanse of sea and looked over the grounds of the Lagoon Hotel, to the other side of the inlet. It was basically the same view we had seen as we sat on the grass outside the Lagoon Hotel the first time we spoke of coming to live in this area. We couldn't see the waterfall or beach as such – they were hidden behind the gardens of the hotel – but over the top of the lawns and banana palms, we could see the mouth of the inlet and the silver coastline snaking away to the north.

The adjacent wall of the room held sliding glass doors onto the balcony overlooking the swimming pool. There was another good-sized, en-suite bedroom upstairs, and a huge bathroom. My mind was already converting the master bedroom into a lounge, and half the bathroom into an open-plan kitchen onto the lounge. It could be a self-contained little flat.

It was absolutely stunning, and I knew immediately that I was home. I looked at Richard, and even though he was trying to keep his poker face on for the estate agent, I could see he felt the same. He simply asked the price, which was within our budget, and said we would think about it and discuss it with him tomorrow.

That evening we had takeaway spare ribs for supper, and sat excitedly discussing the house. We were thinking up names for the B&B, but neither of us liked the other one's choices. He kept coming back to 'Richanval's' (which I thought was awful). In the end I made an executive decision to call it 'Valhalla BnB'. And he agreed.

The next day, we put an offer in a few hundred thousand rand less than the asking price, and after a little haggling, the estate agent phoned us back and told us the owner had accepted it. And then it became necessary to get down to the nitty gritty of deciding how we were going to buy it – together – or not.

Apparently, he'd looked at his pensions, and as it was, he didn't want to cash them in and be penalised for doing so before their due date. He *did* want to buy the house with me, but due to the pension situation, I would, technically, be the actual one paying the money – for now. But in three years' time, he would pay in his share. So, I agreed to do this and to support him for the first three years until his pension came through, when he could buy in to it.

I don't know whether he thought the house was going to go in both of our names from the start, but I thought it best that it be just in my name until he was ready to invest in it.

A month later, we picked up the keys and moved in. The first thing we had to do was go out and buy a bed and a couple of other things, as it would be another couple of weeks before our boxes arrived from the UK.

This would also give us time to do the renovations.

Downstairs, there was a huge lounge with built-in bar that opened up onto the patio and pool, and a big kitchen/utility room. A corridor ran at right angles down the length of the L-shape, off which was a dining room as well as the three bedrooms (two en-suite). And on inspection, if we did away with the corridor, the rooms lent themselves to becoming self-contained, en-suite guest rooms plus a small office – all of which would then open directly onto the pool area.

Initially, we just changed the upstairs into our own, private little flat. Richard good-naturedly went along with the plan, went through the costing with the builders and generally kept an eye on what they were doing.

Max introduced us to 'Princess', one of the security guards on the gate of the Lagoon Hotel. She wanted to know if the maid's room on our property was available, and if so, would it be possible for her to live in it, working for us one day a week in lieu thereof. She looked a good person, with a calm demeanour and an open, friendly smile. I looked at Max, who immediately gave a nod of approval. Richard also nodded, so I agreed. And so, Princess joined us, living in the little back room with shower and toilet, which I had virtually forgotten was there.

Richard's main priority at this time seemed to be to choose himself a local pub, and this involved scouting the area and visiting every bar he could find. And because of the dust and building chaos at home, I joined him for a pub supper most nights.

The places we tried could not be described as 'posh' by any stretch of the imagination. But he managed to find a little bar a five-minute drive away, which he learned from the locals could be reached by a back road, and thereby avoid the occasional police roadblocks on Marine Drive.

It was called the Windpump; tiny, dark, and so smoky you could hardly breathe in there (despite the new no-smoking laws). And noisy, too, with a DJ pumping out music that both he and anybody else so inclined sang along to on a mic. You had to shout to hold a conversation, if that's what you could call the half-drunken ramblings, well-meant verbal abuse and profanities being lobbied around, with which both men and women joined in.

The place was always busy. In fact, it was pretty full from about lunchtime onwards most days, and packed out on Friday and Saturday nights. So, this became his local.

If nothing else, the place had atmosphere. I'd go with him on the weekend sometimes, when the DJ took requests and there would be dancing – or the Afrikaans version, which was called 'sakkie-sakkie'. And sometimes they would clear the tiny dance floor and set up limbo poles, for people to see how low they could really go.

We tried out all the local restaurants too, which were far more civilised, usually stopping for a last drink at the Windpump on the way home.

It was such a wonderful time. I'd never just gone out and bought a car and a house before or had the money to buy nice furnishings and curtains as we did then, including a squishy three-piece, reclining suite in cream, Spanish leather. Richard suggested I open a business account to keep things separate for the taxman. It sounded like good sense, so I did. And with it came a credit card. I felt rich – and it felt good! Richard went online and found a couple of sites on which to advertise 'Valhalla BnB' and I looked at other places in the area to gauge prices and see what we would charge, and together, we came up with a plan.

It was a time of promise. We were realising our dreams, and we were happy. Christmas was just around the corner and although we thought we might be too late to get any bookings, we thought it worth a try. I don't think either of us thought we would actually get one. And then we did!

Chapter Thirty-Three

An Afrikaans gentleman wanted to book all three rooms for a week over Christmas. I looked at the pricing we'd agreed, and told him the cost, with which he seemed very happy, and made the booking. This prompted the urgent buying of beds, sheets and towels, crockery and cutlery. Luckily our boxes arrived with all our kitchen stuff in, two days before they did.

Looking back, we must have had some guardian angel looking out for us then, because never since had such a thing happened. I didn't realise that it's usual to give a discount if people stay longer than a few days. I charged him full price for the whole week for him and his wife, their son and daughter, and their respective spouses and children. Then at the end of the first week, Mr Van Rooyen asked if they could stay a second week, and seeing as it was only them staying there, would it be all right if his other son and his wife came also and took up residency in the dining room? They would supply their own blow-up bed. The breakfast tables were all out on the patio anyway, so it wouldn't be a bother. Apparently, they all worked in the same family business, and Mr Van Rooyen, head of the family, wanted to treat them all.

Knowing no different, I charged him full rate for the extra people, and he paid without complaint. After two weeks, we had made an awful lot of money!

It was not painless, however. I think I aged ten years in those two weeks. Every morning I made fresh fruit salad, then sausage, egg and bacon, fried tomato and baked beans for eight adults and scrambled egg on toast for two kids. Then I would clean up, clean their rooms, change beds every three days and (as they braaied every evening) clean a horrible, greasy braai every day. It was not fun. It was exhausting. And Richard didn't help.

Mr Van Rooyen and his wife, their son and family were pleasant, but the son-in-law was truculent and aggressive. One morning, in a fluster, I tried to open a new box of eggs. My wet hands couldn't tear the thick plastic wrapping, and the whole box went crashing to the floor, breaking all but four eggs and leaving a sticky, slippery mess on the floor. I cleaned up while Richard went, rolling his eyes, to buy more eggs. Breakfast was half an hour late and the Van Rooyen family were unimpressed; the son-in-law especially so.

And had I have given it more thought, I would have realised that I needed to vary the menu – but I didn't think. For most of the two weeks, I was in panic mode. One morning, the two younger women came into the kitchen while I was cooking breakfast, and asked if I ever made 'pap', the stiff, white porridge made from mealies that is the staple breakfast in many Afrikaans homes. To me it looks and tastes like something you might hang wallpaper with. I virtually shooed them out of the kitchen and put a *Staff Only* sign outside the door.

Consequently, the following morning, when I put a plate of sausage, egg and bacon down in front of the son-in-law, he pushed it away and angrily said something in Afrikaans. I don't understand much Afrikaans, but I did understand the gist of his outburst, so I asked if there was something wrong. He pushed his chair back with a loud scraping sound and went to his room, re-emerging with the cold leftovers of last night's braai, which he threw on top of the food I had given him. Then he set about his breakfast without even answering me. So, I learned to vary the menu.

Then halfway through their two weeks, we ran out of water. Apparently, there were always issues with Ugu (the water authority), and especially so at Christmas with the influx of holidaymakers. Whether it was a strike, a burst pipe, or lack of rain, or too much rain, or just plain overloading the system, the result was always the same – no water!

On the third day I had no clean sheets to put on their beds, and it was a toss-up between washing sheets in the swimming pool, telling them they couldn't have clean sheets, or saying nothing and seeing if anyone noticed! Luckily, the water came back on before I had to decide.

In the end, each day became more traumatic than the one before, and Richard was no help at all. I would ask him to clean the braai and he would tell me he would do it later, knowing that I would do it myself before 'later' came. And the more of a nervous wreck I became, the more he withdrew from me, and disappeared down to the pub.

The Van Rooyen family left on the twenty-eighth of December, and I had had my baptism by fire! I had learned some valuable lessons though.

I was so exhausted I couldn't even raise the energy to fight with Richard, even though I was really quite angry with him at this stage – not only because he did little or nothing to help, but also because he hadn't even bought me a Christmas card. With everything else going on, we had agreed not to bother with presents for each other, but I had, at least, managed to buy him a card. When I asked him about it, he said he hadn't even thought about it. And yet he had posted cards off to the UK. When I pointed this fact out to him, he said, 'Well, I *could* have, I suppose.'

'So why didn't you?' I persisted.

He just shrugged. I wondered if it was because I had criticised the last card he gave me and this was his response, or whether he couldn't now produce one of the usual cards in his 'stash' (if he had a stash), in case I asked where he had bought it. In any event, there were no more birthday or Christmas cards after that.

***

Josh and Liesel came down from Jo'burg for a few days in January. They loved the house and the pool (which they spent most of their time in), and if they were not in the pool, they were down on the beach.

We had breakfast at the Waffle House and seafood suppers out on the town, and we went to the Windpump on Friday night, of course. They enjoyed the vibe of the place, danced, and smiled at the locals dancing the sakkie-sakkie (which Josh called 'windsurfing').

Richard was friendly and welcoming, and there was no hint of their previous skirmish. I got to know Liesel a little better. She wasn't quite so shy this time, and (over making salads together) we had a good chat. She was a nice girl, and pretty with her long dark hair and big brown eyes.

Just seeing them again brought life back to normal for me, and it was so good to have them there, even for a few short days.

Late on the evening before they left, when Richard had already gone to bed and Josh, Liesel and I were finishing off the wine, Josh changed the direction of the conversation.

'And how are you and Richard?' he asked.

'We're fine! What makes you ask?'

'Are you going to marry him?'

'Not in the foreseeable future, no. Why?'

'Do you trust him, Mom?'

'Why do you ask that?' I countered.

'I don't know, Mom. I'm not sure about him, hey? And Erin definitely isn't. You know that.'

'Ah! So, she's told you about his past?'

'Was it a secret?'

'No, not a secret. But obviously something he's not proud of and doesn't want everybody talking about. And I guess Mark knows, too?'

'Ja, course. We love you Mom; we worry about you, you know!'

'I know, and I appreciate that, Josh. But I'm all right. I've got my eyes open, don't worry. What does Mark say about it?'

'Well,' he said, with a naughty grin on his face, 'he said to tell you that if you need any knees breaking, him and me have got your back. Right?'

'I'll bear it in mind!' I said, smiling.

Liesel giggled. She must have thought he was joking!

***

By the end of January, all the holidaymakers had gone back home, leaving the coast pleasantly quiet. The traffic reduced by at least half, as did the number of people in the malls; no queues in the supermarket and just locals on the beaches. This, apparently, was the 'norm', and it was lovely.

Richard unpacked our bikes and we started taking rides along the next road down from us, along the seafront. It was a round trip of about three miles, with fresh sea air and a glorious view. Usually there would be a ship or two on the horizon, or we'd see dolphins, or the occasional whale smacking a fin on the surface and blowing water out of its blow hole.

I liked to ride slowly and take it all in, but Richard, of course, liked to 'stretch his legs'. I would usually find him sitting on the bench at the other end, looking out to sea, and where we would drink our juice before heading back.

It became routine for Richard to go to the pub in the late afternoon, 'just for an hour', which normally stretched to two, and then home for supper at about six. I knew he always checked his phone for messages when he left the pub, so it was quite convenient to ask him to bring home bread or milk or whatever.

And the people in the pub became a valuable source of information – anything from where to buy (or not buy) things, or who the best plumber or electrician was. He even found a guy in there who could help him with immigration and went to see him at his office (the backroom of a petrol station), to start the ball rolling on the process. A couple of weeks later, this meant me paying out a few thousand rands for his application. It appeared that he hadn't brought much cash out to South Africa as he didn't think he would need much, the plan being to buy an up-and-running bed-and-breakfast, i.e. a 'sustainable income' already flowing. Not that *he* was doing much to earn any kind of income at all.

He wanted to join a golf club, and we spent one Sunday viewing three close by. Of course, Richard chose the poshest one. We took a buggy ride all around the course, some parts right on the edge of the cliff overlooking the sea, and some laid out around little lakes and waterfalls. We had lunch on the patio of the clubhouse, then went to the office to sign him up. He was like a little boy with a new toy, and I felt a bit like the sugar mommy he'd once joked I was!

'You're getting to be very expensive!' I said, frowning mock disapproval at him.

'Don't worry.' He smiled. 'You'll get it all back.' And he plopped a quick kiss on my forehead.

***

I did start to worry about the finances though. I knew he must have money back in the UK, and I had the ever-increasing feeling that he was making sure it stayed there. When I spoke to him about it, I was given the vague impression that it was all tied up in investments, or in pensions he was loath to access. But I couldn't help but wonder what had happened to the proceeds of his flat and car.

'Well, what about these pensions?' I asked. 'Surely they don't all pay out at the same time?'

'Well, yes. Basically, they do. When I'm sixty-five. But if you're worried about it, I can cash one in. There's one that's worth less than the others anyway. I'll have a look into it. It might take a month or two, but I'll make it paid up now. Leave it with me.'

Immediately, I felt mean for having even mentioned it. I did, after all, still have money in the bank. We would have to start being more careful about spending though, as bills were coming in and guests were not, and apparently, we shouldn't expect many now before Easter! I was glad that I had spoken up though. His contribution would help.

***

February was also very quiet with just two couples for the whole month, which brought in enough to cover the food but not the bills. The credit card was used up and we went into overdraft. I started giving him cash to go to the pub with instead of just handing him my bank card, and he hated being limited like that. He hated having to ask for cash. He made me feel as if I was letting him down; not keeping a promise.

On one occasion he gave me a coquettish little look and said, 'But you promised to keep me for the first three years.'

It was like a spoiled wife sulking for not being kept in the style to which she was accustomed. So, I told him that I, too, had thought we would be taking over a pre-existing bed-and-breakfast business – but the fact was we had not!

But there was hope: an increase in enquiries and a couple of bookings for March.

Chapter Thirty-Four

We were sitting quietly watching television one evening towards the end of February, when my phone rang. It was Erin. It was unusual for her to phone; normally she would WhatsApp me. Unless there was a problem.

'Hello, you,' I said. 'This is a nice surprise!'

'Mom, is Richard there?'

The tone of her voice made my heart rate kick up a notch and I knew, I just knew, that I'd been expecting this call for a long time – whatever 'this call' was.

'Yes,' I said, looking at him. He didn't take his eyes off the TV, but I knew he was listening. Maybe he'd been expecting this call, too.

'You might want to go out of earshot.'

'Just wait a sec, Erin, while I go outside. I can't hear you for the TV.'

I went out onto the balcony hoping he couldn't hear me out there. It would have been too obvious if I'd gone anywhere else.

'What is it? What's the matter?' I asked.

'Mom, the guy who bought granny's bungalow, you know you told him to pass any late mail on to me? Well, he phoned and asked me to go and pick some up, and when I went round there, he was quite angry about it. He gave me a whole stack of envelopes, all addressed to Richard, and he'd opened one. It was from one of these payday loan companies, demanding payment. He wants you to stop the letters coming. I'm sorry, Mom.'

'What are you sorry for? You've done nothing wrong. Have you got the letters there? Does it say anything on the envelopes?'

'No. Most are plain brown A5 envelopes with nothing on but his name and address. And you know what else is strange? His name is spelled in two or three different ways. What's that about?'

'I have no idea.' Immediately, I remembered the brown envelopes that had arrived at the bungalow just before we left.

'Mom? Are you still there?'

'Ja, I'm here,' I whispered. 'I'm just thinking. I think I've seen those plain brown envelopes before. Some arrived the day before we left the UK. He said they were just junk mail, but I had a funny feeling about them.'

'Oh, God, Mom, I'm so sorry. Are you okay?'

'I will be, sweetheart. But I need to find out about this.'

'What do you want me to do with the letters? Do you want me to open them?'

'Not right now. Let me talk to him first and see what's going on, okay?'

'Okay,' she said.

'I'll phone you back tomorrow.'

I went back into the lounge and sat down. He tore his eyes away from the TV just long enough for a quick glance at me.

'Everything all right?' he asked.

'Not really, no. There's lots of mail arrived at Mum's, addressed to you. Do you know what it could be?'

He looked disinterested and shook his head, his attention back on the sports programme.

'Lots of brown envelopes – like the ones that arrived the day before we left, remember?'

'Probably junk mail. How did he know how to get hold of Erin, anyway? Tell them they can just chuck 'em.'

'I gave him Erin's number. He wants you to stop them coming,' I said. 'You need to get in touch with whoever it is and tell them to stop sending stuff. Or can you go online and unsubscribe or something? He doesn't want them coming to the bungalow anymore.'

'Yes, okay. I'll do that.'

'He actually opened one. It's apparently from a payday loan company demanding payment.'

That got his attention. There was a split-second flash of anger, or was it fear in his eyes?

'He had absolutely no right, by law, to open somebody else's mail like that. He could get into big trouble for that! And that letter is obviously not mine. Probably sent to the wrong address.'

'It's got your name on, Richard,' I said, raising my voice a little.

He made a big show of pressing the pause button on the remote and, sighing, gave me his full attention.

'If it's got my name on it...' he started. 'Well... it could be a case of stolen identity. It's happened to me before. It's quite common these days.'

'That's even more reason to do something about it.'

'Well tell them to send it all over here then, and I'll have a look at it.'

'That'll take forever,' I said. 'Erin's going to collect them tomorrow. Can she open them – take a picture and WhatsApp them to you?'

'Oh, for God's sake, just tell her to throw them away. They're nothing! It's just junk mail!'

'They're not nothing, Richard. Identity theft is serious. Doesn't it worry you that somebody else is racking up debt in your name? You need to sort it out.'

Then another thought struck me. 'The envelopes have your

name spelled two or three different ways. How can that be identity theft?' I asked. 'Surely they'd make sure they got your name right?'

'No. That would indicate to me that that's exactly what it is. They can't *even* get my name right!'

I said nothing.

'I'm telling you, it's not me!' he said, getting annoyed. 'It's got to be identity theft, and I don't have to do anything because the onus is on them to prove it *is* me!'

I couldn't believe he'd just said that. I looked at him with absolute incredulity.

'Am I being *accused* of something here?' he asked, getting red in the face.

'We need to sort this out,' I said. 'You have to stop those letters arriving. It's embarrassing!'

'We?' he asked. 'Do what you like! I'm going back to the pub!'

He dropped the remote control in my lap as he left.

I poured myself a glass of wine and went to sit in a swinging pod chair on the balcony. It was peaceful out there; crickets chirped as the sky turned pink and mauve on the horizon, silhouetting the palm trees at the top of the hill. There were lights on in the houses dotted up the hillside, all with their open patios and balconies facing the sea. On one, a family was sitting out having a braai, their distant laughter occasionally drifting across to me.

Nothing had changed, and yet suddenly it felt like everything had. A tightening knot in the pit of my stomach told me it was a different world now than it had been an hour before. But there was nothing to say how or why – just a big question mark. He could be telling the truth. It could all be a mistake, or identity theft – it could be anything! It could be me jumping to conclusions. But I didn't think so.

It felt as though my whole future hung in the balance, and I needed to handle this situation delicately – get it right. Stay calm and reasonable and see how this played out. I knew by then that you get *one* chance with Richard. You reach for the keys a second time, you get slapped. If I wrongly accused him of anything, there would be no going back. We'd be finished.

But I remembered the day the brown envelopes had fallen onto the hall floor at the bungalow, and the expression on his face – and the knot in my stomach tightened even more. *Oh, please, God, let me be wrong!*

He stayed out late, and I was in bed pretending to be asleep when he finally came home. The next morning, he brought me coffee as usual, putting it down beside me without a word.

When I got up, I offered him breakfast, but he said he'd already had cereals. From his quiet, 'hurt' demeanour, I thought I was in for a sulk-day, so took my bowl of cornflakes onto the balcony, away from him. But to my surprise, he followed me out there with two cups of coffee.

He sat in the other pod chair, silent for a minute while he gazed up the hillside and sipped his coffee.

'I'm sorry if I got irritable, last night,' he started. 'But I think you can understand why. I made one mistake many years ago, which I paid for dearly. But now it seems I'm going to be judged for the rest of my life on that. I would have hoped you knew me better by now.'

'I'm not judging you, Richard. I just need to understand what's going on. And sorry, but you must admit, it does all sound a bit odd.'

'I know. But tell Erin to put all the post in one big envelope and send it over. I'll sort it all out, okay? I can't do it from little WhatsApp images.'

'Okay,' I said. 'I'll do that.'

We smiled at each other and the ice was broken. He started to chat about other things as if it was all forgotten – nothing at all wrong.

I WhatsApp-ed Erin and asked her to post the mail on.

***

In that week, things went pretty much back to normal. If the letters were mentioned at all, it was an insignificant matter that he would quickly deal with, and I convinced myself that the whole thing was as trivial as that.

Then at other times I wondered what I would do if he did turn out to be a con man. If I was as stupid about men as Maggie said I was. If this might be the beginning of the end of my happy-ever-after life in paradise? And how would I cope here, alone in paradise? But that idea seemed so far-fetched, it couldn't possibly be true, really. Could it?

I realised I had invested too much in this relationship; everything, in fact. He had become my life. And that was not good. *Rule No 1: don't expect somebody else to be responsible for your happiness!* Whichever way things went, I still needed to be more independent of him. And he needed to know I was quite capable of living without him, if necessary.

Was I capable of chucking him out if needs be? I didn't know the answer to that one myself; but I was pretty sure he didn't think I was.

The more I thought along these lines, the more I felt the urge to find *me* again. I needed to get out more, make friends and have other interests, as he himself had done. I didn't want to tell myself that I needed to *get a life* in case my one with Richard didn't work out, but I suspect it was in the back of my mind. Because Rule No 2 was: *If they're making you* un*happy – it may be time to get out!*

I'd always fancied bowls; lawn bowls, not ten-pin. I'd never tried it, but thought it looked pretty laid-back and civilised – my kind of game. I mentioned it to Richard one evening, who I knew had played bowls himself in the past. He raised a surprised eyebrow but thought it a good idea for me to give it a go. From the bemused little smile on his lips, I don't think he really thought I would.

'It's not expensive, is it? What do you need to start?' I asked.

'Just a set of bowls, basically. And you should be able to borrow a set at the club to start with.'

So, the next time I passed the Uvongo Country Club, I popped in to enquire about the bowling. As I was talking to the smiling receptionist, she waved at somebody behind me, beckoning that person over.

'This is the man you want to talk to,' she said, as he approached. 'He's the captain of the bowling section.'

A tall, lanky man in his sixties, dressed all in white with a white floppy hat, loped towards us.

'Ron, this lady would like to know about the bowling,' she said, and excused herself.

We introduced ourselves and he told me what I needed to know. He seemed very enthusiastic to have a new recruit, even a total novice such as myself. He told me that if I would like to come up to the club on Thursday afternoon, he or one of the other coaches would show me the basics and get me started, and then give me a few lessons before 'hitting the greens!'

That sounded wonderful to me. I thanked him very much, and drove home with a smile on my face.

Richard seemed genuinely surprised when I told him. But his only comment was 'Mmm! Well done!'

***

The letters arrived. I took the large envelope with Erin's bold lettering on and handed it over to him without a word. I was hoping he would open it in front of me, but that wasn't going to happen.

'Ah, thanks! I'll get onto this right away and see what's going on.'

He took them to the sofa in the downstairs (guest) lounge and ten minutes later seemed to be sorting them into various piles. There was no way for me to get close enough to see, without being obviously nosey.

I just smiled from the doorway and asked if I could help. He thanked me, but said he was fine. And ten minutes after that, he came back upstairs, without them.

'Everything okay?'

'Yes,' he said, positively. 'Most of it *was* junk mail, but yes, there does seem to be some sort of scam or identity theft thing going on, as well. I will send a couple of emails and find out what's happening. I'll get to the bottom of it, don't worry,' he said, looking me straight in the eye.

I was truly relieved. I felt like saying 'You see – that wasn't so hard, was it?' but thought better of it.

We went out for a meal at Breakers, my favourite restaurant, and we were happy, relaxed and back to normal again. I was so sorry to have misjudged him. We made love for the first time in a while that night and it felt right, and good, and that we were back on track, together again.

***

The following evening, he came back from the pub in a jovial mood. He came into the downstairs kitchen where I was busy folding the washing, opened a bottle of wine, and poured two glasses without even asking if I wanted one. He told me he'd bumped into the guy who was helping him with his application for citizenship. They had had quite a long chat, and this guy had told Richard that he could get citizenship by either one of two routes.

'One way is to prove that we've been a couple for more than three years,' he explained. 'And to prove that, you have to get letters from family and friends saying that you have been a couple and living together for that time, and a whole lot of other red tape too. You have to put together a whole file of stuff, and it takes a long time and a lot of hassle.'

'And the other way?'

'That we just get married,' he said, the old lopsided smile back again. 'Quick, simple, no problems!'

'I see,' I said, noncommittally.

'It makes sense, doesn't it? And what the hell, we've been talking about it long enough, haven't we? I think we should just get it done now; what do you think?'

I didn't know what to say. I felt I was teetering on a brink and didn't want to say anything that might tip me over.

'So, what do you think?' he repeated, opening his arms wide – an invitation for me to walk in for a hug.

I didn't move. It would have been so easy to let those arms envelop me in a bear hug and feel warm and safe again – pretend everything was okay. Pretend we loved each other? To pretend *something*, anyway, because what I was feeling wasn't love. And what he was offering wasn't love. It was an arrangement convenient for himself, and I was angry that he thought me such an easy pushover. Had it been so in the past? Well, not anymore.

I answered him, quietly. 'I think that ship has already sailed, don't you?'

And I walked away.

***

I spoke with Erin the next day and told her that he'd looked through the mail and was going to sort out whatever the problem was, so the letters should stop arriving now.

She still doubted him and thought I might have jumped the gun in presuming him innocent just yet. But from his demeanour, I felt sure that he was genuine. She was worried because more letters had arrived. I told her he hadn't had a chance to sort it out yet, but that he was on it.

'Okay, Mom,' she said. 'If you say so!'

It was when she asked if I had read them that I realised they had disappeared. I had a look around, even looked in the trash, but they were nowhere. But I supposed it was reasonable to assume he'd put them away safe somewhere.

Chapter Thirty-Five

The following Thursday I went back up to the country club and followed directions down to the bowling greens, where twenty or so white-clad people were playing bowls. As I made my way around the edge, I saw Ron standing with another woman, waving to me from a bench on the side. She and I were the only ones not dressed in white, from which I deduced she might also be new.

As Ron introduced me to Rita, she smiled gratefully, obviously glad to have another novice in the same boat with her – as was I!

She was quite striking to look at: a tall, strongly built woman, probably a little younger than myself, with thick, reddish hair down to her shoulders. She had strong-features and a lively (if not to say 'naughty') twinkle in her eyes.

'Right, ladies!' said Ron. 'Follow me!'

He strode away and we trotted after him to one end of an empty green where there were several coloured bowls lying around.

'Right, you're both new to the game, so let me start by showing you how to hold the bowl,' he said.

Rita looked at me and her lips twitched slightly. This was going to be fun!

When we went back the following week, 'Ruth' became our coach. Ruth reminded me of no one so much as Tolkien's *Treebeard*. She was tall and skinny, with a long face, droopy eyes, droopy shoulders and arms that seemed to dangle around her knees somewhere. She didn't smile much, but apparently had played at national level, and was, out of the kindness of her heart, willing to spend her time teaching us.

I hadn't known that bowls have a 'bias' and were liable (and only too willing) to curve away in the wrong direction if held incorrectly. Ruth taught us where to aim so that the bowl would, hopefully, end up close to the jack – which apparently was the whole aim of the game. She taught us how to stand, walk forwards, crouch and release the bowl off the end of our finger tips in one smooth movement (well, supposedly), and Rita and I would practise this relentlessly each Thursday afternoon while the others played Tabs. (This was a game in which anybody wishing to participate would put their name tab on the counter with the others, so that the captain could arrange them into teams.)

After a couple of weeks, Rita and I were firm friends and started shopping together, and going for coffee. She was of German descent (her parents had come over from Germany when she was little), and she had been married three times. She was now a widow with three grown-up kids and one teenage son, a *laat lametjie* (late lamb). And I soon found out that her interest was not so much in bowls, but in the men playing. She was on the prowl – and looking for a wingman (or woman) to help in the process.

Within a couple of weeks, we had our 'whites', had read the 'Bowling Etiquette Handbook' (well I had, anyway), and were both deemed ready to play with the big kids at Tabs. This was good news for Rita especially, as she and Treebeard were not getting along too well since we had been late for a special practice session with her the week before. We'd forgotten all about it, and when Ruth called to see where we were, we were actually sitting in Rita's kitchen drinking gin and tonics. Rita wanted to cancel, but I thought it too rude at that stage. By the time we arrived we were forty minutes late (and half pissed). Ruth was angry, and Rita unapologetic.

***

The following Thursday afternoon we turned up to play Tabs. It was the first time we had met up with the other bowlers in the little club room, and Rita's eyes scanned the room like a sniper's looking for a target. We were each given our tab and introduced to the other players, who seemed a friendly, lively lot, probably about two-thirds women in their sixties and seventies. But it was obviously the men who ran the show, in a definitely English-speaking, ex-pat kind of way, even though there were quite a few Afrikaans names and voices present, also.

Rita and I proudly put our tabs onto the kitchen counter with the rest of them for Ron to organise into teams for the day. Announcements and results of competitions were read out, we wished Joan a speedy recovery from her hip operation, and we clapped for Fred and Roz having birthdays in the coming week. Then Ron hung up a board off which our tabs dangled, showing which teams we'd been put in, and on which greens we would play.

Then as an afterthought, Ron knocked for attention once again and noted that Eileen and Natalie would be making the tea today. *Me? Really?* I thought, wondering if there could be another Natalie present. But then a woman in a wide-brimmed white hat gave me the thumbs-up sign. Eileen, I presumed.

I was hoping that Rita and I might play on the same team, but it didn't work out that way. With four people on each team, they would play from the worst player through to the best, in order to redeem any boo-boos that any bad players had made.

This being the case, Rita and I were the first players to play, against each other, on opposing teams.

I kept my eye on Eileen, who eventually came and tapped me on the arm to go with her and make tea. We went up to the club room, where she turned the heat up on a big urn, unlocked a cupboard and pulled out a pile of tablecloths. Eileen was a big lady and, probably in her seventies, she moved awkwardly. She had dyed yellow hair set in a tight perm, a pale-skinned, round face (which she obviously kept out of the sun), blue eyes and red lipstick. She reminded me of old, war-time posters of 'land girls' – wholesome, buxom, blue-eyed, blondes. I think that was the look she may still have been going for.

'You do the sugar basins,' she said. 'Sugar's in that big biscuit tin there. We should be four tables today.'

She started laying out tablecloths. I filled a sugar bowl and put it aside and she inspected it as she passed.

'No, not so much sugar,' she said. 'You only need two scoops in each one.' She emptied the whole thing back into the biscuit tin and handed me the bowl back.

'I see,' I said, taking the bowl and realising that there was a pecking order even in the tea-making process. Next, she had me laying out cups and saucers on the counter while she placed little vases of dried flowers on each table. Again, she came over to inspect. I'd put the cups face down and, without comment, she started turning them face up.

'So where are you from?' she asked. 'Are you new in the area?'

'Ja,' I said. 'I moved here a couple of months ago.'

'Where from? Jo'burg?'

'I did spend most of my life in Jo'burg,' I said. 'But I've been in the UK for the past few years, looking after my mum.'

'Ah! Okay. That's why you sound so English still then. Your first time playing bowls, is it?' She smiled.

'Yes,' I said. 'I guess that's obvious, hey?'

She kept smiling. 'And your friend?' she asked.

'Rita? Ja, she's never played before either.'

Her smile suddenly faded and her eyes went hard.

'Well, if you're looking for a man, you won't find one here!' she said. 'Those who aren't married are spoken for anyway – or past caring!'

Then the smile flashed back on again.

'I'm not looking for a man!' I laughed, and was about to tell her that I already had one, when the others started tumbling into the room, red-faced and sweaty, wiping faces with little towels they had hung around their necks. Eileen moved to man the tea urn.

Rita came in and we sat and had tea together. I told her what Eileen had said, and her mouth dropped open.

'Cheeky bitch!' she said.

After tea, we headed back down to the greens.

Both Rita and I were a bit nervous about playing in a proper game, but we seemed to be doing okay. In the first half we were even rewarded with the occasional 'Nice one, Nat!' or 'Well done, Rita!' But then in the second half I think our concentration must have been waning, because both of us sent bowls off on the wrong bias, and they went careening off into the next-door game. The guys joked good-naturedly about this, but even from their comments, we realised it was the biggest boo-boo one could make on the green.

Linda, the woman following on after me (promoted to that position since I was put into hers), smiled kindly.

'Don't worry, love. We all do that at first!' she said. And the woman behind her put a hand on her shoulder, saying, 'And some of us keep on doing it!'

'Oi!' complained Linda. 'I do not!'

'Not you,' said the other woman and she nodded towards the opposite group. They giggled.

The game ended and all the players met in the middle and

shook hands, thanking each other for a great game. Ruth came over to collect the bowls that Rita and I had been using, on loan from a retired member.

'So how was your first game?' she asked, looking from one to the other of us.

'It was good,' I said. 'I enjoyed it. And thanks for arranging for the bowls for us.'

'You might like to look in the club shop,' she said. 'They've usually got some good second-hand ones in.'

'I will,' I said.

'And by the way. Can I just mention that it's the rules of the game that at tea time you sit and socialise with the team you're playing with that day. Not your friends.'

'Oh, sorry!' I said. 'I didn't realise.'

'Well, now you know,' she said, smiling.

Rita didn't say a word, but looked aghast.

'And, Rita,' she continued. 'Your top doesn't comply with club rules, I'm afraid. It needs to be a collared shirt. See?' she said, swinging a long arm towards the other ladies. 'Can you get one for next week?'

Rita's strappy, vest-type top showed a great deal more shoulder than the other ladies' shirts did and I just couldn't imagine her in the more modest, collared version. She tried to smile, but I could see she was angry. As we walked to the car park, she gave vent.

'How ridiculous,' she said, 'that you have to sit where you're told to sit and talk to who you're told to. And "*your top doesn't comply with club rules*",' she mimicked. 'It's like being back in kindergartens!'

'She's probably worried you'll give one of the old guys a heart attack!'

'God, did you see them? It wouldn't take much, would it?'

We laughed.

'It does seem a bit over the top,' I agreed. 'It's not Ruth

though. I think it's in the etiquette handbook. Probably just old rules that go with the game.'

'Well, nobody's going to tell me what I can and can't do,' she said. 'We're not kids!'

One of the guys had come to put his bowls in the boot of his car, then headed back towards the club bar.

'You ladies aren't leaving, are you?' he asked. 'Come and have a drink in the bar with us!'

And then she was all smiles, dragging me along by the wrist, back up to the bar.

***

Things at home were good. Richard hadn't mentioned anything more about getting married, but he was in a good, happy place. It had been weeks since he said he would sort the letter-thing out, and we hadn't heard anything in the meantime, so he obviously had.

The small pension Richard had redeemed finally came through. It was from his very first job working down a coal mine – a job he'd done for less than a year. It was just as well we were doing better financially, as it yielded a pathetically small amount, maybe enough to buy a couple of bags of shopping a week. But we were getting a few more bookings in, and plenty of enquiries for Easter weekend.

Even Richard found the pittance from the coal company funny.

'Oh, well,' he said. 'Just as well we don't need it now, hey!'

'It all helps! We've got an overdraft to pay off, remember, and two credit cards. Your pension can cover your bar bill.' But I actually doubted it would even do that.

***

And it was round about then we decided to get a puppy. One of the guys in the Windpump was in the habit of calling in for one drink after walking his Labrador – a beautiful, shiny-black, soft-eyed dog that I just fell in love with. His name was Rocco, and he would patiently sit at his master's feet, gladly accepting any kind words, pats or treats offered. Bill, his owner, gave us the phone number of the kennels, and I rang them. They had a litter due shortly, and very excitedly I paid a deposit to reserve a pup.

When the phone rang a little later, I thought it was the kennels to confirm they had the deposit, as arranged. I answered it as always, as if it was another enquiry.

'Valhalla BnB, can I help you?'

'Mom?' said Erin.

'Erin?'

'Is Richard with you?'

Chapter Thirty-Six

It was déjà vu. Her words hit me like a sledgehammer as I recognised the tone.

'Mom, are you there?'

'No, he's down at the pub. What now?'

'Mom, the guy who bought Granny's bungalow, what's his name... Mr Ellis? He came round here last night and he was furious! That doesn't even cover it. He went ballistic. He had the bailiffs calling at the bungalow wanting to take his stuff away. And he brought round a bucketful of letters again. He said they're still arriving – more than ever. I thought Richard was going to do something about that?'

I felt physically sick.

'Erin, I don't know what to say. He said he'd emailed the people and sorted it out – weeks ago!'

'Well, I don't think he's done a damn thing, Mom.'

'You know, I can't believe this. When I first told him about the letters, I didn't exactly accuse him of anything, but he knew I was suspicious, and he was mortified. He said he regretted the mistake he made in the past because nobody would trust him now. And I felt awful for doubting him. And now this!'

'Ja, Mom! He regretted his "mistake" so much that he went

to prison and started some sort of money-making racket in there, too. That's regret, hey?'

I hadn't thought about that. And she had a point.

'I'll have to have it out with him again. Find out what the hell he's up to! Can you open the letters, take a photo and WhatsApp them to me?'

'Ja, I can do that.'

I could feel my face was hot with anger, but I needed to calm down before I spoke to him. Just exploding at him wouldn't help any.

He was due home in about half an hour and my mind was going off at so many tangents that I couldn't even think about making supper. So, I WhatsApp-ed him to please bring a pizza home. He had enough money on him to cover it. And that would buy me more time to calm down.

But here it was again. The same anxiety gnawing at my brain and tying my stomach in knots, putting me in something like panic mode. Why would I feel this way if I believed, or trusted him? But I didn't. Not now.

Eventually, I heard the automatic garage door grind open and closed, and I watched him from the balcony, as he came down the garage steps and along the colonnade to the front door. His step was laboured and slow – like a tired old man. And he wasn't carrying a pizza.

I went back inside and heard his heavy tread on each tiled stair as he came up.

'Oh, 'ello!' he said, doing his cute-little-boy voice.

'Hi!' I said, less enthusiastically. 'Where's the pizza?'

'What pizza?'

'The one I asked you to bring when I WhatsApp-ed you.'

'Oh, sorry! I didn't check my phone!'

I knew he always, without fail, checked his phone as he got in the car.

'Well, I've not made anything for supper, so it's pizza or go hungry.'

He sighed. 'I suppose I can go and get one,' he said. 'D'you want to phone and order it? D'you want to come with me? How hungry are you?'

I'd fallen for that one before. I'd agree to go with him somewhere, and then he'd say it was pointless both of us going, so maybe I should go on my own. Not this time!

'Yes,' I said. 'I'm quite peckish. Why don't you just ask them to deliver?'

'No. That takes too long. We'll be waiting all night. Don't worry, I'll go and get it. In a minute. I just need to sit a bit.'

He plonked down into his usual spot at the nearest end of the other sofa, and I knew that he had no intention of going out again. I turned my attention back to the telly and ignored him. I could live without pizza.

After a couple of minutes, he said, 'Or we could just have cheese on toast?'

'Ja, okay then. That would be good.'

He sat forwards and took off his shoes, and stretched out comfortably. I kept my eyes on the telly.

After a couple of minutes, he said, 'So who's going to make it then, you or me?'

'I'm not!'

'Okay. *I'll* go make us some,' he said. But didn't move.

A few more minutes passed.

'Nat?' He waited for me to look at him.

'Ja?'

He gave me his best lopsided smile. 'You know you make the best cheese on toast, don't you, my darling – much better than mine.'

'You're shameless!' I said, and his smile got bigger.

'I know. And you're a darlin'.'

He reached over and patted my hand where it lay on the armrest, assuming that I was now going to go and make cheese on toast. I didn't move.

'So, are you going to make us some?' He smiled again.

'No,' I said, smiling back.

His smile disappeared instantly. He stuck his nose in the air, sniffed in disdain, and turned his attention to the television. 'You're in a strange mood tonight!' he muttered.

'We need to talk.'

'Okay. What about?'

'About these letters that are still arriving at Greenfield Crescent.'

'Oh, Lord! Not this again! I might have known! What now?'

He sounded exasperated. As if it was all a nuisance to him – or a problem that he had already sorted out and I had no right to ask about.

'Mr Ellis has been round to Erin in a foul temper, saying the bailiffs were there by him, trying to take his belongings! And the letters are still arriving – more than ever!'

'Well, it's not my fault! What can I do?'

'Well, it's certainly not Erin's fault, or Mr Ellis's. It's your mess and you need to clear it up. This isn't fair on them.'

'And how would you like me to do that, exactly? I've told you – they must just chuck the bloody things away!'

'Richard, the bailiffs have been round. You said you'd sort it out. You said you were going to email the people concerned and sort it out with them.'

'And I did that!' he said.

'So, what happened?

'Nothing. Nobody came back to me.'

'So, what did you do?'

'What do you mean, "what did I do"?' He was getting agitated and red in the face. 'What could I do? I told you; nobody came back to me.'

'So, you just left it?'

'What else could I do?'

Erin was right; he hadn't done a damn thing!

'Can you show me your emails?' I asked.

'I could. But why d'you want to see them?'

'To see what you said.'

'I told you what I said. Don't you believe me? Are you calling me a liar?'

'No, I'm not calling you a liar, Richard. Don't get all defensive. I'm just trying to get my head around what's happening here,' I said, in my calmest voice.

'Well, I don't know what you want of me,' he said, a little more calmly. 'I don't know what you expect me to do from here in South Africa.'

I thought about that for a moment, and it made me think perhaps he should go back to sort it out.

'I think you're right,' I said. 'Nothing's going to happen from here. You need to go back to the UK and go see these people, find out what's what and get them to stop.'

'And are you going to pay for the ticket?' he sneered.

'I guess I'll have to,' I said. 'If that's what it takes!'

He didn't answer. Then a minute later he got up.

'I'm going to make cheese on toast; do you want some?'

'No, thank you. I'm not hungry now.'

When we spoke the next day, we were calmer, and he had obviously warmed to the idea of going back to the UK to sort things out. No doubt he welcomed the opportunity of a little holiday with the girls, and of getting away from me!

He made a plan to stay with Lea at her place and she would let him use her car also. We found a cheap flight, but he would have to wait till the end of the month for it, two weeks away. That was the longest two weeks of my life. Things calmed down as we tried to get back to normal, but it was just a pretence. There was actually such a tension between us, a big, dark gloom hanging over us. Life was suddenly deadly serious. No more smiles. No more fun. Just agonising politeness.

Erin sent me WhatsApp photos of the letters she opened. There were four loan companies, from which large sums had been borrowed just weeks before we left the UK, and apparently there had been no attempt to start repayment of them. There was a letter from the tax man demanding payment of outstanding tax, and a letter from his accountant asking him to discuss it with them. And there were his two bank credit cards maxed out to the full, neither of which had received repayment since we had left the UK. I wondered how anyone could possibly think this was 'identity theft'.

And the more obvious it was that it was him behind this mess, the more he blanked me out and wouldn't discuss it. I told him that I had copies of the letters and he didn't answer. Didn't even query Erin's right to open them. I made a list of company names, contact numbers, amounts owing, etc., for him to work through, and I handed it to him in a matter-of-fact sort of way, like a shopping list, without blame or judgement.

'There you go,' I said, handing it to him. 'That's a list of the companies involved and all the details. And don't forget your credit cards as well. You also need to go and talk with Linda at the accountants.' (I knew Linda; I had spoken with her when submitting Richard's time sheets and invoices.) 'And you should also go and see Mr Ellis.'

He took it from me, looked at it and said, 'I'm not a child, you know.'

I felt like telling him he was *just* like a child, a naughty little child pleading innocence even while his hand was still in the cookie jar! But, of course, I didn't.

'I know you're not. I just thought that would make it easier for you,' I said.

I think he knew the game was up, but he had a strange response to it all. It was almost as if he believed it was me who was rocking the boat, making things difficult between us – spoiling the 'good thing' we had. His attitude seemed to be that it was my unwarranted distrust that was pushing him to the limit, and it would be my fault if he chose to walk away.

'If you choose to doubt me, Nat, then there is nothing I can do about that, is there? But I won't be patronised. I will go and do what's necessary with this lot,' he said, holding up the list, 'and then we'll have to see where we go from there, won't we?'

It felt like a warning.

'Well, Richard,' I said. 'I need you to prove to me that you have done what's necessary with that lot first, and then, yes, we can consider where we go from there. Okay?'

'And how am I supposed to prove it?'

'Copies of letters, emails, statements – anything to show me that payments have been made.'

'Well, most of it will be done on the phone…' he said, then seeing my face, he said, 'I'll see what I can do.'

***

I knew the right thing to do would be to get rid of him out of my life. That would be the right and sensible thing, the Maggie thing, to do. But emotions aren't right or sensible. Emotions just want somebody to be there with you at the end of the day, somebody to share a smile and a glass of wine with; somebody on your wavelength who can laugh at the same things, and who 'gets you' without judgement, criticism or control. Somebody you can cuddle up to and feel welcome in doing so.

And he had been all of those things once. Hadn't he? But even if we could get past this, could we ever get back there? And if things didn't work out, how on earth would I cope trying to run a bed-and-breakfast on my own, in this big house? Maintenance alone would be a nightmare! How would I cope with difficult guests with no backup? How safe would I be? How lonely would I be?

Then I would think about how he had kept secrets from me.

How, while we were laughing and joking, he had been aware of those secrets. How genuine was our friendship if that were the case? How much did he respect me if he thought he could fool me like that? And twist me around his little finger. That's not how a friend behaves – taking me for a fool. How stupid did he think I was? Was it time to grow that other brain cell?

And so ran my thoughts, round and round all day long and through more than a few nights, also. When I did manage to sleep, I would wake up back into the nightmare of it, and would spend the days trying to keep calm and in control, and pretend that everything was fine. I found myself waiting for him to go to the pub so that I could be alone; and then as soon as he had gone, waiting for him to come home again.

We didn't go out together much anymore – maybe for a drink at the pub, where the noise and other people meant that we didn't have to chat. At home the conversations were pretty much just about practical matters.

***

Towards the end of April, the weekend before he was due to fly, Richard surprised me by asking if I would like to take a drive to Oribi Gorge again. We had once spent a very pleasant day there driving and walking around the nature reserve, daring each other to cross the rope bridge over the gorge, or to try the bungee jump. We'd had a nice meal at the restaurant there, sat out under the trees. I couldn't imagine why he was suggesting we spend a day out together there now. Maybe he wanted to chat – come clean and tell me what he'd done?

We drove and walked pretty much the same route as before, but hardly speaking. We went for lunch in the same restaurant as before, and he chose to sit at the very same table. Then sat looking over my left shoulder, hardly saying a word for the whole time. My mind went back immediately to the old couple we used to see in the Wayfarer, who would sit and eat without speaking. How happy we had been then, laughing at the notion that we would ever be like that, and saying how our relationship would be over if we did become that way. And here we were. Was that what he was trying to tell me? If so, he wasn't going to say it in words. He just sat in stubborn silence. And so did I.

Then a couple of days later he was as different again. We took the forty-five-minute drive to the kennels to pick up the new addition to our family, who was now eight weeks old and ready to come home with us. Richard was happy and smiling, and driving there together felt like we were on another road trip. It brought back memories of happier times, and just for a while we were back there, happy and being kind to each other.

And when they brought forth this round little football of soft, black fur with dark, chocolate-coloured eyes, we both just melted. He was the cutest, sweetest little thing you could imagine, and he somehow forged a mutual bond between us. 'Odin' fell fast asleep on my knee as we drove home.

***

Then the weekend came and I took Richard and his suitcase to meet the airport shuttle bus. He and I were able to say goodbye in a friendly, positive way, both looking forward to his return in two weeks' time.

Chapter Thirty-Seven

Even though we had parted friends, I walked back into the house that day with a tremendous sense of relief that he was gone. And with little Odin wriggling around my feet and following me everywhere I went, it was impossible to be unhappy.

Life carried on. With the Easter holidays over, there wasn't much in the way of bookings, but weekends usually brought one or two couples in for a night or two. And between that, shopping with Rita, and playing bowls, life was busy. Rita told me she was also a member of a walking club and tried to get me to join that with her, but I declined. I liked *strolling* as opposed to the heavy-breathing version, and didn't think that a walking club was really me! But from twelve weeks old, I would take Odin for a walk on the beach every day, in the late afternoon.

Apparently, Rita and a couple of the walking-ladies met once a week for lunch at JoJo's in the mall, and she invited me to join them. That sounded much more like fun.

There were five of us all together scrunched up into a booth at JoJo's. Like Rita and me, the other three ladies were in their fifties and sixties, two divorced and one widowed, and all down to earth, 'tell it like it is' girls. They made for good company and a good laugh. Lunch at JoJo's became a weekly event, during which a bottle of gin would be passed around (under the table), and taken home empty.

***

Richard Skyped regularly to bring me up to date with his news about family and friends, and told me that he was busy sorting things out. He'd been to his accountant to sort out the tax situation, and had 'transferred some funds' to cover this and his credit card payments. And he was also going to contact the loan companies and 'find out what was happening with that story'. He said he just wanted to come home now. I was pleased, and told him I was missing him and looking forward to his return. Although to be honest, I'm not sure that I was.

Now Richard wasn't around, Odin was becoming a bit of a problem. He did not like being left on his own when I went out. I had to lock him inside the house (so that he wouldn't fall into the swimming pool), but I left the top balcony open for him. Whenever I came home, he would proudly show me the trail of destruction he'd caused throughout the house while I was away. I would walk from room to room saying, as crossly as I could, 'Who made this mess? Who made this mess?', and he would just wag his tail with pride at me!

He was a clever little dog, and he'd already learned that the newspaper out on the balcony was for his benefit. But I wasn't sure how I was going to convince him that the lawn was even better!

***

The two weeks of Richard's absence went by very quickly. He was due to fly out of Manchester on the Thursday night, arriving back in Durban late the following afternoon, and I said I would pick him up off the shuttle bus in Uvongo.

He messaged me from Manchester airport as he was about to board and told me that everything had been settled and he was looking forward to getting home. And I *was*, genuinely, looking forward to seeing him again. But the little voice inside was asking, did he really sort everything out?

I was sitting out in the pod chair on the balcony with Odin asleep on my lap, and in the quietness, an idea came to my mind. It was five o'clock in South Africa, four o'clock in the UK. His accountant's office should still be open. I thought the phone number must be on one of the letters that Erin had WhatsApped to me. I checked, and it was.

Purely on an impulse, I dialled the number and heard the phone ringing all those thousands of miles away. But not for long.

'Bradshaw and Dunn, Accountants, how can I help you?'

I recognised Linda's voice.

'Hi, Linda,' I said. 'It's Natalie. Do you remember me?'

There was silence for a second, then, 'Hi, Natalie! Of course I remember you. How are you? We haven't heard from you in a while.'

'I'm fine, and you?'

'No, still surviving. Y'know! What can I do for you?'

'I was wondering if I could speak to Mr Bradshaw? Is he around?' I asked.

'He's not, sorry. He went home a bit early. Can I help?'

'Maybe,' I said. 'Would you know if Richard's been in to see him lately?'

'Richard? No. But it's actually me who handles his books and I've been trying to get hold of him. Do you know where he is?'

'Yes. He's living in South Africa with me now. We moved back here at the end of last year,' I told her.

'Oh, my God! I don't believe it? Really? Richard? No wonder he hasn't been answering my calls!'

'He's actually been over in the UK for the past couple of weeks, and I thought he was going to come and sort his tax matters out with you. But obviously not.'

'Well, I haven't heard from him at all, and I'm pretty sure Mr Bradshaw hasn't either, else he would have told me. Is he still here? He's already missed the end of the tax year, and there are a couple of things we need to speak to him about. So, he does need to come in and see us.'

'He'll be in the air somewhere over the Middle East as we speak,' I said. 'But I will tell him to contact you when he gets home, okay?'

'Okay, yes, if you would. Thanks, Natalie. What's the weather like over there? Glorious, I suppose,' she asked.

'Hot!' I said.

She sighed. 'It's like the slopes of Everest here today!'

We said our goodbyes, and I heard her cut the call.

I didn't move. I don't think I could have moved. I just sat in the tranquillity of the late afternoon, the pool pump churning, a couple of minor birds squabbling, and Odin giving little doggy snores – and in that moment I wondered who it was I'd been living with for the past four years. It certainly wasn't the man I thought I had.

***

When I met him off the shuttle bus the following day he was in a cheerful, 'so-glad-to-be-home' mood.

'Hello, darlin',' he said, kissing me on the cheek. He hadn't called me that in a while.

'Hello,' I answered, smiling. But try as I might to be excited by my partner's homecoming, it felt more like welcoming a guest, a stranger. I opened the boot for him to put his suitcase in.

'Thanks,' he said, straining with his bag. 'So, how's things? Everything okay?'

'Ja, everything's okay.'

I felt him looking at me as he closed the boot, maybe sensing a less enthusiastic welcome than he'd hoped for. He opened the passenger side door and found Odin waiting on the seat.

'Hello, little fella! How are you doing? Look how you've grown!' he said, and Odin wriggled with delight as Richard climbed in and put him on his lap.

'What have you been feeding him?' He laughed. 'He's twice the size!'

'Ja, I'm not surprised! He's a greedy little bugger – and a pooh-machine. It goes in one end and straight out the other.'

His eyes searched mine as I spoke. Then he turned his attention back to Odin.

'Is that so? That's my boy!'

I drove us home and he went straight to the fridge and pulled out a beer, offering me a wine. I declined, and he went to the sofa where he sat pulling off his shoes.

He told me how the girls were, the latest antics of little Izzy, and how the gang in the Brewer were all doing. I listened with a smile on my face. Maybe it was because of his happy mood, or because he'd just got back and was tired, that I held back on a conversation that I knew would end up in a row. Or maybe I knew that this would probably be the last time we could be friends like this – as false as it was. As false as it must always have been.

'How hungry are you?' I asked. 'Do you want something now or do you want to wait for supper?'

'No, I'm not hungry, thanks. I ate on the plane. I'm knackered! But maybe we can go out for a last drink in the Windpump a bit later. What do you think?'

'No, that's fine. Why don't you go and put your head down for a couple of hours?'

'I'm going to have this beer and do just that.'

He went and laid on the bed and not long after was snoring away. I sat on the floor with my back against the sofa, looking out to sea. Odin thought I'd come down to his level for a game, and started pulling at my belt tassels. I played with him for a couple of minutes, smiling at his fierce little growl, but wasn't really in the mood to play. Eventually, he flopped down beside me with his head on my thigh, looked at me with soft, brown eyes and gave such a big sigh that his little body shuddered.

'Ja, that's how I feel, too!' I told him.

As I sat there, I absent-mindedly picked up my phone and found myself looking at the copy letters Erin had sent to me. I looked at the four from payday loan companies again, and noticed that there was a card number quoted.

There must have been an actual credit card, and that card must have been delivered to the address on the letter, i.e. to Richard. And that being the case, how could anybody but Richard get his hands on it? Or use it? It couldn't be anybody but Richard. There was no way it could be identity theft.

Just then there was an incoming WhatsApp from Erin. It was as if she could read my thoughts from six thousand miles away.

The message read: *Hi Mom? How are you? Is he back? Everything ok?*

I wrote back: *Yes, he arrived an hour or so ago. On the bed having a nap at the mo.*

So has he said anything yet?

No, we haven't spoken about anything yet.

Then I tapped out a long message telling her about my phone call with the accountant, and she replied.

Well there you go. There you have it. I knew it! You have to get rid of him, Mom.

I didn't go out to the pub with Richard that evening; I didn't feel like the noise of that place on a Friday night. Richard was happy to go on his own, saying he was only going for one, anyway. But he was gone for a few hours. He must have brought money back with him from the UK.

It was the next day, over mid-morning coffee, that we got into the conversation we needed to have.

'So, did you manage to sort everything out over there?' I asked.

'Yes, pretty much.'

'So, tell me? What happened?'

'Well, yes, looks like somebody was taking out loans in my name. I phoned the loan companies and explained that it wasn't me and they said they would sort it out.'

'What? Didn't you have to go in and see them, even?'

'Yes, I went into one of them, in Manchester. They asked me to sign an affidavit. The others didn't even need that! It's just a formality really. This kind of thing happens all the time.'

'You didn't have to prove it wasn't you in any way?'

'Well, how was I going to prove it *wasn't* me? It's up to them to find out who it *was* they gave the money to.'

'And did you bring any paperwork – anything to say they acknowledge you're not to blame in all this?'

'Like what?' he said. 'There *is* nothing!'

I just looked at him, not knowing what else to say. But I had to tell him I knew.

'And the tax man. Did you go in to see Mr Bradshaw?'

'Old Ernie? Yes, I popped in to see him. That's all sorted out now.' He smiled, and slapped the sofa.

This was it. It was now or never.

'You're lying, Richard. I know you didn't go there.'

'What?' he said, frowning annoyance. 'What are you talking about?'

'I know you didn't go and see Mr Bradshaw!'

'Well, no, technically you're right. It's Linda who deals with my stuff, so it was actually her I had a meeting with.'

'No, you didn't,' I said. 'I phoned Linda and spoke to her, and neither of them have seen you in over a year.'

His face went from shock, to anger, to a cold sneer, in seconds.

'Quite the little sleuth, aren't we?'

I didn't answer.

Odin was chewing on his sandal, so he bent down to pull him away and tickle his fat little tummy. I couldn't see his face then, until he sat up again.

'All right,' he said. 'I didn't go and see Bradshaw because I knew I could deal with that from here and I didn't want to waste time on it. I wanted to get the other stuff sorted out first. The identity theft.'

'And you reckon you did?' I asked.

'Yes,' he said. 'That's all sorted!'

'You know what I can't understand is how somebody applied for a credit card on your name, that was delivered to our address, and yet you didn't receive it? But somebody else at a different address, did? How did that happen? How did they get their hands on it?'

He looked at me and I could almost see the cogs turning in his brain. He shook his head.

'Maybe somebody at the loan company took it? I don't know!'

He was getting angry again. 'You keep asking me questions I don't have the answers to. You obviously don't *want* to believe me, or trust me – so what now?'

'I don't know what now, Richard. You're right, I don't trust you – or believe you. And do you blame me?'

We sat, silent, for a couple of minutes and I'd begun to think the conversation was over. Then he spoke again.

'You know, identity theft is very common. It's not like *murder*, for God's sake! It's what they call a "victimless crime". And to be very honest, I have no sympathy with these loan sharks anyway; just because it's legal for them to steal money off people the way they do – it doesn't make it right. Does it?'

'So, if you can't beat them, join them?'

'No, that's not what I'm saying.'

But it was, and he was looking at me realising I could see his hand in the cookie jar. He was pathetic.

As if he could read my thoughts, his nose came up and with a slight air of disdain he looked away, out to sea.

Neither of us spoke for a couple of minutes.

'So, how do we fix this?' he said, eventually.

I looked at him in surprise. 'Fix it? Do you think we can? You were already supposed to fix it by going back to the UK and sorting things out. But you haven't *done* that, have you?'

'And if I wanted to fix it now? Properly. Make things right?'

'What? Go back again? I can't afford that, Richard. And how many chances do you need, anyway?'

'If that's what it takes,' he said. 'I'll go back. I'll pay.'

'And where are you going to get the money?'

'If you can lend me the fare for now, I will free some money up when I go over and give it back to you.'

'It takes more than that, Richard, it takes *trust* – and I don't think I have any left.'

He didn't answer for a minute or two.

'If you want me to, I'll go back over and sort it out, properly,' he said. 'And bring proof, if that's what you want. Would that make you happy?'

'I don't know! I don't know, Richard. Now *you're* asking *me* questions I don't know the answers to.'

That was the end of that conversation. But it soon became evident that he intended to go back to the UK yet again to make things right. It crossed my mind that he might be planning to go back to the UK and stay there, run away from this awkward situation – and me. And that actually wouldn't be a bad idea. I certainly wouldn't be heartbroken if it were to happen that way.

So I let him use my credit card to book himself a flight. It was a 'Return' ticket.

During the next few days our relationship was in a no man's land where he swung between trying to be cheerful and optimistic and being surly and almost resentful. And I was on a roller coaster of thoughts, emotions, indecision and turmoil, which I am sure was responsible for a handful of hair scooped out of the shower plug – mine!

We were already into the second half of May, and the nights were turning chillier. There was one evening when after a busy day of cleaning, washing and shopping, I flopped down on the sofa in the lounge, hot and tired.

After a while, however, the cool of the evening made me shiver, and Richard raised an eyebrow at me.

'I'm chilly,' I said, 'but I'm too lazy to go and get a jersey.'

Ten minutes later he got up to go to the fridge for a leftover chicken leg, asking me if I wanted one, too.

'No thanks,' I said. 'But while you're up, won't you get my jersey off the end of the bed?'

It would have taken him maybe ten extra steps to do so.

'I'm not going to the bedroom,' he said, flatly, and sat down again without a glance.

Half an hour later he complained of terrible heartburn.

'Have we got anything for it?' he asked, knowing full well we had, but just giving me my cue to jump up and go get it for him.

'Yes, of course,' I said. 'It's in the bathroom cupboard.'

And I gave no sympathetic look as he got up to go find it.

He came and sat down again and, after picking up the remote, started a desultory search through the channels, asking me if there was anything I wanted to watch. He settled on his favourite sitcom before I had even considered the question, both of us knowing that would be the case.

'D'you want to watch this?' he asked.

I didn't answer. I really didn't give a damn.

We sat there five or ten minutes, our eyes on the TV, but I could see he had withdrawn into his own private little world, lost in his own thoughts, probably hardly aware I was there.

Odin tried to jump up on the sofa by me but slid off again. We both laughed then, but it felt awkward. I scooped the little fella up and I chanced to look at Richard as I did. He was looking at me with a strange expression. Fear – distrust – sadness? I felt almost sorry for him then. But his eyes went cold again, and returned to the TV screen. Half an hour later, he went to bed.

I sat wondering where our relationship had gone to, and what the chances were of it ever coming back. But I knew, really.

Chapter Thirty-Eight

The day of his departure dawned. He'd packed his bag the night before, mostly with the same clothes he'd taken the first time, which had been laundered but not even put away in his cupboard yet. The thought struck me that it was an awfully long way to come just to get your washing done!

On that morning, Richard had a bit of a flap on – as much as Richard ever flapped, anyway. But he had on his cheerful, positive, 'Don't-worry-I've-got-this!' smile as, by mid-morning, I drove him to the shuttle bus pickup point. According to the timetable we had a few minutes before the bus was due, but just as he was taking his bag out of the boot, the bus pulled in right behind us and there was no time for much in the way of goodbye. I was grateful for that.

He just gave me a quick hug. 'See you in two weeks,' he said.

And then the bus was disappearing down the road and he was gone. And the nervous energy of him was gone, and there was just a quiet, flat, calmness left behind.

It was strange walking back into the house, now so silent, as if it and I were both listening out for him still. I went upstairs, made myself a cup of coffee and went out on the balcony. Sharing a pod chair with Odin, I let the peace, the Sunday-type quietness, sink in. It felt good.

It rained that afternoon, a soft, soaking rain that pattered gently on the closed slats of the patio awning just in front of me, seen through the plaster columns of the balustrade. It brought a welcome coolness to the air. Odin was half on my knee and half on the seat beside me – a cosy fit these days, the way he was growing. We rocked gently, watching a soft, grey mist drift across the houses on the hillside, bringing with it the strong, seaweedy smell of the sea.

I sat thinking about Richard. I pictured him sitting all alone nursing a beer in the airport. Or maybe he was on the plane already. I thought about our relationship and where it was or wasn't going. But I couldn't come to a decision. You'd think it would be easy, wouldn't you – given all the facts. And I could imagine what Maggie would say to me.

But still… still… I couldn't shake this notion that somewhere inside of Richard there was a decent man, hiding. Yet given the evidence, why would I think that? And all the same old arguments went round and round in my brain while I played devil's advocate with myself.

It rained quite heavily at one point that afternoon, during which a car came splashing through the puddles along the road outside the front gate, and stopped outside the gate of the house opposite. I watched across the top of the garage roof, as the three kids who lived there clambered out of the car, slamming doors, laughing and squealing, and trying to cover their heads with their school bags as they ran up to their front door. What a different world they were in. A parallel universe!

Then the heavens really did open, and the rain pounded down making the awning sound like a kettle drum, and sending a fine (and pleasant) mist over Odin and me. He lifted his head to look at me for a moment, but I told him it was okay and he went back to sleep.

The poor frangipani tree next door was taking a real beating though. The little waxy blooms that had managed to remain so far were being dashed down into a drift of yellow blossoms around the foot of the tree.

After about half an hour the heavy rain stopped, and within minutes the late afternoon sun came out, gilding wet roofs and puddles and banana palms, and casting long purple shadows. The air smelled rich and earthy now.

A broad-beamed Zulu lady with a basket on her head came swaying slowly down the road.

'Meal-lies! Meal-lies!' she cried. But no takers today.

As the sun went down, and one lonely frog started his solo lament, I realised I had been sitting out there for several hours. And poor little Odin had been with me all the time.

'Shame, Odin, do you want some supper, my baby?'

He immediately started thumping his little tail up and down.

I'd spent the whole afternoon thinking about Richard. What a waste of time. I fed Odin. I hadn't eaten since breakfast, but wasn't that hungry, so I fixed myself a slice of toast and a large gin and tonic and went to sit on the lounge floor. I could see the lights coming on over the other side of the inlet, tracing the coast line north, and there was a storm brewing out over the sea.

As dark clouds wiped out the last of the light, lightning flashed far out on the horizon, and within a short while we were in the full throes of a tropical storm. The rain lashed down as a gale churned up the waves, sending them in like cavalry charges against the wind, to dash upon the rocks in an explosion of spray.

The palm trees cowered, their long fronds lashing and snapping like shiny ribbons in the garish pink lightning. And when the thunder came, it sounded like the very fabric of the heavens was being ripped apart, its vibration shaking the house to its foundations.

The storm matched my mood precisely. I sat in the darkness watching the show with Odin curled up on my knee, totally oblivious. I cried, I drank too much gin, and I haven't a clue what time it was when I finally dragged myself off to bed, exhausted.

***

But life goes on. I had guests coming in at two o'clock the next day, so no time to feel sorry for myself. Princess had made up the rooms, and basically, I just needed to put soap and towels, toilet rolls and bin bags in and make sure the tea and coffee trays were topped up and had milk.

Mr and Mrs Dlamini arrived just after two o'clock and Mr and Mrs Botha arrived shortly after. I was surprised how young Mr and Mrs Dlamini were. I doubted that either of them had had their twentieth birthday. She wasn't feeling well, and he lovingly put her to bed before even coming to settle the account. Once he had, he returned to their room and drew the curtains. I sighed with relief; that meant they wanted to be left alone and weren't the sort to be complaining every two minutes.

Some people just liked to complain about everything. 'There's no hot water' (you just have to wait for it); 'The water's too hot'; 'This isn't like my shower head at home'; 'Where are the matching, white-towelling gowns?' (the what?); 'There's a lizard on the ceiling' (a harmless gecko); 'What's that noise?'(crickets); 'Well can't you do something about it?'

And there are those who want things at awkward times: an extra fan, or heater, or pillow, or a cell phone charger, hairdryer, or iron. And 'What time's breakfast? Did I mention that I'm vegan?'

It was no problem, usually, to keep a smile on my face – they were paying for the service. But sometimes, if I wasn't in a good space myself, it was hard.

The guests that weekend were not so bad. I actually felt sorry for the Dlaminis, as *she* spent the whole of her weekend being ill. He was so concerned, but didn't know quite what to do about it. First of all, he came timidly knocking on my door wanting to know where the closest pharmacy was, then he came back to ask where the nearest cash machine was. Then he found he was parked in by the Bothas in Room 2 (whose curtains were also closed). So, in the end, I took him in my car, telling him what to buy for tummy runs! (Thinking, *Sorry, Princess, but I'm glad you'll be in to clean the rooms tomorrow!*)

By ten o'clock on Sunday, those who were having breakfast had had it, and an hour later, everybody had left. I put the dishes in the dish washer, emptied waste bins and stripped beds, putting the first load of sheets on to wash. The pool was looking a bit murky. It needed a backwash, the sides brushed and some chlorine put in, but that could wait till the evening. It's best not to put in chlorine in the sunshine.

There was still some laundry to put away, and among it, a couple of Richard's golf shirts. When I opened his wardrobe, the warm, soapy, cologne smell of him came wafting out, and the first item I saw was the maroon striped jacket he'd worn on our first date. In fact, every shirt and jacket and jersey in there had its own story of happier days: of Dermot and Cathy's wedding, a Caribbean cruise, or the day I persuaded him to wear the pale-yellow jersey. I touched its softness, and so missed the man I'd loved back then, even though that man didn't exist anymore. Had never existed.

I knew what I had to do, but I was putting it off. I knew that once I'd told him it was over, in black and white, that would make it real. Once the words were out there, there would be no taking them back. It would officially be the end of any happy-ever-after. He'd been my last chance, and part of me still didn't want to let go of that.

But I needed to. So, I spent the rest of the day trying to compose an email, which at one point was seven pages long. But in the end, I kept it brief.

Dear Richard,

I don't know whether you're expecting this (I think you probably are), but anyway, this is to tell you that you and I are over.

You will know that this is not a sudden decision, and not one taken easily. But the fact is, I can't trust you. It's no good pretending that this is about 'little white lies' – we both know it's much more than that. It's about you and me. Even if you put things right now, it's not going to work. Because I can't trust you.

I give below the number of the removal company that brought our things out to South Africa (if you want to use them again) – this is their Durban office number. If you make arrangements with them to pick your stuff up, I will show them what they need to pack.

I'm sorry it's ended like this – but that was a chance you took, wasn't it? I won't change my mind, so please don't come back. Natalie

I read it through at least ten times before mustering the courage to press the 'Send' key – and then I did!

At that moment, I thought that was the end of Richard.

Chapter Thirty-Nine

I sent a WhatsApp through to Mark, Josh and Erin telling them that I had 'dumped his sorry ass!' – tapped out with more conviction than I actually felt. They responded, 'Way to go, Mom! Proud of you!', 'Well done. Best news ever!', and 'Shame, Mom, are you okay? But thank goodness for that. You're so much better off without him! Do you want to Skype?'

There was absolutely no response at all from Richard. Nothing.

***

At first it felt a little strange to have the house to myself, but it was a good feeling. And pretty soon, life morphed into a new routine of bowling twice a week, shopping with Rita and lunch with the girls, and taking Odin for a walk on the beach every day, just before supper. He had learned to use the lawn rather than a newspaper. He'd also learned the names of his ten toys, and would fetch 'Monkey', 'Snake', 'Blue ball', 'Red ball', etc., on command. His favourite was his ball though – he lived to play ball. He slept with his head on my lap in the evenings, and on my feet at the bottom of the bed at night, and he woke every morning in such a happy, enthusiastic mood that it brightened the start of my day, too.

He still didn't like being left at home very much, and I was having little success teaching him not to wreck the place when I went out. But with Princess coming and going and Mu, the gardener, coming once a week, he wasn't left on his own that much. And he soon trained Mu to throw a ball for him.

The B&B grew steadily and I started having guests most weekends, especially long weekends, and business people during the week, as well. It was enough to pay the bills.

Princess was an absolute blessing. She cleaned the guest rooms and house a couple of times a week, going through the place like a whirlwind, and did all the ironing. She was a strong Zulu girl, and very good at fixing things. Better than me. And bonus, she and the other guards at the Lagoon would send to my door any guests who couldn't get in there, hadn't made a booking etc., and I was happy to pay a small commission for their referral.

Under Richard's misguidance I had opened up too many bank accounts and credit cards, and the interest on them was killing me. And I wanted to renovate the guest bedrooms to make the place more appealing. So, I decided to sell up my little townhouse in Jo'burg to kill the debt and get the place looking good.

I brought in the same builder who converted the upstairs and told him what I wanted to do, and a couple of weeks later, the work was done. Each room now had a tiled floor, an en-suite bathroom, and its own little kitchenette with a fridge, kettle, toaster and microwave – not self-catering as such, but it would keep a beer cold, provide ice, or could warm a baby's bottle or a takeaway supper. And each room had sliding glass doors that opened up directly onto the pool area.

***

Suddenly it was Christmas, and the B&B was fully booked. But before the main rush, Erin and Dylan flew over from the UK and had two weeks with me. It was wonderful. It was Dylan's first time in SA and he really liked it.

Christmas itself was hectic. Princess's daughter, Nosipho, was staying with her for the holidays and Princess asked her to come in and help me each morning. While guests were at breakfast, she would make beds, empty bins and tidy their rooms, then iron any sheets that needed to be. She also helped with stripping beds and cleaning rooms between one family leaving and the next arriving, which was a tremendous help, and gave me more time to keep the pool and the braai clean. Between Princess, her daughter and myself, we did it. There were a couple of incidents, but thankfully only minor ones. It was all a learning curve.

One such incident was when I was preparing a fruit salad one morning for a full house of guests. I had washed the fruit and was just about to start chopping, when a guest asked if she could use the iron. I took it to her and, on returning to the kitchen, was confronted by a huge, male vervet monkey sitting on the worktop, busily taking a bite out of each fruit one by one, before throwing it to the floor.

He looked at me with tiny, beady eyes and gave me the full up and down look, as if to say, 'Go away, can't you see I'm busy here?'

I 'shooed' at him, and flapped a tea towel in his direction, but he was not impressed – just regarded me coolly as he threw the remains of a mango down and started ripping chunks out of a pawpaw. I picked up the broom and approached him, and he bared long, yellow fangs at me – just for a second or two, just a quick warning, nothing personal. Then he turned his attention back to the fruit. When he had totally destroyed each piece beyond redemption, he coolly climbed down from the counter and idled out of the kitchen door, looking over his shoulder at me as he went.

He was part of a larger group of about eight or ten monkeys that passed through the gardens now and again in their scavenge-hunt for food. And lesson learned: keep the security gate on the back door closed while making fruit salad.

I learned a few other things, too, like don't panic – improvise.

After New Year, Mark and Jen came down from Jo'burg for a few nights. They also loved the area, and the house, and promised to come down often.

They wanted to know all about Richard, and I was not surprised to find out that he (and Josh too, apparently) had not liked Richard from the start.

It was good to relax a little, and sit by the braai fire with them, listening to Mark play his guitar once more.

The holidays were over, the holidaymakers left town, and life resumed its regular routine again. Rita had signed up to an online dating site and wanted me to also, but I 'gave that a swerve'.

She did persuade me on one occasion, however, to go out in a foursome with her. It wouldn't be a *date* as such, she said, but she just wanted some moral support on her first date with a guy she'd met online. 'Johan', my non-date, was apparently a friend of hers and was just coming along to make up a fourth.

I thought it strange that she hadn't mentioned her friend Johan before, and it turned out that she'd also met him on the dating site, but hadn't fancied him, so had told him that she had a lovely friend (me!) who she thought would be perfect for him! So, we had a few words about that, she and I!

I was still in touch with Maggie. We had reverted to our old habit of phoning each other on our birthdays, and spending an hour or so (with glass in hand) catching up on all our news. Her birthday fell a couple of weeks after Richard left, and I was dreading having to tell her what happened. But in the end, I did.

'Well, I won't say "I told you so!",' she said. 'But I fuckin' told you so! Didn't I? But you didn't want to listen, did you?

Was I right? Mmm? Aren't I always right about the plonkers you choose?'

'Yes! Okay! You were right.' I laughed.

'You can just think yourself lucky that you came out of it still with all your stuff. Thank God you weren't daft enough to marry the bastard, at least! He would have had everything off you!'

Her life was pretty much the same. She was working a three-day week and finances were tight, but Alan was now making picture frames for a local printing and frame shop. This not only brought in extra cash, but kept him out in the shed for most of the time, so, as she put it, 'Bonus!'

***

It was some months now, since Richard had left, and I still hadn't heard from him about what he wanted me to do with his belongings, so I emailed him asking him to make a plan. Soon after, the shipping company phoned to ask when they could come and collect. I told them anytime, as long as they gave me a couple of hours' warning, and added that, by the way, they should probably ask for payment up front. I never heard from them again after that.

***

Rita and I were still bowling – and getting better (I thought). And it was around that time there was a kind of coup at the bowling club. Ron was voted out of the position of captain because he was not enforcing the rules strongly enough, and Petra was installed in his place. Petra was an Afrikaans lady, the best lady bowler in the club. She had a small, inner circle of lady bowlers, who quickly replaced the patriarchal, colonial-type rule with matriarchal, Afrikaans-type rule, instead.

Petra, herself, was short and solid; as Richard would have said, 'built like a brick shit-house'. Reena, her vice-captain, was like the caricature of a hospital matron, big and busty and mean, and the third lady of the inner circle was none other than Treebeard (Ruth). Together they made a formidable team – but with not a smile between them.

There were certain rules, more points of etiquette really, which the men had been a little lapse about. The ladies, however, planned to tighten up the ship. For instance, when the first (novice) bowlers had had their turn, they were to move behind the other players and stay out of the way, and certainly not get 'in the head' and give their opinion about whose bowl was closer to the jack. That was for the more important players to decide.

And if somebody on the other team were to make a mistake or throw an obviously rubbish bowl, it was not nice to cheer, or shout, 'D'you want to borrow my specs, mate?' Etiquette required something more like 'Oh, bad luck, old chap!'

They were, even to my inexperienced eyes, being petty. And from the expression on the men's faces, I wasn't the only one who thought so.

That was the final straw for Rita, who gave up bowling then and there. I stuck it out, but it wasn't so much fun after that, and I didn't bother going to the bar anymore.

Rita was keen to try something else though, and we sat discussing our options over a gin and tonic one hot afternoon.

'How about quilting?' she said. 'There's a quilting club right in Margate – wouldn't you like to try that?'

'Nah! I never could sew. DS was one of my worse subjects at school. How about art?'

'Art? Like… painting?'

'Yes. I loved art at school. I've always quite fancied taking it up again. What d'you think?'

'I think if you're artistic, you'd be good at quilting and you could come with me to that? Don't you fancy?'

'I would, if I was any good at sewing, and I would come with you. But I can't sew for a toffee – I'm hopeless!'

'Well, okay,' she said. 'Yes. I'd quite like to do art. Do you know where they do it? I saw an advert on the notice board in the mall.'

'Where?' I asked, already getting excited about the idea.

'I think it said at the art museum, next door to the library.'

'Sounds a bit posh,' I said. 'We only want beginners' classes, don't you think?'

'Well, I'll go back and have a look at the notice again and get the details.'

I was surprised that she had given up so easily on the quilting idea. She normally liked to get her own way, whatever it was about. But so it was that a couple of weeks later, we started at the Riverside Art Club, which met every Tuesday morning at nine and consisted of about thirty-odd people somewhere between the ages of fifty to eighty, and a few older. It was mostly women with a smattering of men. Rita's eyes went around the room scouting out the male contingent and then looked at me with a very disappointed pursing of the lips.

But she sat and listened, did some painting and enjoyed it enough to come back with me the following week. In the meantime, she dragged me down to the local art shop for supplies and bought enough to stock out a studio.

She came to art class more for the social side of it, I think. Whatever the project was that week, she would give it ten or fifteen minutes of her time, and then put her paint brush down and wander round socialising, seeing what the others were doing. She had a very warm, welcoming personality and people were drawn to her. Nevertheless, she gave up art after about three months. We still met for coffee, though, and for our lunches at JoJo's.

I really enjoyed the Tuesday morning art sessions, especially the end of month 'crit', which I found very helpful. Now and again people leaving the club would donate paints, books and equipment to the other members, and one day I came home with a well-used, paint-spattered, easel. The gentle old lady it had belonged to had died, suddenly. I had sat beside her in art just two weeks before, and had had a lovely conversation with her. I took the easel as a personal gift from her, and said *thank you* to her, wherever she might be.

I put it up out on the balcony, and spent many a lazy Sunday standing before it, my bare feet on the sun-warmed tiles, painting the hours away – with Odin lying close by, watching my progress with one eye.

Painting took me to a different world, upon return from which, I couldn't tell where my mind had been, but it was always relaxed and happy.

The people at art club were kind and friendly, and full of ideas. I looked forward to spending time with them on Tuesday mornings – they were good for my soul. My art improved, and I was very proud to have a couple of paintings in the annual exhibition.

One of the ladies at art club, who was also in Rita's walking club, started coming to lunch at JoJo's with us. This was Mattie, a very fit and active seventy-seven-year-old. She asked me if I would like to join her and a couple of others from art club to paint at her place on Friday mornings, which Rita also came to (now and again). Sometimes there would be three or four of us and we would paint. And sometimes it would be just Mattie and I, and then, if we didn't feel like painting, we'd play Scrabble instead.

Mattie also had two sons and a daughter and shared some of the wisdom she'd learned over the years, dished up with a shrewd sense of humour and her delicious, homemade veggie soup.

There came a point where I was out nearly every day, and this was getting too much for me – and Odin, who sulked when he knew I was going out.

So, I didn't really welcome being invited by Treebeard to play as No 1 (novice) bowler in a league match against another team. I'd learned, by this time, that this would be expected in return for the coaching, and so felt obliged to agree. But it didn't help to know that I was her second choice, Linda having not been able to make it that day.

We were to play at and against Umtentwini Club, and on the day, I could tell the normally placid Ruth was obviously pretty intense about it. She did a lot of smiling and pacing about – quite unlike her.

And I was awful! I played like I'd never seen a bowl in my life before. I even sent one off on the wrong bias into the neighbouring green, and as a low groan rippled among my team mates, I wished the ground would just open and swallow me up.

Ruth was up at the other end at the time and I couldn't really see the expression on her face, but the way she threw her long arms up into the air and turned her back on me said it all. I tried to apologise later, and although she told me not to worry, I knew she was angry. We'd lost the game, which was not entirely my fault, but my skill (or lack of) didn't reflect well on her coaching.

The following week up at the club, Tom, one of the old veteran players (and a good one), also bowled on the wrong bias, sending his bowl sailing up the green in completely the wrong direction. When he realised his mistake, he took off his hat and made a deep, sweeping bow, like an actor after a good performance. The other guys responded with applause and whoops and whistles of appreciation. I laughed, too – it was funny! Then the woman in front of me turned around and I realised it was Petra, and she was definitely *not* amused. She gave me a scathing look.

'I don't know what *you* are laughing at!' she said, in a guttural, Afrikaans accent.

And that was the end of my bowling. I left there that day, and never went back again. I concentrated on my art instead, the people at art club never being anything but kind and encouraging, and far gentler on my sensitive ego.

***

By October, most of Richard's things were in boxes under the stairs, but his clothes were still in the wardrobe. It was now getting on for eighteen months since he'd left, so I sent him another email asking if he still wanted his stuff, because if I didn't hear from him by the end of the year, I would assume he *didn't*, and would dispose of it myself.

He wrote back a two-line email, saying he thought I was being 'a little melodramatic', but that he would make arrangements. Nothing happened.

Then suddenly it was Christmas again and I was back into the end-of-year tailspin that that brought. The B&B was bringing in a steady income, which paid the bills, and covered any extras on maintenance; and there was always something like the pool pump giving up, the gate motor, or a geyser (there were three) needing replacement, or the car needing a service, or tyres. But I managed.

And every morning I would get up to Odin's happy face and look out at the ocean twinkling away in the sun and say, 'Good morning, World!' – and know how lucky I was to be here in paradise.

Chapter Forty

That Christmas was even more hectic than the last, and you know what they say about the best laid plans of mice and men! You can't plan for every eventuality, but just when you think you have, something will go wrong!

It was that Christmas the Ross family of six came to stay. In Room 1 was the granny and granddad (about my age), and in Room 2 was their daughter, her five-year-old son, and her boyfriend (who was not the father of the child), and in Room 3 was the older couple's other child, a son of fifteen years, and his best mate.

The whole family seemed to have only one focus, and that was the five-year-old boy named *Damien*. And he was, by far, *the* naughtiest little shit I had ever come across. The whole idea of putting the two teenage boys in Room 3 (where there were also kids' bunk beds) was so that the little boy could sleep in there with his uncle and friend and give his mum and her boyfriend a little peace. But Damien didn't want to sleep with the big boys – he wanted to sleep with his mommy – and what Damien wanted, Damien got!

So, in Room 2 (Mum's room), I made the sofa bed up for him, where he would lie wiping his dirty little feet down the white wall. After the third day, I stopped trying to wash it clean and decided just to repaint it once he'd gone.

At five years old he still had a bottle (which he was never without), a dummy, and wore nappies 'just to sleep in', which he wore for most of the day, too. He was also still breastfeeding, which he demanded whenever and wherever he felt like it, including at the breakfast table when his mother would push her breakfast aside to oblige him.

In fact, breakfast seemed to be a nerve-wracking time for everyone. Damien had endless energy and would run round and round the dining room while I was coming and going with arms full of breakfasts or dirty dishes. Or he would dash outside and run riot out there, usually too close to the pool-edge. So, they had to take turns to leave their breakfast and stand watch while the others ate. I could see granddad and the boyfriend were less than impressed with the situation, but both had obviously learned by now not to say anything.

Even Princess, who had endless patience with children, shook her head and said, 'Eeish! That one!' Zulu women don't believe in smacking their children – but I think even she would have made an exception for Damien.

I heard some kind of ruckus going on down by the pool one morning, and looking down from the balcony, I saw the boyfriend speaking quite animatedly to Damien, and Damien was working up to a full-scale temper tantrum. The mother came out of the room and asked what was going on, and the boyfriend told her that Damien was throwing stones into the swimming pool. Damien flew into his mother's arms screaming and crying as if he'd just escaped a monster, and she scooped him up.

'Did you smack him?' she asked, accusingly.

'I didn't touch him!' said the boyfriend, affronted. And a full-scale row ensued between the two of them, which, thankfully, they took back into their room.

Two minutes later, Damien slipped out of the room and

sauntered slowly around the edge of the pool. Checking that nobody was watching (he thought), he took a handful of soil from the garden and threw it into the water. By the time I got down there, he was standing with a second handful and stopped dead in his tracks when he saw me.

'Put that down, *now*!' I said, pointing at the soil.

He looked at me and frowned, dropped his fist to his side, but did not release the soil.

I frowned back at him. 'If you throw that soil into the water, I will smack your bottom!'

He dropped the soil onto the tiles and ran screaming to find his mother, who by now was coming out of the room again, as was granddad.

Scooping him up into her arms, she scowled at me.

'We don't "s… mack",' she said, as if even the word was abhorrent to her.

'Don't you?' I said, raising my eyebrows. 'I do!'

I walked back into the house, catching a little smirk on grandfather's face as I passed.

But then later that day, the little bugger lay on his bed, feet on the wall, and pulled on the curtain until he managed to pull the whole rail down.

I was very happy when they left!

The vast majority of guests were no problem at all, and a pleasure to host. The problem ones were usually few and far between; except that year!

As the Ross family moved out, the Naidoo family moved in, and we got off on the wrong foot from the start.

They had booked as a family of seven, five adults and two children, but nine people actually arrived, and the 'eleven' year old wore high heels and lipstick and was sixteen if she was a day! When I mentioned that she might not fit into a child's bunk bed, they told me not to worry, they would manage! Not the point – but I didn't push it.

But when the pots, pans and cooking stoves came out, I had to tell them they weren't allowed to cook in the rooms.

'But why not?' asked Mrs Naidoo.

'Because my insurance does not allow for gas rings to be used in the rooms. We are a bed-and-breakfast,' I said. 'Not self-catering.'

'But you have microwaves in the rooms – isn't that self-catering?' put in one of the other women.

'No. The microwaves are there for convenience sake, but they are not suitable for cooking large family meals.'

'Yes, I know, my dear,' said Mrs Naidoo. 'That is why we brought our own gas stoves.'

'But you can't use them in the rooms, I'm sorry. They are a fire hazard.'

'Then how are we supposed to cook?' asked Mr Naidoo.

'You're on holiday!' I smiled. 'Relax – and enjoy – eat out, or have a takeaway. Or you can use the braai.'

'Can we use the braai?' asked another woman.

'Yes, of course!' I said, thinking the problem solved.

'But we cannot braai every night,' said Mrs Naidoo. 'We need to cook our meals as well.'

'Unfortunately, we are a bed-and-breakfast – we cannot allow you to cook in the rooms,' I repeated.

'Well, you have a kitchen here, yes? So can we be self-catering then instead, please?'

'I don't offer self-catering, just bed an' breakfast!'

'Well, how are we to cook our meals then?' asked Mr Naidoo.

'I don't know, but you can't cook in the rooms.'

'So, what if I say to you,' said Mr Naidoo. 'That we don't want you to cook us breakfast. Okay? That we will cook our own breakfast – if you will let us use the kitchen. Yes?'

That sounded okay. They were taking all three rooms so there were no other guests to cook for.

'Yes, that will work. You can use the kitchen.'

'Okay!' said Mrs Naidoo. 'So now we are negotiating nicely. So how much is it for self-catering, if we are making our own breakfasts? How much less will that be?'

'No, the price won't change,' I said. 'I am allowing you to use my kitchen, in exchange for me not cooking for you.'

'But if we came here and we were asking you for self-catering, you wouldn't charge us the same as for bed-and-breakfast, would you?' said Mr Naidoo. 'So, this is what we are asking. How much less is it for self-catering?'

'I don't normally offer self-catering, Mr Naidoo. But if you want the use of the kitchen – my equipment, my electricity and water – I will charge you the same price.'

'So, we must pay for our own breakfasts?'

'Yes.'

'Nah, nah, nah, nah! That isn't right. How about we stick to bed-and-breakfast, and you cook our breakfast, and then because we cannot cook in the rooms, you let us use your kitchen for the other meals.'

'No, I'm sorry, it's one or the other,' I said.

'Then how can we cook our food?' asked Mr Naidoo.

And so the conversation went around and around until, eventually, we compromised. I gave them a tray of eggs, yogurts, bread and fruit, and they had use of the kitchen, which they made *full* use of, slow-cooking curries all day long, and even getting Princess to do a load of washing for them.

I consoled myself with the thought that they were only there for five nights. I could handle that. And from then on, I learned to quote for accommodation only, and offer breakfast 'on request' as an extra cost.

***

In all the years I lived in that house, there were two incidents of theft, both carried out by opportunistic thieves. At holiday times in particular, there is an upsurge in crime as the local criminal fraternity see the influx of holidaymakers as an opportunity not to be missed. I always advised my guests to lock their Trellidors. The sliding glass doors could be left open for fresh air, but Trellidors should be locked.

The Naidoos were sharing all three rooms, going in and out of each other's rooms in a communal way, and with four men among them, what could go wrong?

Mu, the gardener, had been that day and I had unlocked the side gate for him. Normally he locked it again and brought me the key before he left, but on this occasion, he'd left it in the gate. And I hadn't missed its return. My fault, I should have checked. At any other time, this would probably not have been a problem, but during holiday season it was an invitation.

And so it was that on the fourth morning of their stay I was jolted out of sleep at five thirty in the morning, by what sounded like all nine of them pounding on my front door. When I opened it, bleary-eyed and in my dressing gown, I met a tirade of anger, all of them shouting at me at once.

Eventually they calmed down just enough to tell me that they had been robbed: laptops, cell phones, iPad – all gone. Somebody had slipped into their rooms as they slept, and deprived them of their devices. In Rooms 1 and 3 at least, but not in Room 2, wherein stayed a young couple and their baby.

'But how did they get in?' I asked. 'Didn't you lock your Trellidors?'

'Yes, yes! Of course we locked our Trellidors,' they chorused. 'Whoever it was must have had a key!'

'But look,' I said. 'The only spare keys to your rooms were locked up inside. They're here hanging up. Nobody has taken them.'

'Somebody must have made spares,' they said. 'It was probably your maid. You'd better ask her about it!'

'I don't think you can make spares of those keys. And I

would trust Princess with my life. Are you *sure* you locked your Trellidors?' I asked, knowing that they couldn't have.

'Yes, of course we did,' they said.

'But they didn't steal from Room 2?' I asked.

There was silence. Then I think Mrs Naidoo invented a story.

'Because Hijira was up feeding the baby then. The thief probably saw that she was up and didn't go in there.'

'So, you know what time this happened?'

'No, no,' she said, 'I'm just assuming that was it.'

'What are you going to do about it?' demanded Mr Naidoo. 'We need to be recompensed for this loss. It is four cell phones, two laptops and an iPad. That is a lot of money. A very big amount of money.' And everyone started talking over each other again, demanding that I pay.

'Please, everybody stay calm. I will call the police.'

The police came. Officers Thembe and Sithole, two very stout gentlemen whose uniform buttons threated to pop at any moment, and who looked thoroughly bored. They looked all around the property and asked the questions they needed to. They said there had been similar incidents in the area recently, and it was probably the same opportunistic thief or thieves. They even had a good idea who it was. They were just waiting to 'catch him in the act again'. (Again?)

They inspected the doors and confirmed that they had not been broken into, and asked the same question I had – were they sure they had locked their Trellidors? Which sent them off into a gaggle of assurances again.

One of the police officers told me that if I wanted to, I could go down to the station and report the incident and they would give me a case number. They didn't seem too optimistic about catching the thieves, however.

At the end of the day there had been no 'forced entry' as such, and we all knew that the insurance would not pay out in such circumstances.

When the police had gone, the Naidoos weren't interested in whether I reported it or not. They just wanted payment for their goods – from me! I apologised profusely that this had happened but pointed out that perhaps even though they thought they had locked their Trellidors, they obviously hadn't.

This started more argument, which turned personal and nasty, and which only stopped when I agreed to give them their deposit back, which was half the amount of their stay. Then I went upstairs, shaking, and burst into tears.

They left the next morning, still angry but less offensive, saying that they would never come and stay at this unsafe place again. I tried to keep a smile on my face but was thinking, *No, you certainly won't!*

Needless to say, they still wrote a stinking review.

But a couple of weeks later it was all forgotten when Josh came down for a week. Liesel was not with him, and he just said she needed to spend a little time with her family. I didn't ask, but got the impression that everything was not quite hunky dory. No doubt he would tell me about it when he was ready to. In the meantime, it was nice to have him all to myself.

He used Richard's bike to go riding along the seafront and said what a great bike it was. So when he left, I told him to take it with him. I gave him Richard's golf clubs too, to take up to Mark, who I knew would make good use of them.

And then I was on a roll after that. I gave all Richard's clothes away too, and his shoes, some to Princess and some to Mu. Princess came and sorted through them and shared them between herself and Mu. They would be much too big for Mu, but he would be able to sell them. He had three children of his own and two of his deceased brother's to feed and look after, so the clothes went to a good cause.

Of course, it was only a week later when I received an email from Richard saying that he was coming to visit for a week, to sort his stuff out, and would it be all right if he stayed with me.

I emailed him back immediately, saying he was too late, and sorry, but I had already given all his stuff away.

He wrote back that he'd already booked his ticket and was coming for a week's holiday, and would it be okay if he stayed with me. I replied that I didn't think it appropriate that he stay here, but I would book him into the Lagoon for a week as I had some holiday points that needed using up. I told him I would meet him off the shuttle bus.

Chapter Forty-One

I felt quite nervous when I went to pick Richard up, until I saw him again. Pulling his suitcase out from the bus, he cut a tired and lonely figure. When he saw me, he smiled immediately, and transformed once again into Richard-the-charming. I popped the rear door and went to help him. He kissed me on the side of my cheek.

'Hello, darlin',' he said, his voice warm and friendly.

Déjà vu. The voice I'd once fallen for.

We stowed the bags, and he made a big fuss of Odin as he got into the car.

Odin thumped his tail in welcome.

'Well, hello there. Just look at you! Aren't you beautiful? But he was always going to be that, wasn't he!' he said, looking at me.

I pulled out of the car park and onto the main road.

'So, am I in the Lagoon, or at home?' he asked.

'The Lagoon,' I said, thinking that he knew that, and how odd that he should think of my place as his 'home'.

'I had some points which were going to waste, so you might as well use them up.'

'Okay. Thank you. But I don't want you to think I was assuming anything by asking to stay with you.'

'No, I know. It's just easier this way, isn't it.' It wasn't a question.

'D'you want to go for a quick drink first?' he asked.

'Aren't you tired?'

'I am, but I thought we could go for a quick one and then I'll put my head down for a couple of hours. Then maybe I can take you out for supper? What d'you say?'

'Well, I'd have to drop Odin off first anyway, so why don't I drop you off and you go book in, have a drink and a nap, and I'll come and pick you up later?'

'Yes. Okay,' he said. 'That sounds like a plan!'

Later, while I was getting ready, I thought maybe I shouldn't be going out with him at night. Maybe stick to going for coffee in daylight hours; keep it platonic? I didn't want him to think we were on a date or anything. There again, we were both adults and, if the need arose, I would soon make clear to him to forget any such notion.

We went out to what had been our favourite restaurant and shared a seafood platter and a bottle of red wine, and he chatted away easily about the girls, and his life back in England. He didn't mention anything about credit cards, loan companies or the like, so neither did I. It was none of my business now.

'Listen,' I said. 'I'm sorry I threw all your stuff out, but I really didn't think you were going to come for it. It's been eighteen months now, you know. If you'd come just a month earlier, it would still have been here.'

'No, don't worry. It's my fault. I should have stayed in touch and told you. What did you do with it?'

'I gave most of it to Princess and Mu, but your CDs are still there, and your collection of beer mugs.'

He looked slightly appalled for a second, and then smiled magnanimously.

'Well. Never mind. Like I said – my fault!'

He asked if he could come round the following day to look

through the CDs and I told him of course he could. He was so charming – the perfect gentleman – the Richard I had first met before familiarity and sarcasm came into it.

There were a couple of times when I thought he might be flirting with me: a certain little smile as we clinked our wine glasses in a toast, or the way he touched the back of my hand as he made a point. But when I dropped him off at the hotel, he gave me a quick peck on the cheek and thanked me for a lovely evening. And I appreciated that.

The next day he came around mid-morning and there was an awkward moment when I had to open the gate for him. I'd changed the remote settings and his remote control no longer worked. He followed me into the house, his eyes taking it all in again, and I showed him the changes I'd made to the guest rooms. He was impressed.

I made coffee and he sat in the lounge going through the drawer of CDs, picking out just four or five that he wanted to take.

It was Sunday. A quiet, do-nothing day when I had nothing planned and had no excuse to chase him away, and he knew it. So, he stayed for about six hours, chatting, being charming.

At one point, he went into the bedroom. I followed him to the door and saw him fling what had been his wardrobe doors open and stand looking at the empty space within with almost shock on his face, just for a second. I said I was sorry, again, and he just shrugged. Then he closed the doors again and walked out. Did he think I was lying? That his clothes would still be in there?

Eventually, I told him it was time to take Odin for a walk and he said he would go back to the hotel. But before he did, he said that he wanted to visit a few of his old haunts while he was here, and would rather do so with some company – so would I like to go with him for lunch at his old golf club tomorrow. I lied and told him I had bowls in the afternoon, so he suggested we go for morning coffee instead. I had no excuse for that, so I agreed to go. And it was pleasant being with him. There was none of the old friction or tension that there had been before he left.

On Tuesday, he wanted to take me for a drive and lunch at Oribi Gorge again. I had art class so declined. But I agreed to have dinner with him the next night.

We went to a little Italian restaurant we sometimes used to go to, and with its dim lights and romantic atmosphere, it really did feel like old times. The atmosphere was relaxed and we were as two old friends, just catching up.

He told me he'd bought himself a little bungalow quite close to where his daughters lived, and I couldn't help wonder with what money. But I didn't ask. He said he was happy where he was, but missed his life in South Africa. He asked how I would feel if he came out on holiday again someday soon.

I just shrugged, as if I didn't care one way or another. It was really nothing to do with me.

Over dessert, he told me how he wished things had worked out differently and I told him I was sorry, too, that it ended the way it did.

'But there you go!' I said, smiling to lighten the mood.

He put his hand on top of mine and gave me his best smile.

'I don't think you have any idea how I felt when you told me not to come back. It devastated me,' he said. 'I've never been hit so hard with anything like that before!'

I looked at him in disbelief, pulling my hand away. Did he *seriously* think I'd feel sorry for him?

'Have you any idea what you put *me* through?' I asked. 'I went to hell and back in a bucket, twice, over that little lot!'

'I know,' he said, recapturing my hand and holding it. 'And I'm sorry, really. If there was anything I thought I could do to make things right, I would do it.'

'Well, we can't put the clock back, can we? We *are* where we *are*, and we're both over it. So…'

He still held on to my hand and, smiling a sad, sweet smile, looked into my eyes.

'It wasn't all bad, was it?' he asked. 'I seem to remember the sex was pretty good. Don't you think?'

Not answering, I looked down at his hand on mine, and gently pulled away from his grip.

'I'm sorry,' he said, as if he hadn't noticed he'd been holding on to me.

The waiter came over just then. Richard ordered us an Irish coffee and the conversation returned to a lighter note.

A few minutes later I excused myself and went to the loo, and when I came back, he was on his cell phone.

'Okay. Right. Okay. Goodnight, darlin', I'll talk to you again tomorrow. Okay. Yes. Goodnight... You too.' He slipped the phone into his pocket.

'That's Jackie. I suppose you could say she's my girlfriend. She phones me this time every night,' he said, with a coquettish little shake of the head.

I just smiled. *Well good luck with that one, Jackie*, I thought, and wondered if she knew where he was tonight.

After a second Irish, we left the restaurant and I drove him back to the Lagoon, stopping outside the door.

'You coming in for a glass of wine?' he asked.

'I think the bar is probably closed by now.'

'I've got a nice bottle of Merlot in my room,' he smiled, putting his hand on my thigh.

'Oh, have you now?' I laughed.

He gave me the crooked smile again.

'You're not really going to make me sleep on my own in there, are you?' he said, repeating the words I'd once spoken to him.

'Afraid so!' I said, looking him straight in the eye.

His smile faded to one of mock sadness, as if that might change my mind. And realising it wasn't going to, he reached over, cupped my chin in his hand and moved in for a kiss. I know I should probably have avoided it, but I didn't. But neither did I respond. I just let it happen.

He stopped mid-kiss, his face very close to mine.

'Are you sure?'

'I am,' I said, flatly.

He looked into my eyes, hoping, no doubt, to see a glimmer of indecision.

'Good night then,' he said.

And just like that – he was gone.

I was feeling a bit depressed when I got in, and knowing I wouldn't sleep immediately, poured myself a glass of wine and sat on the floor in the lounge with Odin. He came and sat up against me and I put my arm around him, glad of his company.

I assumed now that Richard had come back over here to try to worm his way back in again. I had thought that a possibility from the start, but thought there would at least be an apology. I should have known there wouldn't be. But the casual way he had gone about trying to win me over was insulting.

He'd said he missed his life here – not that he'd missed me. He said he'd been devastated when I told him not to come back, but didn't acknowledge how I'd felt. He hadn't tried to explain himself at all, and actually tried to make me feel sorry for him! Or jealous? Really? Did he think that was all it would take to charm me into bed again. How easy! What a pushover I must have been for him the first time around. How right were Erin and Maggie, and how stupid was I?

I sighed deeply and Odin went to fetch his ball. He sat trying to push it into my hand, his eyes full of anticipation.

'I'm sorry,' I said, stroking his black, velvet head. He flopped down, head on my thigh, sighing as deeply as I had.

Richard phoned again the next morning. He wanted to come round again, but I told him I had too much to do. He asked if we could grab some pub grub at the Windpump later, and I said I didn't think that was a good idea. But I did promise to take him to the shuttle bus the next morning.

And it was with great relief that I did.

He was friendly and charming as ever and as the shuttle bus pulled into the bus stop, he gave me a quick kiss on the cheek.

'Maybe see you again soon?' he asked.

I pretended that in the haste of the moment, I hadn't heard him.

'Bye!' I smiled.

And I waved him goodbye – forever.

Chapter Forty-Two

Life went back to normal again. Easter came and went (with a full house), followed by a tropical winter of warm days and chilly nights.

I loved the winters on the coast, which were never really that cold. Every afternoon, Odin and I would walk down to the beach and then in a figure eight, with the fishing pier at the centre. This path took us through a strip of windblown mangrove alongside Beacon Rocks, then down onto the beach itself to backtrack to the fishing pier and then complete the figure eight by walking up towards the waterfall and back. We would regularly bump into fellow dog walkers up by the pier, stop for a quick chat or just nod hello. Odin was a very sociable soul and was friendly with all.

Mostly I would enjoy the peace and solitude of the beach, where I'd sit on my rock and watch the waves and contemplate the universe, while Odin dug holes and chased crabs; or I'd sit looking at the waterfall and beach, enjoying the rugged beauty of the place, and throwing a ball for Odin, of course. He would get side-tracked now and again, and chase the odd dassie (rock rabbit). But it was all about the ball, really.

I loved living in Valhalla, which I normally had to myself during the week. I never grew tired of the view from my upstairs nest, as the sea had so many moods and changed with the days and the seasons. Most mornings it would be a dark, twinkly blue, which by lunchtime became a shimmering silver disc. Some days the sea would be grey and angry and thrash about, and on windy mornings, white horse-heads of spray would gallop to the shore.

Whatever the weather, the sea was usually calm by the evening. Big white clouds would catch the last rays of the sun and turn pink and orange, and the whole scene would be washed in their glow. And as the light faded, breakers would lazily roll in and crash, translucent white against the gathering darkness.

On autumn evenings you sometimes couldn't even see the sea – just the disembodied spit of land across the inlet, rising out of the mist with its lights flickering through the distance, like a ghost ship.

And on dull winter days, I would see dolphins and whales enjoying the cooler waters, especially towards July, which brought the annual sardine run. This was the time when huge shoals of sardines would travel up the South African coast, so many that the water would boil and churn with them – and they became the prey of all the bigger fish and seabirds, too, not to mention the people. When news travelled that the sardines were running, the locals would go down to the beach and spread the net wide, each person helping to hold it in place – then they would drag the bulging catch of glistening, squirming, silver fish up onto the sand for all to share.

The evening was the best time of the day for me, when I would sit out on the balcony with a gin and tonic, watching the sun go down behind the palm trees at the top of the hill. On summer evenings, the scent of the frangipani trees was intoxicating, and the frogs and crickets would serenade late into the night.

I would sometimes sit on the lounge floor and watch the full moon rise, casting a silver pathway across the water straight to me, and sending a shining ripple down each little incoming wave as it broke.

On more than one moonlit summer's night (if there were no guests), I would skinny dip in the pool, floating flat on my back on the satin-soft coolness of the water, watching the moon sail across the sky.

Odin was my constant companion, full of life and fun. He was the happiest little soul from the moment of his first stretch and sneeze of the morning. But he still hated me going out without him, and he let me know it! His MO was to get nice and wet in the swimming pool, roll around in the garden to get muddy, and then run around the house and roll on any suitable surface – like a bedspread or white leather couch.

One day, when Princess had cleaned the guest rooms and changed the sheets, she'd left the sliding doors in each room open to air the rooms – and Odin had been in each one and jumped all over the clean white duvet covers.

He knew it was wrong. When I came home he would run to greet me at the garage door, and I could immediately tell from his guilty look and subdued tail-wagging that he'd been up to mischief again.

And I tried everything: bribes, threats, shouting at him and showing him a rolled-up newspaper, or totally ignoring him and not making eye contact. But then he would look at me totally heartbroken, and I would hug him and apologise!

There was only one thing for it – he needed company while I was out. So, I phoned the breeder and asked if she had any pups available. Luckily enough, she was expecting a litter soon, and ten weeks later I picked up Runa – Odin's half-sister (the same father but different mother). She looked just like Odin had – a little round, black ball of energy!

From the word go, Odin was everything a big brother should be, and instinctively gentle with her. But within a couple of weeks, Runa picked up a virus and we nearly lost her. At one point I brought the water bowl to her so that she could drink, but she was so weak her little head flopped in the water. I had to use a syringe.

Odin never left her side, but gently licked her clean and kept her warm. And between our joint efforts, she pulled through – and eventually grew bigger and stronger than Odin, who had been the runt of his litter. He always remained the alpha, however, and Runa a lolloping, gentle soul who followed his lead. The three of us were pretty much inseparable. Odin had his pack and he never made another mess again. (Well, rarely!)

One of the ladies I quite often sat with at art club, Liz, had two boxer dogs, and invited me to join her and her friend Ann (who had a blond Labrador) on their Monday morning, doggy play-dates. We met in the conservation area just up river from the waterfall, and we spent many happy hours chatting away at a picnic table there, while the dogs ran free and had a ball. It was more about us ladies getting together for a chat, really – but the dogs enjoyed it just as much!

***

The seasons changed, and the years rolled by. Erin and Dylan came to visit again, and we had a lovely two weeks together. It warmed my heart to see her so happy and Dylan was such a nice guy. By now, though, I understood that Dylan was part of a big, very close-knit and supportive family, and the family had embraced Erin also. I knew there was no chance that they would come to live in South Africa. If she was happy, then I couldn't wish otherwise, but it made saying goodbye to her even harder. I cried all the way home from the airport.

Mark and Jen came down from Jo'burg quite often, when their jobs allowed. They always seemed so laid-back and content with each other, and it was always a pleasure to have them around, even though their visits were short.

Josh also came down for the holidays, sometimes on his own, when he would spend his time surfing and scuba diving. But more often than not he would bring a girlfriend – a different one each time – and I would wonder if he would ever settle down. I smiled and welcomed them and refrained from asking what happened to the last one; the sheepish grin on Josh's face would say it all.

But Princess would give him stick.

'How, Josh!' she would say. 'Why have you got another girlfriend? When are you going to stay with one girlfriend and get married? You can't go on with this new girlfriend and that new girlfriend and like that. You're not a little boy now. When are you going to get married?'

But he would just grin his way out of it.

***

Rita eventually decided to sell up and go live with her son in Cape Town, and despite her being a bossy madam, lunch at JoJo's was not the same without her and I stopped going every week. Then Mattie suffered a stroke, after which she couldn't drive, and her daughter took her to live with her a little further up the coast. It was too far away for me to go and paint with her. With both her and Rita being absent from the JoJo lunches, I went even less – and eventually, not at all.

But at about the same time, five or six of us in the art club had formed a break-away group that met to paint together, at each other's houses, once a week, as well as going to art club for the Tuesday morning session. Our break-away group was far less formal. We called it the Paint 'n' Sippers: a mixed group of at least four or five, and sometimes six. We would sit around a table painting together, listening to music, chatting and drinking wine (or homemade brandy), and generally being down to earth and real with each other. No word or subject was off limits, and by the end of the afternoon, we'd usually set the world to rights.

Of the four regulars, three of us were born in the same year. The fourth, George (short for Georgina), was half our age – but in her head she was just as old as the rest of us. We had all been through life's mill in one way or another: surviving a bush war, abuse, the loss of loved ones, divorce, or a crazy, murderous partner – and we enjoyed being absolutely politically incorrect about it all. We had many very special times together, healing times.

***

One New Year's Eve, Odin, Runa and I sat in the dark lounge and watched the fireworks and Chinese lanterns light up the sky from the beach parties all around, and I realised I'd been living in this house, in this paradise, for seven years.

The B&B was running well, making more income year on year, although I was never going to get rich from it. But that was fine, as long as it paid the bills.

I'd certainly had a few strange guests come to stay at the B&B in those years. On the one hand, there were people like Thabo, who stayed two nights per month, paid for by the ice cream company he worked for. He always had a cheery smile on his face, never complained about anything, and ate everything I put in front of him, for which he always thanked and complimented me.

Then there were the three dark-skinned beauties who booked for three nights and then stayed for a month – before I actually clicked that they were 'ladies of the night', street workers, and that I was effectively housing a brothel. To look at them, you would never have guessed so; they were beautiful and elegant. Although I guess the stereotype image I had in my mind probably belonged more to the movies than to real life. These ladies were very sweet, well dressed and gently spoken.

Although I didn't appreciate one of them sifting through a jar of breakfast muesli, with long, painted talons, pulling out all the fruity bits!

And then there was Rashid. Rashid was booked in by his company for one night mid-week, but assured me that he would be staying for at least two or three nights per month in future. He was small in stature, but big on aftershave.

I didn't normally socialise with guests unless they initiated it, and not even then if it was a single male, as was the case with Rashid. He was sitting out by the pool that evening as I was doing my rounds, making sure everything was as it should be. He insisted that I have a glass of wine with him, which he had already poured for me. So I sat down with him. And we were having quite a pleasant conversation until he came behind me and started giving me a neck massage. I thought it time to say goodnight then, and went up to my nest.

But a little while after that, he messaged me asking if he could have another pillow – despite the fact that he was in a double bed with four pillows to himself already. I took a pillow down and knocked on his door, which was open, but the curtain closed, and he called for me to go in. Pushing the curtain aside, I saw him reclined on the bed, arms up behind his head on the pillows, and wearing nothing but a very small pair of red jocks, which did nothing to hide the fact of his arousal. So, keeping my eyes on his face, I very casually put the pillow on the end of the bed and got out of there fast.

A while later, he came sneaking up the stairs. Or at least, I think he did, judging from the low-pitched growl Odin gave, followed by a double speed-wobble as both dogs went to chase something down the stairs – followed by the quick slam of Rashid's Trellidor! I then went down and locked the Trellidor gate at the bottom of *my* stairs.

But at breakfast the next morning, all was revealed. He (rather petulantly) told me about the 'sweet deal' I'd missed out on. His company would pay for his accommodation, which money he would pocket (or perhaps give me a small percentage of) as he would not even be using a guest room. He would share my room, my bed, and 'pleasure the body very nicely'. Everybody would be a winner!

It was at times like these that I began to ask myself how long I could carry on with the B&B on my own. It was hard work, and there was the forever ongoing maintenance of the place. But where to from here? The kids were all settled in their own lives, and much as they liked to come visit, none of them actually wanted to take over the B&B.

One beautiful evening in early spring, I sat on my favourite rock down on the beach watching a line of sea birds fly in silhouette against a lavender-coloured sky. I loved this place. I could sit here doing nothing but taking in a sensory feast of beauty, tasting the salty air and listening to the rhythm of the sea. It was almost as if the earth was breathing, the waves flowing in and out like breath.

Odin was busy digging holes in the sand close by, and Runa was helping him. I sat watching them, and the gentle little wavelets that ran up the beach with such enthusiasm, and then trickled back again. And those little wavelets seemed to be a metaphor for my life. As if I had spent half my life rushing in blindly, reaching a turning point, and taking a moment to reflect before slipping back into the sea to be a part of the big whole again. And that would be my life, my moment in the sun, as somebody sat on a rock and watched me and contemplated their own mortality.

The thought of dying was not a depressing thought, but it did make me feel as if life was slipping by. That there was something else I should be doing. This beautiful place, which I knew I would miss forever if I ever left, was somehow becoming somewhere I *must* leave. It was becoming *not enough*. And I realised then that it was not about changing beds and cleaning swimming pools, awkward guests and getting things fixed – it was about something that was missing. And I knew that *something* was family.

I patted my rock as I climbed off it. 'But I *will* miss you,' I told it.

A couple of nights later the phone rang, and when I heard Erin's voice at that late hour, I immediately thought there was something wrong.

'Erin? What's the matter? Are you all right?'

'Yes, Mom, I'm fine. How are you?'

'I'm also fine. I was just thinking about you actually. How come you're phoning at this time of night?'

'Is it that late? Sorry, I didn't realise. But, Mom?'

'Yes?'

'Guess what?'

'What?' I said, but I knew what she was about to say.

'I think I'm pregnant!'

'Oh, Erin! Are you serious? How do you mean you *think* you are?'

'I just did a home test kit, just now, and it says I am!'

'Oh, my word!' I said, my eyes welling up and a big lump coming to my throat.

'That is amazing! Oh, Erin, I'm so happy for you. How do you feel?'

'I feel excited – and scared. I wasn't expecting this. We weren't trying. I'm on the pill. I don't know what Dylan's going to say. What if it's not what he wants, Mom? What if I can't do this?'

'Well, you won't know till you tell him,' I said. 'But I'm sure he'll be fine with it. But you know, boyfriends come and go – *husbands* come and go – but a baby is forever, for the rest of your life. So, the only question you have to ask is "Am I ready for this?"'

Eventually, she decided she was, with or without Dylan. But happily, it transpired that Dylan was, also.

I wanted to go over there and be with her for the birth, but she said she would rather I go a month later, when she was back at home, Dylan back at work, and she would need me more. And that made sense.

Over the next months we chatted over Skype and I watched her slowly blossom (or 'balloon' as she put it) into pregnancy.

***

That Christmas the boys both came down again, and in the new year, Dylan and a very pregnant Erin came over for two weeks. It was so lovely to see them together and I thought what a close little family they were going to be.

I think she was getting really fed up towards the end of her nine months, but then in mid-February, two weeks early, he arrived! They sent me pictures from the hospital, and we Skyped, but it wasn't the same as being there. I couldn't wait! So, I booked my ticket for the following month.

I asked Herman, my handyman (who had also become a friend over the years, and who the dogs loved), if he and his wife would like to come and live in my place for the month I was away. And they were quite happy to do so, so that was settled.

***

Four weeks later, standing in the weak March sunlight in Erin's living room, she placed this tiny, perfect little bundle into my arms, and I wanted to cry. He stirred in his sleep, struggling to open his eyes against the brightness. When he managed to, he considered me for a moment, frowned deeply, and then went back to sleep. I rocked him in my arms as I had once rocked his mother, and I could hardly believe I was holding my little girl's child.

Erin positively *glowed*. She was like a rose in full bloom, and so full of emotions that she was a bit like a time bomb at times, too. But that was okay.

Dylan was like a dog with two tails. I don't think he stopped smiling the whole time I was there. I met all his family and they were, indeed, a warm, welcoming body – especially his parents. They were friends as well as family, and I envied that.

The whole family lived dotted around a beautiful little village in North Wales (with an unpronounceable name). The houses were built of the local stone and clustered around the River Clwyd that ran through the bottom of the valley, and was surrounded on all sides by rolling green hills. And sheep – millions of sheep! Everywhere!

Dylan returned to work and I had Erin and '*Sprog*' (who had not yet been officially named) to myself for most of the day. I had a wonderful time playing 'granny': changing nappies, burping him, folding washing and generally doing whatever I could to help. It was lovely to be with Erin again in a domestic situation and not just on holiday. But we did get out and about as well.

At the top of the village was an ancient, mediaeval castle, and bundling *Sprog* up in several layers in his pram, we took a walk all around its gardens. I took lots of photographs of rugged, broken stone walls, dungeons, and beautiful old trees and woodlands alive with daffodils, promising myself I would paint them one day.

On another occasion, Dylan and his dad took us all to a sheep farm, which belonged to another family member. The steep, winding road that climbed up to it reminded me of an enchanted forest from some fairy-tale, with archways of moss-covered trees and tight bends leading to the farm itself, which sat on top of the world. From the top, we looked out forever across green hills and valleys – at least as far away as the snow-covered peaks of Snowdonia, anyway. Everywhere, there were sheep and lambs frolicking in the fresh breeze.

***

And all the time there, I had this growing feeling inside of me that I couldn't put a name to, but which, when I got back to South Africa, I knew was called 'hiraeth' (in Welsh). Longing!

Chapter Forty-Three

It wasn't long after my return to South Africa that I decided to sell the B&B.

However, it wasn't going to happen quickly. In the end I had about six different agents trying to sell it, all of whom kept telling me how bad the market was.

A year passed by. It was in the April that Odin started having fits. The vet said it was epilepsy and it was awful to witness. I thought he was going to die. But then he recovered and was perfectly fine again, back to being his usual happy self, so full of life. I forgot all about the epileptic fits until about six months later, when they started again.

I took him up to the vet, and he put him on medication, which seemed to be working. And then one Thursday morning, Odin had a long and violent fit. I phoned the vet and asked if he could come. He couldn't – and Odin was too heavy for me to pick up. I called Princess and she left her job on the gate at the Lagoon, and in full uniform she came running to help. Nearly in tears, she picked Odin up and put him in the car for me, and I drove him to the veterinary surgery. By the time we got there, the fit had passed and he was pretty much himself again, but the vet took him in for the night anyway, to monitor him. It was at nine o'clock that evening I got the call – Odin had had a massive fit and had died.

It broke my heart. I couldn't believe that my beautiful boy had gone.

And Runa knew something had happened. She came to me very quietly, not her usual fussy self, and just sat facing me on the lounge floor where Odin normally sat. It was almost as if she was asking where he was. I put my arm around her and she licked my salty cheek, then lay down with her head on my lap. I believe we grieved together, and it took a while. She and I became a pack of two – and we were closer because of it. But I know she missed Odin just as much as I did.

***

The art club had swollen in numbers to about forty or so people. There were now more males and even a few young people, and as a result, there was a whole new energy and enthusiasm, not to mention fresh ideas and projects. We started communicating with other clubs and sharing mutual arty ventures and occasions.

One of these occasions was a four-day workshop being given up at our art club, which I attended along with about fifteen other people from various clubs. For me, it turned out to be a bit of a disaster because it was probably not the best time or place to try out oil paint for the first time – which I managed to get all over me. I fell way behind everybody else and was feeling pretty miserable.

I was glad to find a familiar face sitting at the easel next to mine – Drew, who I'd met before and was on speaking terms with. He was a tall, wide-shouldered man with a white moustache and kind eyes, and had a certain bearing about him. I felt safe sitting next to him, and when he leaned over and asked what colours made grey, I felt a little less useless and pathetic; much better, in fact.

We seemed to bump into each other at quite a lot of arty functions after that, and became quite good friends. He even joined us for Paint 'n' Sip on a couple of occasions.

Then Covid struck!

The art club closed for several months. It was a case of wearing masks every time you left the house, sanitising hands at every shop door you entered, and not being allowed to buy booze or cigarettes. It was ridiculous, really, as every Tuesday morning there would be a long queue of people standing outside the post office waiting for their government pensions, and there would not be a mask in sight. They would be sharing the same cigarettes and same cans of coke, as they always had.

Non-essential businesses were obliged to close their doors but I kept the B&B open, being careful to sanitise everything between one guest and another. For the first three months there were very few bookings, but after that, it was business as usual. I think I even picked up a few extra guests because some of the other B&B's stayed closed.

A second year had passed since putting the house on the market, and still no buyers. The estate agencies were closed, so nobody even came to look. And I wasn't going anywhere anyway, because international travel was still prohibited. I began to wonder if I would *ever* get back to the UK.

It wasn't all bad news though. Paint 'n' Sippers carried on, even though we were not officially allowed to visit each other's homes. One of our number made himself a still, and the moonshine ran freely – and so did the fun.

Slowly, the restrictions began to lift and people were allowed to meet again, but not to gather in large numbers. Mark and Jen, and then Josh with yet another new girlfriend, came down to visit. All seemed happy and well and life seemed to be getting back to normal again.

***

One day in November, a couple came to stay just for one night. They were from Jo'burg and had come down to the south coast to look at properties, intending to buy a holiday home. They had spent two days looking, and had found a place, but just needed an extra day to think it over. Hence their booking into Valhalla.

Over breakfast the following morning, I asked them what kind of place they were looking for, and they told me they wanted somewhere they could invite his kids and her kids to come for family vacations together. They wanted four bedrooms.

Half-jokingly, I said, 'Well this place is on the market. Why don't you buy this?'

They looked at each other, and said, 'Really?'

I showed them around, and as they say in the movies – the rest is history! I had a buyer.

I had to drop the price a little to get the deal done, but there was no agents' commission, and I was happy. The money wouldn't buy me much after it had been converted into pounds, but hopefully enough to buy a little two-bedroomed cottage in Wales.

An estate agent friend helped me with the paperwork, certificates for the electrics, the gas fire, and to say we had no wood infestations. The deposit was paid, and all we were waiting for then was for the registration to go through.

Things happen very slowly in Uvongo, however. The registration office was closed and nothing was going to happen now until the new year. So, we were probably looking at March/April for the actual handover date, and the new owners agreed that I should stay on till after Easter, to honour the bookings I had made (and be paid for them).

Mr and Mrs Nkosi had also decided to keep the place as a B&B and have a go at running it themselves. Mr Nkosi was some sort of government adviser and the government were apparently giving out grants to black entrepreneurs, which Mrs Nkosi, as the new owner, could take advantage of.

They told me that if I wanted to stay in one of the rooms until I was ready to fly, they would be happy to let me – in which case I might perhaps be able to show them the ropes. This suited me just fine. It would also give me a chance to convince them to keep Princess on.

Christmas came and went in its usual madness. You couldn't drive anywhere for the number of cars on the road, and combis and taxis parked anywhere and everywhere while their occupants got out and had a braai right there on the roadside.

Once more you couldn't move in the shops because of the number of sun-burned holidaymakers walking round the aisles in their masks, shorts and flip-flops. Shelly Beach and Hibiscus Malls were claustrophobic; the noise and the heat of so many people milling around was a nightmare. And there were queues everywhere. The queue for the ATM machine in Shelly Beach was so long that I nearly fainted before I got to it.

The beaches were worse! But at least they were open again. During the lockdown, the beaches had been closed – I have no idea why – but, of course, the local dog walkers still used them. You just had to dive into the trees and bushes along the beach if you heard the coastguard's helicopter coming over. If he spotted you, he would hail through a loud speaker and tell you to get off the beach.

Josh and 'Ash', and then Mark and Jen, came down to stay again. They were sad that I was selling the place, but I think they understood why. I was sad to be selling it, too. But it was time.

Then New Year came and went, all the holidaymakers went home, and the place reverted back to normal. But there was still no news from the registration office.

I started looking at furniture removal prices (I was leaving most of the furniture behind, but I had quite a few boxes to go over). I was looking at flights, and I had to find one for Runa, also. There were few and far between international flights getting off the ground at that point, and the red tape to get on one was awful, and even harder for a dog. Runa was vaccinated up to date and all her records were in order. But before she could fly, she would still have to visit the local vet, have vaccinations and wait ten days to see if they worked, then visit the state vet, with all her records stamped and dated, before she would be let on a flight. The good news was that she wouldn't have to go into quarantine in the UK.

The bad news was I *would* have to go into quarantine when I reached the UK, and I would have to pay for it myself. And that was only on condition that I'd had a negative Covid test two days before I flew.

***

I phoned Maggie and told her I was coming home. She knew I'd been thinking about it so no surprise, really.

'Oh. Yes? How long for this time?' she asked.

'For good, this time.'

'Mmm!' she said, obviously unconvinced. 'So, have you got somewhere to stay?'

'Yes, I'm going to stay with Erin while I look around for somewhere.'

'Okay. Well, you know there's a spare room here if you need one, don't you?'

'Thanks,' I said. 'But Runa will have been waiting for ten days at Erin's, so I need to get there.'

'You're not bringing the bloody dog with you, are you?'

'Of course!'

'So, when are you coming?' she asked.

'Don't know exactly,' I said. 'Hopefully in the next few weeks.'

'Well let me know when you've got a date and Alan will go and pick you up at the airport. Or is Erin going to pick you up?'

'I've got to fly to London and quarantine in a hotel there for ten days. But what I was thinking is that if I got the train up from London to Chester, maybe he could pick me up at the station and bring me to yours for the night? Then we could have a bit of a catch-up and Erin could come and pick me up from yours the next day. What do you think?'

'Yes, that's a good idea,' she said.

So that was the plan.

***

It was all starting to feel real to me by now, and I was getting excited about the move. But by the end of February, registration had still not gone through. Apparently, due to Covid, there was a backlog in the Deeds Office and there was nothing anyone could do about it. We just had to be patient and wait. It was very frustrating.

And then something happened that would turn my life upside down, rock my world, and make me not worry about how long registration took.

Chapter Forty-Four

It was the middle of March. It would have been a normal Paint 'n' Sip day, if Martin hadn't been having his seventieth birthday – which automatically made it a party day. Three of us (not George) were turning seventy in this year, so we'd decided that each event should be celebrated with a little fancy-dress party. On this occasion, it was a military theme, and the birthday boy entered under an arch of toy guns and swords.

The fact that it was my turn to host was convenient, as there would be a couple of extra art club people coming and the pool/stoep/braai area was perfect for entertaining. Everybody was told to bring their swimming costumes with them also.

It was a lovely, funny, friendly day, most of it spent in the pool. The Paint 'n' Sippers had done the birthday boy proud. But by the late afternoon, everybody was just about partied-out. Strong coffee was dispensed to those who were driving, and in ones and twos, they started to leave. Eventually, there was just Drew and I, and Runa (who had also spent most of her day in the pool and was now sleeping), left sitting on the stoep.

He didn't look like he was about to go anywhere soon, so I offered to refill our wine glasses and he nodded in agreement. We chatted easily. He said what a good day it had been, and it *had* been – but I was glad to sit and share a quiet glass of wine and wind down, and Drew was a very easy person to wind down with.

Eventually he asked how the sale of the house was going and I brought him up to date on the details.

'We'll miss you,' he said. Then, '*I'll* miss you!'

'Aw, thank you, Drew. That's nice of you.'

'You know what? If I was thirty or even twenty years younger, and in different circumstances, I would have made a play for you.'

I must admit, I had had such thoughts myself over the couple of years I'd known him. But I knew he was married.

'And I would not have rejected you,' I smiled.

He looked at me a little sheepishly. 'And if I hit on you now?' he asked.

What? My mind scrambled to work out if that was merely a theoretical question or if he was actually hitting on me. What if he was? Was he about to say something that he would regret when he woke up totally sober, in the morning? But I loved those kind, green eyes and would have loved to have them gaze into mine. I pictured us both naked, then, shocked at myself, put that thought aside. But I fancied him. And I was leaving in a few weeks anyway. Would it have been so wrong?

'I'm sorry,' he said. 'I didn't mean to…'

'I'll tell you what,' I interrupted. 'Before I go, you and me will have a skinny dip in this pool together.'

His eyes crinkled into a cheeky smile, three inches in front of mine.

'Why not now?'

And two minutes later, like two naughty children, we were stripped off and wading into the pool hand in hand. The water was chilly, but his body was warm – and it felt so good wrapped around mine.

And minutes later we were on the bed, and considering we were both seventy years old, the sex was pretty impressive! But even better was the way we held each other – as if we hadn't felt the warmth of another human being for a long, long time. Which I suspect was the case.

***

I often think back to that day and am still shocked by how it happened. Was it the booze? Was it an inevitable and undeniable attraction? Was it two old biddies flattering themselves that they were still desirable to the opposite sex? Or the thrill and excitement of being naughty? Did it make us feel still connected to the world – still viable? Was it all about the sex? My guess is that it was all the above. But more than anything, it was about the sex. At first anyway.

We talked very candidly about what we were doing and both agreed that it was a short-term gift for us to just enjoy. Nobody would get hurt, and there would be no regrets at the end of the day.

Then something happened. For both of us, when we least expected it.

We fell in love!

From the first moment I lay in his arms, I was 'home'. My body was his to do what he liked with. And I couldn't get enough of him: his skin, the feel and smell of him. I looked into those gorgeous green eyes and saw a beautiful soul – and saw that other soul looking back at me as if I was beautiful. That is how he made me feel.

It was a very small village, so we had to be careful. My upstairs flat became our private little world where our relationship could exist with no expectation of each other, or wondering where the relationship was going; no nitty gritty shittiness of daily life. There was nothing but to accept each other and just to love each other. And we did, deeply and beautifully.

We were in a secret little bubble, safe from scrutiny and

judgement, and society's codes of conduct, both agreeing that we'd earned the right to decide such things for ourselves. And what was right for us was to be lying next to each other, skin on skin, loving each other. And we didn't waste a second. He would come round when he could, and we would spend the next three, four – five, six – hours making love.

The sex went from impressive to utterly amazing; well, most of the time anyway. At our age you had to maintain a good sense of humour about body bits that didn't always behave in the way they once did. We just accepted and trusted each other, and in such a totally natural and unselfconscious way, took such joy in each other's bodies. And we explored every avenue of that joy! I had never felt so relaxed, free – positively wanton – in all my life.

I remember we were on the bed one morning, me on top, looking out across the top of the slatted bedhead into the next-door neighbour's garden. I was a little preoccupied at the time, so was not focused on anything in particular, and then I was – our old neighbour standing in his garden below, looking up at me through the window. Old Fred never came further than the edge of his stoep, so he was the last person I expected to see. I bobbed my head down, peeping out between the vertical slats of the bedhead and there he was, smiling up at me and giving me two thumbs up!

On one occasion I asked Drew, 'Can you imagine what we would have been like together if we'd met each other years ago?'

'We'd probably never have come up for air!' he said. 'But we wouldn't be the people we are today – and it wouldn't have been this good.'

And that's how he made me feel. So, I decided then and there to just go with the flow and enjoy the ride, as it were.

In our quieter moments, we would tell each other stories of our youth, or lie stark naked on the bed eating lasagne out of breakfast bowls, chatting and laughing as if we'd done this all our lives. He cooked me prawns and stuffed mushrooms in between kisses and sips of wine, and we'd marvel at the relationship we had, the love we had for each other; we were soulmates.

And then there were the times we would just lie quietly in each other's arms just kissing – long, slow, tender kisses, gently stroking fingers over skin and falling asleep together. Even in sleep, his eyes looked kind. He looked like an angel! (Even though I knew he definitely was not!)

When we *accidentally* came across each other at art functions, nobody would have guessed there was anything going on between us, which made it deliciously naughty knowing that there was. Even more so, the accidental little touches, or little kisses stolen out of sight.

We began to say the words, 'I love you' – which we knew were said in the context of our bubble, which inevitably had to burst one day. But the words were no less true. He said that for him, they had never been truer. I know sceptics would say that what we had wasn't love, just lust. But they'd be wrong. Safe inside our bubble, we had a love that asked nothing of each other, but just each other.

We spoke about staying in touch when I was living in the UK. What we had was about touch, tactile, physical, and real, and I didn't know how long we could survive on WhatsApp, especially knowing we would never see each other again. It was bound to peter out, and it might even be better to just cut it dead when I left, just say goodbye, keep our bubble pristine and beautiful. But that was too brutal. Neither of us could do that.

And then the sale went through. We'd been together just three months and yet it felt more like three, or possibly thirty-three, years. I could hardly imagine being without him now. And the reality that that was about to happen hit home like a physical blow.

***

Mark and Jen came down the weekend before I left to spend a couple of days with me and see me off at the airport. Josh couldn't make it, but he phoned to say his goodbyes, and that he would come visit me in the UK pretty soon.

I was leaving on the Wednesday and saw Drew briefly on Monday morning, but was so busy with last-minute preparations, getting Runa's paperwork done and my car sold, that I didn't have much time to give him. He had made me a gift, and gave me a letter, which he told me to open when I was on the plane. I wanted to give him something to remember me by, but there was nothing that he could keep. But I had a letter for him too, a long letter, which started…

My darling, darling Drew

Our time together is coming to an end and there is so much I want to say before it's too late. I am sitting here in the lounge looking out at the blue, blue afternoon – just the slightest breath of breeze (which wasn't there earlier, when we lay skin on skin, in the bedroom). The bed is still all mussed up, and I will fall asleep tonight with the smell of you on my pillow – and I will hug the pillow.

I know our parting is going to be sad – and we will tell ourselves that we always knew it had to happen. But I know once I am on that plane, there will be tears. Sorry for that – and don't feel bad, it's not your fault. I think my tears will be testimony to what we have today – and the memories that will be with me forever, forever. And they are sooooooo worth a few tears.

***

The next day I was an emotional wreck – and in a tailspin. I was supposed to be seeing Drew one last time, but I was actually dreading it. It was going to be a terribly sad occasion and I wondered why we had arranged to meet again. It was going to be awful. Why were we stringing it out like this, making it so painful for ourselves?

I was standing in the queue in the bank, nervous and frustrated that it was taking so long, when my phone rang. It was Drew, and in a very sad, quiet voice, he said that he didn't think he could bear to come and say goodbye – and how did I feel? The thought of not seeing him again was awful, but it was the right thing to do. And so we said goodbye there and then, over the phone.

***

The next day Mark and Jen took me to the pickup point for the shuttle bus. We'd just about pulled in when the bus appeared behind us, and as the driver stowed my luggage in the back, there was just time for a quick hug.

Travelling the familiar route to Durban, I wondered how many times I had driven this road taking the kids to the airport. It was always me being left behind feeling… left behind! Now it was my time to leave.

By the time I boarded the plane, I was exhausted. I ordered the requisite double gin and tonic, read Drew's letter – and cried my eyes out.

Chapter Forty-Five

The plane descended through grey mist and rain to the runway at Heathrow airport. As we landed, the captain made the usual announcements, including one to passengers who were required to quarantine, to please stay on the plane until last.

When everybody else had departed, we were allowed to disembark and go through customs, after which we collected our bags and were shown onto a shuttle bus, and then to a coach waiting outside the main building. There we waited – about three hours – for more quarantinees to join us. Eventually, after an hour's drive across London, and a chat with rather a nice lady who was also going to quarantine, we arrived at the hotel. I was exhausted. But then there was another wait as we filled out forms, including a menu from which we had to choose our meals for the next full ten days. I was so tired I was just ticking off the items that seemed vaguely familiar.

And then at last, we were shown to our rooms. And I was very happy to see that I had a big bay window, which overlooked the River Thames and the bright lights of London on the other side. Then I collapsed on the bed and slept.

Sometime later I woke, and all was quiet. I guessed it was

late at night. And I was hungry. I peeped out of the door into the long corridor, but there was nobody in sight. There were, however, three brown paper bags on the floor outside the door of my room. My supper. A chicken wrap and salads, and a little chocolate pudding, juice, fresh spring water and cake – all wrapped up takeaway style.

Once I'd eaten, I had a lovely hot bath with plenty of hotel smellies in it, and put my dressing gown on. Then I fished out my bottle of homemade moonshine (carefully disguised in a normal brandy bottle for me by the Paint 'n' Sippers), and now wide awake, sat watching the nightlife on the river.

And that, basically, is what I did for the next ten days. The lady I had met on the coach was in the room across the corridor from me, and sometimes we would happen to open our doors at the same time when we heard the knock that announced the arrival of our food – and then we would have a chat across the divide of the corridor. But if there was a guard on duty (and there quite often was), he would saunter up the corridor and ask us to stay in our rooms.

We were allowed to leave our rooms for ten minutes once a day for a walk outside in the fresh air. But to do this, you had to phone down to ask if they would send up somebody to escort you to a place that looked like a delivery area around the back of the hotel – like a prison yard, complete with high walls and barbed wire. I went down once, and didn't bother again.

Twice while we were there, we had to give ourselves Covid tests, which were then put in a tube with a stopper on and a label, and left outside our doors to mysteriously disappear.

Staff were not allowed in our rooms; there were no bed changes or cleaning done at all. If you used the limited crockery in the room, you washed it in the bathroom.

I liked my room, and I had my laptop or the TV to keep me occupied. I spent a great deal of time just watching the tug boats and other craft going up and down the river. But I was very glad to get out of there after the ten days were up.

A coach took us to Euston station. I had bought my ticket online, and pushing my luggage in a mobile trolley thing, I wandered around the crowded central area looking at train arrival times. Eventually, I found my train and a kind gentleman lifted my luggage on for me. I found a seat nearby.

I have always loved trains. To sit back and do absolutely nothing but watch the world go by for a while is most agreeable. But the best was the feeling that I was back out in the world and that things were moving again.

The view was pretty grimy at first as we headed out of London, but soon transformed to the English countryside; under weak sunshine and milky skies, green fields stretched to the horizon, fields of sheep and cattle, fields of pale gold with round haybales dotted all over them, rivers with longboats and swans drifting along, willow trees dipping into the water, a man cycling slowly over a bridge as we sped underneath it, and little towns with little houses and little gardens. A woman hanging her washing out on the line, people in white playing bowls, people offloading beer barrels into the basement cellar of a pub. Life. Life in England.

When we arrived at Chester, I found a trolley and hauled my bags up the platform and into the station. I hoped Alan hadn't had to wait too long. I knew he wouldn't mind though. He was one of the most patient people I knew. But looking round, I couldn't see him anywhere.

As I stood there, a young woman came rushing up to me, out of breath, and I saw it was Debbie.

'Hello, Debs. What are you...'

'Hi, Nat! Sorry I'm late. Have you been waiting long?'

'No, I've just this minute got here. I was expecting your dad? Is he here, too?'

'No, he couldn't make it.'

'Oh. Okay. Well thanks very much for coming for me.'

'No problem,' she answered. 'I don't know about you, but I'm parched. I haven't had a cup of tea since lunch. Do you mind if we just grab one to go?'

'No, not at all.'

She started to push my trolley.

'I can do that,' I said. But ignoring me, she made off to a coffee bar near the ticket office, and I trotted after her.

We ordered, and she asked if I wanted to sit a minute while we waited.

'No, I'm fine. I'm sure it won't take long.' *I must look as tired as I feel*, I thought.

'No, I think you must sit a moment, Nat,' she insisted. 'I need to tell you something.'

I sat down, knowing from her tone that it was something important. She sat opposite, and seeing she had my attention, she leaned forwards, arms on the table.

'Dad died,' she said.

Two words. I heard them, but they didn't make sense.

'What?'

'Dad died. He had a heart attack.'

'No! I only spoke to him a couple of weeks ago? It can't be! What happened?'

'Ten days ago. Playing golf. He had a massive heart attack. He didn't even make it to the hospital.'

'I can't believe it. I'm so sorry. Oh, God! How's your mum?'

'Not good, but she'll be okay.'

'Do you think she wants me there, or do you think she wants to be on her own? God, I can't believe this!'

'No, she wants you there. It may not seem like it – you know my mum. But believe me, yes, she wants you there. Me and Julia have been with her since it happened. But she'll be glad to see you. If you want to stay, that is?'

'Yes, of course,' I said. Although this was obviously not going to be the catch-up session I'd anticipated.

'It's actually the funeral, tomorrow,' she said. 'I don't know whether you want to come to that, or what you want to do. You don't have to feel obliged to. If you're tired from the trip, you can just stay and sleep while we go, if you like.'

'No,' I said. 'I liked your dad. I would like to be there. But I must phone Erin and tell her the plan.'

A waitress came and gave us two takeaway cups.

'I spoke to Erin,' she said. 'She picked up Runa okay and she's going to call you later.'

'Okay, that's fine then,' I said.

'Okay,' she said, obviously relieved to have it said. 'Shall we go?'

***

Maggie came out onto the doorstep as we walked up the garden path, and I just took her and hugged her. There were no words to say. And for once in her life, she didn't push me away. Eventually, she broke free.

'Hi,' she said. 'How are you doing? Did you have a good trip?'

'How are *you*?' I asked, although I could see the answer on her face. Dry-eyed and without expression, but I could see the distress in her eyes.

'Yes, I've been better,' she said.

A pretty, young girl looking very like Debbie appeared.

'Hello,' I said. 'Julia?'

She came forwards, smiling, showing teeth braces.

'Yes,' she said. 'And you're Natalie, aren't you? Hello.'

'My word! You're a young woman already. How old are you?'

'I'm fourteen.' She grinned, and I felt really old.

'Mum,' said Debbie. 'Do you mind if I go and do a few things and I'll come back later, if you like?'

'No, you go, Debs. It's fine. I know you need to get on with stuff. I'll be fine. Really.'

'Do you want me to come back?'

'Not unless you want to. I'll be fine now, really.'

'I can come back if you want?' persisted Debbie.

'Debbie, piss off!' said her mother.

'Right!'

Five minutes later she and Julia were gone and Maggie and I were ensconced in our usual places on the sofa and chair in her lounge, vodka and coke in hand.

It was just like old times, except there was no Alan falling asleep in the other chair. The emptiness of the house was palpable.

'So, what happened?' I asked.

She shrugged. 'He went to golf Sunday morning, as usual – and didn't come back!' she said. 'That's all there was to it.'

'Do you want to talk about it?'

'Not really. Nothing to say.'

I didn't push it, and we chatted about other things.

It was much later, with a few more vodka and cokes inside her, that she started to talk. 'This house is so quiet. He wasn't a noisy man, was he – but you'd know when he was around. You'd know he was down in the kitchen making the tea, or in the shed working even. Now, it's just dead quiet. Debbie's been here with me most of the time, but she can't stay here. And when I'm on my own the quiet gets to me. I just want to scream. But I'll have to get used to it, won't I?'

'So, will you stay here, or move somewhere else?'

'Like where?' she said. 'I've lived here since we got married forty-odd years ago. There're so many memories here, but I don't know whether I want to live with them or not. Not on my own. I don't know. Debbie has hinted a couple of times about me moving in there with them, but the boyfriend is there more often than not, now. I don't know. I don't want to even think about that just yet.'

'Yes. One step at a time.'

'Are you coming with us to the funeral tomorrow?' she asked. 'You don't have to if you don't want to.'

'Of course I am. I liked Alan. I'd like to be there.'

'D'you want to go instead of me? Make my apologies.'

I smiled, knowing she was joking.

'I'm dreading it,' she said. 'His mum and dad and his sisters, and all the golf club and his mates from the Black Bull and God knows who else. Everyone asking how I am!'

She downed the last of her drink. 'And you know how I am? Really?'

'How are you?'

'I am so fuckin' angry I could kill him – if he wasn't already dead!' she said.

I just smiled.

'It wasn't supposed to happen like this. I was supposed to go first – not him. How fuckin' selfish can you get to just up and die in the middle of the golf course and just leave me to it. Typical. It's so bloody typical of him. Didn't even say goodbye! So bloody selfish! If I knew he was going to do this, I'd have put arsenic on his cornflakes years ago!'

'I don't think he had much choice in the matter.'

'What's that got to do with it?' she said. 'I was supposed to go first and he was supposed to wait until I did. And then just to go and do it like that, without a goodbye! I am so fuckin' pissed off. How am I supposed to manage now?' And the tears welled up in her eyes. She got up, took my glass out of my hand and went to the kitchen. I followed.

'You'll be all right, you know,' I said. 'You think you won't manage, but you will. You'll see. You've got me. You've got Debs. You'll be fine.'

'I'll have to be, won't I?' she said.

***

I woke up the next morning feeling jet-lagged and hungover, and really not feeling like going to a funeral. Maggie looked awful too, but we got through it.

It was a cremation actually, at the same crematorium where we had Mum's. We sat on the front pew, Maggie in the middle with me on one side and Debbie and Julia on the other. Maggie was very quiet. She didn't cry. It was almost as if she was in shock somehow. Just 'not there'.

Her son, Andrew, was in the pew behind, obviously up from Milton Keynes for the occasion. I remembered him as a handsome young man with a full head of hair, and now he was middle aged, pot-bellied and balding. He was with a woman with ratty features and stringy, blonde hair. Slapper-bitch, I presumed. We nodded to each other as they had a quick, whispered conversation with Maggie.

There were lots of people there. Three or four guys told funny little anecdotes of Alan's life, tales of what a good friend he'd been, about his loyalty to golf and his reliability in all things; all testimonies to the kind of man Alan had been.

Maggie didn't say a word. She didn't move. But when the coffin started moving towards the little red curtains, she grabbed my wrist and squeezed it, until the coffin disappeared. She just wanted to get out of there after that, but we convinced her to come into the hall for the tea and snacks.

Maggie doesn't do 'tea', and she didn't want anything to eat either. She didn't even want to sit down. I grabbed a coffee and stood with her. There were so many people who wanted to come and offer their condolences and Maggie didn't know what to say to them a lot of the time, so I jumped in and took over now and again.

At one stage I went to the loo, and when I came back, Andy and Slapper-bitch were talking to her, smiling, looking sheepish. Maggie was also trying hard to crack a smile. I took my time walking over and as I did, they moved away.

'Okay?' I asked, and she just shrugged.

At last, we got her out of there and took her home, where she immediately collapsed on the sofa.

'Has she eaten anything?' whispered Debbie.

'Not a thing.'

'Well, I brought a doggie bag. Here,' she said, handing me two brown paper bags. 'Maybe later. There's one for you.'

Debbie brought us a glass of brandy and Maggie perked up a little. Debs and Julia stayed a while talking about the service, the people and the 'do' afterwards. She had arranged it all, and she had done a good job.

Eventually they left. Maggie curled up on the sofa and fell asleep, so I pulled the throw over her and sat and watched TV with the sound down. I think I actually nodded off for a while, myself.

It was good to get a WhatsApp from Drew. We messaged for a while and I told him what was going on. And we told each other, again, how much we were missing each other. It felt like I hadn't heard from him for ages, even though it had been just the night before. I didn't tell Maggie about him. I thought she had enough on her plate to worry about. And I didn't want her to burst my bubble – I wanted it to be the one that floated free, away up into the sky.

Maggie was much better the next day. It was a lovely, slightly blustery day at the end of June. So, I dragged her, kicking and screaming (well, complaining bitterly), for a walk around the little park close by, which she hadn't been to since Julia was a toddler. She actually admitted that she'd enjoyed it.

A couple of nights later, we were just sitting watching TV (although I don't think she was, really), when out of the blue, she asked, 'So where do you think you go when you die?'

'I don't know,' I said. 'But I don't think it's the end. There's something more. Too many people have seen stuff and had "near-death experiences" and then come back saying they saw… something. There must be something.'

'So, what do you reckon happens?'

'I don't know,' I said. 'I don't think anyone does. But I think there's some part of us, spirit, if you like. Maybe it goes back to where it came from, gets absorbed back into some big energy or something, or maybe it goes on somewhere else. I don't know. They say you see all your dead relatives there and you have a big party!'

'Umhh!' she said. 'There's a few I don't want to meet up with again.'

'No, I think it's all cool there. Like, everybody gets "wisdom" and you don't bother to fight about the things you fought about here. They don't matter anymore.'

'Have you ever seen anything spooky?' she asked.

'No, no ghosts. But I told you, didn't I, about the day my dad died?'

'Yes, that's right. You did.'

'Why?' I asked, wondering where this was going.

'Do you reckon he was saying goodbye?'

'Yes, I think so. Why? Has something happened?'

'I don't know,' she said. 'But I was just getting ready for bed last night, and thinking about Alan, and then all of a sudden I felt him so strongly there with me. I didn't see anything, just felt him there with me. Like he was comforting me,' she said, tears welling up in her eyes again.

'Ja,' I said, tears pricking mine, too. 'That'll be Alan.'

'I wish I'd had time to say goodbye,' she said, wiping her tears away. 'And that I loved him.'

'I know.'

'I hadn't said that to him for years, you know. I didn't think it was true anymore. But you know what? I did. I still do love him. And now it's too late to tell him.'

I put my hand on her forearm as it rested on the sofa.

'You know what?' I said. 'Alan knew you better than you know yourself, and he loved the bones of you. He loved you as you are, and as you are, he knew that you loved him. That's probably what he came to tell you, so don't beat yourself up about that one. He knew.'

More tears escaped and ran down her cheek and she freed her arm to grab a tissue and blow her nose.

'I don't know what I'm going to do with my life,' she said. 'There's no job to go to, and no Alan to come home to; what the fuck am I going to do with myself?'

'You'll do something,' I said. 'Don't worry about it.'

'I feel like those bloody Red Indians,' she went on. 'Like the tribe is walking away from me and leaving me by the waterfall.'

I couldn't help it. I laughed.

And she couldn't help give one little chuckle herself.

'Well, me and Debbie are going to be right here with you. You are going to be absolutely fine,' I said. 'You'll see.'

And she actually smiled a little.

The following day was Friday and I had been with her for four days. Debbie had popped in most evenings to see how she was, and had invited us to go shopping with her on the weekend. I didn't want to, really. I wanted to see Erin and the baby. And Ru.

'Listen,' said Maggie. 'I know you're dying to get to Erin's and see that little *Sprog* of hers, and probably the bloody dog, too. You've been here long enough. I'll be okay.'

'Ah, trying to get rid of me now, are you?'

'Of course! I've had four days of you, you know. What do you think!'

'Are you sure?' I said, smiling. 'I can stay longer if you want?'

'No. You can bugger off now,' she said, giving my arm a squeeze. 'And thanks for staying.'

So, with that, I phoned Erin, and arranged for her to pick me up the following morning. She arrived at the same time as Debbie and Julia, and had *Sprog* (now named Glyn) with her, now two years old already, who was made a big fuss of by us ladies.

And amid promises that she would phone if she needed me, whenever that might be, I left Maggie with Debs.

Chapter Forty-Six

It was so good to be back with Erin and little Glyn again; he was such a little character. And I was also surprised to see what an attentive father Dylan was. He changed nappies, spoon fed and played with his son; he even put a wash on! I was impressed. They were good together, a happy little unit.

And I think Ru was as pleased to see me as I was to see her. She pranced about in circles and then it was wet kisses all over.

The first thing I needed to do was to buy a car, and this was sorted out in the first week. Erin and Dylan showed me some sites online; I compared what they had to offer and ended up with another Hyundai Tucson. It was the same model I had in South Africa and had about the same mileage on it. But this one was shiny black, and had a sunroof.

The following Monday morning, the house hunt began. Erin offered to come with me, but I told her to stay with Glyn, and if there was anything I liked, I would ask her to come and take a look then.

The search started online, and there then followed visits to local estate agents, followed by the endless driving around to look at the places they had on their books, and there were quite a few. Trouble was, the ones I particularly liked were out of my price range, and the ones I could afford were either nicely renovated but small or a little bigger and 'in need of a little TLC'. As each day passed, we were going further and further afield.

Every day, we would come back into the little town and drive past what looked like an old shop, but it was closed and derelict. It was not in the centre of town but on a bend at the top of the sloping high street, looking directly back down the street.

Just in passing one day, and for something to say as much as anything else, I asked the estate agent, Sue, if she knew anything about it. She told me that it used to be a baby shop, with prams and toys, but that it had stood empty for years now.

'I'll find out about it for you,' she said.

'Oh, don't worry,' I said. 'I don't want a shop.'

But a few days later she told me that the old lady who owned it had died and had left it to her family, none of whom were interested in it. If I liked, she could find out if it was for sale. I thanked her, but again told her not to worry about it.

However, the next time she took me out she told me that she had actually spoken to one of the children, and she had the keys to the place if I wanted to take a look.

She'd been to so much trouble, I felt obliged to. And I wouldn't mind seeing it. It looked an interesting place.

So, on our way back into the village after yet another futile search, we pulled up in a little car park at the back of the old shop, then we walked up a couple of cracked and weed-infested steps onto a raised pavement area that ran to the side and front. There were two, big shop windows downstairs, one either side of the door, but they were so filthy dirty that we couldn't see in. She managed to turn the key in the old lock though, and in we went.

As our eyes adjusted to the dimmer light, we saw a good-sized room with a long counter at one end. It was bigger than the usual little shops in the village. She must have read my thoughts.

'This was apparently once two shops, which the old lady knocked into one,' she said.

'They must have been very small.'

'Well, yes. Probably. That's why she did it.'

There wasn't much to see downstairs, just a bare wooden floor, a fairly big kitchen with broken tiles and cupboard doors hanging off their hinges, and a storeroom. The whole place was filthy and smelled musty and dank. I was just beginning to wonder why I'd even let her bring me here, when she led the way up a dusty staircase, our footsteps sounding hollow on the bare wood.

The stairs opened up into a good-sized room, which had two big windows in and was pleasantly light and airy. One window was wide and deep, nearly to the floor, and faced straight down the high street. The other was not so deep and faced the back, with a beautiful view of green fields and hills; and to the left and right, there were separate little suites, each with its own bedroom and *en-suite* bathroom, and its own spare room. At the back of the main, central room was a small kitchen, with a back door leading out onto a wooden deck, again, looking out on the hills.

'This would make a lovely sitting room,' said Sue.

And as we stood looking, the late afternoon sun flooded through the window and transformed the room with its warmth and brightness. I could picture it with a carpet in, and curtains and furniture. And it was lovely.

'You know,' I said. 'I love the light and the airiness and the views. If you could find me a little place like this without a shop underneath, and maybe that's liveable in – that would be perfect.'

'Well, the beauty of a place like this is that you could probably get it at a really good price, and with the money you save, you can do it up the way you want to; put your own stamp on it. And you could always rent out the shop below. That would generate some income for you. I admit it doesn't look much at the moment, but this place could be a real investment.'

'It could be a lot of hard work, as well.'

I thanked her and said I'd think about it, and she took me home.

And I did think about it. I told Erin about it. I even drew it for her and Dylan.

'Like that,' I said, finishing my explanation of what was what. 'It's very run down. And the kitchen is disgusting.'

'But why would you want such a big place, Mom?' asked Erin. 'That's work and maintenance again, isn't it?'

'Yes. You're right,' I said. 'I don't need such a big place. But it would be nice to have a second bedroom for when Mark and Jen, and Josh and whoever, come over to visit, or maybe when Sprog can stay over so that Mum and Dad can have a night out.'

'Oh, ja! I like that idea!'

'And it would be nice to have somewhere where I can keep all my art stuff out, so that I don't have to pack it away all the time.'

'Yes,' she said, looking at my sketch again. 'It would have been perfect if it didn't have the shop underneath it or need so much work doing on it. You don't need a shop, do you? Or the hassle of tenants.'

***

After a while the estate agents had nothing else to show me and I had to wait for new stock to come on the market. But when it did, it was still not what I wanted, and inexplicably, my mind kept going back to the old shop. I didn't say anything though.

'Well don't worry, Mom,' said Erin. 'Something will come up. There's somewhere out there with your name on it. We just have to be patient until we find it.'

'Tell you what,' said Dylan. 'Why don't you ask my dad to

go take a look at that old shop you liked? He's done a lot of renovation work in his time and he could give you an idea of what needs to be done? I'll ask him for you if you like?'

'That's an idea!' I said, surprised at my own words. 'Would he mind?'

'Not at all.'

'Great! I'll ask the estate agent for the keys.'

During the week that followed, I went with 'Taid' ('Granddad' in Welsh) and Sue, the estate agent, back to the old shop. He had a good look around but didn't say much in front of Sue.

When we got home to Taid's, he and Enfys and I sat down with a cup of tea (and a slice of her freshly baked coffee cake), and he told me what he thought.

He felt it was structurally sound, and that it wouldn't need an awful lot doing to it to bring it back up to scratch.

'The wiring looks okay, but you'd best get it checked if you're thinking of buying it. You'd need to gut the two kitchens,' he said. 'And re-tile them and put new fittings in. Maybe the two little bathrooms also – modernise them, you know? But if you can get it at the right price, it could be worth doing.'

'And what would the right price be?'

'Well, I have a friend who's a handyman, renovator, does that kind of thing, you know. He'd do a good job and he wouldn't rip you off. He's a good bloke. I could ask him to go and take a look at the place, if you want. Give you an idea of how much, like.'

I thanked him very much and he said he would get in touch with his friend.

***

I phoned Maggie the following week. She was 'coping'. She asked how I was doing, and I brought her up to date on things.

She mentioned that Debbie had won a spa day for two people at a fancy spa in North Wales, quite close to where I was staying with Erin. Debbie had wanted to take her mum, but Maggie had said she didn't feel like it at the moment, so Debs was going to take Julia instead.

I thought she must be mad to turn down a free spa day – and Erin agreed. But then Erin came up with another idea.

'Why don't you invite Maggie here to spend the day with us while Debbie and Julia go for their beauty treatment?' she said.

'That's a fantastic idea.'

I phoned Maggie back to suggest it, and she seemed pleased at the thought. After arranging things with Debbie, she phoned me back to say she would be arriving at 7.30am on Friday morning, as Debs was due at the spa at 8.00.

Maggie was looking much better. It was a lovely morning, and she and I sat at the table in Erin's sunny little kitchen, having coffee and watching Glyn eat his breakfast. Dylan popped his head around the door to say goodbye as he left for work, and then Erin came to join us. I made fresh coffee and we sat and chatted while she cleaned Glyn up.

Maggie commented to Erin that she thought we lived in a very pretty little village, and I told her about the various properties I had looked at here. Erin offered to take us for a drive around if we wanted and maybe go out for lunch. That sounded like a plan to me. And to Maggie.

I couldn't remember exactly where the houses were that Sue had shown me, but we had a general drive around and I recognised a couple of them and pointed them out. Of course, I knew where the old shop was, and asked them if they'd like to see that.

'Although it looks awful from outside,' I added. 'So maybe we should give it a miss, rather.'

'Well, I'd like to see it,' said Erin. 'Why don't you phone the estate agent and ask her if we can have a look? And then maybe we can go and get some lunch.'

I rang Sue, said I was very sorry to trouble her yet again, but could I have the keys just one more time so that I could show my daughter and my friend?

She was there in ten minutes. She opened up for us and we all trundled in, little Glyn wriggling out of his mum's arms to toddle freely.

Erin and Maggie walked around not saying a word, while Sue gave her pitch again. I could see from Maggie's face what *she* thought though, especially when she saw the kitchen.

Erin was walking around with a more positive expression.

Sue excused herself to take a call, and Erin whispered to me.

'Mom, this place is just crying out to be a coffee shop. Look at it! Take that window out and put sliding doors onto that veranda out there…'

I looked, and realised she was right.

'Don't you want to start a coffee shop, Mom? I'd help you. Wouldn't it be great? I'd love to do that!'

Maggie looked at her with wide-eyed scepticism, as if she expected her to have more sense.

Sue finished her call and invited us to look upstairs. While the others went off in that direction, she touched my arm to hold me back.

'I managed to get in touch with the owners,' she said. 'They'd be willing to negotiate a good price.'

'Do you know how good?' I asked.

She gave me a ballpark figure, and I did a quick calculation according to the figures Taid's friend had come up with, and what they wanted was not all that much more than he had recommended.

'If they could bring that down by a couple of thousand,' I said, 'I think I might be interested.'

Her eyes sparkled as she asked by how much exactly, and I told her.

She excused herself again to make a call and I went upstairs to the others, both of whom were looking more impressed with the place than they had been downstairs.

'Mom, you could make this so beautiful!'

'It's in a good spot,' said Maggie, 'with the town on one side and the hills on the other.'

'You like it?' I asked, incredulously.

'I think it could be fantastic!' said Erin.

'Cleaned up and fixed up,' said Maggie, 'I think it could be quite nice.'

'So,' I said. 'Why don't you come live here with me?'

'What?' she said, totally amazed.

'Come live here with me,' I repeated.

I could see by Erin's face that she thought this was a fantastic idea, too.

'Look,' I said, pointing to one of the rooms. 'You could have your own little suite, bedroom, bathroom and a hobby room, and we could share this lounge and kitchen. Maybe help out in the coffee shop?'

'What coffee shop?' she said. 'And I don't have any hobbies.'

'Well turn it into a lounge then, or a second bedroom.'

Her eyes went even wider. 'You're serious, aren't you?'

'Deadly serious!'

'Can I come help with the coffee shop?' said Erin. 'I would so love to do that.'

'It was *your* idea. It's going to be your shop. I'll do the renovations and you can rent from me – at mates' rates!'

'Yes!' she said, punching the air.

Sue joined us again at that point, and overhearing the comment about a coffee shop, she chirped in.

'A coffee shop! What a splendid idea. Of course, there would be certain rules and regulations, and health laws…'

'I know about the regulations and compliance and all that,' said Maggie, and told Sue that she was a cook.

Erin went to catch Glyn while Sue took yet another call and Maggie signalled for me to go out on the wooden deck with her. I followed her out there.

'Tell me you're not serious about this?' she said.

'Deadly serious!'

'Well, I would have to think about it. It would mean selling my house, and I'm not sure about that.'

'It doesn't mean selling your house. You can rent yours out, or let Debbie and them live there. Just come live here with me. No rent. Just go halvsies on the bills with me, that's all.'

'And the coffee shop bit?'

'Erin can run that as a separate thing, but I'm sure she wouldn't mind a bit of help. She'd probably need quite a lot of help, actually. But that would be entirely up to you and her. It wouldn't be expected of you, put it that way.'

And then remembering what Alan had once told me, I added, 'I can help also. I do happen to make wonderful cream scones.'

I took a sneaky look at her and waited for the explosion.

She looked around to make sure nobody else could hear.

'*You?* Make fuckin' cream scones? That'll be the day. You haven't *seen* cream scones till you've seen mine, let alone taste them!' she said.

Then she saw my face.

'Oh. I get it,' she said. 'How did you know?'

'Alan told me.' I smiled, and she teared up.

Erin and Glyn followed us out onto the deck.

'Oh, Mom! Just look at that view,' she said. 'This place is just perfect for you. And look, there's a little garden down there for Runa.'

'And over there,' I said, pointing, 'is a public footpath. And it leads straight through into the fields.'

'Oh, Mom. This *is* perfect. You have to buy it.'

Sue joined us out on the deck, smiling broadly at Erin's words.

'And we can sell hot dogs, and buffalo biltong and spring water to passing tribes,' said Maggie. 'Now all we need is a waterfall.'

The other two looked at her perplexed, but I smiled.

'Private joke,' I explained.

'There is actually a waterfall up there somewhere,' said Sue, indicating the public footpath. 'Just a little one. I believe it's quite hard to find, but some of the locals know where it is. And I've got some good news for you,' she said. 'They've agreed your price. It's yours if you want it!'

We all looked at each other in shock.

'The Waterfall Café.' Erin beamed.

Maggie looked at me and I spread my hands wide.

'What can I say?' I said, smiling. 'Come on, you said you wanted adventure. This is it! What do you say?'

She broke into the biggest smile I had seen on her face in years, and it was wonderful to see.

'I'll take that as a "Yes" then, shall I?' I said.

Erin stood smiling too, knowing what the answer would be, but holding her breath all the same.

Maggie looked around at our expectant faces and rolled her eyes to the ceiling.

'Oh. Fuck!' she whispered, still beaming, while the rest of us high-fived.

Acknowledgements

My thanks to the Pinboard Writers' Club for their knowledge, friendship and encouragement, and in particular my gratitude to Peter Jones for his kind contribution to the proof reading/editing of this book.

My thanks also to Peter Read, for his advice and guidance also in the proof reading/editing process.

Thank you all so much